£2-50

CW01018638

# CHIMERA

# CHIMERA

*by*
*Simon Mawer*

HAMISH HAMILTON
LONDON

# HAMISH HAMILTON LTD

Published by the Penguin Group
27 Wrights Lane, London W8 5TZ, England
Viking Penguin Inc., 40 West 23rd Street, New York, New York 10010, U.S.A.
Penguin Books Australia Ltd, Ringwood, Victoria, Australia
Penguin Books Canada Ltd, 2801 John Street, Markham, Ontario, Canada L3R 1B4
Penguin Books (N.Z.) Ltd, 182–190 Wairau Road, Auckland 10, New Zealand

Penguin Books Ltd, Registered Offices: Harmondsworth, Middlesex, England

First published in Great Britain 1989 by
Hamish Hamilton Ltd

Copyright © 1989 by Simon Mawer

Extract from 'East Coker' from *Four Quartets* by T. S. Eliot reprinted
by permission of Faber & Faber Ltd

1 3 5 7 9 10 8 6 4 2

All rights reserved. Without limiting the rights under copyright reserved above, no
part of this publication may be reproduced, stored in or introduced into a retrieval
system or transmitted, in any form or by any means (electronic, mechanical,
photocopying, recording or otherwise), without the prior written permission of both
the copyright owner and the above publisher of this book.

Cataloguing in Publication Data is available from the British Library

ISBN 0–241–12744–0

Typeset at The Spartan Press Ltd
Lymington, Hants
Printed in Great Britain by
Richard Clay Ltd, Bungay, Suffolk

*For my mother; too late*

# I

## *Autumn 1943*

THE drop was like an act of birth. Sitting in the fuselage on his parachute pack he had become resigned to a passive existence, dependent for all his needs on others. The battering, the pitching, the racket of engine noise, the cold had all washed over him as though they were external to the womb in which he lay. Then the engine note had risen to new heights of mechanical anguish and the whole machine had dipped and shuddered, and the dispatcher, a kind of Charon, was mouthing words at him:

'We're approaching the Dee Zed,' he read.

He was a creature in their hands, a foetus to be delivered. He sat at the hole in the floor with his legs out in the slip-stream and his mind numbed by the blast of air, while a red light gleamed steadily from the fuselage roof. The green came on. He felt the dispatcher's hand in his back; a great tempest of air; a sudden stop as the rigging lines snapped taut. Ahead and above a second parachute – his equipment – deployed like a sudden second moon. Below him the ground tilted, swung back gently, paused, then reached up and hit him.

Something – rock, earth, scrub – slammed against his body. He fell sideways, fought to get his hands on the quick release buckle, struggled onto his knees to collapse the billowing silk. Only then could he get back his breath and feel the newness of his existence, the strange sensation of being reborn. Far away, high against the stars, there sounded the drone of aero engines. That was his umbilical cord now severed, the last scrap of a life in which he had been both watched and pandered to, led and cajoled, treated like a lord and like an imbecile. Now he was on his own.

He stood up gingerly and breathed in the warm, scented air. Around him was an anonymous hillside, monochrome in the moonlight, angling down into a pool of darkness which was the valley. The far skyline was an undulation of black hills, Italian hills which in England would almost pass as mountains.

Cautiously he tested his limbs. The first nightmare was over: there was no damage beyond the inevitable bruising. He rubbed a smarting knee, and gathered his thoughts together. It was two forty-seven, which gave him less than four hours until dawn, four hours in which he would try to catch some sleep before making a move. He stumbled around for a few minutes 'doing the housework', as one of the instructors used to put it: folding the parachute canopy into something like a manageable bundle and concealing it temporarily in a thicket, then setting off along the hillside in the direction in which the other parachute had come down. He found it soon – another nightmare over – and opened the CLE container to retrieve his equipment. Then he could bundle the second parachute away and find somewhere on the hillside where he could lie up until dawn. He wondered whether he would sleep. He rather supposed he would not, but in the event he did because the next thing he knew with any real awareness was a greying of the dark and the first sound of birds.

Dawn was a new world: an eastern skyline flushed flamingo pink; opalescent mists in the folds of the hillside; a dampness on the ground and on his clothes which the first breath of the sun would dispel. He remembered many such Italian dawns – climbing in the hills of the Mugello, waiting in a hide in the Maremma for the first flickering of duck against the sky, fishing for trout in the river Sieve – but there had been no other dawn so expectant. No childhood or adolescent diversion had ever matched this.

Amongst his things were a loaf of grey bread, some sausages and a piece of *caciotta* cheese, but after taking a few bites he felt full. Not far away a *fontanella* was spouting icy water into a cattle trough; a drink was all he needed. Then he turned back up the hill, picked up his Italian army webbing pack and the battered suitcase which held the wireless set, and set off across the hills with the sunrise on his left. He felt quite absurdly happy.

It was almost ten o'clock by the time he found himself looking down onto the town. Walking across the open downland he had barely needed to refer to the military map which was folded in one of his pockets: at the Club he had gone over the thing often enough to know the route by heart, and just as the pilot had promised they had dropped him exactly where planned. From dropping zone to town he could follow the contours in his mind, name each hill as he breasted it, each stretch of open *macchia* as he strode across it: Poggio Cucchetto, Poggio del Forno, the sinister Piano della Femmina Morta, Colle Lungo, the pious Ara di Santa Maria. They were names, he fancied, which he would take with him to the grave. He was very fit and his bruised knee was not giving him any undue trouble so not even the tedious slopes of Colle Lungo could tire him: the four-hour walk was almost exactly as he had calculated weeks ago back at the Club. The only delay was when he stopped at the edge of a copse below Poggio del Forno to examine the road for the first time. A convoy of grey vehicles was grinding its way towards the coast. His binoculars showed machine-gun crews searching the skies, ranks of men sitting in the open half-tracks as solemn and correct as a congregation in church, the black crosses against the grey, the helmets as bleak and threatening as a hoplite's. He found himself, quite automatically, counting.

The town to which he walked lay in a saddle in the hills astride the road. Long ago it had been built by the Romans for precisely that purpose, to dominate one of the new roads they had carved through Etruscan territory; but the town which David Hewison looked down on that sunny day of late autumn in 1943 bore little trace of those origins. The foundations of the walls might have been Roman but what still stood above ground was mediaeval, while the gate proclaimed itself baroque:

MDCLXXIIII. CLEMENTE  X. PONT. MAX

Within the confines of the town there were some quarters where the narrowness of the streets and the poverty of the houses suggested mediaeval, but for the most part a freer spirit prevailed: the centre had been laid out in an expansive rectangular *piazza*. The buildings which fronted this space had a French air about them which hinted at a Napoleonic interlude, while the dominant edifice, seated four square in the very centre of the *piazza* where one might have expected a church, was late nineteenth-century civic. MUNICIPIO, proclaimed a carving over the main entrance, thus demonstrating what the burghers of Vetrano had expected the populace to revere in the early days of a united Italy. A plaque beside the entrance celebrated the glories of the King, Victor Emmanuel II, Count Cavour and Giuseppe Garibaldi, Fathers of the Nation, and gave another date: MDCCCLXX. The orphanage directly opposite announced, on yet another plaque, that it had been founded under the blessing of PIO IX. PONT. MAX., which provided an interesting little sidelight on Italian history for those visitors able to appreciate it; which wasn't many.

On the morning of his first arrival there David Hewison saw little of this. He skirted cautiously around the hills on the northern side of the town until he reached a track leading down amongst the buildings. Then he humped his pack from one shoulder to the other, grabbed his suitcase, and strode down into Vetrano's history.

# II

THE bus from Viterbo left me on the hillside and continued around the curve of the hill. From where I stood an avenue of cypresses led upwards, but at the top the house itself was almost hidden behind a copse of umbrella pines. I looked up at its shadowed mass for a while, thinking of Poggio Sanssieve as it stands out on its own hillside for all the world to admire, and wondering at the contrast. Then I slung my jacket over one shoulder, picked up my suitcase, and walked past the sign:

VILLA RASENNA. PROPRIETÀ PRIVATA.

The avenue was hot and steep, striped like an awning with the regular shadows of the cypress trees, floored with white dust. Halfway up I had to pause in the shade to transfer the suitcase from one hand to the other. I had travelled down that morning from Florence, a journey of three hours on the train followed by a further hour on the bus which had finally brought me to this unknown corner of Italy. I was hot and tired and more than a little uncertain of my motives. If I had to put it into words, and I was not inclined to because that made the whole enterprise seem faintly ridiculous, I was in pursuit of a tiny piece of my past.

At the top of the avenue the house stood quietly in the circle of pines with the light around it as cool and green as bottle glass. There was a gravel forecourt strewn with pine needles and a driveway continuing around the building to the right; to the left was a wall of box with the hint of gardens beyond. The façade itself was solemnly symmetrical, but indeterminate in period and style because, like so many Italian buildings, it had been worked over again and again throughout the centuries until it had become a kind of architectural palimpsest.

From the main entrance a fan of basalt steps spread out onto the gravel. One side of the double doors was open. I crossed the gravel, put down my suitcase and folded my jacket over it, then tugged at the bell-pull. The bell, if there was a bell, must have sounded far away in the depths of the house. Out on the steps I heard nothing.

I wondered if the open door meant that I was expected. Through it I could see an archway, and through that into a paved courtyard where a stone fountain played despondently in the still air. On the other side of the courtyard was another archway leading further into the heart of the building. Leaving my suitcase I stepped through the entrance.

The desk and filing cabinet of some kind of office were visible through a half-open door on the left. On the right a wide stone staircase led up to a landing where a dusty terracotta amphora stood. The second flight of stairs rose back overhead to the *piano nobile*.

From the edge of the courtyard I looked round. The dominant tone was grey – grey basalt paving, grey stone fountain, grey Tuscan order columns. An eccentric rectangle of sunlight illuminated part of one wall and half the floor of the courtyard. The edge of shadow cut straight across the fountain. The space was as quiet and sombre as a cloister, and again there was that contrast with Poggio Sanssieve, the contrast of mediaeval cloister with renaissance court.

'Good morning. Welcome to the Villa Rasenna.'

The voice startled me. For an instant, before I looked round, I wondered who it might be; but when I saw her on the landing beside the amphora I recognized her even though I had only seen her once before, twelve years ago, and then at a distance across a crowd of heads.

'Good morning. I'm sorry, I didn't know if the bell was working.'

'*Non fa niente*. I was not sure whether you would come. You are Anthony? I'm Lara.'

She came down the stairs and we shook hands formally even though, strictly speaking, we were nephew and aunt. I don't know if the thought occurred to her but to me it seemed faintly ridiculous: there was no difference in our ages.

She glanced down at my dusty shoes and crumpled trousers. 'Did you have a bad journey? How did you come?'

'By train to Viterbo. Then a bus.'

'A bus? Why didn't you telephone? We could have sent a car.'

I shrugged. 'The driver stopped right outside.'

'Your things. . . ?'

'I left them on the steps.' I went to retrieve the jacket and the single suitcase. When I returned she was in the office speaking on the telephone.

'Leave them there. Palmiro will take them to your room.'

'Palmiro?'

'He works for us.'

I watched her curiously as we went up the stairs together. She talked all the time, apologizing that there was no one else to welcome me – 'They are all at the excavation' – commiserating with me, almost apologizing for the heat of the day and the inconvenience of the journey as though somehow she was responsible. Her face was animated as she spoke, brilliantly warm when she smiled, sombre when she did not: very Italian in its contrasts. And I found her strangely familiar. She was not a blood relative of course, so it was not any family resemblance that I recognized. Rather it was as though, quite unconsciously, a closed loop in my mind had played over and over my one previous sight of her until I knew intimately the curve of her eyebrows and the slope of her nose and the particular turn of her mouth. Yet even at that first meeting I felt there was more than that; some knowledge too of the person behind the face.

At the top of the stairs we reached a beamed gallery which overlooked the courtyard. The place would be cold in winter but then, in the first heat of spring, it was pleasantly dark and cool. Lara opened the doors to the drawing room.

'I remember your mother at my wedding,' she said unexpectedly. 'She showed me kindness. David always said how fond he was of her.'

I weighed her words. 'I'm glad she was kind. She wasn't very good at it.'

'She was then.' Her smile was sympathetic. 'These days must have been difficult for you.'

'Yes. I'm afraid they have been.'

The small reference to family was allowed to die as we went into the room.

The drawing room of the Villa was a large room with three window bays along its outer wall and a canopied fireplace as high as a doorway on the inner side. The window frames and fireplace were of the same iron-grey stone as the pillars in the courtyard. The furniture was worn and well-used, the armchairs and sofas gathered around the fireplace and the tables rather in the manner of a public room, a club lounge or a college common room perhaps. There was a writing desk, some low tables piled with journals, a few standard lamps. But what made the place different were the artifacts from the excavation which lay around the room, the vases and urns and bronzes scattered about as though they were nothing more than the ordinary objects of domestic life; and the full-length portrait which hung between the two doors in the far wall.

Lara noticed me glance at the painting. 'They call it the Lucri treasure,' she said as she sat in one of the chairs by the fireplace. There was a hint of irony in her tone and her smile.

'Impressive.'

The painting was, quite obviously, a portrait of Lara herself. She was standing four square to the viewer wearing a loose white robe. Her face was blocked in strong masses of black and white. Her hair was gathered up and braided. The only real colour in the whole painting was the red of her lips and the yellow of the gold: a gold fillet holding her hair in place, an elaborate gold pectoral in the form of a scallop shell splayed across her chest, gold fibulae at both shoulders, gold earrings, gold bracelets.

'Like Schliemann's wife wearing the treasure of Troy,' she said. 'Would the English think it in bad taste?'

I laughed at her anxiety. 'Undoubtedly. But it isn't.'

The answer seemed to please her. 'That was two years ago. The jewellery is in the Villa Giulia museum now. Perhaps you remember the discovery? It was quite a news story.'

'I remember reading about it.'

'And now they're making some kind of film for television.'

'About the jewellery?'

'About the whole excavation. The mysteries of the

Etruscans.' She made a disparaging face. 'They come in here with their cameras and peer around as though the house were a museum. Is that how it seems?'

Beside her chair a bronze beast, a chimera with a goat head, a lion head and a snake tail, snarled at me. It was the size of a small cat, twisted and contorted, sprung tight with rage. Lara patted its lion head and smiled ruefully at me as though seeking reassurance. My denial was heartfelt. Certainly the pieces which lay around the room would have graced any museum, yet somehow they fitted their present context more perfectly. In the Villa Rasenna they were being taken for what they really were. I reached out and picked up a bowl from a nearby table. Across the glossy black of its inner surface a red Hercules pursued a pair of Amazons with intentions which had been equivocal for two and a half thousand years. Dredging through my memory I turned it over in my hands.

'Fifth century?'

'About 460.'

'Are you an archaeologist as well?'

She shook her head. 'I help with the clerical work sometimes, sometimes digging. Was that just a good guess?'

I replaced the kylix carefully. 'A long time ago I studied for a while under Elwyn Davies.'

'Elwyn is a great friend of David's.'

'I was little more than a child. Quite rich, over-indulged, over-privileged. I didn't learn very much, I'm afraid. Not Elwyn's fault.'

Whatever she was about to say was interrupted. A door opened at the far end of the room and a girl came in with a tray.

'Rosa is Palmiro's sister.'

The girl bobbed.

'If you would like something?' Lara gestured to the tray. There was *acqua minerale*, fruit juice, some cold beer. 'Then I will show you to your room. I'm afraid I cannot be with you for lunch because I have an engagement in Vetrano. But you must make yourself at home. Villa Rasenna is quite used to having guests.' She paused, smiling. 'And anyway you are family.'

*

The room she showed me to, the one which I always came to occupy at the Villa, lay towards the back of the building on the south side. Its windows looked out over the gardens. There was the rather anonymous air one expects in guest rooms or hotel bedrooms, the smell of polish, a faint hint of damp. On the wall were some Piranesi prints of romantic ruins, in a bookshelf a typical guest room selection: a few volumes of poetry; copies of *Il Gattopardo* and *Cristo si è fermato a Eboli*; some travel books, including Lawrence's *Etruscan Places*; a few thrillers of the more intelligent kind. On a desk beneath one of the windows I found writing paper headed 'The Hewison Archaeological Trust, Villa Rasenna'. I remember laughing at that. Thomas's face, taut with fury, floated before my eyes. I even toyed with the idea of writing him a letter of resignation from here; but the joke was stillborn.

I ate lunch alone in the great beamed dining room, served by a self-conscious Rosa and watched from the door by the youth called Palmiro. After the meal I found my way back to my room and tried to sleep. I was tired, physically tired from the trials of the last few days, mentally tired from the oppressive rituals which had attended my mother's death and the guilt-laden remorse with which the family had surrounded me; but sleep did not come. I was haunted by phantoms of my past and by a dozen voices with their conflicting claims on me, and eventually I abandoned the room and any attempt at sleep.

My tiredness brought with it a strange sense of detachment. I wandered through the unfamiliar house as though I was walking through a dream. I met no one. Shafts of sunlight cut through a myriad of undisturbed dust motes in the empty corridors, shining on nothing more than deserted corners and vacant staircases and the curious artifacts from the excavation. And I recalled a similar lonely sunny afternoon when I had invaded my uncle's room at Poggio Sanssieve . . .

With the quiet determination of the slightly insane Nonna Angelica had always kept her son's room ready for him. When I used to spend summers there he had not stepped inside the house for more than a decade, probably he never would again; and yet there the room was, waiting. The maids swept and dusted. The bed was remade every day, the sheets turned down, the pillows plumped. There was fresh soap on the wash stand – Lifeline; in my family one notices such details – fresh water in the jug, fresh flowers in the vase, newly laundered pyjamas folded on the counterpane. The room which I entered on that day was a mausoleum in which David Hewison lay preserved in all but body.

I still remember the photographs on the wall: 'Placid House, 1937' in which he stood gaunt-faced but youthful behind a grim Benedictine monk; 'University College Freshmen, 1939' in which he appeared in the back row in immaculate subfusc; and a signed studio portrait of him at the same age, but now wearing the very uniform which I discovered in the wardrobe along with an old dinner jacket and a herring-bone tweed overcoat – the uniform of a subaltern of the Ox and Bucks Light Infantry. I still remember the cap badge, a hunting horn. In the bottom of the wardrobe was a pair of brogue shoes with the initials H.H. in tiny brass tacks hammered into the sole. There was also a hickory-shafted golf-club, a niblick or some such. And the smell of moth-balls.

The child which I was had gazed on these relics with wonder. How had they fitted in with my half-apprehended images of an Uncle David whom I had seen only once, and then dimly, at my grandfather's funeral? A prodigal; a traitor to the family; a spy floating down through the Italian sky beneath a parachute; a discoverer of lost civilizations; a hero.

'Strange chap,' my father had observed in that brisk, military manner which memory has doubtless caricatured for me. 'I've known a few of these Special Operations fellows in my time. Find it damned difficult to settle down.'

I tiptoed around his bedroom in wonder.

In a chest of drawers lay carefully folded, carefully moth-balled shirts. In a drawer in the bedside table was a box of collar studs, a stack of hand-tinted postcards of Italian cities all held together with an elastic band, a lapel badge of the Italian Touring Club; and a revolver.

Everything stopped: my heart, my breathing, time itself. A revolver.

The weapon lay there like a guilty secret. I reached out and took it up, startled by its weight and by the thickness of the steel, awed by the sullen power of its spring. What feeble mimics my toys were! Using both thumbs I cocked it so that the firing pin reared up like a single carnivorous fang. It seemed awesomely potent, but mute, unyielding of any story. I never pulled the trigger. Amidst the faint interior sounds of dust and decay and the exterior whisperings of the breeze that hammer would have sounded like the crack of doom. Breathlessly I returned the thing, still cocked, to its drawer, and was left only with fantasy . . .

I found myself on a terrace overlooking the gardens of the Villa. The youth called Palmiro was at work in the garden, irresolutely weeding a flower bed.

'*Salve.*'

He straightened up. '*Salve.*'

'Hot work.'

He shrugged. 'It gets hotter.'

I recognized his type from Poggio Sanssieve: bored by the country, fed up with the low pay, convinced that the city has more to offer; ripe for delusion. We talked for a while in a desultory way about the garden and his work.

'How long have you been with Signor Hewison?'

'Since my father died. He was a Communist. I was named after Palmiro Togliatti. When my father died Signor 'Ewison took my mother on as housekeeper. Now we all work at the Villa. There's no other work here.'

'You must owe him a lot.'

Again that shrug. 'He and my father were companions in the war, in the resistance.'

'Was that round here?'

'Of course. They were leaders together, but my father was poor and Signor 'Ewison is rich, so now we work for him.'

I nodded at his worldly wisdom and contemplated this little fragment of the past which chance conversation had thrown up. But when questioned further Palmiro was either quite ignorant or deliberately evasive about what had happened.

'It's the stuff of history books,' he said dismissively. 'They gave my father a medal of some kind and that was that. It didn't make him rich.'

12

He was about to return to his work, but without any great enthusiasm for when I asked the way to the village he said, 'I'll get the car,' and looked eager to drop his trowel.

'If it's not far I'd prefer to walk.'

'Walk?'

'Walk. On foot.' I actually pointed to them.

Faced with such determination Palmiro grudgingly admitted to the existence of a path as one might, after much evasion, eventually admit to a minor transgression of the law. 'Through that gap in the hedge over there.' He pointed across the garden. 'But it's probably overgrown once you get beyond the olives.'

'I'll take a chance on it.' I thanked him. He shrugged and turned morosely back to his weeding.

'No one goes that way these days,' he complained. 'Not since cars.'

The path was clear enough. It followed a meandering line along the contours of the hillside, at first amongst the olive trees of which Palmiro had spoken, then above a small vineyard and through a chestnut coppice. The hillside was in the full flood of spring, the Italian spring which I had almost forgotten amidst the grey constancies of life in a big city. Within twenty yards my stunted mind had been assaulted by a dozen unfamiliar sensations. I felt like a visitor wandering through a street market on his first day in a foreign country, confused by the noise and overwhelmed by the smells, bewildered by the colours and the shapes; and for the first time I began to understand how long ago those childhood days were when I visited Italy every year with my mother.

Some way beyond the trees the land fell abruptly away into a deep gorge. I stopped at the edge, arrested by the sight as much as by the space at my feet. Far below me was the motor road. Directly across from where I stood, crowded onto a stump of volcanic rock at the same level as myself, was the village. The walls grew out of the rock and the houses grew out of the walls so that it was almost impossible to tell where one stopped and the other began. Some of the windows were vacant sockets, some of the roofs had caved in to show a litter of broken beams. It was a grim, decaying place like a pile of skulls on a funeral pyre. Above the rooftops there was a drift of woodsmoke which might have been the final breath from a cremation.

I shivered. I was in shirtsleeves and the breeze suddenly seemed cold. This was neither the place I remembered nor the kind of place I was familiar with from the hills around Poggio Sanssieve. Here there was none of that Renaissance optimism which, for all that the twentieth century has done, one can still feel in the Florentine countryside. Here, in the place where David Hewison had made his home, there was something altogether darker and less reasonable.

As I turned to go a bell rang out from the village, a desolate tolling on the spring air which might have been sounding for Mary or Juno or Etruscan Uni, or any one of the goddesses who have ruled the place throughout the millennia, back to nameless clots of clay moulded by nameless hands.

# III

# *Autumn 1943*

His first contact was with Dottore Egidio Pellegrino, *Medico Chirurgo, Malattie Generali. Orario Clinica 17–20.* This man, who ever since the Armistice of the eighth of September had had dozens of wandering Allied soldiers pass through his hands and had only just finished treating an Urdu-speaking Indian for blistered feet, at first viewed Hewison with suspicion: it seemed that the one combination of race, occupation and language which he had not yet encountered was English parachutist speaking native Italian. In his rather bewildered mind – he was assisting fugitives more from a vague and generalized loyalty to his Hippocratic oath than out of any political calculation – the phrase *agente provocatore* sounded a warning. Only the day before the *maresciallo* of *Carabinieri*, a man as confused as anyone in the town, had warned him of 'certain SS officers who are posing as Austrian deserters from the German army'.

'But where should our loyalties lie, *dottore*?' the *maresciallo* had asked in a plaintive voice. 'I have heard that in Rome they are arresting my colleagues and deporting them to Germany. What should we do, we who have sworn loyalty to a monarchy which has deserted us? What do such things as oaths of allegiance mean these days?'

What indeed? Doctor Pellegrino had thought. And he thought it again as he examined the papers of a man who claimed to be English but by his accent was clearly Italian.

'How can I believe this story?' he enquired finally. He might have added: 'And, if I believe it, what do I do about it?'

'Because I can get Colonel Stevens to tell you it's true,' Hewison answered with a smile.

15

And so it was that BRUNO went on the air for the first time, and so it was that on that evening's BBC Italian language transmission from London the avuncular 'Colonello Buonasera' included amongst his messages '*ai nostri amici in Italia*' the sentence: Tarquin the Proud was the last King of Rome.

Doctor Pellegrino, who had chosen the sentence himself, turned off the wireless and regarded his unexpected and, if the truth be admitted, unwanted visitor with what he hoped was a welcoming expression.

'If you don't include the house of Savoy,' he added wryly.

He possessed enough foresight to see that soon he would be faced with much more difficult decisions than whether to treat an English airman's broken ankle, or whether to give shelter to an Italian soldier trying to evade the new call-up. These questions were simple enough if one applied the only real standard which Pellegrino knew: that of simple humanity. But when the time came for fighting then the choices would become more tortuous, the conflicting motives more vicious. A medical analogy came most readily to the doctor's mind as he explained to the Englishman that he would have to take him to a safer place in the morning. He even voiced his fears and that analogy when they were sharing a precious glass of *grappa* later that evening.

'What I am doing now is straightforward enough. What worries' – he meant 'frightens' – 'me is what happens when cancer breaks out.'

The journey the next day was noteworthy for involving Hewison's second view of the enemy. It was one thing to stand unseen on a hillside and watch a passing convoy through binoculars, quite another to lie in the back of Doctor Pellegrino's ancient Fiat and hear heavy feet crunching towards it as it waited at a road block. The face that peered through the window at him wore the black cap of the newly-constituted republican Fascist militia and the loose-mouthed expression of the street-corner louts who were all that there was left to recruit.

'Who is this, *dottor*'?'

'A patient.'

'What's his problem?'

The youth flicked his fingers for Hewison's documents. 'Egisto Pascucci,' he read out loud. Then, 'Class of '21. Why haven't you reported for military service?'

'Medical discharge,' the doctor answered. 'Rheumatic fever with cardiac complications.' He handed the militiaman more documents. The man frowned at them.

'What are you doing here?'

'Trying to get home. I was discharged from military hospital in Genoa a fortnight ago, as you can see. Then the Americans bombed the railway line at Grosseto and I had to walk.'

'Not a good thing with a bad heart,' added Pellegrino.

'He looks healthy enough to me.'

'Tachycardia. His heart beats fast, far too fast for his good. That gives him that colour. It's a bad sign. He needs rest.'

The militiaman shrugged, handing the documents back. '*Beato lui.* Maybe he's the lucky one, who knows?'

'Maybe,' said the doctor.

The militiaman pushed himself away from the car and waved them through. Pellegrino grated the Fiat into gear.

'They will have to go north with the Germans when the Allies come,' he said over his shoulder as they left the road block behind. 'But we are not a nation which has much belief in the future so what do they care? For the moment they have clothes, food, freedom from arrest and deportation, and a little bit of power. That's not a bad bargain.'

The village to which they drove was unlike Vetrano in every way. Astride its main road Vetrano had felt the passage of history, and bore the marks on its face. Sabazia, at the far end of a desolate, unmetalled track, had been avoided by every one of those influences and had thus retained, almost unblemished, the complexion which it had acquired at its beginning. The word 'mediaeval', with its imprecision of date and its connotations of an introverted and ritual world, fitted the place exactly.

The house to which the doctor took Hewison was the only building apart from the church which had any pretence at design. All the others appeared autochthonic, mere remouldings of the volcanic stump on which they stood, their walls indistinguishable from the cliffs which ringed the place; but this house, Il Castello, bore the mark of a nameless and long-dead architect. It stood at the upper end of the village where the cliffs ran into the general hillside and where, therefore, the construction of walls had been necessary. It was in the manner of a citadel, facing down the single village street but cut off from that street by a narrow ditch. In the past – the not so recent past, Hewison guessed – there had been a wooden drawbridge. Now lemon trees grew in the ditch and a stone bridge connected castle to village, but it still remained a building apart both in position and spirit.

It was in this building with its squat tower and its swallow-tailed crenellations – 'Ghibelline,' he explained to Gianluca once. 'Square means Guelf, swallow-tailed means Ghibelline' – with its flock of jackdaws and its deep inner courtyard where the winter sun barely shone, with its maze of rooms and passages and its postern gate giving secret access outside the village walls, that David Hewison was to make his base in the coming months.

He confronted his hosts that first morning across an expansive table in the dining room of the house, beneath a high-beamed ceiling and under the sceptical gaze of a stuffed boar's head.

'This place is too cut off,' he said angrily. 'It's absurd.'

His hosts were a young boy of about fifteen and a middle-aged woman who was the boy's mother. They did not seem a likely couple to begin the formation of a resistance group. The boy was smiling excitedly, which suggested that he little understood the gravity of what he was doing; the woman seemed withdrawn and stern, as though maybe she understood only too well. There was no one else in the place beyond a woman of the village who cooked, and her daughter who swept, and an old man who tended the garden. His hostess's husband was 'away on business'.

'What type of business?'

She was a fine-looking woman, in her forties Hewison guessed, but her face was austere and hard. She had the manner of a widow.

'He is an official of the government.'

'What government, for heaven's sake?' Italy was beset by governments at that time, governments of liberation, governments of occupation, governments of mediation, governments of indecision.

'The Italian Social Republic,' she replied. Which was how he discovered that he was in the house of a prominent Fascist.

'You must understand,' the doctor explained calmly, 'that in this house you are perfectly safe. *La Signora* Clara has assisted many Allied soldiers in the past two months. Even now there are two of your fellow-countrymen hiding in the cellars. So you see, the *signora* is dedicated to the cause of freedom. And the fact that her husband is an important official means that she is above all suspicion.'

'That doesn't make the position here any better.' Hewison felt angry and frustrated. All those months of patient training, first in England and then at the Club near Algiers, were being reduced to this: two middle-aged people and a child playing a game of charades. 'This place is altogether too isolated, too remote,' he insisted. 'I need to be able to make contacts easily, I need anonymity and the flexibility of choice. Here I would have my hands tied. I am sure that the *signora* is a very brave woman' – *la signora* smiled thinly – 'but that does not alter the unsuitability. It will not do.'

'I think perhaps,' the doctor replied with his customary patience, 'that we ought to wait for the meeting of *il Comitato*.'

'*Il Comitato*?'

'*Il Comitato per Liberazione Nazionale*.'

'Here? Who the hell are they?'

The local Committee for National Liberation was a curious, heterogeneous group of men whose authority derived from little more than the fact that they had proclaimed themselves what they called themselves, a group of citizens who at other times might have been involved in the most trivial of local politics. They gave the impression of men who had been for a long time inside a cave, now blinking in the sunlight.

'We wish to bury all political conflict in the struggle for liberation,' Pellegrino explained on their behalf. The group nodded almost as one. Only Orlandi, a young man who did not blink against the light, disagreed:

'That is falling into the habits of the past. Politics can never be buried, least of all in a struggle for liberation. It was the Fascists who tried to bury politics, and now what we are facing is more than just a struggle for liberation. We are facing civil war.'

The others began to mutter amongst themselves. Orlandi's voice rose a pitch: 'A war between the forces of reaction embodied in the Fascist puppet government, and the forces of progress symbolized by the Red Army and the People's resistance in Yugoslavia. We are, *compagni*, in a revolutionary situation.'

This man was the only one with any proven constituency. Pellegrino might lay claim to being a liberal – 'Call me a Giolittian,' he said with typical Italian reference to a now obscure past – but he could not claim any following; another man, a railway official, claimed socialism as his creed, but it was his knowledge of the railways which made him important. It was only Orlandi who had any following. '*Un Gruppo di Azione Patriottica*,' he said. 'Twenty-five men, trained and armed.'

'Deserters from the army,' murmured the shcoolteacher who was a monarchist.

'Deserters from the forces of monarchist-fascist oppression!' Orlandi shouted.

The meeting hovered on the edge of disintegration.

'*Signori*,' said Hewison. Since being introduced it was the first time he had spoken. All eyes turned to him, eyes in which he saw a painful blend of resentment and hope. '*Signori*, let us take Signor Orlandi's determination and spirit for our example, while putting aside his polemics for the moment. Whether we are in the grip of the historically inevitable revolution I cannot pretend to know, but we are certainly in the grip of history. Perhaps for the moment politics are irrelevant in the face of this war.'

'War is the pursuit of politics by different means,' Orlandi interrupted grandly.

'Quite so.' Hewison smiled round at them. 'Then perhaps we can settle down to getting those means on the road.'

It was a feeble enough pun on the use of the word *mezzi* in Italian, but those half a dozen men and one woman around the table were willing to laugh at anything at that moment. So they laughed; and having taken the initiative from Orlandi Hewison went on to keep it. He moved them by appealing to their innate sense of wonder, their instinctive willingness to believe the stranger who calls forth signs and portents. Like the messianic protagonist of some cargo cult he spoke of communicating with the deity, of gifts which would drop from the sky into their arms if only they would get down on their knees and worship him; and in their condition of despair this is what they did. Even Orlandi was swept up in the fervour of this thrilling revivalist religion.

The change from mere exhortation to actual planning was not perceptible. When he looked back on that meeting Hewison could not identify the moment when the hypothetical had metamorphosed into the concrete, but such a moment there must have been because suddenly he was appealing to their reason rather than their emotion, talking about a command structure, a division of tasks within the area, the collection and transmission of intelligence, the setting up of cut-outs and couriers and safe houses, the planning of sabotage, the training of a guerilla group which could operate from the hills when the moment for uprising came, all the paraphernalia which had been drummed into him again and again in briefings at the Club. And, more than that, there would be a name:

'I suggest that we be mindful of the past, when men of this country were stirred to fight another powerful invader by similar means two thousand years ago.' Like all Italians they were powerless in the face of appeals to the past. 'We will take our name from that first great guerilla leader, Quintus Fabius Maximus.'

The schoolmaster, who was a teacher of classics, nodded earnest approval at this idea. There was a moment's hesitation from Orlandi, who would have preferred 'Gramsci' and who was very uncertain of the party line on Ancient Rome, but, it being explained that Quintus Fabius Maximus had been a republican rather than an imperial hero, he finally agreed.

Thus network FABIOMASSIMO was born, and Hewison was never able to tell exactly how he had taken this course when, at the time he first opened his mouth to speak, his intention had been to explain the total unsuitability of Sabazia, or even Vetrano, as a base for operations.

That evening he carried his wireless set up to an attic of the *Castello* and beneath the wide-eyed gaze of the boy Gianluca he made his first transmission on behalf of 'Fabiomassimo'. The morse key chattered and buzzed like an insect in the dusty space under the rafters; while in one of the beach houses at the Club des Pins outside Algiers a wireless operator of the First Aid Nursing Yeomanry heard the sounds in her headphones and began scribbling down the letter groups.

'It's Bruno on the air,' she announced with a little stir of triumph, recalling a visit to Djemila in his company. Hewison's conducting officer was there, peering over the shoulder of the cypher clerk as the letter groups resolved themselves into clear English.

'There are his security checks,' the clerk said. 'Network "Fabiomassimo" is born.'

'Bloody classicist,' his conducting officer muttered; but he was grinning.

# IV

THE archaeologists returned from the excavation in the early evening. Emerging from a convoy of dusty vehicles they filled the house with noise. Doors opened and closed. The plumbing sounded through the fabric of the building and the tones of north Oxford were heard in the corridors and in the drawing room. The place lost its mantle of desolation and put on instead a faded academical gown.

'We accommodate all the permanent staff in the Villa,' Lara had explained. 'They say it is the atmosphere of a university college.'

Perhaps. Certainly they were not unlike the little court of disciples which used to gather round Elwyn Davies in the pub near the Taylorian: the same tones, the same jokes, the same self-satisfied pedantry. One voice I recognized.

'Of course Protheroe was a most absent-minded fellow,' it was saying. In this case the accent was Mancunian. 'I remember watching him at work in a trench, at Tiryns it must have been. He had picked up this sherd and was scrubbing at it with an old toothbrush. Then he stopped and stared . . . like this. "What is it, Professor?" I asked. "Early Helladic?" He shook his head miserably. "No," he answered. "Toothpaste."'

I'd heard the story as well, in that very pub.

'Meredith,' I said.

He looked round in surprise. It took him a moment to recognize me. 'Well I never, it's the bloody dilettante himself. It must be all of twelve, thirteen years.' We shook hands warmly enough. Amongst a crowd of strangers all on their home ground it was pleasant to find someone I knew, if only as a vague acquaintance. 'What brings you here then? Surely you're not in the trade.'

I shook my head. 'Family.'

Recognition dawned. 'Of course. You're the great man's cousin or something, aren't you? Nephew. I remember Elwyn mentioning it.' He turned to the girl who had been his audience, whom I later came to know as Hannah. 'Old Elwyn Davies. I always used to say that . . . Anthony, isn't it? . . . Anthony here was living proof that intellect is not inheritable.' We laughed dutifully. 'No doubt you've proved him wrong?'

I shrugged. Meredith did not need an answer. He was enjoying himself.

'And then there was that girlfriend we were all so envious about. Now that can't just have been the attraction of riches, can it, Anthony? That required talent. What was her name?'

'Helen.'

'Helen, that's it. What happened to her, I wonder?'

I was spared having to respond. A hush had fallen on the company. I turned and saw that my uncle had come into the room. I watched as he stooped to talk to Lara for a moment: then he looked across at me.

'Anthony Lessing.'

His presence was not just a quality of his height, but also an effect of his face. It was an arresting face, almost a caricature of those features which I knew in his brother Thomas, remembered in my grandmother and even my mother. Perhaps I too have them in some measure: the long chin, the full mouth, a certain heavy hoodedness of the eyes. In H. D. Hewison all these qualities seemed exaggerated, so that his feature had something of the quality of a classical acting mask, an archetype.

We shook hands in the middle of the room with the people around us watching.

'An emissary of the family,' he said. His tone was uncertain.

'An emissary of no one.'

He regarded me thoughtfully. 'Well at least we meet again under happier circumstances.'

At dinner I sat between Lara and the wife of the excavation administrator, Jane van Doren. There were others at the table whose names I barely took in at the time although I was to

24

become familiar with many of them in the coming months. Goffredo Macchioni, an immaculately-suited Italian who was introduced as 'our man from the Ministry' and whom I therefore unjustly consigned to some personal limbo reserved for bureaucrats, was one such, and I am sure there were others; but the Villa always played host to a shifting population and I no longer remember exactly who sat down to that first meal. What I do remember was the sensation of being an outsider intruding on their introverted little society. They saw me as a bringer of news, both good and bad; as possible adjudicator in long-standing and obscure disputes; as a curiosity from a remote world; as a threat.

'So you're one of the famous family,' Jane said, more as a statement than a question.

'Nephew. My mother was David's sister.'

'Of course. She died just recently, didn't she? David went to the funeral.'

'That's right.'

'I met her once, I think. At David's wedding. Good-looking woman: what they used to call a beauty.'

'I suppose so.'

'She can't have been very old. David said it was cancer.'

'It was.'

'Bloody disease. And what do you do, Mr Lessing? In the great family empire, I mean. Sell under-arm deodorants or something?'

'I think we ought to call him Anthony,' Lara suggested. '"Mr Lessing" sounds awfully formal.'

'Anthony then.'

'Public relations,' I answered. 'Presenting the acceptable face of drugs to the public.'

'Sounds impossible.'

Jane's complexion was dry and dusty, witness to too much summer sun in too many hot places. Names like Kenyon and Woolley were scattered around as she spoke of excavation seasons in Greece and Palestine and Mesopotamia and visiting professorships at Boston and Chicago. It was quickly made clear that she was a power within the Villa Rasenna, a corner stone of the excavation:

25

'I was here right from the start really. The very first person hired by the Hewison Archaeological Trust, the first supervisor at Lucri. Before you were born, I expect. Since then, however much I've travelled, I've always come back. I consider what I've done here to be my most important work.'

Lara was a contrast.

'Unlike Jane I've lived here all my life,' she explained with a gentle irony. 'She makes me feel very provincial.' The disparaging little face which she made amused me. She seemed reserved and watchful, sometimes wary of what people might say, always reflective about what went on around her. Occasionally her expression would be lit by a vivid laugh, but more often when something amused her an ironical smile glided across her mouth. I have always been fascinated by the shape of mouths and the way they reveal what is in the mind. Eyes are dead, glaucous things, mere receptors; mouths transmit.

'The trouble with archaeologists,' she said while I watched that faint, ironical uplift of the corners of her mouth, 'is that in order to understand something they have to destroy it. Doesn't that seem like a – what is the English? – *un bimbo viziato?*'

'Spoilt child.'

'Exactly. Spoilt children.'

From the start I enjoyed her company. From the start I felt that I knew her far better than my previous glimpse of her and a generation of family gossip could possibly justify. From the start, perhaps because we both shared illusions about her husband, I felt a bond grow up between us. I sensed the dangers inherent in this, and I ignored them.

'Is David a spoilt child?' I asked, and watched the lips curve ever more delightfully.

'Oh, quite the worst kind.'

I looked at the man sitting at the far end of the table, arguing with Jane's husband. I had seen little more of him in the past than I had seen his wife but I knew him too, in the way that all children come to know those things that adults try to hide: he had always loomed in my mind as a mythic figure, half noble, half cunning, wholly inimical to those relations who had

26

peopled my childhood. It was not easy for the adult to change the child's perception.

'But isn't he something of a hero?' I asked. 'There were always stories in the family about his war record. They didn't sound like the exploits of a spoilt child.'

Jane was quick with her laughter. 'What prodigious forces we had in Florence! Don't worry, you'll hear all about it when he gets going: battles across the Ponte Vecchio, snipers in the streets, all that kind of thing.'

'I meant here, not in Florence.'

Her amusement died. 'That was a small thing,' she said. 'Nothing really.'

'Yet this was where he came back, when it was all over.'

'It was a long time ago,' Lara said quietly. 'My whole life.'

I let the matter rest, but thought about it as I watched him at the far end of the table. He was protesting at something Charles van Doren had said, accusing the man of pedantry.

'Hiding behind barricades of humbug!' he cried. 'You don't just sit on the fence, you build them all around you.'

Jane's husband replied with elaborate patience, as one might treat with someone one does not quite trust, whose humour is only skin deep.

That evening as every evening the conversation at the table revolved around David Hewison as though held by a gravitational field. Sometimes the talk was academic, sometimes anecdotal, often it was wide-ranging and contentious as he hunted the sacred cows with relish; but always there was that undercurrent of unease. He was, I quickly came to understand, respected rather than loved by those around him, feared for the cutting edge of his tongue and a temper that was always uncertain. And he had all the exile's prejudices: an abstract longing for things which no longer existed, and a violent loathing of things which were little more than fables.

'Can it be true?' he would ask incredulously. 'Seventy-five per cent of children in Britain under the age of fifteen have never been inside a church?' or some equally bizarre and unanswerable statistic. 'Can it be true?'

I, the visitor from England, was called upon as expert witness. It was my duty to respond, to defend the country against accusations of paganism and barbarism and a dozen other 'isms' which infected the England of his mind.

'Where is the national soul?' he cried as though referring to some index, a moral equivalent of the gross national product. 'In 1941 we put it in pawn to be redeemed after the duration; but we lost the ticket.'

And there were the inevitable references to the family and to the firm which my grandfather had created. He had, I discovered, many metaphors to hand:

'Like a minotaur,' he explained to his audience. 'The beast which came forth after my father played foul with commerce, the beast which demands sacrifice and loyalty, but against which no Theseus seems able to prevail.'

When, later in the evening, he led me into his study to talk 'about the world outside my ivory tower', I knew that he only meant the family and the firm, that indissoluble hybrid which, even though he had deliberately run away from it, still occupied a central chamber in the labyrinth of his mind.

Sitting at his desk amidst the relics of his life's work – a scene which was later to appear photographed in some colour magazine – he gestured me to a chair with the invitation, 'Tell me about my brother Thomas.'

I didn't know how to respond. I too had run, but only for a few days and in pursuit of a shadow. If it came to a matter of loyalties I did not know where my own lay.

'He's something of a recluse these days. He lives on his own in Albany. We rarely see him.'

'He broods, does he? Worries about whether he's going barmy like our father, I've no doubt. Does he threaten violence?'

I laughed. It was the family nightmare, memories of Sir Gordon in his decline assaulting his attendants and raving about plots and betrayal. Despite the reassurance of experts there remains within the Hewison family the lingering fear that it might have been something in the genes, something deep down where no medicine can reach, a blot fused into the escutcheon.

'I think he's just an ageing and rather lonely man with

nothing much left to do now that the running of the business has passed to Honjohn.'

'Honjohn? Can it really be Honjohn?'

I smiled. 'A backstairs nickname. You don't use it to his face.'

The idea amused him. He sat at his desk and repeated the name 'Honjohn' a few times as though it were the most wonderful joke.

'And what is this Honjohn creature like? I remember him only as a pimply youth.'

'He was at the funeral.' He must have known perfectly well.

'Not Farmer Bill? Not that amiable rustic in brown tweed?'

'He wasn't in brown tweed.'

'Well, he looked as if he ought to have been.'

'That's his image,' I explained, almost defensively. 'Gentleman farmer.'

'Image. A fine public relations word. Well, his image seemed to be dairy cows and frozen embryos. That's all he would talk about.'

'It's one of the new things: the Agrotech Division. And Dinatech.'

'Frozen food?'

'Recombinant DNA technology. Gene splicing, plasmid manipulation, you name it and Hewison Pharmaceuticals can mutate its genes for you. It's meant to be the next big growth area.'

He laughed. 'You sound as if you believe it.'

'It's my job to.'

'Ah. That's your price is it, nephew? A comfortable sinecure in the family business. Pimping for Sir Thomas and –' he pronounced the name with careful distaste – 'Honjohn.'

I stood up, irritated by his manner as well as by the truth which lay behind his jibes. It was Helen's voice which sounded in my head as I walked away from his desk to examine a group of bronze figurines which I had noticed on the mantelshelf. I knew all the arguments in defence of the firm, all of them. I had practised them a thousand times on her.

'Where would Lucri be without it all?' I asked my uncle; and received no answer. Distractedly I picked up a silver-framed photograph which I had found behind the bronzes. I peered at it, not really noticing it.

'She was fifteen then.' He had been watching me from across the room. 'I'm afraid the photograph doesn't really do her justice, but she was a difficult subject. She hated having her photograph taken.'

I realized that it was a picture of Lara, Lara in the ingenuous clothes of a schoolgirl who has not yet come to terms with her womanhood – floral print dress, plain shoes with low heels, white socks – but Lara already with the darks and lights of her adult beauty. She was standing beside a stone gateway, squinting against the light and half-raising her hand as though to shield her face.

'Does it embarrass you?' he asked.

I looked round at him. 'Embarrass me?'

'It embarrasses many people, you know; outrages some. The family for example, my mother particularly. An older man marrying a younger girl, I mean.'

I could hear Nonna Angelica's voice, querulous with spite, denouncing her: 'A mere girl, a peasant girl!'

'It's very common. I think it always has been.'

'But still people don't like it.'

I shrugged. 'As long as she is beyond the age of consent it can't matter. Isn't it just a question of compatibility?'

'Indeed.' He nodded. 'And we are compatible, in our way.'

'I'm sure.'

There was another silence. He gazed unseeing from behind his desk. I looked at the face in the picture, beautiful in its contrasts, in its brilliant smile and its shadows.

'She lived in the village, didn't she?'

His gaze came back into focus. 'Her family owned the big house which they grace with the title of *castello*. Her brother still owns it in fact, although he doesn't live there. Her father . . .' He paused. '. . . died in the war, before Lara was even born. That photograph,' he pointed almost belligerently, 'that photograph was taken on the day when Lara and I became lovers.'

His look was a challenge.

'How would the family have felt about that, I wonder? How

would they have felt to have had all their little suspicions confirmed? That at the age of, what, forty? I was the lover of a fifteen-year-old girl.'

I shrugged. 'You are still happy. It's only when unhappiness results that such things are bad, isn't it? It's that which makes it wrong.'

'You are proposing a morality with happiness as the only criterion, are you?'

'I suppose so. I'm not a moral philosopher, still less a theologian.'

'No religion? Lapsed?'

There. You could liken it to an inherited disease. It manifests itself in strange ways throughout the generations: in a maudlin craving for grace in my mother, in the ritual, self-conscious piety of my grandmother, in genuine devotion in some of them: one of my cousins was studying for the priesthood at the time; one of my aunts was a nun. But in one way or other the disease usually breaks out. Here was David Hewison, bereft of faith perhaps, still looking for a confessor.

'You never lose everything, do you?' I answered him. 'I've still got a sort of residual Catholicism left, something of the form and the moral framework but little of the spiritual belief. A few years ago I found that I was enjoying being a Catholic because it was exclusive rather than universal, like being a member of a club. It didn't seem a very good reason for professing a faith. Now . . .' I shrugged. 'It's not so easy to regain one's belief just because you need it.'

He nodded, and for a moment there was a sympathy between us that had not been there before.

'Then maybe you'll understand Lara and me,' he said. 'It's not a very fashionable thing to admit these days, but for me her love was an almost spiritual experience, some kind of substitute for the faith which I too had lost. It was rather disturbing for a forty-year-old to discover this in a fifteen-year-old girl, but that doesn't make it any less true. I found in her a . . . perhaps "sense of continuity" is the best I can do to explain it. Despite her youth she seemed to have an instinctive wisdom which I had not met before, a sense of her own place in the course of things.'

He smiled ironically, conscious that the mask had slipped a little. 'I'm sorry, I must be embarrassing you. The habit of confession dies hard, you see.' I realize now that that is what he wanted out of me: an outsider to confess to. The trouble is that we never really understand the burden which lies on the shoulders of the man on the other side of the grille.

Propelled by our awkwardness the conversation veered away to other things, and soon enough it came round to my mother.

'Did she speak much about me?' he asked.

'In recent years she didn't speak much about anybody but herself. But when I was a child . . . I suppose she was the only one who ever spoke well of you.'

'Was she indeed?' He seemed pleased, as much by the idea of the others' disapprobation as my mother's approval. Helen would have loved this conversation, I thought: the Hewison family inspecting its wounds. 'What did she say?'

I shrugged. 'I remember once – I suppose I was shocked to hear such words being used about adults – I remember she said, "They are all fools, but at least your Uncle David is an honourable fool."'

'Was she including herself in that? She was the biggest fool of all.' He watched me closely, waiting for a reaction. When none came he seemed to soften a bit, became almost solicitous:

'I'm sorry we drifted apart really. Maybe I could have helped her . . . but when a family fragments – bang!' He made a gesture with his hands of something exploding.

'Was it like that?'

'More or less. And then one finds that one cannot make good the damage done even when there is a need, when she was ill for example. I suppose I should have visited her or something . . .'

'She wouldn't have wanted it. She didn't want anybody except me. She said I was the only one who had no interest in her looks.'

'I suppose it was difficult.'

'Of course it was difficult.' I felt suddenly angry. 'It was bloody difficult. They gave her a colostomy, you know? But

32

the thing had already spread. "Metastasis" they call it. Very classical. So then they filled her full of drugs to try and keep it under some kind of control, which they didn't. Her hair fell out. She lost weight, became like a figure out of Belsen, her head shaved like a criminal. Oh, it was difficult all right, but not as difficult for me as it was for her. "It's a punishment," she said to me once. "Eventually we are all punished for what we have done. This is my punishment."' I smiled thinly at her brother. 'Well, if it was a punishment it was a pretty bloody one. Not the kind of thing you'd respect the Almighty for.'

'I didn't realize.'

'No, few people did.'

He watched me without expression. I had the impression that in his carefully controlled world he approached everything on his own terms. There was never anyone or anything to discomfit him.

'It's ironical,' he said at last, 'that the only thing the family seems incapable of buying is bodily health. Anything else they can manage, even spiritual comfort if you are worth it. Look at Sister Agnes of the Sacred Heart of Mary. Didn't they practically buy her a convent? But not bodily health. Not my father, not your mother. Not with all the wretched pharmaceuticals in the world.'

He began to tidy up the papers on his desk. Perhaps he was tidying away the past.

'Anyway tomorrow I'll show you Lucri,' he said briskly. 'No problems there. No people.'

'There were,' I said. 'But they're all dead as well.'


Later on in my room, going over the events of the day, wondering about my uncle and the curious little world which he had constructed about him, I looked through the bookshelf beside my bed. Between *Etruscan Places* and something called *Daily Life of the Etruscans* a narrow spine caught my eye.

*Four Quartets*, it read. T. S. Eliot. Faber.

A memory stirred. I took the book down and flicked through the pages to *East Coker*.

'In my beginning is my end.'

Turning more pages I discovered that someone had been there before me: the lines I had been looking for were neatly underlined in pencil.

> 'But a lifetime burning in every moment
> And not the lifetime of one man only
> But of old stones that cannot be deciphered.'

In Faber's rather pedantic fashion the title page said MCMXLIV, so I assumed that it was a first edition. On the fly leaf the initials H. D. H. were written, again in pencil. But below that in black ink was the inscription:

'To L. A. You are the music while the music lasts.'

I guessed that they were Lara's initials, and the book had been a love gift from David Hewison. Now it was forgotten, in the way that all such signposts of a courtship, once of inestimable significance, become forgotten. How many such memories of Helen could I have discovered then, could still discover now?

The little artifact intrigued me. I turned it over in my hands, trying to visualize more of its associations by a mere examination of its cover, like an archaeologist with a potsherd. But its context, what it might have meant before it was consigned to the rubbish heap of a bookshelf in a guest room, remained obscure.

Later on other little pieces were to present themselves like that to me, like fragments found in the floor of an excavation trench. Some proved to be nothing more than flakes of oxidized bronze, green with verdigris and without form or substance. Others were treasure.

I returned the book to the shelf and finally slept.

# V

# *Winter 1943/44*

SOON autumn, with its absurd hopes of a rapid end to the war in Italy, gave way to winter. The Allied armies were held fast on the Gustav line far to the south and seemed little more than a distant myth. With growing confidence the Germans began to move reinforcements down from the north and take Italians, those who had tried to ignore the call-up, away to labour camps beyond the Brenner pass. For much of the male population there was nothing to do but try to lead a secret life hiding in the villages and the farms, a fugitive in one's own country; for the others there was nothing to do but hope. It was a hard and bitter winter, with the country on the edge of an anarchy of despair.

'If only they had acted at once,' said Clara. 'The whole thing might have been over by now.'

Since the founding of the group she had become something of a confidant to Hewison. Surprisingly, for he had never really believed all the stuff he had been lectured about at the Club, 'Fabiomassimo' had evolved in much the way he had proposed at that first meeting of the *Comitato per Liberazione Nazionale*. It had begun passively, mainly collecting and transmitting information on German troop dispositions and road and rail movements, but it soon became more active: telephone lines were cut, railway points were smashed, caltrops were strewn in the path of German vehicles, a fuel dump was burned. He requested air drops of equipment, and Orlandi and his men found themselves out in the hills at night, flashing signals at circling aircraft and watching parachutes drift down like great jellyfish floating in on the tide. When

Orlandi had pleaded for boots, the sky rained boots; when one of their number, an advocate, suggested that bribery was a weapon which would free them from the attentions of the local Fascist militia, gold sovereigns showered from the heavens; when a port official at Civitavecchia revealed that ships were about to dock bringing with them the armour of a Panzergrenadier Division which had been diverted from Sardinia, the night roared and shook with bombs; and, when it was decided that they were ready for acts of real destruction, the containers which floated down were packed with Sten guns and plastic explosive, time pencils and detonators.

Thus David Hewison fulfilled his messianic utterances. He was a god who distributed money as needed, a seer who spoke with war lords a thousand miles away, a Solomon whose uncompromised position of neutrality meant that he, and only he, could establish rule over the divisions of his factious little army. But, faced with the continual war of words and balancing of tempers and ambitions which his position had come to involve, he had discovered the need for someone with whom he could talk, a kind of secular confessor. In Clara Alessio he had found the perfect listener. His life was one of constant movement between Sabazia and Vetrano and other villages, and the farms in the hills where Orlandi's group was in hiding and training, but always the Castello provided a refuge and a moment's sanity. He would talk with her about the most trivial things, but also the most vital; and always she listened to what he had to say with sympathy and perception. Despite her connections with the Fascists he had come to trust her implicitly, and he knew that, while such total trust was stupid and dangerous, it was justified.

'They will move soon enough now,' he told her. 'One can tell from the messages.'

'You mean another landing?' It had been the main topic of conversation for months, ever since the armistice.

'I'm sure so.'

She smiled thinly. She always avoided asking him about details. Often he told her anyway, but she never asked. She never put any demands on him.

'There's another thing. I've asked for a pianist, if they can spare one. I need some help.'

'A pianist?' She raised her eyebrows. 'Your jargon again.'

'I'm sorry. It's infectious. A wireless operator. I'm rushing around like a scalded cat at the moment, and I can't keep doing two jobs. I'll have to turn more of my attention to Orlandi's lot or they'll begin to get dangerous.'

'So you will not come here?'

'I won't be here as often.' There was a silence, but it seemed as much a part of their conversation as talk. Much of their stunted little relationship was of things left unsaid.

'Perhaps it is a good thing. I have heard from Vincenzo: there is a chance that he will be coming south.'

He had often wondered about her husband. He used to watch her sitting at her desk – she wrote letters often, although the postal service was almost non-existent – with a photograph of the man in front of her. It showed him being presented to the king. The two men made an absurd contrast: Alessio, tall and dominating, stooping down to shake hands with the silly, pompous little monarch. What she thought about her husband, now shut away in that lunatic asylum which Mussolini had created around himself on the shores of Lake Garda, she never said.

'Will he come here?'

'If he can. But his work will take him to Rome or somewhere, maybe to Soratte. Something to do with liaison with the German High Command. He is very guarded when he speaks on the telephone.'

'Why does he put up with it?'

She regarded him steadily, her pinched, thin face like a mask. 'You understand the word *virtù*?'

He shrugged. 'Machiavelli, Castiglione, that kind of thing?'

'Exactly that,' she agreed. 'That is his reason, *virtù*; an old-fashioned Renaissance concept which we can barely compre-hend now.' Despair lurked in her eyes, and for an awful moment he wondered whether it would overwhelm her. Then she laughed humourlessly and began putting things in order on her desk. 'At least *Il Volpe* will be pleased to be doing

37

something active. Gathering information and cutting tele-phone lines is hardly the stuff of which heroes such as he are made.'

*Il Volpe* was Orlandi's nom-de-guerre. At first he had wanted to call himself *Lupo* but Hewison had persuaded him out of it. *Volpe*, the fox, had been by way of a compromise.

'It's also a farmer's word for blight,' Clara had observed on hearing the name. That had been one of the few times she really laughed; Hewison loved to see her laugh.

'Well, now he'll have his opportunity. If the landing comes in this part it will be something like that civil war he is always advocating.'

Clara's expression was heavy with irony as Hewison rose to go. She was Italian, with all the Italian's fatalism.

'*In bocc'al volpe*,' she said with a shrug. And laughed.

# VI

'MALARIA,' Hewison explained. He was at the wheel of the Land Rover driving towards the excavation the next morning. The vehicle pitched and rolled on the rough track but he seemed quite oblivious to the discomfort. 'One thousand five hundred years of malaria, give or take a century,' he said generously. 'And before that the *latifundia*. Remember the Gracchi?'

He had that trick of the tutor about him, the sudden question to see whether a pupil is following what is being said.

'Land reform in the republican era?' I hazarded. 'Tiberius Gracchus and . . .' but memory failed me.

'Gaius Sempronius. They battled against the big landlords, but without much success. Nothing changes. Anyway they weren't fighting on behalf of the Etruscans. Those poor devils had long been driven off the land to make way for cattle and sheep.'

'Like the Highland Clearances?'

'Not unlike. Nineteenth-century Ireland, I always think. A foreign but half-familiar religion, a barbaric language, the same kind of peasants peering out of the same kind of hovels at their masters, sometimes amusing them with funny dances, sometimes telling them strange stories about a vanished but glorious past. And possibly, just occasionally, throwing up a Shaw or a Joyce.'

'That's something.'

'Is it? Bloody traitors I would have thought.'

He laughed, but without much humour. I looked away at the passing landscape, seeing, I suppose, nothing more than deserted hillsides covered with scrub oak and the despairing flags of asphodel. I know now that I would see more. Now I

39

would recognize the pock-marks of long-past eruptions in that exhausted volcanic landscape, and see in them a metaphor: although the volcanoes are dead and oakwoods flourish in the river gorges, yet in many places the stench of sulphur still hangs in the air as a reminder of what once was and what might be again. They still build thermal baths over some of the worst leaks, just as the Romans did. People with sinusitis go there to inhale the massive farts of the underworld.

But it was the Etruscans who made this land blossom and it has never been as prosperous since. They found easily defensible sites for their cities and a rich volcanic soil for their harvests. There was copper and tin and iron in the hills, and when they were at their height Rome was less than a collection of shepherds' huts on the banks of a nearby river.

'Over there somewhere.' Hewison gestured vaguely towards the south, almost as if the place did not exist even now. 'About thirty miles away. This is the same route which the Romans took when they finally invaded after the fall of Veii towards the end of the fourth century BC. You can argue for years about the exact date. They came over the hills from Sutri' – he pointed over his shoulder and the Land Rover lurched dangerously – 'Cortuosa and Contenebra are Livy's names for the towns which they attacked. Which of the two is Lucri is anybody's guess at the moment. Perhaps one day we'll find out.'

It was not difficult to picture the grim and arrogant soldiery marching across the hills to the rhythm of drums and cymbals, their standards waving in the air. Somehow they were still figures in that landscape for in two thousand years it has never regained its population. It still looks as though the inhabitants have just fled and the Roman army is still marching. The Roman conquest, the clearances, the malaria. Echoes of that ancient destruction still ring in the landscape of Etruria like vibrations in a sheet of steel.

The site of the excavation of Lucri is a narrow tongue of land approachable only from the east along an undulating ridge. On all other sides it is ringed by steep slopes and cliffs.

Where the ridge narrows and the pastures give way to woods a sign announced:

'ZONA ARCHEOLOGICA. VIETATO L'ACCESSO AI NON ADDETTI
AI LAVORI.
SOPRINTENDENZA ARCHEOLOGICA PER ETRURIA
MERIDIONALE.'

Past the sign and beyond a chain-link fence was the excavation village. It had something of the air of a military camp: paths running between rows of tents and pre-fabricated huts; a sign which told visitors in two languages that they should report first to the excavation office; a military-style marquee with a notice announcing: 'Mess Tent. *Mensa.*' I almost expected the bawling of a drill sergeant, the tramp of fatigue squads, that kind of thing. But the main path had a sign saying: '*Decumanus Maximus*', an academic joke.

Hewison strode through the place like a senior officer visiting the regimental lines, with head thrust forward and hands clasped behind his back. Passers-by won a brisk smile and a word of encouragement as though he was intent on maintaining morale.

'We call it the *tendopoli*,' he said. 'Underpopulated at the moment but if you come here during the long vacation you'll see the place in top gear. We've broken new ground in Italy by using mainly volunteer diggers, about three hundred in all. Some of the regulars have been coming here for years now. We offer them board and lodging under canvas and one day off a week; not that they take it. It's a sort of kibbutz atmosphere, I'm told.' His mouth turned down. 'Can't say I've ever visited one myself. Anyway, they seem to enjoy it.'

We looked in at the office. Charles von Doren was arguing with an assistant about the repair bill for one of the vehicles. Hewison pulled out some plans from a map drawer to indicate the salient features of the site. The map was meticulously drawn, cross-hatched with surveying datum lines, intricately underpinned with a network of trenches and the tiny details of masonry. His finger swept from one feature to another.

'Necropolis; fourth-century habitation site; sixth-century habitation; acropolis; you can see the lines of the walls; this is the temple area.' He might have been indicating troop dispositions.

41

'And now, dammit, let's go and see the actual thing.'

At the far end of the camp there was a line of trees. He went through a gap. Beyond was a broken path and a stretch of bare rock leading between two moss-encrusted boulders; then a carved ramp which ran steeply down the hillside, turning suddenly through narrow defiles, funnelling any invaders into tight, awkward corners. It was not hard to imagine soldiers looking down from the over-hanging rocks, raining spears and arrows down and boiling pitch or what-ever they used: the kind of thing which archaeologists pay only half-heed to – they prefer the trivial waste of ordinary life – but which happened, century after century; and happens still.

For a big man my uncle moved quickly down the ramps as though straining away from the present practicalities of the excavation and into its substance. When he passed through the final gate and threw out a hand to display the intricate traceries of the excavated town in front of us his face was alight with something more than mere satisfaction: a light of pure possession.

'So there's Lucri.'

If the *tendopoli* had been like a military camp then the excavation itself resembled a building site: the same maze of walls and trenches, the same waste of bare earth. Its twenty acres of tapering land were dominated by two hills, the acropolis at the far end and the necropolis, the cliff of tombs, in the centre. Once the whole area must have been a land-scape of holm oak and thorn bush, an almost arcadian place of rock and vegetation bordered by the glitter of streams and the silence of ancient woods. But all that had been doomed when David Hewison and the Welshman Elwyn Davies had first walked over the undulating ground and felt its strange echoes and reverberations, and decided that here, plain enough, was a site. Now the vegetation had gone and the earth had been laid bare. Over the decades, like anatomists flaying a corpse, the archaeologists had meticulously stripped the promontory of its skin of soil to lay bare the bones and sinews of the ancient city, the shadowy substructure of its houses and streets.

It was through this fossil skeleton of Lucri that Hewison led me on that spring morning. The place was almost deserted. Only in one trench, in the strange aqueous light which corrugated fibreglass roofing cast over them, a few diggers were already working.

Meredith looked up at us, tugging at his forelock in mock salute. Hannah, the girl he had been with the evening before, said, 'Welcome to the *taverna*. No drinks, I'm afraid.' Her fingers were stained with grey dust.

We talked about their work for a while. Hewison studiously referred to the network of stones which surrounded Meredith and his little team as the '*taberna*'. For Meredith it was 'the pub'.

'We're working through an ash layer into the last habitation levels,' he explained. 'Fourth century.'

'Ash layer?'

Hewison nodded. 'Fire. It's not continuous throughout the site and the evidence is inconclusive, but it seems likely. Etruscan buildings were all wood, you see. The Romans burned the place down.'

We watched the diggers for a while more. Looming over the area where they were working was the gaunt cliff of the necropolis. The tomb entrances – toothless mouths and sightless eyes – recalled my view of Sabazia from across the gorge. It was a sight the inhabitants of Lucri would have had to live with, a reminder of death in the midst of their lives, like a skull on a philosopher's desk. And then the Romans with their fire.

'Let's make a start over there.' My uncle was impatient to get going. He pointed towards the farther hill, the feature which formed the bulbous end of the site. Its southern flank was a sheer face of rock dropping down into the gorge on our left.

'That's the acropolis which I showed you on the plans. Actually the word "arx" is more appropriate. Like many Latin words it's probably Etruscan in origin. As it was the best defended site that's where the earliest settlement was. We have evidence of a Chalcolithic burial – Rinaldone culture of about two thousand BC – and Apennine culture huts dating to around one thousand two hundred BC.'

43

We threaded our way through the maze of trenches with Hewison talking in that driving, didactic manner of his:

'In the same levels we also found four potsherds of Mycenean ware, which give positive evidence of cultural links at that time between central Italy and the Aegean. There is some controversy over their origin but Meredith seems convinced. If you add them to the similar sherd found at another site near here by the Swedish Institute then you have a fairly strong case.

'Of course anything you see now above ground is Etruscan, that pylon for example; difficult to date with any precision. The main walls were erected against the Romans, but I'd put that gate considerably earlier.'

And so David Hewison explained the excavation of Lucri to me, the first member of his family who had ever seen it. He was tireless in both word and limb. His hand would sweep out to indicate a particular feature and suddenly he was clambering his way across the foundation walls to show a specific aspect of the city, or dropping to his knees in a trench to demonstrate some subtle aspect of stratigraphy. And I found my self dragged back by his enthusiasm to my university days, recent in years but somehow long-dead in memory, when I would find myself following an archaeology lecturer around a dig trying to master facts and hypotheses as they came like missiles. We leapt the centuries as though they were narrow ditches, went back and forth over the periods as though playing hopscotch, and all the while I tried to fit the whole together into some kind of schema, or worse, because my knowledge of the Etruscans was miserably vague, to build a schema as I went along.

But Hewison spoke well and there was no doubt that he had an impressive life-work of which to speak. The excavation was a huge piece of work, thrilling in its concept, anachronistic in its scale. It seemed to hark back to the almost legendary excavations of the past, to Schliemann's Troy and Mycenae, to Evans' Knossos, to Woolley's Ur of the Chaldees, each one of them the realization of a vision in which the act of excavation becomes so much more than a mere dissection of the past, becomes an act of empathy and communion.

From the high and windy arx with its reconstructed temple, to the narrow streets and alleys of the city beneath, to the necropolis with its rock-cut tombs, there was everything I could have envisaged as a child first hearing about this strange, estranged uncle: here was imagination, vision, mystery. Here, I realized, was a legend in the making, and the legend found its perfect image in the man. I still retain a vivid picture of him striding over the bones of his obsession, his voice urgent, convincing, supremely convinced.

'Imagination is the key,' he insisted.

We stood before the temple of Turan on the summit of the arx. The building had something of the look of a Chinese pagoda. Its glaring primary colours presented a stark contrast to the diffused spring colouring of the woods and the surrounding hills.

'Imagination,' he repeated, pointing up at it. 'It still offends people, you know. However much you cite the evidence it offends them because they are too tied up with our misconceptions of the classical world. Imagine if you tried to repaint all the extant Greek classical statues. Can you wonder that they can't stomach this?'

Demon faces in bright polychrome terracotta leered down at us.

We went back to the narrow ridge below the arx. To the right was the way we had come, back to the city itself; to the left another way wound steeply down through the trees.

'Where does that go?' I asked.

He shrugged. 'The valley. The railway line. Disused now. There's an abandoned station there but it's nothing more than a ruin. Now, up here is our prize.'

Ahead of us was a sign saying:

'NECROPOLIS. VII – IV sec. AC.'

There was a staircase cut into the rock and at the top a platform in the hillside. At its back a short cliff guarded the summit. It was not difficult to imagine the funeral processions halting on the platform, perhaps for a ritual purification before making their way up onto the summit. There would have been cymbals and pipes, the flame of sacred fires, the keening of the mourners. Now there was just this short stretch of bare rock edged by blackthorn and holm oak; and Hewison standing with his head thrust forward and his hands on his hips, challenging with his smile.

'You should have come here years ago, when you were fooling around at university. Look.'

He swept out a hand to encompass the view. From where we were we could see across to the arx with its temple, down onto the streets and houses, down again even further to the stream which had cut the gorge on the south side of the site.

'It's a pretty place, isn't it? Woods, rocks, running water, the sort of thing which Poussin might have painted. *Et in arcadia ego.* In a way it is a shame that I've been at work here for the last two decades spending the family fortune. After all there is nothing very beautiful about bare earth and trenches, or half-buried stones. Or security fences and guards if it comes to that. But the point is that this place lives for me. Lives. In here.' He tapped his forehead. 'It's a self-indulgence, I suppose. A bit like going back to a place which you knew in childhood. Those things you had forgotten coming back bit by bit, you know what I mean? Putting yourself into some kind of context, any context. It's better than none.'

And suddenly I understood why the family hated him so. Not only had he stolen his own present from their grasp, and used the Hewison money to do so, but with the Villa Rasenna and the excavation of Lucri he had taken back his own past as well. It was not to Poggio Sanssieve that he returned to do obeisance: it was to Lucri. And with that hold gone they had lost him completely.

Pleased that in some way I had solved a little riddle I followed him up to the summit of the hill. Thus explained he seemed less daunting, almost companionable. Together we crossed the summit platform to the edge of the cliff and together we peered over the precipice to where, almost directly below us, Meredith and his colleagues were working beneath the plastic roofing.

'Now here, for example. Don't you feel it? The holy of holies?'

Was there something numinous about the place? I was prepared to accept it for his sake: it was his shrine and one is always polite about another person's religion.

Perhaps he saw my scepticism. 'Follow me.'

We went around a boulder and down, down between vertical rock walls as though into a deep well, our feet slithering on the steps which the Etruscans had carved. Then equally suddenly we emerged into the sunlight of a narrow terrace. There was a row of doors in the cliff like a street of troglodyte dwellings, comic rather than numinous. Hewison ducked into one of the doorways to point out the stone platforms where sarcophagi had once lain. 'Most of the tombs were already empty when we got to them which made them difficult to date. Stripped by the Romans in all probability. I'd guess they're quite early, say seventh century.'

He stood silently for a moment, a big man stooped beneath the roof of the cave with his face as solemn as a mourner's. The dusty floor, the absolute bareness of the place, seemed only to emphasize the dead centuries which lay between the original occupiers and the present visitors.

He looked up. 'But occasionally we've struck lucky. Come.'

I followed him back out into the light and further along the terrace, past the row of gaping doorways to the far end where a great slab of rock had slipped from the upper cliff. With remarkable agility he climbed down to a lower level. Following warily I found that he had gone on out of sight around the foot of the slab.

'Come on,' he called. He was enjoying himself. When I reached him on the other side of the rock he was grinning like a child.

'Bit awkward at the moment, isn't it? We'll have to put in steps when the tourists come. Look there.'

At first sight there was nothing. The rock face he was pointing to was a blank, except that carved into the rock was the outline of a door, the jambs and lintel alone without any opening.

'There. That's our latest.' He pointed at the ground.

At the foot of this dummy door was a shallow opening about three feet high.

47

'They started this kind of entrance at the beginning of the fourth century. We don't have any firm explanation for the false doors. Perhaps it was nothing more than fancy, perhaps it was an attempt to hide them from grave robbers. Perhaps the poor devils knew that the Romans were coming and that their days were numbered. If that was the reason then occasionally it worked.'

He crouched down and lowered his legs through the hole. 'It's a bit awkward, I'm afraid. There should be a lamp inside somewhere. Hang on a moment.'

He disappeared, a Lazarus in reverse. I waited on the small ledge with the wind buffeting around me. Far below my position, below the excavations where Meredith was working, the Vesca stream sparkled in the sunlight as it made its way through the gorge to join the main river beyond the point of the arx. Eventually my uncle's voice summoned me from the depths:

'Duck your head until you are right in. Then you can stand upright.'

I lowered myself after him. The air was suddenly cold. It had the still, dead feel of the centuries about it, like a cold grave cloth wrapped around one's body. I straightened up in the darkness.

'There we are.' His voice was loud, confined by close walls. He was standing a few feet away along a short passage, holding a small lamp above his head. The sphere of light showed up the brown walls of the passage, the earth floor, the vaulted ceiling. There were chisel-marks in the rock. Beyond him was an entrance of the most absolute and all-absorbing blackness.

'This is the dromos, the entrance passage. There's a step down into the chamber itself so be careful.' He grinned. The light cast diagonal shadows across his face giving him the harsh, angular look of a hallowe'en mask. Then he turned and led the way into the black.

When he spoke again his voice resonated in the volume of the tomb.

'We're here.'

The light wobbled in the darkness like a globe of incandescent matter floating in water. Huge shadows staggered and lurched across the walls and the floor. The light fell on a collection of pots, some bronze figurines which were green with verdigris, a dagger and helmet, a candelabrum. Then it rose upwards in his hand.

I had to stifle a cry. On either side of the chamber, looking up from low couches, where two life-size human figures.

'I forgot to mention the owners,' Hewison said with a soft laugh.

The figures, a man on one side, a female on the other, were moulded in reddish terracotta. Each was reclining on an elbow and looking towards the entrance with a faint, archaic smile of welcome. The male even held out one hand as though showing something to the onlooker.

'Maybe they were expecting to be disturbed,' Hewison said softly. 'It's hard not to feel for them, isn't it?' His amusement at his little surprise seemed to have evaporated. Standing over the male figure he gave the impression of a priest called to the deathbed: his expression was infinitely tender, his movements solemn, almost hieratic. I remembered him in the church at Farm Street, standing like this over my mother's coffin.

'His name was Lars, of the gens Lethna.' His finger ran along the inscription on the base of the sarcophagus. 'This word is *zilath*, a political post corresponding to the Roman *praetor*. This part gives his age: *lupu ril huth zathrum*, died twenty-six years old.'

With the lamp held up he crossed to the other couch. The woman looked impassively up at me, perhaps as she had looked impassively at her forthcoming death. Her features were elegant and fine, her gently slanted eyes faintly amused.

'She was Sethra Velznath. That's the gentilitial form of *Velzna*, Volsinii. The name survives in modern Bolsena. So Lars had married a woman from a neighbouring city.'

It was impossible not to feel an intruder on something private. I sensed a great ocean of time lying all around me in that claustrophobic chamber and tried to search for a landmark, something to ground the thing in my own experience. A date? What did that mean? These people had existed, palpably existed. To them their own time had not been a

49

cypher in an archaeological chronology. They had stood at the very pinnacle of their past, at a moment which subsumed all that had gone before. An eternal present. To fix them in some temporal framework, like flies in amber, seemed to reduce the significance of their own particular existence. They had existed; in some metaphysical way I felt that they still did exist. That was enough. Never before had I felt so vividly the import of the word eternity.

Hewison asked softly, 'Are the two-thousand-year dead any further away from us than last month's dead?'

Then without waiting for an answer he made his way out towards the daylight.

That evening he was full of enthusiasm for our tour of the excavation.

'Anthony loved the place, didn't you? Stunned by it. Amazed.'

I admitted as much. Even his own over-enthusiasm seemed justified. 'Particularly the two sarcophagi in that new tomb. What are their names?'

'Lars and Sethra.'

'They seem as fine as the husband and wife group in the Villa Giulia.'

'Better,' he insisted. 'Less stylized. Closer to the truth. Look, you can see.' Lara was passing his chair. He reached out and caught her arm. 'A living Etruscan. Aren't the same features here?'

He held her for inspection, and I sensed a hint of unease behind her good-humoured protest. I wondered whether it was for this that she had first attracted him, this facile resemblance to the dark-skinned, long-nosed people who dance stately steps across the walls of dozens of painted tombs at Tarquinia or lie at their ease on sarcophagus lids from Cerveteri or Tuscania or Lucri. 'Isn't this the same bone structure, the same skin texture? Look at the slant of those eyes. Who is to deny it?'

'Any anthropologist, I would have thought,' Charles van Doren answered him. 'You might as well look for Roman blood in a modern Italian.'

'That's it: blood groups!' Lara no longer seemed to matter. Pursuing this new idea with all the enthusiasm of a dog after a rabbit, Hewison let her go. 'We need a survey of blood groups. That would show them up. Blood groups can show racial migrations, gypsies, Bretons, Basques, that kind of thing. Why not the Etruscans?'

'About two thousand years why not,' replied Jane, but Hewison ignored her.

'What about thalassaemia? Or something else. Who has ever investigated the people of this area to find some genetic marker which would put them apart from the rest of the country? Then one could find other groups with the same characteristics and show how they related. For God's sake they speak differently here – think of the *gorgia toscana* – so what's to say they don't have identifiable gene differences? Isn't that what modern anthropology is all about?'

This was the obsessive side to the man's nature, the farmer's stubbornness which for over twenty years had driven him to till his few acres of excavation, and which also drove him to extract the maximum from every passing idea. On that occasion the blood group question soon died away in sheer ignorance but the subject was not forgotten. Later the idea re-surfaced, this time cloaked in further information:

'Beta-amino isobutyric acid,' he declared with immense satisfaction one evening when everyone was on the terrace. 'A substance excreted in unusually high concentrations by people of Asian origin. Now if we could show that people living in Tuscany and northern Lazio were similar excreters, then that would confirm the eastern origins of the group.'

'Are you proposing to test Lara's urine?' asked Jane. There was embarrassed laughter.

'Why not? For God's sake why not? We have run excavation into the ground. Without a bilingual we are making no headway with the language. We need a new approach.'

There was a feeling that he might just demonstrate his conviction by demanding that Lara squat down and urinate there and then amidst the tables and chairs.

Hannah said, 'It sounds mediaeval to me, like analyzing the humours.'

'Watch it,' Meredith warned her, 'or you'll end up as one of the control group.'

Mercifully laughter took over, but it was plain that Hewison was only half-amused. From time to time thereafter he would bring the subject up and try to fire people's interest in it without success.

Yet when he was within his own field his enthusiasms were moderated by a genuine and touching sensitivity. Later on that evening following my first visit to the excavation he showed me some of the pottery. He cradled the pieces in his huge hands with the gentleness of a father with a new-born baby, and his talk was far more than the merely analytical talk of an expert like Meredith. He loved the pieces, and loved the strange people who had made them, perhaps because he saw in them a people who, like him, had not quite fitted into the world which they had inhabited. But he was honest about them.

'No Lawrentian sentimentality,' he insisted. 'No mawkishness. They were as dangerous and nasty, and doubtless as posturing and deceiving as any people ever was or ever is. But what life, eh? What vitality! And what a brilliant sense of the sheer terror of nature.'

And the bronze chimera was almost a pet for him. It crouched beside his chair in the drawing room of the Villa while he caressed its lion head as though nuzzling a puppy.

'Look at her. She hates herself for the awful mess which nature has made of her, and she hates you for being half-way normal. But my goodness she lives!'

The bronze creature snarled and twisted under his hand.

I believe it was the same evening that I first heard him talk about the war, not the war which had taken place around Sabazia but rather the public one which Jane had warned me to expect. I forget how the subject came up, but I remember that he grabbed the opportunity with enthusiasm:

'You should have seen us, Anthony, with our operational HQ beside the Boboli Gardens and land lines laid across the Ponte Vecchio to the partisan groups on the north bank. Every street south of the river choked with rubble. Snipers in every *palazzo*. Machine-gun emplacements on the Lungarno. We infiltrated men over the bridge by the Vasari *corridoio*, did you know? The Germans had blown all the other bridges and mined the Ponte Vecchio itself, but they never seemed to think of the *corridoio*. Hadn't read their Baedekers.'

It was a story I was to hear often enough. The time of day would dictate the tone: early in the evening it was tales of derring-do which might have come – the illusion was his own – from the autobiography of that other Florentine, Benvenuto Cellini; but later on a grimmer note would intrude: dead bodies would appear amongst the rubble, a colleague had his leg blown off before his eyes, a convent was invaded and the sisters raped, partisans were put up against a wall in the Palazzo Vecchio and machine-gunned.

'And then the Germans withdrew to the Gothic line in the mountains . . . and suddenly I could go home.'

I remember his expression as he looked at me: a challenge, but at the same time a look of derision. For I knew where home was, and I knew *what* home was.

'The Pontassieve factory kept working throughout the war, did you know?'

I shrugged. 'What else could it do? It must have been needed: dressings, disinfectants, drugs, all kind of things. The wounded don't have any nationality, do they?'

He laughed. 'Is that the voice of public relations speaking? I inspected the books, you know. Oh yes, I stood over Signor Orsini and inspected the books, the real ones which are not available to government officials of any kind. And do you know where all the profits had gone?'

The question was purely rhetorical. Those others who were listening – Jane, Charles, Lara and the rest – had surely heard it all before.

'Switzerland,' he said flatly. 'All over the border into the Swiss operation. Nice and safe. For the duration. Pimps, you see, dear nephew, pimps the lot of them. And do you know what they all pimp for?' He looked round the company. No one seemed disposed to answer. 'They pimp for what my father called, rather quaintly I always thought, the "patrimony", and brother Thomas refers to as the corporate personality. Isn't that right, nephew?'

'In a way,' I answered.

'In a way,' he repeated. 'It is exactly right. I had found it out long before, at the age of fifteen. I told my grandfather, my Italian grandfather that is, that I would rather run his broken-down old estate in Tuscany than make toothpaste and soap. So my mother told my father, and my father sent me away to boarding school. "Some discipline is what he needs," they said. They sent me to the Benedictines, and lo and behold I found quite the wrong discipline for in an access of piety I announced to the whole family that I had decided to enter the novitiate.'

He looked for a reaction. A few people laughed nervously.

'My mother screamed, I swear she screamed with horror. Anyone would have thought that I had confessed to buggering juniors. "Whom have you told about this?" she demanded. "You irresponsible boy, whom have you told?"

'"God," I answered. Do you know there was relief all over her face? "Is that all?" she asked. "Just God?"

'"Yes, just God."

'She pursed her lips, like this. What I always used to call the satisfied arsehole. "Well," she said. "Then at least no damage has been done."'

Now the audience laughed freely, sensing that the threatened storm had dispersed.

'So it was back to the private tutors and as soon as possible pack me off to the university where my brother Thomas could keep an eye on me. And do you know the only one of them who showed me any sympathy?' He looked round the gathering and his gaze came to rest on me. 'My sister. Flicky, I used to call her. No one else called her that. To the rest she was Felicity, and to our mother Perpetua, for heaven's sake. But to me she was Flicky. And she told me that she thought my vocation a great and noble thing, and that Mamma was a *putana*. I don't really think she knew what the word meant, but the spirit was right.'

The court was enjoying itself. Hewison was enjoying himself. Lara was smiling at me. 'See how fond of her he was?'

But behind the acid jokes lay half a century of bitterness which, of all the people present, perhaps only I could taste.

# VII

# *Winter 1943/44*

ORLANDI and Hewison pored over the maps. They followed the black line of a railway as it wound through the hills from east to west until Orlandi's finger came decisively down.

'That's the place,' he said. 'I know the area like the back of my hand, and that's the place.'

There was no denying that he was right. From a town on the Via Cassia the branch-line left the main north-south railway and meandered across country to link up with the coast. It was a monument to the idiocies of planners, its existence dictated, like so much else in pre-war Italy, by theory rather than the needs of the people, for barely anywhere in its thirty-mile course did it pass usefully near a village; indeed from the map it seemed at times that it deliberately avoided each *paese* that lay near its route. But it had not been built to serve the people. It had been built in concordance with an idea, the theory that geographical barriers could be broken down by modern communications, that the natural and ancient north-south polarization of the peninsula should be cut across from east to west, and that thereby, by some mystic catalysis, Italy would become a progressive European country like Germany or France. So the trains, empty for the most part, had shuttled back and forth by order of a ministry in Rome without anyone taking very much notice of them until the war came. Then, of course, the silly single track suddenly became important, and guns and armour and troops took advantage of it and Orlandi and Hewison followed its route with fascination, as though examining some newly deciphered text; and Orlandi's finger came down on the most significant symbol along the whole thirty miles: the girder bridge over the River Mignone.

'That's the place,' he repeated. 'Immediately after Vetrano station.'

The station was a little box in the midst of crowded contour lines. It was so far from Vetrano itself that they had to refer to the adjoining map to find the town.

'Six kilometres. Look: all the way along the valley. No road, not even a track worth the name. Then up over the hills to the town. A piece of Fascist lunacy. The Germans would hardly get a half-track to that station.'

Orlandi's finger came back to the little box. 'The station is stuck in a narrow valley, see? Immediately afterwards the track passes through a rock cutting and goes directly out onto the bridge. A double-span simple girder construction with masonry arch approaches,' he added, displaying an unexpected knowledge of such things. His eyes were alight with visions of the explosion. He could hear the awful clangour of riven steel, see twisted girders flung pell-mell into the air and a train plummeting into the gulf below.

'And after the bridge?'

'It keeps to the far wall of the valley for a while, and then there's the tunnel.' He pointed to where the black line gave way to a row of dashes. 'A good kilometre long.'

'Maybe the tunnel would be better. It's further from the station.'

'The tunnel!' Orlandi's tone was derisive. Tunnels did not embody the spectacle of bridges. 'Too easy to repair,' he said. 'You'd only bring a bit of rock and earth down and they'd soon bulldoze it clear. And don't worry about the station: there's nothing there. Half-a-dozen railwaymen. It's a real dead end place, only there's water there for the engines, that's all.'

Hewison rubbed his chin. 'We'll have to take a look. Blowing a line is one thing, but an entire bridge . . . God knows how much plastic we'd need.'

'So let's take a look.'

The walk took a morning. It was a fine winter day with a cloudless sky of intense blue. The air shifted gently down from the north bringing with it a bite of frost. They started from where they had passed the night in one of the farm huts above Sabazia and made their way beside the river Vesca, following the edge of its gorge until Orlandi suddenly announced: 'We cross here.'

There was a gap in the brambles beside the track and a steep path running downhill. They slithered down amongst the *macchia* and the litter of a decaying hillside, down to the stream at the bottom. At the water's edge they drank, cupping the icy water up to their mouths. Then they balanced on boulders across the stream, and stepped into the past.

The first sign was small: a neat series of steps cut in the rock of the far bank, steps bevelled off by time and over-lain with moss. These led, now vanishing, now re-emerging from the grass, to a short plateau beneath the cliffs. Great mossy boulders stood like menhirs amongst the scrub. There was something deliberate about them, an elusive quality of design which made it certain that they had not just fallen at random from the cliff above; and yet it was impossible to say why they were there, what significance they had.

Orlandi pointed to the trees ahead. Above their crowns the cliff loomed implacably. 'That way.'

His grin betrayed him: he knew a secret.

The trees were holm oak, evergreen symbols of immortality. In their dense shade the boulders crowded in on the two men, jostling them like huge, silent guards, pushing them into a narrow defile.

'A gate!' Hewison exclaimed.

On either side of the gap he had found sockets some twenty centimetres across, each corresponding exactly with its opposite number on the other side. The most stunted imagination could supply the bars to barricade the way. The word 'pylon' floated up into his consciousness. A whole section of his mind was awakening, a part which had remained dormant ever since he had joined the army. His other life. He peered into the trees on either side. Bearing in mind the earth movements which plagued this part of the world it was easy enough to imagine the chaos of boulders re-formed into a wall. Another word was there: 'cyclopean'.

Orlandi's voice came from above, somewhere up the cliff face:

'Where the hell are you?'

Hewison pulled himself from the undefined past back into the twentieth century. He pushed on through a narrow corridor of stone, through a second gateway, then around a sharp corner to the foot of the cliff.

The face was shrouded in moss and oozing with damp, but the way ahead was clear enough, a diagonal ramp carved out of the rock and slanting upwards towards the skyline. In places there were shallow steps. A drainage channel ran down one side. From halfway up *Il Volpe* beckoned impatiently.

'What kept you?'

Hewison gestured around. 'This place. It's a fortified passage up from the river.' He had already dismissed Roman with ease. This was older, simpler, cast in bold slabs of stone rather than painstaking ashlar or brickwork. 'Etruscan. It must be.'

Orlandi shrugged. What was the past to him? 'Get a move on.'

But Hewison could hear the mules snorting and stamping on the ramp. There was the cursing of the drivers, the crack of whips, the swaying of the loads: bales of cloth perhaps, sacks of grain, baskets of metal-bearing ore from the Tolfa hills. And the helmeted guards standing impassively at either end of the narrow gangway.

At the head of the ramp was a square-cut platform and another gate of monumental rock. They went through onto the plateau, into a field of thistles beneath a great expanse of winter sky.

'We're here.' Orlandi pulled the map out and showed the stream and the hatching which marked the cliff. 'Over there' – he pointed across the plateau – 'is the other valley, with the railway line. We'll get a good view of it from the far end of this ridge.'

He set off westward, cursing the thistles, with Hewison in his wake. After a while they reached a rough track which ran along the crest of the plateau between the derelict fields. Whenever they could see down into the valley on their right they caught a glimpse of the railway, and once they stood and listened as a train went past; but otherwise there was no sign of life and no sound beyond their own footsteps and the rustling of the wind in the thistles.

Later they heard the distant rumble of aero engines and looking up they could make out a formation of a dozen aircraft, silver crucifixes against the blue, moving northwards; Americans, going to bomb Livorno or somewhere.

'Fortresses,' said Hewison.

'Bastards,' said Orlandi.

Then the land dropped down sharply and they were on a narrow neck between the two valleys, with their path climbing up ahead to a rock escarpment. This feature seemed both natural and artificial, a natural scarp across the plateau which human hands had improved, carved steeper where necessary, built up with boulders where the rock had eroded away. It was impossible to say whether the narrow gap which broached this defence had been cut or whether it was natural, so intimately did these distant people know their landscape, so perfectly could they mould it. Here there was no intrusion on the land: nature and man's work seemed an organic whole.

With a growing sense of excitement Hewison followed Orlandi through the gap and across another field towards a line of trees. They halted. Through the trees they could see down onto the stream which they had crossed earlier. It was larger now, almost a river meandering through a narrow flood plain between steep wooded slopes and cliffs, heading for its junction with the main river. But what Hewison was looking at was the acropolis.

It was as if the buildings still stood above the cliffs on the high, domed summit. Orlandi pointed to it and referred to it as 'that hill', but for Hewison it was quite plainly the acropolis, the final boss of rock at the end of the ridge, the inner citadel of the city upon which they had intruded, the arx.

'We can get a perfect view of the station from that hill,' said his companion. 'But from now on we must be quiet.'

The hill was entirely cliff-bound except for the neck which connected it with the bulk of the plateau. To reach it they were forced down from their vantage point and across a narrow space beneath cliffs. The place was thick with holm oak. They clambered over lichen-shrouded boulders up through the trees and onto the summit of the hill.

The hill was covered with grass and scattered with narrow spears of asphodel. It had the blighted look of the *garigue*, the impoverished scrub which signals a meagre soil; and for Hewison it was a moment of revelation. Across the plateau there were anonymous mounds which reverberated under foot. In many places piles of stones broke through the grass like eruptions of psoriasis. He knew, with an excitement that was almost suffocating, that he was walking a mere six inches above the bones and cavities of a city.

Orlandi was beckoning urgently from the line of trees which marked the north boundary of the acropolis. He seemed quite oblivious to the fact that he was standing behind a metre and a half of carefully constructed fortress wall.

'Down there,' he was whispering, pointing through a gap in the trees. 'Down there.'

Vetrano station was an unexceptional place in an unexpected situation. Tucked in the bottom of its narrow valley, it consisted of a single box-like station building, two platforms, two water towers and a siding. The name VETRANO blazed in bright yellow ceramic tiles across the front of the building, but it seemed unlikely that many passengers would ever read it. Behind the station a scrub-covered hillside rose to a rocky summit. There was no trace of track or path or any other connection with the world of man, save the single-track line which ran away up the valley. This little outpost of the twentieth century had been dumped in the midst of an ancient wilderness.

'*Tedeschi*,' Orlandi whispered. He spat fatly into the bushes.

There were indeed Germans. From two hundred feet above it was easy to see their *feldgrau* uniforms, their characteristic helmets. Through binoculars it was even possible to make out rank badges and regimental insignia. One of them was smoking as he leant against the wall of the building, while the other picked his nose with elaborate curiosity. The nose-picker looked to be at least fifty years old; his partner seemed a bare eighteen. They were guarding, if that was the appropriate word, two empty flat-cars which lay alongside one of the platforms. It did not appear to be the most onerous task currently faced by the Wehrmacht.

As Hewison and Orlandi watched, a bell rang out like the angelus bell from a church. A second before the brassy little sound reached him up on the plateau Hewison had noticed the soldiers move. The nose-picker spoke to someone within the building; the smoker threw away his cigarette and picked up his rifle.

'A train,' whispered Orlandi.

Down on the platform a man in the uniform of the Italian State Railways – 'bastard collaborator,' muttered Orlandi – had appeared. He wandered over to a signal lever and pulled. They heard a signal clang somewhere out of sight to the right. Except for the soldiers' uniforms and rifles the little dumb show might have been a peacetime scene at any remote country station.

'Come on,' urged Orlandi. 'Let's go and watch it. It's coming from the coast, it'll cross over the bridge.'

How he had worked that out, or whether he had merely guessed, Hewison did not know. Dutifully he turned from the vantage point and followed his companion across the hill.

This would have been the temple area, he thought, as he stumbled in the man's wake. What gods did the Etruscans worship? He searched his mind and found it appallingly empty. There was Apollo, he felt sure, but he must have been borrowed from the Greeks; and he had an idea that Minerva was the Etruscan goddess Menvra. But nothing else. He stood in the midst of an ancient acropolis, on top of the foundations of temples and shrines, and found that he had no real knowledge whatever of the Etruscan pantheon, indeed almost no knowledge of the Etruscans themselves. They were just the stuff of legend: the Kings of Rome, Tarquin the Proud, Lars Porsena – vague, mythic figures perceived uncertainly through the funerary objects he had seen before the war in the museums in Florence and elsewhere, and now consigned to the scrap-heap of his memory along with Arthur's knights and Charlemagne's paladins: mere literary conventions. And yet

61

the Etruscans had lived. All about him there were impressions of them in the landscape, like a potter's thumbprint preserved for millennia in a piece of clay. He felt them. It was the present century, the absurd *volpe* pushing ahead through the brambles, the railway with its cargoes of war, the high-flying bombers, the committee for national liberation, his own presence here, which all seemed insubstantial and dream-like.

He waded through brambles after Orlandi.

The plateau of the acropolis came to a point like the prow of a ship. On either side the cliffs dropped sheer, but at the very place where Orlandi was crouched was a small pulpit of rock. Beyond it there was a gulf before the rocks rose up again like the hunched vertebral column of some giant archosaur. Hewison crept forward to join his companion.

It was a remarkable position. Peering over the lip of rock he found himself looking directly down onto the railway line where it cut through the ridge. There was a concrete water tower and a signal gantry almost at their level. To the right the line went back along the valley to the station. To the left it ran out over six masonry arches and onto the girder bridge which strode, with massive incongruity, over the waters and water meadows of the river Mignone. Beyond the bridge the line continued high up on the valley wall for half a kilometre, before vanishing into the tunnel. In their little hollow in the rock they seemed to be suspended above this view as though in the gondola of a balloon.

'Here it comes,' Orlandi whispered.

A whistle announced the train's appearance. Moving like a snake with slow, reptilian certainty it emerged from the distant tunnel and strung itself along the side of the valley. For a while it clung to the hills as though reluctant to leave their security, and then the engine had turned towards them onto the bridge. Its plume of smoke blew away down wind.

'Goods wagons,' whispered Orlandi. 'Do you see those guns?'

The train consisted of fifteen plain brown wagons and one passenger car. Just behind the tender and again at the very rear of the train were thirty-seven millimetre anti-aircraft guns mounted on flat-cars. Through the binoculars Hewison could see the crews watching the sky.

The noise increased. It spread towards them and enveloped them. The bridge rang with the vibration. The engine's whistle shrieked in their ears and steam surged up around them, cutting off their view so that their only sensation was the thunder of the train through the gap below, a sensation that was both sound and feeling at the same time, like something taking possession of their bodies.

'Quite a place!' Orlandi shouted above the racket. He was grinning exultantly, like a little boy on a railway bridge.

# VIII

JANE van Doren wielded her power within the world of the excavation with some subtlety. Her commands masqueraded under the guise of requests; a careful interrogation passed for solicitude.

'Do come and help me if you can spare a minute,' she said, and soon I found myself in that part of the Villa which was her own special preserve, the Finds Room with Jane humming to herself as she worked, occasionally smoking a cigarette – 'started during the war before all this publicity about the health risk, and never managed to give it up' – and exhibiting that curious mixture of the maternal and the martinet which was her stock-in-trade.

'Do this, will you? If you don't mind getting your hands dirty. When they are clean put them to dry over there. But be gentle with them.'

'They' were pottery fragments, a whole collection of that litter which is the stuff of excavations. Like a library the room was walled and sub-divided by banks of metal shelving, but there were no books. It was a library of potsherds, a library of domestic disaster.

'You can bring those over here if you like. And I'll begin entering the others in the catalogue. I hope you don't mind.'

No one did. She had a brisk humour and a sharp irony which persuaded people into doing for her almost as much as she did herself.

'What does Jane want now?' they would ask in mock exasperation; but always they did what was wanted.

'I suppose you wanted to get away from things for a bit?' she asked me.

I looked up from the plastic basin in which I was washing

64

dirt from formless chunks of terracotta. 'Intimations of mortality,' I answered. 'I feel rather backward not having had them before. Watching my mother die was like . . . looking in a mirror for the first time. An uncomfortable experience.'

'No family? Immediate family, I mean. Wife, children.'

'I'm married, but . . . we're breaking up.'

'I'm sorry.' She could be sympathetic when required. She looked at me with a motherly smile. 'Not a good moment.'

'Not at all. But it had been coming for a long time. We met at university and it was too early, I suppose. We grew up and apart.'

'Someone else?'

I shrugged. 'Politics. She got in with some sort of radical Marxist group. You know the kind of thing: middle class intellectuals calling themselves the Proletarian Action Party or something. That makes PAP: it can't be that. Anyway the kind of thing you can't take seriously whatever it calls itself. But she does.'

'I can't imagine that she was very popular with the Hewison clan.'

'Disastrous.'

'And why did you come here?'

I went back to the washing. 'I wanted an escape. David's something of a symbol in the family: the man who got away; the prodigal who never returned to eat humble pie.'

'Are you tempted to follow him?'

I ignored that. 'I was already here in Italy. I had to bury my mother at Poggio Sanssieve – do you know the place?'

'I've heard about it. Rather splendid by all accounts.'

'It used to be, before they restored it and turned it into a company showpiece. Anyway I couldn't really face going straight back to London so I got on the first train to Rome. On a whim.'

'And what do you think?'

'Of what?'

'The prodigal.'

I evaded the question. 'I knew something of what to expect. I read his book about Lucri when I was at university, and Elwyn Davies –'

'You know Elwyn?'

'I used to go to his lectures.'

And so we talked about that, content for the moment to occupy neutral ground while I wondered about her own place in the past, and her relationship with Hewison in those early days when Elwyn Davies had been here. She had the kind of bleached, durable good looks which one does not see amongst Italians: in her thirties, doyenne of the Lucri excavation, she would have been striking. When I asked her about her husband her tone was faintly patronizing, faintly deprecating:

'Oh, Charles . . .' They had 'bumped into' each other in Crete, he a bachelor migrating between the British School at Athens and Cambridge University, she 'at a loose end after working at Lucri . . . and we helped each other down from the shelf, I suppose.'

'And eventually you brought Charles back here?'

She shrugged. 'This is where my heart is. I know Lucri is almost all David's, but at least a part of it is mine.'

As we worked she was happy enough to reminisce, but they were neutral reminiscences which gave little away: the first survey, the battles with Italian bureaucracy over permits, the gathering of the first volunteers, the first trenches cut, that kind of thing. The Villa itself had been an empty shell in which the staff had done little better than camp, spending much of their time battling with leaking roofs and decayed fittings. But when I mentioned Lara there was something else, a hint of evasion.

'What about her? She was just a young schoolgirl. You know: pleated skirt, white blouse and ankle socks. She used to help. No one took much notice of her really.'

'Didn't they?' I smiled, but she didn't seem amused.

'You know what I mean. There were lots of young people around during the summers. Her mother was a friend of David's – people often stayed at their house in fact – and Lara used to join in the digging. Nothing more than that.'

There was an edge to her voice. Jealousy? By chance I had been at Poggio Sanssieve when the momentous news had arrived. I had been looking on as Nonna Angelica cast discretion to the winds and read aloud from her son's letter:

66

'. . . a girl for whom I have acted almost as guardian over the years . . .' and then, quivering with outrage, had delivered the dismissal: 'A peasant child.'

I also remembered the moment on the steps of the church in Sabazia when even that illusion had been dashed. Had Lara, in her innocence, dashed others?

I finished the washing. Leaving the potsherds to dry I wandered around to examine the pottery. On one shelf I discovered lumps of clay crudely shaped into bits of anatomy: limbs, noses, ears, like the broken parts of so many dolls. There were some triangular slabs of terracotta, each with a narrow groove incised downwards towards the point.

'Female pudenda.' Jane had been watching me from across the room. 'You'll see that some of them have a little clay bead inset into the groove. Clitoris. Question: does the absence of a clitoris in some of them imply that the Etruscans practised female circumcision?'

'Does it?'

'Who knows? Those other things, the pear-shaped lumps, are uteri. They all come from a shrine we excavated two years ago beneath the arx. It must have been a healing cult.'

'Things haven't changed,' I said. There are modern shrines in Italy which are little different: abandoned plaster casts, leg-irons, crutches, all sorts of things hanging on the walls. Looking over the collection of bits from Lucri I saw just so many pathetic illusions.

'And now we put our faith in pills,' I said, 'and the Hewison family gets richer.'

Jane shrugged. 'No doubt there was a family who made the votive objects for the shrine. No doubt they were rich as well.'

It was after I had been at the Villa for three days, helping out in an ineffectual way at the dig and in the Finds Room, that Lara announced that she would take me to see something of the rest of the countryside.

'Anthony has not come here just to slave away for you,' she declared. 'He is our guest.'

Jane looked at us both with bright curiosity. Hewison didn't seem to care.

'You won't find much to enthuse about,' he warned. 'It's not like Tuscany here. None of your tourist attractions. This is one of those parts of Italy which the tourist board forgets.'

So we escaped one morning, feeling like schoolchildren let out of bounds. Or at least that was my mood. Leaving the Villa in Lara's battered little Renault was a blessed release from that web of obligation and patronage by which Hewison bound others to him, and also, in my case, a release from unnamable ties of blood relation.

Perhaps my own feelings communicated themselves to Lara. In a bantering way we had often talked about our families and our own absurd relationship – 'Listen to what your aunt tells you,' she had taken to saying when we disagreed over something – and her tone was heavily ironical when she suggested that she show me her 'ancestral home':

'You must see how David married above himself.'

We drove around the hill on which the Villa stood and down past cliffs into Sabazia's valley. Beside the road were caves which might have once been tombs but were now filled with farm implements and hay; bridging the stream was an old stone arch which Lara called the 'Ponte Etrusco'.

And then we rounded the corner and came in sight of the village itself.

This was the view I remembered from my previous visit all those years ago, the crumbling pile rising up above the road on its stump of volcanic rock. As the car ground up the ramp towards the gate I recalled it all quite vividly: the same gatehouse with the same rotting gate still hanging on its hinges, the same casemates overhead from which, presumably, boiling pitch and the contents of communal piss-pots had once rained down on would-be invaders, the same hairpin bend taking us round and into the village square. But then I had been driving and it had been Helen sitting beside me in the car.

Lara parked in front of the church. Two other cars and some advertisement signs on the village shop were the only concessions to the present century. Everything else was of a piece: grey and mediaeval.

She pointed. 'The church where we were married.'

I looked at her, wondering how she would react.

'I was there.'

'Where?'

'At your wedding.' I laughed awkwardly. 'It was a sort of adolescent joke. We were staying at Poggio Sanssieve at the time. My grandmother decided that my mother would accompany her and she would get Thomas to come from England.'

'I hated Thomas.'

'He's not the kind of man people love. Anyway my grandmother decided that,' I broke into a passable imitation of Nonna Angelica's querulous voice, '"the children shall not come." So we made up our minds that we damn well would.'

She smiled uncertainly, wondering whether she had been the butt of some joke.

'It was curiosity really. After all David was the mysterious lost relative, the black sheep. We wanted to see.'

'We?'

'Helen and I. It was before we were married. I suppose it was her first time at Poggio Sanssieve.'

Helen was the type of person in whom honesty, far from being a virtue, becomes a kind of vice. 'I cannot resist the possibility of seeing the Hewison family tearing itself to pieces,' she had said, but I didn't tell Lara that. I just told her how we had borrowed the *fattore*'s old Lancia and driven down from Florence early in the morning, arriving in time to edge round the back of the *piazza* and peer over the heads of the crowd to catch sight of the family group on the steps of the church: Nonna Angelica in black silk as though dressed for a funeral, my mother smiling vaguely at the pushing and shoving peasantry, Thomas looking as appalled as if Hewison Pharmaceuticals had just been nationalized, which was the current nightmare; and David Hewison himself, the *pècora nera*, nodding solemnly at the villagers as though he only half-recognized them. He had shown the same presence as he often exhibited at the Villa Rasenna: a half-distracted authority, like an impatient adult amongst children.

What had I seen of Lara then? It is difficult to recall now. Memory gets overlain with memories of memory and with later prejudices. I think now that I saw a figure of splendid, dark solemnity walking between the grey pillars of the church, with a white veil encompassing a profile as fine as a classical marble and eyes of an almost too intense blackness. A Beatrice. But I suspect that much of that is an illusion, and anyway I have since discovered that her eyes are green. Probably I did just catch my breath because she certainly made any English rose such as Helen look pale and etiolated, but probably that was nothing more than a passing impression, one of those momentary infidelities to which men are prone. Yet I did see her smile more condescendingly back at Nonna Angelica than ever Nonna Angelica did at her – which gave Helen and me hilarious delight – and then smile in genuine happiness when my mother bent to kiss her. I do remember that. I do remember the glimmer of thanks breaking through.

We left before anyone spotted us. The amusement was over. H. D. Hewison, standing as wooden as a statue at the altar rail, had been married to his 'peasant child', with a jolly little fellow whom Helen thought she recognized as one witness and a handsome and beautifully dressed young man as the other.

The crowd outside was cheering and clapping and throwing rice and rose petals around us as we pushed our way back to the car.

'No drama,' Helen had said. 'Everyone *very* well-behaved.'

I asked what she had expected.

'Expected? Nothing. Hoped for? Some Italian histrionics.'

I smiled at Lara now to show that it had all been a harmless joke.

'Nonna Angelica would have been furious if she had known. She had turned jealousy into a kind of philosophy. She would have hated to think that there had been others there to share her disgrace.'

'Why didn't you mention it earlier?'

'I didn't quite know how to.'

'Is there anything else you know about?'

'Is there anything particular to know?'

We looked at one another without speaking. For a moment there was a tension between us, the first little tension of intimacy. We both recognized it, I think, saw it in each other's faces; and tried to dismiss it.

'There's always something more, isn't there? You never know everything.' Then she looked away. 'Will you excuse me for a moment? There's someone I must go and see, an old lady who was my mother's maid. I won't be long.'

I watched her cross the *piazza*: the girl for whom the villagers had thrown rose petals, a bright figure in a white cotton dress who stood out in vivid contrast amongst all that was grey and mediaeval. Yet there was no doubt that she still belonged here. Two men sitting outside the small bar called out a greeting in which familiarity was mixed with an almost feudal respect; a woman stepped out of the door of the only shop to make some offering which seemed like an act of homage. This was her *paese*, something which, however many times I had visited the place, the village of Sanssieve had never been for me; nor anywhere else.

I wondered how Hewison had come into this small world, the booming intruder, the dominant figure amongst so much that was involuted and self-sufficient. How had he fared?

Over at the bar the two men nodded at me: '*Buon Dì.*'

Beyond the plastic fly curtain an *espresso* machine gleamed in the darkness. A shadowy figure served me. Carrying my cup of coffee I went back into the daylight.

'*Un bel paese,*' I suggested to the two men.

One of them shrugged. 'There's nothing here.'

The other added something in a rush of dialect from which I could only pick out a few words. I looked helpless.

'*Non è italiano?*' the first asked.

'*Un quarto. Mia nonna era italiana. Sono un cane bastardo.*'

He laughed.

'Like *Signor* Hewison,' I added.

There was no sign of recognition. 'Like *Signor* 'Evison. I'm his nephew.'

'Ah, Evison.' The two men nodded, as neutral as trees leaning in the breeze.

'The rest of me is English.'

'From London?'

I admitted the fact.

'I,' the man tapped his chest, 'was in South Africa and Australia. Then England. Prisoner of war.'

I smiled sympathetically and took the opportunity offered.

'*Signor* Evison was here during the war, wasn't he?'

The man shrugged. 'There was everybody. Germans, Americans, Moroccans, Poles, everybody.'

His companion grumbled something and stared pointedly away across the *piazza*.

'But wasn't he with the partisans?'

Did the word mean anything to them? The man's face was impenetrable, as rough and brown and cracked as the wall of the building behind him, and no more forthcoming.

'*È un bel signore*,' he said. 'Very clever, very rich. They say his family makes soap.'

'That's right,' I answered. 'And toothpaste.'

Would Hewison have understood them? Would he have been able to sit at the table with them and drink their cloudy wine and match their views of the world with his own? Or would he have been a man apart, *un forestiere*? I felt the barrier of incomprehension between us as absolutely as if it had been an iron grille.

Lara appeared shortly, the clipping of her shoes on the paving announcing her approach long before she turned the corner of the alley where her old lady lived. She smiled and waved.

One of the men called, 'Is he your cousin?'

'Nephew,' she replied. '*zia* Lara.'

We all laughed at the joke, but it was a fragile point of contact.

The place which had once been Lara's home was in the upper part of the village at the far end of the main street. There was a small square where a holm oak grew, then a ditch spanned by a narrow bridge, and beyond the ditch was the *castello*.

The building was a hybrid between a fortress and a large house, or perhaps it had once been the former and was now caught midway in its metamorphosis into the latter: the curtainless windows which looked down on Lara as she searched her handbag for the key were those of a *seicento palazzo*, but high above us swallow-tailed crenellations were etched against the sky like a row of dragon's teeth.

'It seems a sad place now, but it is my home. I will not allow it to die.'

She produced the key with a gesture of triumph and the massive door swung open to reveal what had once been an entrance archway. Recently it had been glassed in at the far end to create a hall but the transformation was only partial: the glass doors at the far end seemed a fragile barrier between the new interior and the inner courtyard with its carved well-head and damp walls, and the flagstones underfoot were worn concave by the passage of horses. There was the smell of damp in the air.

'It is sad, not lived in,' she said, 'but who would live in such a place so far from the city?'

'Why not you?'

'Us?' In her expression resignation battled with sadness. 'Well, really it is my brother Gianluca's, but he cannot work from here. He is a city person, I suppose. And David . . .' Her voice trailed away. 'David feels that it is not his house, I think. Not to live in. There are memories.'

'Aren't they happy ones?'

She smiled wryly. 'Such things are not simply happy or sad. They are memories; as many facets as a diamond.' She beckoned me in. 'Come.'

The whole house was vacant, stripped of furniture and fittings, inhabited only by dust and cobwebs and the myriad of organisms which patiently reduce such places to powder. Walking ahead of me Lara seemed a small, distracted figure searching for something irretrievably lost amongst the desolate rooms and the deserted corridors.

'This is where we used to play hide-and-seek; here was my mother's work room; here was her bedroom – she died here in 1964; here was Gianluca's room . . .' here this memory, here that. Each room was as vacant as the next. No artifact brought any of the *Castello*'s past to life, and yet quite obviously the

73

past was living vividly in her mind. From one closed door high up in the building she turned to me with a smile of excitement: 'The stairs to the attics.' But the door was locked and a search through her handbag brought no key to light.

'Gianluca must have it,' she said sadly. Then, 'I must be boring you with all this. *Dio mio*, other people's lives . . .' She smiled brightly. 'It isn't good, this concern with the past. But at Lucri we get so used to it that we forget about the future.'

'I'm not sure I believe in the future,' I replied. 'In my work I always have to make appeals to the future. Most of the time it seems to be doing little more than covering up a lie about the present.'

Lara closed her handbag with a snap. 'Perhaps that's why David always makes appeals to the past. He claims that now he has lost his faith the past is his only philosophy.' She looked around the dusty landing on which we stood, the cracked window-pane, the flaking walls. 'Do you think that one day other people will search around in these relics of our own past in order to understand us?'

Light came from the window behind her as she looked at me. Against the light it was hard to make out her expression, but I sensed her ironical smile. 'Is that what you are trying to do, Anthony?'

'Perhaps. And understand myself as well.'

'But your past isn't here. It's in England, with Helen.'

'A piece of it is here, a bit of the background if you like: the other side of the family feud. And there's a personal moment too, a significant one. When I saw you that time.'

And so my present experience worked its way back into my own past to become a kind of memory, replacing the previous dormant image of a beautiful but bewildered girl by the Lara I saw now, a woman whose slightest appearance could stir me, a woman with all the power and frailty of her sex.

She was silent for a long time. When finally she spoke it was as though she had reached a decision.

'Come.' She led the way purposefully back down the narrow stairs and along another corridor. I could barely orientate myself in the building. Glimpses of the inner courtyard or across rooftops or towards distant wooded hills

74

gave few clues. Then she stopped abruptly and flung open yet another door to display yet another empty room. The wallpaper that remained was pale pink, mottled with damp like an abstract pattern; beside the fireplace it had become detached from the wall and now hung over in a great curving strip.

'This was the room where we first made love,' she said flatly. 'My bedroom.'

We stood looking into the unexceptional room with its bare floor boards and grey mantle of dust. There was a curtain rail above the window and a piece of wood, perhaps the shelf from a long-broken bookcase, lying in one corner; otherwise the room was quite deserted. But in her mind she could fill it: with a bed with a flowered coverlet, with curtains and carpet, with a dressing table cluttered with all the paraphernalia of adolescence, with chairs and a bedside table and the bookcase whose sole surviving shelf lay now, a reproach, in the corner. And with herself; and David Hewison.

'He had come from the excavation. He used to visit us unannounced quite often, sometimes with a friend, maybe Elwyn. But that time he came alone. My mother was out. There were servants in the house of course, Rosa's mother for one and there was also my brother, I think, but he would have been in the library. That's where he spent most of his time. So really we were alone.'

I tried not to picture the scene. After a while she shrugged and closed the door. I followed her away from the memory, back along the corridor, down another flight of stairs – wider and shallower this time – and along another corridor. She opened double doors onto a long, high-ceilinged room which was lined with empty bookshelves.

'The library.'

Then on and down, and we were once again in the entrance hall where the grey light penetrated from the courtyard and the flagstones were worn concave from the passage of centuries.

'He promised to marry me that day,' she said as she fiddled with the main door. 'There's an appeal to the future for you. I suppose he was frightened of what might happen after what we had done. "Is my Toy" – Toy was his pet name for me – "Is my Toy all right?" he kept asking. He was nervous, but I was happy. I didn't care about anything else, not the future nor the past, nothing except that moment with him.' She smiled, holding the door open for me. Outside the light was glaringly bright. She pointed across the bridge, across the small *piazza* to where an old archway led down through the village walls. 'Then we went for a walk together and over there he took a photograph of me. He told me you noticed it.'

We stepped outside. She closed the door behind her and locked it, as though locking those particular memories away. But as she crossed the bridge it was not difficult to imagine her in a floral print dress and white ankle socks and sensible shoes, smiling and laughing with the man who had just initiated her into womanhood, so little had changed in her face since the photograph. Not difficult either to imagine her stumbling with her guilt in the fusty darkness of a confessional in the village church . . . 'Bless me, father, for I have sinned . . .'

'Why did he take so long to fulfil his promise?' I asked.

'His promise?'

'To marry you. Why did it only take place after your mother's death?'

'There were difficulties.' She smiled as though to show that really they had not mattered. 'I don't know when she noticed that things had changed with David. You see his visits had always been events of great excitement; he was always a favourite uncle, if you like. Little changed there.'

'Except that you were fifteen, sixteen instead of twelve.'

'Of course, and that was when she became difficult. His visits were less frequent and her presence became . . . more intrusive. We began to arrange meetings in secret. By that time he had bought the Villa and of course the dig had begun. I used to work there at weekends and during holidays. There were arguments with my mother.' She tossed her head, a girl again. 'You can imagine the kind of thing. They happen to everyone.'

'What was his relationship with your mother?' I threw in my guess. 'Did it date from the war?'

We had reached the main *piazza*. One of the men at the bar

76

called out, 'Have you been to the *Castello*? When are you coming back to live there?'

'Who knows?' she answered him.

I wondered whether my question had been deliberately ignored, but as she opened the car door and climbed in she began to talk, about her mother, about David, about the war; a story which was far removed from his accounts of the battles in the streets of Florence. This was a furtive war in which people lived a kind of looking-glass life where nothing was what it seemed and few were what they claimed to be.

'So they first knew each other *in extremis*, I suppose. And when he came back in peace time . . .' she shrugged. 'Imagine, it was only then that she found out his real name. Think how much importance you give to knowing someone's name. Yet when he came back he was no longer Egisto Pascucci or whatever it was, but David Hewison. An Englishman with a fortune.'

She started the engine and turned the car away from the old church. The engine note sounded harsh against the stone walls, like an intruder hammering at the castle gates.

'Did your mother resent him?'

'Perhaps that was it, I don't know. In a way I think she was a bit frightened of him. All Hewisons are a bit frightening.'

'Am I?'

She glanced sideways for a moment. She was smiling, but there was little humour in it.

'Yes you are. You all are. You have an inbred sense that whatever you want is possible.'

'What was it that David wanted?'

'I suppose he wanted to find a new identity, create something for himself – his own personality, his own life – that would not just be part of his family.'

'And what is it that I want?' I asked.

The car wound its way down through the gateway towards the bottom of the valley. She drove hunched forward over the steering wheel as though concentrating on the road.

'Perhaps you are at your most frightening,' she replied, 'when you don't know.'

# IX

# *Winter 1943/44*

RUMOURS of a second Allied landing spread like an epidemic in the first weeks of the new year, fed by both the desperate hopes of the Italians who saw every ship on the horizon as the vanguard of an Allied fleet, and the fears of the Germans who knew that their Tyrrhenian flank was hideously exposed and that there was little they could do to counter such a landing.

'We must strike at once against the forces of Nazi oppression!' Orlandi shouted. At that time they were using a deserted farm – *il casolare* – out in the hills to the west of Sabazia. It was here, in the smoky main room of the building that he would address his men, rising to uncharacteristic heights of demagogy when confronted with the comrades. They would nod surly agreement as their leader gesticulated at them from in front of the fire. They were a decent enough group of men, their appearance of out-and-out villainy more a product of grime and tattered army battledress and unkempt beards than any innate unpleasantness, but they were frustrated by inaction. The blowing up of the occasional telegraph pole and the scattering of caltrops on roads had lost their savour. These men wanted war, and the only war was away to the south on the River Garigliano; they wanted it here and they wanted it now.

'It is a vast undertaking,' Hewison replied calmly. 'Blowing up a bridge that size would take pounds and pounds of plastic, and it'd need an expert to place the stuff.'

His position with these men was a curious one. They could not but admire a man of his powers, or respect a man who could teach them to strip a Sten gun or tamp and prime plastic explosive or render a car useless in five minutes with just a screw-driver. Abilities like these were worthy of immense respect. But they were wary of him. He spoke Italian like a *signore*, and yet he was English. Occasionally nowadays he would lapse into a very convincing *romanesco* dialect, yet he was a *signore*. He would argue politics with them expertly, more knowledgeably than *Il Volpe*, and yet he claimed to have no politics. He must be an anti-Fascist – was he not there to fight Fascism? – and yet he consorted with the Alessio woman who, for all she seemed to be, had a husband who was *un gerarca*, one of the leaders of Mussolini's new republic. In all he was an enigma, a man who claimed no sides in a world where everyone had some side to take, a mass of contradictions, an object of suspicion. And now he was trying to discourage them from their bridge.

'I certainly couldn't do it. Even an expert would take hours, right under the noses of the Germans at the station.'

'It could be done. It must be done,' Orlandi insisted. 'If necessary we could take the station from them. They are nothing there.'

'It would be better done with an air raid. I could call for an air raid.'

There was a ghastly silence: as though he had just declared King Victor Emmanuel the saviour of Italy.

Orlandi spoke very slowly. 'That is not possible.'

'Certainly it is possible. It will guarantee our aim, destruction of the bridge – that is our aim, isn't it? – much better than trying to blow it ourselves. It seems a perfect solution.'

'But it will remove our target.'

'Exactly. In a cloud of dust.'

'But it is *our* target. Ours. We are fighting the glorious war of liberation.'

'So is the RAF.'

'The RAF is an instrument of imperialism,' interrupted a new voice. 'It would be an imperialistic act to bomb that bridge. That is an Italian bridge, and therefore it is ours to destroy.'

The voice belonged to a young man called Tobasi who had styled himself the ideologue of the group. He had joined 'Fabiomassimo' a week earlier, and possessed an influence which stemmed from his claim, the truth of which could not

79

be tested, to have been sent from Turin by the Party with the express purpose of bringing the spirit of revolution to the peasant masses in the south. His arguments gained a great deal from the fact that they were so larded with Marxist-Leninist jargon that no one could really understand them. It was a particularly powerful form of debate.

'It would be contrary to the historical dialectic of the situation,' he announced.

'Heavy bombers have a way of ignoring historical dialectics,' Hewison observed mildly.

There was an awful silence, but this one had the stench of defeat about it.

'*Signor* Egisto,' said Tobasi quietly. He had a narrow, rodent face that at other times Hewison might have described as sensitive. His eyes looked coldly at the Englishman through round, rimless spectacles, like fish swimming in two glass bowls. '*Signor* Egisto, our group operates in a spirit of proletarian unity and within a true consciousness of the national-popular characteristic of the Italian class struggle, as propounded by our late leader and comrade, the martyr Antonio Gramsci.'

Around the room men nodded slowly at the mention of Gramsci's name, like a monastic chapter at the name of Jesus.

'That bridge was built on the bones of the Italian proletariat. It is a symbol of oppression by the capitalist exploitative classes, and a reproach to those who would obstruct the historical inevitability of revolution: but also a rock against which such counter-revolutionaries will be smashed by the tide of history.'

Perhaps Orlandi had understood the import of what Tobasi was saying. He looked uncomfortable, glancing anxiously from one man to the other, his eyes pleading. Hewison felt quite sorry for him.

'A compromise, Egisto,' he whispered quickly. 'You say that at present we are unable to destroy the bridge. What compromise can you suggest?'

Hewison rubbed his chin thoughtfully. 'Maybe we could go for part of the rail. That is what we have the ability to do. We do it at night, and we do it as secretly as possible without disturbing the people at the station.'

'But that is the work of saboteurs, thieves in the night.'

'That is precisely what we are, Agostino.'

'Volpe.'

'I apologize. Volpe. We are saboteurs. We are a guerilla force, Quintus Fabius Maximus, remember? The delayer who stings his enemy, and then vanishes in order to sting again. Let us just destroy the rail with plastic, but with a pressure fuse so that a passing train sets it off. It will do an enormous amount of damage like that.'

Orlandi snorted. 'They will clear the line, repair the rail.'

'But it will take them time and men, and then we will cut the line again, but the next time somewhere else, the tunnel maybe.'

The balance of the debate tipped gently back and forth. The remainder of the group was a mere audience watching Tobasi, Orlandi, and the Englishman. They had no understanding of the tensions which lay below the surface of the argument.

'This idea lacks the bold stroke,' said Orlandi, knowing that it was the only possibility.

'But it might just work,' urged Hewison. Orlandi sighed with resignation. Tobasi said nothing.

So Hewison and Orlandi spent a night watching the bridge. They crouched in the little pulpit amongst the rocks at the point of the old acropolis, and throughout the night they watched to see how the bridge was guarded.

It wasn't.

Morning found them bitterly cold – it had snowed briefly at three o'clock – and as stiff as boards. Orlandi was muttering about frostbite. They made their agonized way back from the observation post feeling a strange mixture of triumph and disappointment. At one point, only half-jokingly, Orlandi suggested that they invent a guard roster for the bridge in order to justify their vigil. Hewison understood exactly how he felt.

That afternoon Hewison made a transmission from the *Castello*. He crouched beneath the sloping rafters in the attic much as he had when the birth of 'Fabiomassimo' had first been announced to Algiers. Just as on that occasion

Gianluca's eyes watched him steadily from the shadows. When the irritant buzzing of the morse key had stopped the boy suddenly announced, 'My father is returning.'

Normally he was as silent as his mother about such matters, more so perhaps. Hewison had never been able to fathom his silence, his faintly ironical outlook on the world, his disturbing age-in-youth.

'Does that please you?'

The boy's eyes followed him like a cat's. 'I will see that your wireless is safe.'

Hewison was packing things away. It was always important to have everything ready for immediate removal, just as it was important not to transmit for more than five minutes at a time and never from the same place twice in succession. 'You haven't answered my question.'

'My father is a Fascist.'

Hewison looked up, smiling. 'And what are you, Gianluca?'

'I am a nihilist. My only belief is that there is nothing left to believe.'

'That's a despairing creed for a young boy.'

'You sound like my mother. That is the kind of thing adults always say: patronizing.'

'All right then; why do you not believe in anything? Don't you even believe in the love of your mother, or the cause of freedom, or something?'

'I believe only that one can make a decision for every moment, but that the reasons for one's decisions are not necessarily consistent. Do you understand me?'

'You mean you might decide to betray me tomorrow, if the circumstances were right?'

The boy laughed. 'But you don't know why I help you. You don't understand the circumstances. I mean that I have to make the decision to help you every minute of the day, but in this case at least one influence on my decisions remains constant, so really there is no choice.'

'What's that?'

Gianluca looked at him curiously, smiling faintly as though the whole conversation might be a joke. 'I can always see the disadvantages of not helping you.'

'That sounds rather cold-blooded. And rather difficult, I should have thought. It is easier to have a creed and be carried along by it.'

'You are being cynical.'

Hewison patted his shoulder. 'Not half as cynical as you.'

They went down the narrow stairs from the attics. The upper rooms of the *Castello*, presumably once populated by servants and children, were deserted: room after room of bare tiled floors, small windows, dust motes dancing in the shafts of light.

'You are a Christian, aren't you?' the boy asked suddenly. He meant 'Catholic'. 'I have seen you going into the church.'

Hewison paused at the head of the stairs which led down to the inhabited part of the building. He hesitated a moment before answering.

The boy said, 'I know you are. I followed you in and you were making your confession to Don Ignazio.'

'I was born a Catholic, yes. I am not sure of my faith any more.'

The boy smiled in triumph. 'So you are just like me.'

When Hewison found Clara in her study he told her about the strange conversation.

'At least he can talk to someone,' she remarked. 'He needs a man to talk to. Being shut up in this village is like being in prison: just that fool of a priest the only half-educated male for miles around. And the doctor, of course.'

'You think he misses his father?'

She looked weary. 'He says he hates his father.'

'That's what he told me. It seems that he will have the opportunity to put it to the test soon.'

Clara nodded. 'He told you, did he? Yes, he comes in about a week. He wasn't sure when. That job I told you about.' She made a small derisive sound. 'It is like waiting for someone to die. There's no hope, but the person hangs on.'

'What do you mean by that?'

'I mean everything by it. Until this cursed war is finished nothing can happen: no human being can love another, no one can grow up, no one can grow old. Everything is held in pawn, to be redeemed by something called "liberation". Except that now that word is taking on a sense of fantasy. One might just as well say "the day of judgement".'

He was helpless in the face of this despair. He mumbled something about the end not being far away, 'They have just given orders to move against lines of communication. We are going to bomb the bridge tonight,' but his words sounded hollow. However soon the Allies arrived, for many it would still be too late.

'I think we had better take the wireless away,' he said. 'Until your husband leaves, at least.' She nodded. 'And for Christ's sake keep an eye on Gianluca. I'm not happy about his state of mind at the moment. He knows far too much for anyone's good.'

# X

THE town of Vetrano is a contrast to Sabazia in almost every way. It has none of the village's compactness and little that remains of its antiquity. It sprawls across a shallow saddle in the hills to the north of Lucri and successive phases of reconstruction and remodelling have emptied it of any beauty it may once have possessed, whilst the boom years of the nineteen-fifties have infected it with a rash of apartment blocks around the periphery.

I visited it by myself on the last day of my stay at the Villa Rasenna for no other reason than that it was here that David Hewison proposed to build the Lucri museum. It was easy enough to imagine the tourist buses flocking into its extensive *piazza* as they did already into Cerveteri and Tarquinia nearby, even easier to imagine how eager the *comune* was to win its share of the tourist trade. But the place itself was undistinguished. There was a large, grey municipal building and a large, grey baroque church. There was a bus stop with a blue Fiat coach waiting for passengers with the promise 'Viterbo' hung in its windscreen. There were women in the grocery shops and the fruiterers, and youths gathered outside the bars. Traffic passed often enough down the main road. There was about the place a small-town bustle.

*EVITA L'ODORE APOCRINO CON EVIT-O*, a notice exhorted from the window of the pharmacy. *UN PRO-DOTTO DI EVISON FARMACEUTICI SpA*.

BAN-O by any other name would smell as sweet.

Beside the pharmacy was a building which sported a papal tiara and crossed keys on its façade. Italian town buildings grow inscriptions like the symptoms of a disease. This one announced *Opera Pia della Fanciullezza* to the world. I watched a pair of nuns hurry up the steps, and I could picture an interior of bare, shining tiles and an atmosphere of sanctity and disinfectant.

My glance went from the orphanage across the other dull nineteenth-century frontages back to the *municipio*.

There were the inevitable inscriptions here too. One of them celebrated the glories of the unification of Italy; it or its sister could be found on every single such building the length of the peninsula. But the other was different. It gave a date – 26 *Gennaio* 1944 – and a list of fifteen names. Beneath the date was inscribed the sentence:

*Da Mano Nazi-Fascisti Furono Barbaramente Trucidati.*

Some of the letters were missing so that with the passage of time the inscriptions were taking on the appearance of a half-completed children's game or an archaeological puzzle. I read through the names one by one almost as though I might recognize one, but they remained mute witnesses to an event about which I knew nothing. Then I noticed a sign at the side of the building announcing the existence of a tourist office.

The room was grey and dusty, an almost forgotten adjunct to the operations of the *comune*. A poster on the wall announced a display by the Vetrano *Gruppo Folcloristico*, but the date was from the previous month. From a desk beneath the poster a grey-haired man looked up with scant interest at my entrance. He may have been reading the book which lay open before him, but just as likely he had been asleep. Whichever, it was clear that I was little more than an intrusion.

'*Buon giorno.*'

The man considered the proposition thoughtfully, without committing himself to an opinion. In front of him on the desk was a pile of badly printed local guide books.

'*Mille lire,*' he said as I picked one up.

I produced the money. He smiled a faint smile of triumph as he stowed the note away in a drawer, as though he knew more about the value of the thing than I did. Under his gaze I flicked through the guide to the final pages. And there it was. I still have the book and so I can offer an accurate translation:

During the last war Vetrano endured tragic days. Battles

between Allied forces and the retreating Germans took place in the surrounding hills in June 1944 following the liberation of the Eternal City, and the town was much damaged by artillery bombardment. The most sorrowful episode came earlier, however, with the brutal reprisal of the twenty-sixth of January ordered by the German High Command following a partisan action against the railway station of Vetrano. Fifteen innocent citizens were machine-gunned in the fields outside the town. To these fifteen martyrs a dignified mausoleum has been dedicated.

'Now the Germans come as friends,' the man said. Perhaps he was concerned about my origins. I nodded encouragingly at him and turned the page.

Excavations of World Importance, it declared.

'This railway station,' I said. 'It's the one at Lucri, isn't it? Just beside the acropolis.'

The man agreed. 'Excavations of world importance,' he suggested. He began a ritual discourse on Lucri, but I interrupted him.

'Was *Signor* 'Ewison there? He was a partisan. Was he there at the attack on the station?'

The man's voice trailed away helplessly, as though all the time he had been expecting trouble from this stranger.

'The archaeologist David 'Ewison?' His eyes were hostile. The excavations of world importance were forgotten. 'Yes, he was there.'

It was like a key. I inserted it into the lock, turned it, and the lock snapped open. There, exposed in my hands, was the whole intricate mechanism of Lucri and the Villa Rasenna and David Hewison's life.

'I am not going to work my fingers to the bone just to finance David's bloody hobby.' Thus Uncle Thomas, overheard through closed doors one family weekend long ago.

'Who were the partisans?' I asked the man in the tourist office.

He waved a dismissive hand. 'Communists, *contadini*, deserters, everybody.' His expression implied a whole rag-bag of humanity, the flotsam of a civil war. 'It was stupidity. They tried to destroy the railway bridge.'

I had seen that on the excavation plans. It lay just beyond the railway station, just beyond the point of the arx, just where I had not gone when Hewison had guided me round.

'A stupidity,' the man repeated. 'Three days later the Americans came with bombs. They destroyed it, just as they destroyed everything.'

The mausoleum was at the end of a cul-de-sac called Via dei Quindici Martiri. It was a plain building faced with a grey granite which must have come from somewhere in the north. Its manner was faintly gothic, yet neither the style nor the material was intrusive: they lent the building an air of detachment from its environment which seemed appropriate: gothic amidst the baroque, granite amongst the volcanic tuff. All around the building was a lawn as immaculate as a bowling green.

Inside the porch there was a small table with a book for visitors to sign. I noticed that the last names were German, from Düsseldorf. I went on through the inner door.

After the bright sunlight outside it took my eyes some minutes to accustom themselves to the light from the high lancet windows; at first I thought that this was why the place seemed so bare. But then I understood. There were just names and a cross, nothing else. Just fifteen names in plain bronze letters set into the walls, five on one side, five on the other, five on the end wall opposite the door, and above these last five a slender cross incised into the granite. There was nothing else, no inscription, no self-righteous exhortation to forgive, no prayers for mercy, not even a plea for eternity. Just fifteen names and vases of flowers on the floor beneath. The little chapel was less a religious memorial than a simple statement of fact, an embodiment of the fatalism which permeates the Italian mind. These fifteen had been killed. That was all. The posturing, the carefully engendered outrage, were left to the plaque on the council building. In the mausoleum there were just the fifteen names.

I stood for a long while reading over them and feeling the burden of someone else's guilt almost as vividly as if it had been my own. Hewison's own words, subtly transformed in meaning, came back to me:

'Are the two-thousand-year dead any further away than last month's dead?'

I signed my own name in the book beneath the unknown Germans from Düsseldorf, and then on a sudden thought turned the pages back to January. Beneath the arms of the *Comune di* Vetrano and an elaborate dedication in the name of the people of the town was a list of signatures headed by one Francesco Tardini, *Sindaco*. But on the opposite page, set apart from the pieties of officialdom, was the signature I expected to find: David Hewison.

The word 'atonement', with its echo of a funeral bell, sounded in my mind as I made my way back to the main square.

Lara was working in the office as I came in. She looked through the open door with a smile.

'How did you find the metropolis?'

'Interesting.'

'Not many people do. Meredith says that it is as exciting as Wigan on a Monday night. I don't think that is very exciting.'

'I'm certain it's not.'

She leafed through some invoices on her desk. 'So what interested you?'

I didn't answer at once. I watched her as she ran her finger down a list of figures, entering them into a calculating machine with practised rapidity. The machine whirred and chattered and spat out its conclusion on a strip of paper.

'Prices,' she muttered. 'I don't know how we keep going.'

Ask Thomas, I thought.

'I visited the mausoleum.'

There was a fractional pause in her work. Another row of figures was digested by the machine. The paper strip stuttered round once more.

'And?' She tore the paper from the machine and looked up.

'I also spoke with a man in the tourist office. He mentioned David's involvement.'

She was watching me carefully, as though trying to read my thoughts. Until now I had seen her as the focus of my uncle's life, but my new understanding had shifted the perspectives.

89

'He mentioned it?'

'I suggested it.'

'And now you understand?'

'I think so.'

She nodded. 'It's not something we talk about. None of us. It was one of those incidents with which any war is littered. There was nothing remarkable about it, except that it happened here and that relatives are still alive and still remember . . .'

'I saw the flowers.'

'. . . but really it was nothing much. A month or two later they killed over three hundred at the Fosse Ardeatina, later on in the north they murdered thousands, almost two thousand in Marzabotto alone. You could say that Vetrano was lucky.' She gave a bleak smile. 'The man in the tourist office lost his father. Did he tell you about the bridge?'

'I read about it in the guide book, put two and two together. I've not seen it.'

'It's not a view which David ever shows to visitors: you have to go right to the point of the arx. Of course they rebuilt it after the war: an ugly black thing which doesn't even have the redeeming feature of being useful any longer. The station is a ruin.' Her expression was puzzled, like a child who doesn't understand adult emotions. 'It all seems so much of a stupidity now, doesn't it? A battle for a station and a bridge which would not even be in use a dozen years later. And we have had to live with them beside our work for the last twenty-five years.'

She fiddled with the mechanism of her calculator. 'Anyway, now you can see something of what lies behind Lucri. It is, I suppose, an expiation, a kind of offering to the people of Vetrano. You see until Lucri they were nothing, a people without significance, without a history. With Lucri they have gained a past.'

'Redeemed from time,' I suggested, but I don't know whether she caught the allusion. Her ironical smile was back in place now, part of her armour.

'I know it interests you, Anthony, this past. But be careful. Time is no healer.'

\*

Mid-afternoon was the dead time at the Villa Rasenna. The great house sat solid and immutable within its circle of umbrella pines. It took on the lineaments of eternity. Within the public rooms and corridors no one walked. No footsteps sounded beneath the vaulted ceilings. Sunlight shone into deserted rooms and picked out no movement except the random dance of dust motes in the air. In the drawing room the chimera snarled at no one.

Lara had excused herself and disappeared into the depths of the house. To do what? Wondering at her and her husband, and the vicious little drama of the past, I lunched alone again; or at least almost alone, for towards the end of my meal Meredith appeared from somewhere with a delighted smile at the prospect of a captive audience. I waited patiently until the man had trapped himself with a plate of spaghetti – 'Diet of Worms,' he said, forking up his first mouthful – and then got up and left him alone.

Outside the gardens were as deserted as the house. Only the rasp of my footsteps on the gravel paths intruded on the cricket song and the screaming of the swifts. Palmiro was taking his siesta somewhere at the back of the building and for the moment there was no other movement between the flower beds. The air was heavy with the smell of box, vividly redolent of the gardens at Poggio Sanssieve. I picked a sprig from one of the immaculate hedges and broke it beneath my nose, but the smell evaded me. It was as elusive as a vague memory. When I did not pursue it I sensed it all around the hedges and the flower beds – a heavy, resinous scent – but, when I went in search of it, it vanished. I recalled this capricious quality too and wondered whether there was some mystic significance in it, some symbol of knowledge. I thought of the archaeologists painstakingly peeling away successive deposits and exposing a new truth at each level. Was an understanding of the recent past like that? Or was it – I had come back to my own knowledge – was it simply that fifteen villagers had been machine-gunned, and a man had thus been turned in on himself with guilt, to spend a lifetime and a fortune trying to absolve himself?

I had reached the far border of the garden where the box

hedges grew as big as a wall. A gap like a doorway showed the way through into the trees beyond. A glance back at the house showed nothing stirring. No face looked out of any window. The terrace was deserted. I could identify the windows of my own bedroom and guessed that others to the right, towards the front of the building, must belong to Lara's; but those that weren't shuttered were just blank reflections of the sky, like cataracted eyes.

I turned. Through the gap in the hedge a clear path led away through the trees, steepening down the hillside. Where there was a break in the leaf canopy I could see across to the track which Palmiro had shown me that first afternoon, the way to Sabazia; but soon my own path curved away to the right around the spur of the hill and I was out of any contact with what I knew.

Yet the path led somewhere. It had an insistence about it, a definition which suggested that it was not just a casual sheep track ambling around the hills. It had a destination and I pursued it with the vague curiosity of someone who has more important matters on his mind.

When finally I emerged from the clasp of the trees and into the clearing I was dazzled by the sudden light. There was a lawn of dense grass at my feet, but the margins of the clearing were just formless shapes against the glare. All around was the sound of running water. Only when my eyes had adjusted could I make out the border of holm oak and the mass of rock which emerged from the hillside to stand at the back of the clearing like a sentinel. From the base of the rock a small stream issued to cross the open space and plunge down through the woods towards the valley far below.

A primaeval stillness seemed to fill the opening, like water filling a deep pool. The air possessed a limpid, water-bright clarity in which every shape was etched exactly. Every colour shone as though infused with light: arrow-heads of ivy clinging to the cliff, chicory flowers as blue as turquoise amongst the grass, poppies like gouts of blood. The heavy scent of honeysuckle lay on the air.

'Beautiful.' I had said the word out loud. It sounded a discordant note amidst the stillness, giving a momentary dimension of time to a place which bore the imprint of eternity. But the vegetation swallowed the sound up, expunged it from the face of the day as though it had never been. I felt a sense of relief that the solecism had gone unnoticed.

Then I noticed the cave. The rock at the back of the clearing was a spout of lava, frozen to stillness aeons ago, but its monumental wholeness was an illusion: at its base, bearded with ivy, was a vertical cleft from which the stream issued.

I dismissed the immediate idea of a tomb. The cliffs of the countryside were so honeycombed with them that they became a commonplace, but this cleft was no artificial opening. It was a natural grotto.

A clash of languages sounded in my mind as I stepped past the moss and maidenhair fern into the cave. The word in Italian is *grotta*. Is it for shame that the northern mind has rendered masculine what is so obviously female? Beyond the opening was an amniotic darkness. Aqueous reflections wobbled and pulsed across the roof. Running water sounded all around, like a flow of blood.

I stood still while the shadows resolved themselves into shapes: a bowl of rock from which the spring issued, a runnel which led the flow towards the daylight, a buttress of rock which hinted at ancient chisels; and then the figure. At first this was a shapeless thing in the back recess of the cave, a blot. But slowly, like an embryo growing, it took on form, discovering arms and legs and head, until finally it was delivered from the shadows whole: a god.

The statue was about three feet high, mounted on a plinth of rock and carved of the same brown stone as the cave itself so that it seemed hardly a created thing but rather some chthonic being sprung from the earth. Its eyes had the solemn stare of archaic sculpture, its lips that faint curve which modern critics have tried to dismiss as a failure of technique, but which here, quite plainly, intended an arcane wisdom. The head was adorned with a crescent beard and a wreath of crudely carved triangular leaves. The body was draped in a long robe. In its hand was a staff, tipped with what appeared to be a pine cone; the other hand held a rough cup. I remembered enough to recognize the staff as a thyrsus, the cup as a kantharos, the god himself as Dionysos.

The Dionysos smiled ironically out of the shadows. Under that unmoving gaze I tried to assemble what I knew of him. I recalled he was a great deal more than the effeminate wine god of popular myth, pursued across so many classical vases by drunken revellers: he was a vegetation deity, a god of fecundity and birth, but also of death, a nature god whose identity and cult were far from the Olympian pantheon, more mystic and less mythic, distant from Olympos in both mood and origin. Orgiastic? But sexual ecstasy has long been a pathway to mystic knowledge, a fact which puritans know only too well.

I made a wry face back at the god in the shadows. Nymphs and satyrs: a vulgar joke.

A careful examination of the cave revealed something more to the still-born archaeologist in me: the place was not the natural grotto it had appeared. Like a Roman nymphaeum it was a painstaking imitation of nature. The interior walls bore the marks of chisels, the bowl of the spring was carved, the shallow depression in the rock at the statue's feet was a deliberate shaping and included a runnel which joined it to the stream. Libations poured to the god? Sacrificial blood? The thing about the simplest archaeological assessment is that it demystifies. Looking up at the god now in the detached manner of the pure rationalist I wondered how the statue came to be there, what its origin was, what its age. Its gaze held no power any longer, the curious staff no potency. I would ask about it at the Villa. It was an artifact such as one finds in museums; perhaps it should be in a museum itself lest it be damaged or stolen.

So I walked back out into the blinding daylight confident of the centuries during which the demons had been put to flight and the darkness flooded in a cold and reasonable light. But as I returned along the path towards the Villa something shifted in the depths of my mind like the earth moving beneath the foundations of a house; as though the whole framework of time had trembled.

*

94

'I found a statue of Dionysos this afternoon. In a cave up the valley.'

There was a momentary lull in the conversation. Lara looked up from her plate. Meredith was saying to his audience: 'So Saint Peter said to the archaeologist, "To you it *may* just be a primitive expression of the fear of death within an essentially pessimistic eschatology, but to us in here it's Hell. And that's where you're going."' His audience laughed.

'Pacha,' said my uncle. 'An Etruscan deity which merged with the Greek Dionysos towards the end of the seventh century.' He reapplied himself to his food.

'But that statue –'

It was Charles van Doren who answered. 'Late Archaic, say sixth century BC. All the usual early Greek attributes of course, before the god became clean-shaven and effeminate. Classical representations usually show him naked. There are some rock-cut tombs a bit further on but their relationship with the Dionysos isn't at all clear.' He glanced at Hewison. 'There are alternative suggestions to the origin of the name Bacchus of course. The word is of Greek derivation.'

'Borrowed,' retorted Hewison. 'You know that as well as I do, Charles. "Lydian" is the usual attribution.'

'Well, there is little doubt that the Dionysiac cult was eastern in origin . . .'

'There's little doubt because there's so little information. Certainly there were eastern influences, Phrygian, Lydian –'

'Sabazia,' I said in surprise, an old memory reawakening.

Hewison bowed slightly in my direction. 'Exactly. All seems not to be lost with you. Sabazia. And Bassareus and Zagreus. In fact a whole complex of bronze age deities. But the question is, how did he get *here*?'

Van Doren made a dismissive sound. 'Introduced during the Greek trading expansion of the sixth century.'

'But Pacha?' Hewison eyed his colleague with scarcely disguised anger.

'Etruscan borrowing from the Greek.'

'But you admit the Greeks borrowed it from the Lydians, and they perhaps from the Phrygians. And what happens if you go far enough back and find that it comes out of the pre-

Indo-European substratum? That he was, maybe, an early bronze age deity spread over a wide area?'

Van Doren snorted. 'Evidence, that's all you need to support an argument like that. Evidence.'

The argument spluttered on like a firework, now dying away, now bursting into renewed life. I confessed to Lara that I couldn't understand how the statue could remain there in its cave.

'How could you move it?' she asked.

'Shouldn't it be in a museum or something?'

She shook her head and smiled. 'For the villagers it is still a figure of importance.'

I stared at her in disbelief. 'A pagan hangover? Surely that kind of thing is the stuff of nineteenth-century romance.'

She shrugged. 'Is it nineteenth-century romance to celebrate the Roman feast of Sol Invictus and call it Christmas? Or the festival of Diana the virgin huntress and call it Maria Assunta? Or the feast of Lupercal and call it the Purification of the Blessed Virgin? The list is almost endless.'

'So what is your Dionysos' name?'

'San Sabbatino.' She smiled her ironical smile. 'Until a century ago there used to be a mass celebrated at the cave some time in April for engaged couples. The practice was suppressed by the diocese.'

'I'm not surprised.'

'But they were all Indo-European speakers,' van Doren was saying loudly. 'Lydians, Hittites, the whole Anatolian complex. Probably even the Phrygians as well. You've got nobody else to go with your Etruscans, David. They are out on their own, isolated; one of those unexplained quirks of history.'

'There was a satyr and a maenad in the middle of a Dionysiac orgy,' said Meredith to his audience, 'and the satyr whispered in the maenad's ear: "How about you and me going off by ourselves for a bit of fun?" "All on our own?" the maenad asked in horror. "Without anyone else? Ooo, you're nothing but a dirty old man!"'

Thus the matter of the Dionysos died, demythologized by a prehistoric argument, emasculated by church sanction, reduced finally to a feeble joke. And yet in my mind the small god smiled his faint, knowing smile, and the challenge still seemed to be there.

Before I left for the airport next morning I went to the excavation alone. I walked through the skeleton of Lucri and up onto the narrow neck which joins the necropolis to the arx, the city of the dead to the city of the once-living. I climbed the rough steps through the ancient pylon up onto the high and windy plateau of the arx. There, possibly for the last time, I took it all in: the block of the Tolfa hills drawn in two dimensions in the background, the River Mignone curling through the nearer hills and running across the prow of the arx, the narrow stream valleys which cut back on either side to delineate the promontory on which the city had been built, and the network of foundation wall and pavement which were all that remained of the place and which might have stayed buried for ever if it had not been for David Hewison.

The axis around which the whole of this revolved was the Temple of Turan.

'In principle it is no different from the rebuilding of, say, a broken vase,' my uncle had asserted.

It squatted toad-like on its stepped base, more oriental even than it had seemed at first sight, the terracotta gargoyles leering and grimacing from the eaves like sacred monkeys. When I turned my back I expected a cackle of manic laughter. No classical rationalism there, I thought.

At the head of the main steps a sign read:

TEMPIO II. TEMPIO PUTATIVO DI TURAN (AFRODITE)
6° SECOLO AC.

All ready for the first tourists. Through the yawning doorway I looked into the empty cella.

'We found no trace of the cult statue,' Hewison had explained mournfully. 'Taken by the Romans, one presumes.'

No trace of the statue and no sense of the numinous either. Just a room with plaster walls and a floor swept bare as a barn. In the ceiling the beams and the bronze bindings looked bright and new.

I went back outside into the daylight and down the temple steps to the paving stones of the street.

What was all this like before, say in 1944? I tried to picture the trenches filled, the low walls buried, the whole plateau grassed over, perhaps with clumps of bramble and scrub oak, perhaps dotted with the blade-like leaves of asphodel. Asphodel is not a magic bloom of the Elysian fields; it is a tough member of the lily family which grows everywhere and stinks of cat's piss. But I couldn't make it regrow in my mind over the naked and dissected plateau of Lucri.

I walked on through the skeleton of:

TEMPIO IA. TEMPIO PUTATIVO DI TIN (ZEUS)
5° SECOLO AC.

heading through the trees towards the point of the promontory, where I had not gone with my uncle three days earlier.

Beyond the final scraps of excavation was a stretch of grass and the finish of the plateau. The cliffs converged to form a sharp prow. There was a gnarled oak clinging like an arthritic claw to the rock. I climbed around the trunk into a narrow pulpit which overlooked the precipice. And there was the bridge.

This was why I had come. From immediately below me, in a superb gesture of futility, the structure strode out across the river to the far side of the valley. Its black girders seemed brand new, but the rails were brown with rust and the stonework was bearded with grass. Like the Dionysos it too was a shadow of the past, a spasm on the face of nature; and, like the Dionysos, by its incongruity it disturbed. Here was an object with a ritual and obsessive purposiveness which ranked with any cult statue, any temple, any altar. Just so, men had died for it. I felt something like fear stir deep inside me. Here, in this gaunt construction of steel girders, was the sense of the numinous which the reconstructed temple lacked.

I looked back into the narrow valley towards the station. The name was quite clear, inscribed in ceramic tiles across the front of the single building:

VETRANO.

While the building itself crumbled away into dust the yellow tiles were fated never to fade. Already the roof had part collapsed. Grass now grew on the platform and between the sleepers, but those tiles would always keep the gloss of their firing, just as bronze age faience may be recovered from an excavation trench still as luminous and fresh as when it was made.

Further up the line where earth had slipped from the bank and buried one rail a large grey cow stood and cropped grass. Nothing else moved in the valley. Behind the station building was a steep slope of volcanic ash and an outcrop of rock; beyond that more hills running away to a skyline over which lay the town where the Via dei Quindici Martiri led to a little gothic chapel with fifteen inscribed names.

I stood looking for a long time. On the siding down below the cow shifted her grazing. Her cow-bell gonged mournfully in the empty air. The archaeologists were squatting in trenches with toothbrush and trowel, or crouching over broken pots with brush and glue, trying to find their own pattern of the past. But here there was another pattern. Partly it was in the fabric of the place – railway bridge, station, acropolis, a bizarre juxtaposition of distant centuries with the present one – but part of it was an event, as transient as a reflection in water.

# XI

IN THE afternoon I flew back to England. The airliner pulled up from the Roman Campagna into a sky of fused enamel blue; two hours later it was descending through sepulchral gloom over southern England and discovering London sprawled under layers of cloud like a corpse under a shroud. Neon signs and sodium lights glimmered in the wet tarmac. Pallid tourists in incongruous summer clothing shuffled through the halls towards delayed charter flights to Ibiza and Majorca.

'Should have stayed where you were, mate,' said the taxi driver, not knowing where I had been but assuming that anywhere else must be better. 'Bloody cricket season started two days ago.'

The taxi nosed through the traffic in Kensington like a barge up a canal. Beyond the windows and the screen of rain was a hard, literal world whose brilliance and warmth came from electricity and whose myths were the fables of television and advertising. Here the past was simply yesterday's newspaper.

REMEMBER TO BUILD THE FLUORIDE BARRIER, exhorted one hoarding.

SPRAY AWAY APOCRINE DECAY, cried another. CROWD-CONFIDENCE FROM HEWISON LABORATORIES.

Names and phrases which have eaten like tooth decay into a nation's mind. As I unlocked the front door to my house I had the sensation that I was intruding on someone else's life.

There was a pile of mail on the carpet – circulars mainly, some letters from the lawyers about my mother's estate, a few letters of condolence. I tossed them onto the hall table. The hall itself was clogged with tea chests containing her posses-sions. I manoeuvred my way around them and humped my suitcase upstairs to the main bedroom. In contrast to the clutter downstairs this room seemed bare, stripped of those small tokens by which, even in her absence, Helen had signalled her presence: her pictures, her things on the dressing table, her shoes thrown under a chair.

I wandered round the house as though seeing it for the first time: a museum visitor peering at the little artifacts that were the only remaining evidence of what there had once been. There was nothing belonging to my father, but then that was not surprising. Being unbound by Catholicism he had long gone to another wife, another family, no doubt bequeathing to them his own junk. Somewhere there were half-siblings whom I had never even seen. All he had left me was half my genes, disjointed memories of a military manner, and a childhood shadowed by borrowed father-figures: my grand-father barely; Uncle Thomas obtrusively; even, I suppose – the proximity of ages between, say, twelve and twenty-four meaning little – Honjohn; and men who did not age at all as she got older, and scarcely varied in character: my mother's 'friends'. Never Uncle David.

In the sitting room my mother's bureau stood beside the fireplace like a malevolent intruder. In the top drawer was the letter which, only ten days earlier, I had found amongst her papers. I took it out again. It was written on low-quality paper, brown with age: OHMS. The words 'From Algiers, by hand' had been scrawled in pencil across the top left-hand corner in my mother's writing. The text itself was in faded black ink:

Darling Flicky,
   I shouldn't be writing this to you and you will guard it with your life. Does that not sound grand? Maybe it will frighten my Flicky into obedience. Anyway by the time you receive it I am sure that things will have been resolved for me, but at the moment the weather and other nuisances have condemned me to wait.
   I have spent most of the last weeks dropping out of aircraft, at first into the sea but later onto dry land because 'they' have once more changed their minds about what we are finally going to do. I think I know what a cow feels like being prepared for the

*mattatoio*; but a beautifully-treated cow. We live like royalty in an exclusive club which, it is rumoured, was once a nudist camp for jaded Frogs and their paramours. Would my Flicky be happy to disport herself unclad amongst the sand dunes, I wonder? The girls who look after us are. They have a rude name which is an acrostic of their official title and therefore entirely the fault of the stupid official who invented them. I cannot tell you the name for fear of embarrassing you. But, when they disport themselves thus, you may see it.

Do you see how the lascivious atmosphere of this place warps my mind? In a few days, dearest Flicky, I will be back at home amongst people who do *not* think like that at all. I will have to mend my ways. I feel a great sadness with them. They need what little help I may be able to offer.

War is a wonderful time for pharmaceuticals, is it not? Here we wash ourselves with Lifeline and treat the wounded with the new wonder drug which dear Papa goes senile about. Bandage sales must be at an all time high. Don't take my joke about the *mattatoio* too seriously. In a strange, rather tightly-strung way I feel immensely happy. Like waiting to go on stage. Above all people, I love you,

David.

Could I fit it better into context now? Or are the two people at either end of that letter too distant to mean anything? I find it difficult to picture that angular and elegantly dissolute woman who was my mother as a 'dearest Flicky' to be teased about her prudishness, but there was an echo of such childish affection in the presence of David's gaunt figure beside her coffin at Farm Street, his face drawn tight as though against a gale.

'Darling Flicky' said the note attached to his wreath; that and nothing more. A voice from thirty years past.

Some time that evening Helen rang:
    'I've been trying to get you for days.'
    'I took a short holiday, went to visit David Hewison.'
    'Good God. I thought he was *persona non grata*.'
    'It was just a whim. I needed a change.'
    'And how was it?'
    'Interesting.'

There was a pause. Doubtless she was remembering. Doubtless she was deciding that it no longer mattered.

'Well, I was just ringing to see how you were.'

'I'm fine.'

'And I thought perhaps we ought to meet to sort some things out. Next week some time? Would you mind?'

'Not really.'

So we agreed on dinner together, on neutral ground. We were breaking up as adults ought to, Helen had said: no recriminations, no sentimentality.

I passed the next days in that curious limbo to which the bereaved and the separated are so often condemned. People at work were painfully polite. They didn't know whether to commiserate with me about my mother, whether even to mention Helen. Their conversations were evasive and distant as though they had only just made my acquaintance.

Friends with whom I went to the theatre were similarly awkward. From accidental hints they dropped it dawned on me that only the evening before they had seen Helen at a dinner party. It was a party to which, in the normal run of things, we would have been invited together. Our own split was having the effect of splitting those we knew: there were some who came down on her side, some who came down on mine, and this despite the fact that there were no sides. I felt like a pariah.

I retreated to the seclusion of my house, and in the evenings to the anonymity of a nearby wine bar which we had never frequented. There the talk was all about holidays in the Lot, and health food restaurants, and 'have you seen the new callisthenic dance troupe?', but I didn't mind much. The place was a kind of Lethe. Someone asked me what I did for a living and I explained that I worked for a firm manufacturing homeopathic medicines. Had I said 'a drug company' I would have been ostracized.

My attendance at the plate glass and steel tower which houses the head office of Hewison Pharmaceuticals was perfunctory. Even Honjohn noticed it. He called me in for a 'chat' and spoke at length about farm subsidies and the

Common Agricultural Policy which were matters close to his heart. It was apparent that dealing with a member of the family was distasteful to him. Had I just been an ordinary employee he would have given me 'a week to pull yourself together, or find work more suited to your particular talents', but with family he had to tread warily.

'You've been under a lot of strain recently,' he observed. 'Poor Aunt Felicity going. And then your wife.'

'It was the other way round, John.'

He flushed. 'Of course.'

He is a short, pugnacious man with tufts of hair on his cheeks and a brush of a moustache. He doesn't look like a Hewison at all. As his Uncle David had recognized, his true ambition, realized in the slightly comic manner of all such ambitions, is to look like a country squire or a gentleman farmer rather than the managing director of a pharmaceutical company; and the backstairs wisdom is that he treats his employees like his prize Guernseys: feeds them well, milks them hard, and sells those with a low yield. He has always considered my yield particularly low. I was thought to possess a certain wayward talent for explaining away the more unpleasant aspects of the drugs industry to journalists and the like, but the accent is on the word 'wayward'. I was regarded as dangerously flippant, even – my connection with Helen being cited as evidence – subversive.

But now he was positively solicitous. 'A double blow like you've had is bound to have an effect on a fellow. Rosamund suggested we invite you down to Guerdon House for a weekend, and of course I'd be delighted to see you. But I think you need more of a break than that. What do you say?'

'As a matter of fact, John, I have been thinking about things.'

He looked relieved. 'Jolly good. Got a plan then? A project?'

'In a way. I thought I might go back to Italy for a while. When I was there I took the opportunity to go to Rome for a few days.'

'Rome. Excellent. Fascinating city. Can't really say I like the place much but some people seem to.' He was always faintly embarrassed about his Italian blood, as if he had a fear that the Italian genes might get out of control and run amok, shattering for ever his gentleman farmer image.

'I went to see our uncle.'

'Our uncle?'

'David. He was at my mother's funeral, remember?'

'Yes, of course. Rather embarrassing really.'

'I don't see why.'

'Well, my father. I mean brothers cutting each other at a family funeral like that.' He flapped helplessly.

'No better than children.'

He flushed, but not with embarrassment. This was the farmer about to give vent to righteous anger. 'You don't seem to understand what Uncle David has done. He's nothing better than a parasite on the firm with his bloody archaeological trust. Do you know what it costs every year? Do you know? Just to grub around in the dirt?'

I left the anger to blow away in a cloud of inane bluster.

'Sold his birthright . . . blackmailed his own family . . . spat on his father's memory . . . mess of pottage . . . fatted calf . . .' Eventually the storm, familiar enough but minor of its kind, died away and left him with nothing more than vague hissings and rumblings. 'And you are proposing to join him?'

'It depends what you mean. I'm not proposing to join in a family feud, if that's your worry. They use lots of volunteer workers on the dig during the season. I just thought I might go and help.'

'Digging?'

'You make it sound like manual labour.'

'Isn't it?'

'Not in the way you intend. And it's a very different world from production quotas and marketing policies and agonizing over whether all grades of employee should eat in the same canteen.'

He looked at me with eyebrows raised. 'Do I detect an echo of your wife there?'

'Don't be absurd.'

'Well anyway, Anthony, remember this. I don't much like coming the elder cousin and that sort of thing, but I can't ignore my position.' He meant more than just managing director: he meant heir-apparent to the Hewison family. 'Remember that it is all very well to turn your back on the company and all too easy to sneer at it. But you owe it a damned lot. We all do. Just ask yourself where you would be without it, eh?'

'Of course, John.'

'And don't use that tone with me either. And another thing. Whatever you do, don't tell my father where you're going.'

Dinner with Helen was conducted in the brisk manner of a shareholders' meeting when liquidation has already been decided and there remains only the division of the assets.

'I'm only interested in those things which were really ours,' she said. 'Just the things, not your interest in the bloody business.'

I watched as she shifted our possessions, under the guise of pepper mill, salt cellar, oil bottle and the like, around the restaurant table. At one point a waiter glided across to us and courteously borrowed an oil painting by Ruskin Spear for another table to use. Eventually, the Ruskin Spear restored, Helen achieved the disposition which suited her. She looked up with a bright smile.

'Your Italian trip has done wonders for you, you know. I was worried about you before.'

'Gratifying.'

'Don't be bitter. You seem to have fallen for your aunt.'

'What on earth do you mean?'

She raised her eyebrows in that calculated manner which used to aggravate Honjohn so. 'Don't be so touchy. It's just that you've hardly stopped talking about her.'

'I hadn't noticed.'

'Well, I got the Spear without a murmur of protest just as you were going on about how detached she seemed from . . . oh, something or other.'

'She is *simpatica*, certainly.'

'I do wish you wouldn't use Italianisms like that. It sounds so pretentious.'

'It is my second language.'

'How exotic.'

She always looked like porcelain and that was what made her so dangerous: porcelain, one forgets, is hard and sharp. Our meeting hovered on the edge of rancour until, in an unusually pacific gesture, she reached across the table and touched my hand. Maybe that showed how matters really had come to an end. 'What are you going to do now?'

'Back to Italy probably, I don't know when. I might help out on the dig. It'll give me time to think things over.'

Again the raised eyebrows. 'What about the job?'

'I saw Honjohn the other day, told him I needed a holiday. He said he understood.'

'I bet he doesn't. Did you tell him your plans?'

'As a matter of fact I did.'

She laughed. 'I should think that will stir them up. Dear Uncle Thomas will be raving about corporate loyalty or whatever the phrase is. They'll probably sack you.'

'Maybe. But since my mother's death I actually own part of the business. They'll remember that.'

'I'm sure. Anyway I hope that you have a good time. Better the archaeological branch of the family than the commercial one. And now I must be off.'

She rummaged in her purse and pulled out some notes. 'My share,' she said.

Years ago I would have argued, but I knew by now that it wasn't worth the effort. We kissed and I watched her walk to the car, a slight, almost delicate figure who had changed little in appearance since the days when I had first met her at university.

The next day she came with her friend to collect her remaining things. The friend had a knowing smile and eyes which went everywhere.

'Nice place you've got here,' she said. 'Must have cost a packet.'

'It would if it were for sale.'

She peered into the various rooms. 'You could get two families in here at least.'

'It would cost them a packet,' I replied.

She looked at me with that knowing expression. 'Money can keep people alive,' she said, 'but it kills people who have too much.'

'You sound like Saint Paul.'

'Come on, Robin,' said Helen. She seemed a bit embarrassed by her companion. 'Let's go.'

As they drove away in their hired van I could see them laughing together.

I was thirty-six years old and I was turning a corner in my life. Some people turn it much younger, some – Honjohn for one, I suspect – never. It was a disturbing, disorientating experience. I had discovered that the world around the corner looks exactly like the one just left behind; it is just that all the values have changed.

I wrote a letter to Hewison asking if I could come, and while waiting for a reply I began to do some reading, books from the public library which caught my eye as I searched along the shelves of Ancient History, Anthropology, Archaeology: *Etruscan and Early Roman Architecture*, *The Etruscans*, *Central and Southern Italy before Rome*, titles like that. As I read about *lucumo* and *zilth*, about Tachuna and Caere, about the divinities Uni and Turans and Tin, about Tages the demon child who sprang from a furrow near Tarquinia and instructed the ploughman Tarchon in the secret art of divination, I began to understand something of David Hewison's search for a past. I entered a strange world, a world suffused with magic and a submission to the forces of nature which was almost oriental in character, almost Hindu. The ancient Romans must have seen themselves as the future when they confronted such archaic fatalism: religionists displacing magicians.

'Remember what Seneca wrote,' Lara had said one evening at the Villa, '"The Romans believe that lightning is caused when clouds collide, whereas the Etruscans believe that clouds collide in order to release the lightning."'

And there it was, this mysterious sense of pattern and design, permeating everything I read. Ever since the Romans dispensed their blend of Greek rationality and farmer's common sense man has attempted to dominate nature – what else is the whole rationale of a drug company? – but for the Etruscans the rule was to submit and endure. I began to wonder how much things have really changed. In London, in

England, the past is little more than a gloss on the present; but in Italy an older spirit prevails. Reading those books – Boethius, Pallottino and others – I felt that I was looking back through two thousand years of reason into the shadows where the chimera still lurks and Dionysos still smiles his enigmatic smile, and finding there my own reflection. Or Lara's.

It would be dishonest of me not to admit that Lara was part of this. I thought of her a great deal while I was waiting for a reply from the Villa. I would reconstruct conversations with her from the scraps I found in my memory and try to read into them a significance that was surely not there; or picture her features – the particular shape of her mouth and the curve of her cheek, the dark line of her eyebrows and the colour of her eyes – and attempt to find in them hints of a budding intimacy. Like any courtship it was a frustrating experience: the closer I examined my memories of her the more elusive they became, like objects in a darkened room. Then, in pretended relief, I would look away to other things . . . and there she was again visible in the forefront of my mind, smiling that faint, curved smile, the smile of the Dionysos.

It was a blessing to find a distraction. One day a passing comment to the librarian brought mention of a newly-published book about the work of the Special Operations Executive during the last war.

'Now that there's this thirty year rule they can publish a bit more,' he explained. 'The subject's becoming quite popular.'

I seized on the book eagerly, but the indexed entry for Italy had little more than 'The story of what SOE achieved in Italy is yet to be written in English', along with some half-stories and a few names. There was a bare mention of the fighting in Florence; nothing at all about H. D. Hewison. Maybe it was this very silence that awakened my curiosity. I searched elsewhere and in a book called *Secret War in the Midi* turned up this hint. I quote it in full:

At the club in those days there was also the classical scholar Elwyn Davies, who came from G(R) in Cairo following one of the periodic Cairene blood-lettings. Apart from his official work at the Club he organized trips to the local archaeological sites such as Djemila and Tipasa which were welcome breaks from the grim business of training and dispatching agents.

I experienced a little snatch of excitement. Flicking through the pages I quickly learned what I had suspected: the 'Club' was Le Club des Pins, sometime beach club for the French rich, in 1943 SOE Headquarters in Algiers; and that day I contacted Elwyn Davies for the first time in twelve years.

'I've found him,' Helen had announced one lunchtime. 'The witness at the Wedding.'

In our language the event had assumed a disproportionate significance. We always spoke the word as though it bore a capital letter. 'I told you I recognized him. He's a Reader in Mycaenean Archaeology or something. One Elwyn Davies.'

'Let's go and see.'

So we sat in the back of a not very crowded lecture theatre and listened to the Welshman make jokes about Minos and Ariadne, and do a reasonable job of rendering the more arcane aspects of pre-classical Greek history palatable to a few dozen undergraduates.

I approached him as he gathered up his papers at the end.

'I believe you know my uncle.'

He looked at me with bright and penetrating eyes.

'I know many men, my dear. Doubtless a considerable proportion of them are uncles of some kind or other.'

'H. D. Hewison.'

'Ah!' He had the most remarkable knack, the Welshman's trick, of putting great expression into an essentially non-committal remark. That is why they make such fine actors.

'We saw you at his wedding last summer.'

'We?'

I ushered Helen forward. 'My girlfriend.'

'Girlfriend,' he repeated, as though he had not heard the word before. 'But I do not remember either of you.'

'We were . . . amongst the crowd.'

'Spies.'

I laughed. 'Spying. You remember my mother, I'm sure. His sister Felicity.'

He nodded. 'Felicity Perpetua. A lady who is perhaps not always happy.'

'Do you know him well?' I asked.

'Your uncle?' He smiled and turned the question back: 'Do *you* know him well?'

'Not at all. I suppose that was only the second time I've seen him. The first would have been at my grandfather's funeral, but I barely remember that. I don't think I have ever spoken to him.'

'Then I know him better than you.' He picked up his papers and tucked them under his arm. 'He seems to me to be spending a personal fortune in the most responsible way imaginable.'

'You should hear what the family says about it.'

'You should hear what he says about the family.'

We watched him stump out of the lecture room.

'Gosh,' said Helen admiringly. 'He bites.'

The pursuit of Elwyn Davies became something of a game. I suppose it was an extension of our joke about the Wedding. Now we had the Witness. We heard him lecture in his college and I even attended a course which he gave at the Ashmolean on Mycaenean pottery. Finally we ran him to earth one Friday lunchtime in a little pub near the Taylorian Institute.

'Wretched children,' he said loudly as we brought beer to his table. 'You are not pursuing me for my wisdom but for tittle-tattle about your ancestor. What is the metaphor he uses? *Una piòvra*, an octopus.'

'Metaphor for what?'

'His family.'

I laughed. 'I look upon it as far more passive than that: a spider's web.'

'Who is the spider?'

'My grandmother, Nonna Angelica.'

'Ah!' He lit his pipe and wreathed his face in thick clouds of smoke. He had a gnomic air about him which entirely delighted us: a gnome's wisdom, a gnome's humour, a gnome's strange malevolence. We would not have been surprised if he had magicked a pot of gold in place of his flabby steak and kidney pie. But instead what he did conjure up that lunchtime was an outsider's picture of H. D. Hewison and his work, the first I had ever heard:

'Oh, seminal, my dear, seminal. You see there has never been anything like it before, never: the complete excavation of an Etruscan habitation site, I mean – unless you count Marzabotto, which was a *colonia* and therefore a very different animal. Perhaps some of the reconstruction work has been a little . . . questionable, but taken as a whole I'd say that the criticism is nothing more than academic sour grapes. After all, the latter part of the twentieth century is not much enamoured of rich men's hobbies however constructive they may be. And when it's difficult enough to find adequate money for a mere field survey, well! You may imagine the back-biting.'

'Have you known him long?'

He puffed at his pipe and regarded me through a haze of smoke. 'Known him long?' His laugh was more of puzzlement than amusement. 'You want a date, do you? That gives a kind of spurious significance, I suppose. Think what it has done for my subject. Perhaps I could give you dates and thus imbue my words with wisdom, but I don't know how much truth I'd be talking.'

'Is he that mysterious?'

'As curious as the next man. Which means far more imponderable to me than, say, a minyan potsherd. You could say that I first came to know him professionally when we were together at the British School just after the war. We were in different fields of course, but interested enough in each other's work. I was involved in the cities of Magna Graecia – Metapontum, Sybaris and the like – whereas he was doing research into early republican Rome. He was an ancient historian you see, not an archaeologist. But even in those days his interests were leaning towards the Etruscans. And he certainly advertised them.'

He nodded enthusiastically, sifting through his memories to find the right piece. 'For example, I recall one evening how he delivered a great diatribe against the classical historians, accusing them of re-writing history just like the Ministry of

Truth; which caught us all out at the time because none of us knew the Orwell book then. But, you see, that wasn't really the way to do it, as though it were a modern political issue. Not the way at all.' He raised his eyebrows questioningly. 'We all of us know the limitations of Livy and Dionysius of Harlicarnassus anyway, don't we?'

Some people came into the bar and hailed him from across the room. For a moment I thought we were going to be interrupted, but he waved them away with his pipe.

'There was the suspicion – more than a suspicion in fact – of emotional involvement, don't you see? Anathema!'

'And Lucri?'

He nodded. 'There's an emotional involvement for you. Lucri. Well, he did a lot of walking in southern Etruria at the time, poking around the old Etruscan sites, frequently camping out. Much of his work paved the way for the South Etruria Survey which the British School carried out later under Ward Perkins. But by then Hewison had found Lucri. He took me to see the place right at the beginning.'

The noise in the bar had increased as more customers came in. People were jostling against my chair. The place was full of that baying noise which is the celebration call of the English middle class.

'So you saw the place even before he bought it?'

'Oh certainly. Lovely spot, typical Etruscan habitation site, of course: a small plateau almost entirely surrounded by cliffs. Streams on both sides, you must know the kind.'

'I hardly know the area at all.'

Davies shook his head in disbelief. 'The opportunities which the privileged miss. Not your uncle though. I remember standing with him on the very summit of the plateau – you could see the stones amongst the grass – as he said: "I could buy this place, Elwyn. Buy the bloody place and dig it. Like Evans with Knossos."'

Davies took the pipe from his mouth and laid it in an ashtray.

'And that's what he did.'

That almost signalled the end of our conversation. Some of the people who had originally hailed him came over to us through the crowd. This time the Welshman welcomed them.

'What about the war?' I asked.

'The what?' He looked round at me.

'The war, the last war. There's always been a family story that he did something in Italy, parachuted behind the German lines or something.'

Did the bright amusement in Davies' eyes really fade for an instant? Was there a moment of pain amongst the artificiality of an over-crowded Oxford pub? Or is that just a false memory, the kind that gets written back into the past and hallowed as truth? It is too easy to colour the past with present, all too easy.

'Yes,' said Davies. 'There was something. Special Operations or some such. He never spoke about it.'

Then the other conversations broke in.

There was a sequel. A week or two later I found a package waiting for me at the porters' lodge.

'Mr Davies of BNC left it for you, sir. He said not to keep it too long. It's his only copy.'

It was an academic publication, a weighty paperback of the kind you only find in university bookshops and libraries.

*Lucri; the Excavation of an Etruscan Acropolis.*

The author was H. D. Hewison and the publisher was an organization whose name, until that moment, I had only heard muttered amongst the family as a kind of oath: The Hewison Archaeological Trust. Subsequently I found out more, in particular the exact wording of Article Fifteen of the Trust's constitution because I later suggested to Honjohn precisely what it forbids:

'The Trust shall not be used, by way of advertising or publicity, to the advantage of the parent company Hewison Pharmaceuticals Ltd. or any of the subsidiary companies thereof.'

'It's a damned parasite,' Thomas declared. 'A leech. And we can't even take any credit for it.'

Now, twelve years after, I wondered whether Elwyn Davies would remember me, indeed whether he was even still alive; but his voice on the telephone was unchanged.

'Anthony the dilettante, after so many years! But of course you may come.'

# XII

So I travelled up to Oxford again with a feeling of anticipation and something of a pilgrim's emotions: curiosity mingled with reverence.

It was one of those May days when the weather lies on the borderline between spring and summer, a peculiarly English day. Shafts of sunlight illuminated the gothic limestone of the Bodleian and the Roman baroque of the Radcliffe Camera. There was some kind of ceremony going on and gowned figures stalked through the archways or congregated like rooks in the quadrangles, giving the place that strange sense of continuity because of change rather than despite it: an air of defiance that is peculiar to the city. In Davies's rooms, sitting in a chair at an angle to the lancet windows, looking down onto the perfect square of lawn which is the navel of the college, I felt that nothing could ever bear the hard stamp of reality in this place; that was why Helen hated it so. Scholastic, Royalist, Jacobite, Tractarian, now it was Logical Positivist, which is just scholastic by another name.

'Do you know they put some damned papier-mâché fountain in the middle a few weeks ago,' Davies remarked in mock outrage, pointing down to the quadrangle. 'Some television film they are doing. I spoke out against it of course, but the bursar was adamant.' He turned a faintly amazed expression on me. 'Said we need the money.'

'And do you?'

He laughed. 'I believe we do. Capital is one thing, they tell me, but unless you sell your property to the developers it is all somewhat theoretical. Liquidity –' he pronounced the word with relish – 'is the problem. So instead we prostitute the Old Quad. And that's why the Principal is so keen to meet you: he can sniff endowments out like a bloodhound. But never mind all that. Tell me about you. It must be ten years and more since you were wasting your time here.'

I nodded. 'Something like that.'

'And what about that girl? The political one. Didn't you marry her?'

I was surprised he knew. 'I did, but . . .'

'Finished?'

'Finished. It seems so.' I shrugged, not wishing to talk about it.

'Can't say I'm surprised. Happens to everyone these days. Reaching the proportions of an epidemic. It wouldn't surprise me if one of those fellows in the new Zoology Laboratories doesn't discover a virus.'

He chuckled and settled himself into his wing-back chair to regard me with that bright expression which had delighted us both so much. 'And you have made contact with your uncle at last.'

'Just a few days ago. Getting away from things here. I was made quite welcome at the Villa.'

'Ah, the eponymous Villa Rasenna. How has that place come on, I wonder? I remember it from the very first days when it was a bare barn of a place in which you could do little more than camp. In the early days it was the *castello* in Sabazia that was the centre of things.'

'Lara showed it to me. It's deserted now.'

'Of course. But when her mother was alive . . .' He shook his head. 'She was a remarkable woman, you know.'

'So I have gathered.'

'Great force, great personality. The only person whom I have ever known dominate your Uncle David.'

'What was her relationship with him?'

Davies' eyebrows rose a fraction. 'Relationship? Now there's a word which positively reeks of euphemism. But of course they were almost a generation apart, more like mother and son I would say. Like any such relationship there was an element of carnality there, the suggestion of physical contact, if you see what I mean; but maternal and filial rather than erotic. And then in some ways she was often faintly hostile towards David, as though underneath everything she resented him.'

He leant forward and poured tea. There was something of the fussiness of the spinster about him. Perhaps the genders, which move steadily apart during puberty, come back together in old age. I guessed that Davies was in his seventies by now: an old man being looked after in his failing years by the only family he had ever known – his college.

'She died of a carcinoma of the stomach, you know. When would that be? It seems long ago now but that's just a manifestation of age: these days I find the greatest difficulty in recalling any dates that aren't BC.' He chuckled at his joke. 'I think her death would have been in the middle of the sixties.'

'Nineteen sixty-four.'

He nodded. 'You've been doing your homework. Anyway it was not a pleasant thing to witness. David offered her any medical treatment that was available, flying her to England, all that kind of thing. But she refused everything except the ministrations of the family doctor, an old fellow called Pellegrino. That was typical of Clara, you see. A woman of great determination, great self-sufficiency. And that resentment of David.'

He reached forward to pick up a plain chocolate biscuit from the tray.

'My only vice. Smoking is a ritual and wine a necessity; these things are merely pleasurable and therefore constitute a true vice.'

When I refused his offer of the plate he seemed delighted.

'You knew him during the war, didn't you?' I asked. My tone was pitched carefully midway between question and assertion.

He ate his biscuit methodically, examining me from the depths of his chair. Eventually he said, 'She was a comrade-in-arms of his, you know.'

I pretended surprise and there was a gleam of triumph in the Welshman's eyes. 'You didn't know that, then? Oh yes, Clara Alessio was a member of Hewison's group, a most significant member. Indeed after the war we tried to get approval for a decoration for her, an OBE or something equally inadequate. But there were problems.'

He paused, finishing the last of the biscuit and then, quickly and precisely, licking the tip of each finger in turn to remove every trace of chocolate. 'How did you find out? About me, I mean. Did David tell you?'

'No. I put two and two together. I knew he was in Algiers in 1943, and I found a reference in a book to your being there at that time.'

'A book?'

'*War in the Midi* or something. I forget the author's name.'

'Ah, Philipson. Garrulous old fool. Well, of course you are right. We were both in the Special Operations Executive. I was David's conducting officer in fact. More than that, I actually recruited him to the firm.'

'The firm? Was it really called that? It sounds like *Boy's Own Paper*.'

'Well, it was, my boy, it was. The post-war generation has had so much spy thriller nonsense that it can no longer imagine the truth. In those days the whole business was organized on a personal basis, the old-boy network, the Great Game, you know the thing. Then from those foundations we came to recruit all imaginable types, eccentrics beyond belief, from professional safecrackers – petermen they were called. Interesting etymology that, to do with Saint Peter, fishing things out, but also, surely, with modern allusions to saltpetre, don't you think? – all the way to circus dwarves.' He paused, tapping his chin thoughtfully and gazing out on the Old Quadrangle as though on a host of dwarves all awaiting employment. 'I'm not really sure what we did want the dwarf for, in fact,' he admitted ruefully.

I smiled. 'And Hewison? Had you been his tutor?'

'What? Oh no.' Davies repeated the 'no' two or three times as though it needed emphasis. 'No, no. Shortly before the outbreak of hostilities I had fled to Cambridge to escape the overpowering influence of Beazley, you see, to work with Protheroe on a revised prehistoric chronology of the Aegean. Fascinating study, really. I don't recall the details now, but anyway carbon dating blew the whole argument to pieces shortly after the war. Our own atomic bomb, I suppose.'

He looked sharply at me. His expression was, as ever, bright and cunning. 'I'm wandering, you say? Well, let me. It's a privilege of old age, and besides it sets the scene for me, brings it all back. And, let me tell you, it's vivid. In here.' He tapped his forehead in a gesture reminiscent of my uncle's, then pushed himself out of his chair.

'Come, my boy. Let us leave these things for the good Young to clear away. We need a brisk walk to enliven our bodies before the ordeal of sherry with the Principal, who will doubtless make references to the Hewison fortune and try and interest you in biomedical research or something. That's what comes of electing a scientist.'

We made our way down into the open air and through the quadrangle, Davies nodding greetings to people as he passed by. The High was thick with cars and bicycles. As we gained the haven of the narrow streets on the far side and made our way towards Corpus and the entrance to Christ Church Meadow he came back to the original subject.

'It was on a train journey as a matter of fact, one of those interminable and squalid wartime train journeys which you may thank God for having been spared. Reading and sleeping were the only escapes from such purgatory and with little success I was essaying the latter. Opposite me, trying to avoid my knees, was a lieutenant from some infantry regiment. But he was a subaltern reading Dante, which you may imagine put him out of the ordinary run of things. The usual level was "Comic Cuts". Perhaps appropriately what this man was reading was *Purgatorio*.'

Recall of the incident, with its donnish exchange of quotes – 'I am delighted to say that my knowledge of Dante was quite equal to his, although naturally his Italian was vastly more fluent' – obviously gave the old Welshman much pleasure. While the six other occupants of the compartment dozed fitfully around them the two men had started up a conversation in a mixture of English and Italian, and soon discovered acquaintances in common, interests shared, opinions satisfactorily at variance. Finally Davies suggested that Hewison's life as a junior officer in a line regiment might be less than stimulating. He offered the younger man his card.

'Come and see me at this address and we'll see about something more interesting,' he had suggested.

He wagged an admonishing finger at me. 'Mark my words, we were not complete amateurs in those days. Not only did I immediately check up on him, but I discovered that as soon as he rejoined his unit the next day he put in an enquiry about me through the battalion Intelligence Officer. That was the kind of thing we loved in our recruits, a natural caution. For he was a natural, you see. By that time we had come to recognize them: reserved, sociable enough when required, but with an immense self-sufficiency. He needed no one, no one with whom to share his thoughts if you see what I mean. And of course he was highly intelligent.'

We had paused, looking south across the Meadow. Wind rushed through the great elms which bordered the paths. The sudden sunlight was only a simulacrum of summer. Setting off towards the river Davies gave an account of Hewison's first interview in an anonymous office in Northumberland Avenue, his training in Arisaig on the west coast of Scotland, his move out to North Africa, the days of preparation at the beach club outside Algiers which had become the base for SOE's operations into south-western Europe. It was a strange story, an almost mythic tale that seemed to animate Davies' frame as he related it. He spoke quickly and accurately, a young man again.

'Southern France was our main preoccupation at the time. The Balkans operation was run from Cairo, and although Italy was our concern in Algiers it was a bit of a side show in the early days. Apart from anything the OVRA, the Fascist secret police, was startlingly efficient. But then came the invasion of the peninsula and the capitulation of the Badoglio government – Mussolini had gone in June you remember and the Salerno landings coincided with the Italian armistice. Our first big success came exactly then with Operation Monkey. It was completely fortuitous but a feather in our cap neverthe-less. One of our agents, Dick Mallaby, had been captured by the Fascists near Lake Como in the spring of forty-three and most of the armistice was negotiated through him and his wireless, operating from the Quirinal palace. It was really only then, once Italy had done her celebrated volte-face, that we began in earnest. David Hewison was one of our first agents to go. Bruno was his code name. He made a blind drop in the Maremma, between Tarquinia and Vetrano. Dangerous business, dropping agents blind, but it had to be done if you were opening up an area for the first time. Any sort of accident on landing, a broken ankle or something equally silly, and you'd probably had it. Finished. Months of preparation gone up in smoke. That was why sometimes they were dropped in lakes – like Mallaby himself into Lake Como – but therein lay another danger because if you were spotted coming down you were almost certain to be captured. It was a toss-up really. With Hewison we did consider the lakes in the area, particularly Bolsena if my memory serves me right; but finally we decided to risk dry land. The River Marta valley I think. His first contact was in Vetrano.'

'Where the massacre took place.'

Davies was patting the pockets of his tweed jacket. He found his pipe and began to ream the bowl with an old penknife.

'You've heard about that, have you? Well, that was the kind of thing that happened in our war, the kind of thing one had to . . . not accept; come to terms with, I suppose.' He put the pipe in his mouth and blew sharply through it, then produced an old tobacco pouch.

'You must understand that one of the main reasons we had put Hewison in was to disrupt communications through to the coast.' He began to fill the pipe, packing the tobacco down with a thick, capable thumb. 'The planners were already thinking ahead of Salerno, you see: Anzio, Ostia, Ladispoli, Civitavecchia, there was a number of likely beaches around Rome, and in every case it would have been necessary to break the road and rail links with the coast in order to hinder the inevitable counter-attack. In the Vetrano area communications are particularly poor, as I'm sure you've seen: just the one road linking the Via Cassia with the Via Aurelia, and the one railway line running roughly parallel a little way to the south. The Tolfa hills get in the way, you see. Personally I think the Allies made a mistake in choosing Anzio. I always said that the Civitavecchia area would have been the best. But . . .' He shrugged.

'So what happened at Vetrano?'

'The killings, you mean?' The Welshman was fiddling with matches. The small, distracting action seemed designed to give him time to assemble his ideas. 'By that time – it must have been just before the landings, towards the end of January 1944 – Hewison had a small group in operation. "Fabiomassimo".' He glanced up from his pipe, with amusement in his eyes. 'A good classicist, you see. Quintus Fabius Maximus.'

'Cunctator.'

Davies nodded. He tamped the tobacco with a nicotine-stained finger then cupped a hand against the wind. A match flared.

'I never really got to know the details. Obviously I was hundreds of miles away at the time, in Algiers . . . no, Bari it would have been by then. Maryland; Number One Special Force. Our only direct contact was through the wireless and naturally there was not much opportunity for giving details by that means. There was even a standing order that transmissions were not to last more than five minutes if I remember rightly. Besides, what was exceptional? "Fabiomassimo" tried to bomb the rail bridge at Lucri – you've seen it, of course? – and ended up killing some German soldiers. I can't even remember how many, but it was only two or three. The Germans took hostages in reprisal and shot them. Simple. Happened all the time, didn't it? They killed three hundred at the Fosse Ardeatine.'

'And that's it?'

'What more do you want?' Davies was suddenly brusque, almost angry. 'When we got to know about it we even tried to get a leaflet drop, claiming the raid as an operation by a British commando or something equally implausible, but there were better things to do with aircraft at that time.'

'Of course.'

'And anyway the thing is long since over. Dead and buried.'

'Not for the people of Vetrano. Not for Hewison.'

'How so?' Davies was standing four-square in the path, his teeth clamped onto the stem of his pipe. He was a small figure, but somehow indomitable. A group of oarsmen coming back from the boathouses parted and flowed around him like water around a rock. I heard one of them say, 'Old Elwyn at bay'. I shrugged, wondering at the sudden, uncharacteristic anger of the man.

'The town still remembers, and he still seems affected by it. In some way it seems to provide a motive for the excavation, a form of atonement maybe.'

Davies snorted. 'A conceit.'

'Lara herself suggested it to me.'

'What,' the Welshman replied, 'does Lara know?' He puffed away and regarded me with that caustic eye which had so often glared at undergraduates caught out in some elementary error. 'You should know well enough, Anthony, that you must go to primary sources.' The glare had developed a spark of amusement.

'That's why I'm here.'

'Oh, but there are others apart from me.'

'Who?'

'Well, Jane for one.'

'Van Doren?'

The Welshman chuckled into his pipe. 'Jane MacAllister. She was one of my FANYs.'

'Fannies?'

'First Aid Nursing Yeomanry. They were the girls' – his Welsh intonation would have rendered the word 'gels' anyway, but he deliberately exaggerated the sound and thus created a picture of much more than a neutral, classless group of young women – 'who assisted us in the Firm with, oh, any number of jobs, from signals to bed-making. Our own private sisters of mercy. Jane joined me from F Section, the French operation. We had any number of French speakers you see, but Italian speakers were rather rarer. She had been to school in Locarno at the beginning of the war. Her father was a diplomat, and her brother too, come to that. He's Ambassador in one of the Scandinavian countries at the moment, I believe. Oslo?'

123

Davies turned and stumped back up the path in the wake of the rowing eight. I followed him, trying anew to fit Jane van Doren into the intricate little puzzle, wondering about her relationship with the man at the centre of everything.

'Jane, let us say, "mothered" Hewison while he was doing final training at the Club; despite the fact that she was a bare eighteen years old. Even then she was the kind of woman who organized men. You've noticed, no doubt.'

'I've noticed.'

'Well, you can imagine how she took him under her wing.'

'Just that?'

Davies looked sideways at me. 'Meaning?'

'I thought perhaps there had been something –'

'Between David and Jane MacAllister?' Davies shrugged. As far as I knew the old man had always lived alone, a life which seemed neutral in the matter of sex. He, who was so awake to the slightest subtlety of Helladic or Cycladic chronology, hardly seemed the person to be aware of the secrets between men and women.

'Well, we used to keep a fairly close eye on such things, of course.' He sounded as though he was speaking of some disease. 'Sometimes it was harmless enough, to be sure, but on occasion the thing could become dangerous. One had to be aware. But I remember nothing particular between Jane and Hewison. Anyway, how could it be of significance, all those years ago?'

'It would be rather uncommon to have your husband's former lover living in your house. If that's what she had been.'

Davies' expression denied all knowledge of such things. 'I think I detect a certain fondness for Lara, don't I?' he remarked. 'A certain defensiveness about the lady?'

'Maybe. But that's not the point.'

'I'm sure not. Anyway, do not imagine you are alone. *Mater pulchra filia pulchrior.* There's barely a man involved with Lucri who has not felt himself . . . bewitched, shall we say?' It was not clear whether he included himself or not. 'And your uncle more than any. It disturbed him, you know; deeply disturbed him. Once he even confided to me about it, when perhaps he had had more to drink than was good for him. He

124

asked me whether I thought he was . . . unnatural was the word he used. She was young, you see, very young: a mere fifteen or sixteen I suppose. But bewitching: great green eyes, black hair – what is the cliché? As black as a raven's wing?' He chuckled faintly, shaking his head at the memory. 'And a kind of mystic, capricious mind, full of strange intuitions and flights of fancy. I recall seeing real anguish in his face when she was with us in those early days, anguish whenever she touched him or smiled at him. She looked upon him as a kind of uncle and that only made it worse for him. Her father was not alive, you see; killed in the war.'

'She told me.'

'It made it difficult, made it difficult. But I don't think that Jane figured. Not beside Lara.'

At the end of the path Davies hesitated. 'Is there time for the Botanic Garden? Are you fit enough?'

I laughed and turned right with him along the Broad Walk. Our talk drifted onto other subjects – Helen, my life in London, his own retirement which, as was to be expected, was fully occupied with work – and we only mentioned David Hewison again when he talked about my mother. It transpired that he had met her more than the once when I had seen the two of them together on the steps of the church in Sabazia.

'When David came back from Italy in 1945. I thought her an unhappy woman then.'

'You weren't wrong.'

I followed him through the gate into the gardens – 'The Physick Garden,' he announced. 'Stone pines from the Pincio, gingko from the Permian, and everything a physick for the mind. This is where I come when I am troubled by thoughts of mortality. I will die and they will bury me and the worms will eat me up and their faeces will feed magnificent plants like these.' He laughed, a great shout of a laugh which was full of real humour. Together we went through the entrance portico and emerged onto the High, stepping in one stride from the seventeenth century into the twentieth.

He touched my elbow. 'If it really interests you, speak with Gianluca,' he said unexpectedly. 'He was there during the war, you understand. A most courageous boy, most courageous.'

125

# XIII

I RETURNED to Lucri just as the season was beginning. The daytime temperature had risen. Clouds became a rarity in a sky of oppressive blue. The streams on either side of the site shrank back to leave white boulders standing out of the water like polished skulls, while all across the site, around the walls and the trenches, up on the arx and alongside the huts and tents of the *tendopoli*, the grass browned off. Dust rose like smoke from the trenches where a growing army of volunteers worked amidst the shriek of cicadas.

The work satisfied me – by its discomfort and monotony as much as anything else.

'Just navvying really,' was how Meredith described it. He had the kind of two-dimensional view of things that pleased me at the time. Life was simply a matter of deposits and potsherds; anything else was just an inconvenience. 'Trouble nowadays is that no one who is willing to do the work even knows how to use a bloody pickaxe. I have to show them everything: I practically have to show them how to pee.'

In the *tendopoli* the skeleton population which I had seen on my first visit was expanding as the university terms finished and the students flocked to the place. It was the 'kibbutz' atmosphere of which David Hewison had spoken with scant understanding: a babble of talk in the mess tent, young people trooping off towards the dig like workers going out to the fields, suntanned figures wallowing and shouting in the pools of the Vesca stream when there was any free time, bonfire parties in the evenings at which liaisons were made and broken with cheerful promiscuity. Charles van Doren pronounced the whole thing pagan.

I worked on the habitation site where Meredith was

126

supervising. They had cleared the top soil from the wall footings and floor of what they called the *taverna*. It was just a hollow square of ashlar blocks with an opening onto the ancient street. Shop, tavern, storehouse, it might have been anything.

The work was largely conducted on hands and knees. Dust got into eyes and mouth. The sun drummed incessantly on one's back or on the corrugated plastic erected as a roof above us. Our little team included Hannah, who was working for a doctorate at Birmingham University; two teachers from London who were married, they said, but not to each other; and a Fulbright Scholar from Louisiana called Henry.

He was the comedian of the group. He shook his head in dismay when we found the rubbish tip behind our tavern.

'Litterin' don't have nothin' on this.'

'Domestic rubbish deposit,' Meredith corrected him. 'Important.'

Under his patient instruction we scraped our way into the litter centimetre by centimetre as though searching for gold nuggets.

'Never thought I'd end up picking through trash cans,' said Henry. 'What would ma ole mamma say?'

We worked under the gaze of frequent visitors whom we treated with a kindly impatience, as though they were children. Sometimes, having broken away from the usual round of Tarquinia and Cerveteri, an enterprising gaggle of tourists would appear; more often Goffredo Macchioni would bring officials or guests of the Ministry – 'We have to toady to them,' Hewison explained; but our regular audience was the camera team from British television which Lara had mentioned, and a Mr Harris of the British Council. This man peered into our *taverna* as though expecting treasures.

'Excavations of world importance,' he said to reassure himself.

An exhibition of the Lucri work was being set up jointly by the British Council and the *Ministero per i Beni Culturali*, to open in Florence in the autumn. I was detailed to show him around.

'Excavations of world importance,' I agreed encouragingly.

He was a worried man with hair just the nicotine side of grey. The sun bothered him, the dust bothered him, above all the time bothered him. He seemed to navigate his way around the dig by means of a compass which he carried in his wrist watch.

'Must get back to the Council,' he kept saying. 'Extraordinary work, extraordinary work. Do you know the jewellery? Do you know how much the Italian Government has insured it for? *Miliardi, miliardi*. And then they say it isn't enough and we mustn't lose it.'

'Have you seen this?' Henry asked solemnly.

Mr Harris hadn't.

'It's a sewer.'

Only in one respect did I not work as one of the other volunteers: I accepted Lara's invitation to stay at the Villa.

'. . . unless you'd prefer the *tendopoli*. There's more life there.'

Henry had put it less euphemistically: 'There are women here'd work the ass off Priapus,' he asserted with enthusiasm, but despite such attractions I preferred the even tenor of the Villa Rasenna. I had convinced myself that its constancy of shade, of cool, of quiet, was the palliative I needed.

'I don't think communal living is what I want at the moment,' I told Lara. 'Folk songs round the camp fire aren't really my thing. I need to work things out of my system.'

She laughed at that. 'How very Anglo-Saxon, to describe everything in terms of plumbing. It's just what David always says about the British archaeologists: they forget about the people of Lucri and instead spend all their time arguing about the layout of the drains.'

'Henry as well.' I gave a poor imitation of his accent: 'These guys sure spent some time on the john.'

I enjoyed her easy laughter. She was so many things that Helen was not. Above all she was magnificently and naturally female, without that continual glance over her shoulder to detect the first hint of sexual prejudice. Helen had always been ready to mobilize sex as a weapon when required; but Lara simply remained confident in the strength of her gender, that quality of woman which has always been inaccessible to the male.

'Maybe I should give way and weep on your shoulder,' I suggested jokingly.

'Maybe you should.'

A dangerous thing to say, except that there were people all around to render it innocuous, Meredith telling jokes, Charles lecturing a captive audience about some tedious detail of technique, Jane bustling and organizing. Lara and I had no age gap and no history of family familiarity to give a ready and acceptable framework to our relationship, so we wavered between the formal and the dangerously intimate and our feelings lay at the mercy of circumstances which seemed out of our control.

The discovery of the new grave was the great event of that season. Like so many such things it was fortuitous: a violent rainstorm, a freak among the cloudless days, loosened the soil on a precipitous wooded slope on the southern side of the excavation site. There followed a small slide of rubble and earth which revealed, to the first person who scrambled along the stream bank at that point, a hole at the foot of a short, newly-exposed cliff.

Hewison was the first to examine it properly. Word had got around and a small crowd had gathered on the far bank of the stream to watch. It included the van Dorens and Macchioni, and a Cambridge archaeologist named Arden-Tillyard who had made the discovery; there was also the man from the British Council and, of course, the ubiquitous television camera crew. We all looked up at the figure of Hewison, in battered plimsolls and khaki shorts and shirt, climbing carefully up through the trees to the landslide debris.

'For heaven's sake go carefully, David!' van Doren barked.

'Chisel-marks, definite chisel-marks,' Arden-Tillyard kept saying. 'Wish to goodness I'd had a torch.'

I found Lara standing beside me. She was wearing the uniform of the dig – denim shorts and tee shirt – and her hair was pulled back by a plastic clip. She looked very young and very beautiful as she stared up at her husband climbing over the unstable rubble, and I suddenly realized that I was jealous of that look.

'I'm certain it's not natural,' said Arden-Tillyard to anyone who would listen. 'The edge is bevelled. Clear chisel-marks.'

Hewison paused in his climb, the black hole three yards above him. One of the boulders at his feet shifted. Loose stones skittered down through the trees.

'This lot's bloody unstable,' he called out. 'I'll go round to the left.'

I recalled his easy movements across the tiered cliff of the necropolis and smiled reassuringly at Lara. 'He'd have made a mountaineer.'

She turned an anxious face towards me. 'It is a tomb,' she said. Her voice was very soft. Unlike Arden-Tillyard's it did not carry to the rest of the crowd; unlike Arden-Tillyard's it was not hedged about with doubt. 'It is a tomb,' she repeated in the manner of someone stating a fact.

'Certainly man-made.' Arden-Tillyard stood just behind her. 'No doubt in my mind at all. Wonderful luck.'

'Major importance,' said Mr Harris.

Hewison had reached the hole. He produced a torch and shone the beam into the opening, then cautiously put his head in.

'Careful, old man!' van Doren called.

'Oh shut up, Charles,' his wife snapped. 'What do you think he's being?'

Slowly Hewison crawled into the hole until only his feet remained out in the daylight. There was a long pause. The camera crew left off filming and began to fiddle with their machine. The only other sound was the trickling of water amongst the boulders of the stream bed and the muttered assertions of Arden-Tillyard: 'I'd swear it's an artifact. No doubt in my mind. Chisel-marks.'

'We'll name it after you, Francis,' Jane suggested. 'The Arden-Tillyard hole.'

'Come on, he's moving,' said the director of the film crew. The camera began to whirr again.

As cautiously as he had entered the hole Hewison began to extract himself. There was a sigh of relief from the watchers beside the stream, a shout of 'What about it, old man?' from van Doren, but Hewison made no reply until he had moved sideways away from the scar of rock and soil. Then he looked down on his audience.

'It's a burial,' he confirmed. 'The chamber goes about eight feet into the rock, say four feet high.'

'Bloody marvellous,' muttered the television man. The directional microphone was aimed like a bazooka at the figure above them amongst the trees.

'I knew it all along,' Arden-Tillyard said triumphantly.

Van Doren called, 'Are there grave goods?'

'It's a multiple burial. No grave goods that I could see. Nothing. Just bones, hundreds of bones amongst the dust.' He made his way down the slope and emerged from the trees on the far bank. The crowd watched him in silence. 'It's just bones,' he repeated. 'Nothing more than bones. A dozen skulls or more, I'm not sure. Just heaped.' He was breathing hard, as though the climb had taken a lot of energy; but, more than that, there was a haggard look to his face, a pallor beneath his weathered complexion.

Lara had slipped her hand through my arm as though for security.

'Is there nothing else, David?' van Doren asked as Hewison picked his way towards us over the boulders of the stream. 'Nothing else at all?'

Hewison shook his head. 'Not that I could see at a glance.' He climbed up onto the bank beside van Doren and turned to look back up the slope. 'We're going to have to do a lot of work on that slope to make it safe.'

'It's very strange, just bones.' Van Doren's tone was petulant, as though the tomb had somehow let him down. 'Very strange indeed. It'll make it damnably difficult to date.'

'Some of the skulls,' Hewison was saying, 'some of the skulls have . . .' he paused, as though lost for words, jabbing his fingers against his own head '. . . great holes in them. Holes, depressed fractures.' He shook his head and uttered a small sound which might almost have been a laugh. 'It was a massacre,' he said quietly. 'A bloody massacre.'

He turned from us and walked away through the silent crowd. The camera whirred, watching him.

'Bloody marvellous,' murmured the television man.

In the evening speculation was rife. The archaeologists gathered in the usual informal group on the terrace overlooking the garden of the Villa. Their voices were animated.

'It's going to be a dreadful headache,' Van Doren complained. 'If what David says is true and there are no artifacts then we'll have the devil of a job dating the thing. For heaven's sake, it may be neolithic.'

Hewison was disparaging. 'How on earth could they be in that state of preservation if they were neolithic?' he asked.

'Well, Apennine culture at least, or Proto-Villanovan. Who the devil knows?'

Hannah asked, 'What about a test on the bones themselves? Surely a nitrogen assay would give an idea.'

Van Doren looked dubious. 'It might be better than nothing, but I wouldn't place much reliance on it alone.' He swept his lank forelock from his eyes and turned his didactic manner on the company. Nitrogen assay, it seemed, was something he knew a great deal about.

'They're not children, you know,' his wife interrupted.

He looked faintly surprised at this idea. 'Aren't they? These days all adults are exactly like children. They all seem to believe that science can do anything. The word of Science has replaced the word of God.'

'Whose is that?' Jane asked. 'Yours?'

I was sitting quite apart from the group on the balustrade of the terrace and I suppose I should have kept out of it, but the combination of academic smugness and conjugal bickering annoyed me.

'Do you think they might be modern?' I asked.

My words brought silence.

'Modern?' my uncle demanded. He glared at me as though I had made an indecent remark. 'What on earth do you mean, *modern*?'

I shrugged. 'An idea, that's all. Probably silly. But what have you got? A dozen-odd skeletons which seem to be hacked about a bit. It just occurred to me that the ancient world does not have a prerogative in massacres. They have happened in modern times as well, haven't they?'

My uncle's face was the colour of putty. He drew a deep breath and his mouth moved as though to say something, but it was Arden-Tillyard's languid voice which broke the silence.

'Do you think we ought to call the police perhaps?'

There was laughter.

'No, my dear fellow,' the Cambridge man went on, 'there is no doubt that we are dealing with an ancient burial. As bone ages it loses its organic component and along with that its flexibility. All you are left with is a mineral *skeleton* of the original bone, if you take my meaning. This is quite fragile. However, I believe the other thing is far more pertinent to the question of dating.' He looked from me to his colleagues. Putting a finger up to stroke his blond moustache he said, with a portentous air, 'It is all a question of chisel-marks.'

'You haven't stopped talking about chisel-marks all day,' said Jane.

'What one needs,' Arden-Tillyard explained, 'is a thorough statistical analysis of chisel-marks from tombs of known dates. Then one could compare unknown data with known standards.' He spoke with a faint smile lurking beneath his moustache, as though everything he said were some kind of private joke. His left hand, describing lazy circles in front of his face, seemed to be plucking his ideas ad hoc from the air. 'It would all depend on acquiring a reasonable sample and identifying a number of reliable parameters – width, depth of stroke, that kind of thing – to which you could apply a rigorous statistical analysis, but the idea itself seems quite sound.' His tone was of faint surprise. Maybe at the beginning of his discourse the whole thing had appeared unlikely, been in fact some kind of donnish joke designed to divert the flow of the conversation.

Later that evening, after supper, it was the same man who rescued me from an argument with my uncle. During the meal Hewison had become belligerent.

'I wanted privacy,' he said at one point. 'When I began my work here I wanted privacy. I wanted to be left alone with the past. And what do I get? I get journalists, I get television cameras, I get government ministers. Do you know that the present luminary's sole claim to fame is that his putrefying little political party obtained four per cent of the national vote at the last election? And he could revoke our excavation licence on a whim –'

'It is an intricate thing, the internal politics of this country,' Mr Harris interrupted. He felt that he understood such things. 'An almost Byzantine system of checks and balances –'

'And I get the British Council. As much guts as a frozen chicken, that's how someone described it to me once. As much guts as a frozen chicken.'

Harris winced and glanced at his watch. 'I don't think that our function is actually to have guts, Mr Hewison . . .'

But the Council man, once mauled, was tossed away as of no further interest. 'And now, to cap everything, I get relatives.'

His eyes lighted on me. 'Do you know what my mother said to me once? She said, "You are a bad family man."' He glared around the terrace at the nervous company. Jane was smoothing Harris's ruffled feathers. The others just watched helplessly.

'Oh, but you must not misunderstand. My dear mother did not mean that I ran around making other men's wives pregnant, or didn't help my own with the washing up. She had a very different sense of family. Family meant Empire. It meant reverence towards dead ancestors – my father and grandfather – and living relatives, in particular herself and Thomas. It meant a whole lot of things which the Romans expressed in those dreadful epithets that haunted my schooldays: *gravitas, pietas, humilitas*. It meant loyalty to the cause. "You do not," she said, "take your share of the patrimony and run away like the prodigal son. You do not sell your birthright for a mess of pottage." She was very good with Biblical allusions, you see. "A man must face up to his responsibilities." Responsibilities!' He made the word sound indecent. 'Are you a good family man, Anthony Lessing? Are you a good family man?'

I had seen the bile well up in him before, but then he had swallowed it back down. This time it spilled over.

'My marriage has just failed, so by those standards I suppose not.'

'That's not what I mean and you know it. *The* family, *our* family, our little septic pool of genes. Where are your loyalties there?'

'It doesn't really mean much to me, I'm afraid. I've always been on the edge of things. The power lies with Thomas, Honjohn, others.'

'But you sold out to them, didn't you? You took their offer of a sinecure. Did you also take their thirty pieces of silver?'

In Italian Lara said, 'David, this isn't fair.'

'*Zitta!*' He didn't shift his glance from me. I saw her look – as though he had just struck her.

'Did you?' he persisted.

'I don't know what you mean.'

'Are you here to spy on me? Like you did twelve years ago at my wedding?'

There was a small cry from Lara. Her hand went to her mouth and she stared at me in horror.

'I offered you hospitality,' her husband was saying. 'I thought you needed it, the only child of my sister. She was little better than a whore but she was the only one of them I ever loved. And now has her son betrayed my trust?'

There was a confused movement between Jane and Hewison and Arden-Tillyard. I found Arden-Tillyard at my side, taking my elbow.

'Perhaps a stroll in the garden is in order.'

'I have not betrayed any trust,' I answered Hewison. I looked pointedly at Lara.

Arden-Tillyard continued to edge me away. 'After all we haven't really talked much,' he said. 'And David is not really very sociable at the moment,' he added in a masterpiece of understatement.

He led me down from the terrace and into the garden. It was suddenly quiet and cool, a blessed relief from the scene above us. Hewison shouted something at our backs. I heard Jane's voice telling him to let the matter drop.

'I have a cousin who works for Hewison Pharmaceuticals,' my companion said unexpectedly. He lit a cheroot and drew in the smoke. 'Does that surprise you? Mind you, I've never told David. Don't think I'd dare.' He chuckled. 'The fellow found the name too much of a mouthful, so he dropped the Arden. Or the Tillyard.'

'Not Geoffrey Arden?'

'Good Lord, do you know him? He's in the States, isn't he?'

'He's head of' – I almost said 'our' – 'the North American operation. I don't know him very well but we've met from time to time.'

Voices were raised behind us. Chairs were being moved. I heard Charles and Jane talking loudly, then Hewison's voice:

'I will do as I bloody well please! This is my home!'

Arden-Tillyard's voice drifted on blithely. 'Geoffrey and I are what in other days would have been the black sheep of the family. The fate of most of the clan is the Guards or the City – nothing disreputable,' he added quickly. 'Merchant banking, although these days even that's beginning to look little better than bookmaking. But Geoffrey and I . . .' He shook his head in disappointment. 'Academia and Commerce. Frightful.'

We had reached the fountain at the axis of the paths. Behind us the terrace projected from the backdrop of the Villa like a Renaissance apron stage. In the lights figures moved back and forth. My uncle's voice was the only one which reached us.

'I suppose you don't realize why David got rather . . . overwrought this evening?' Arden-Tillyard enquired.

'You tell me.'

'My dear fellow, don't snap.'

'I'm sorry, I didn't mean to. I'm just a bit on edge. I'd like your explanation.'

'Your intonation suggests that you already have one of your own.' He smiled in the darkness. I could see his features in the backwash of light from the terrace. 'Mind you, I thought you handled him well enough under the circumstances: orderly withdrawal seemed to be the order of the day. A concept which my father seemed to spend most of his military career perfecting.'

I wondered how old Arden-Tillyard was. He had that deceptive kind of looks which seem unaffected by ageing: his fair hair would never grey, his spare frame would never develop a paunch, and yet his narrow, bony face must have seemed that of an adult even in his youth. Surprisingly and quite inconsequentially he alluded to this very impression when he next spoke.

'I remember when I was a child – that fact alone people find remarkable. "You a child, Francis?" they ask in amazement. "Surely never." But I have to disillusion them: even I was young once. So, I remember when I was a child a particular Uncle Harry. Uncle Harry had been an officer in the family regiment, the Coldstream, during the Great War. He must have been, I suppose, my great-uncle, but let us not worry about the finer points of genealogy. All I remember of Uncle Harry was that if there was so much as a mutter of thunder on the horizon he would go as pale as death and begin to shake all over. It really was remarkable. Had to be led away to his room.'

The man drew reflectively on his cheroot. 'Now that was a phenomenon of the utmost fascination to us children. I even remember praying for thunder just to see Uncle Harry go queer, actually praying. Dear God, please make it thunder tomorrow. In an ecstasy of anticipation we would watch thunder clouds build up. "Was that thunder?" we would ask one another within Uncle Harry's hearing.

'It was shell-shock, of course, but we children never understood that. In 1917 Uncle Harry had sat in a dug-out somewhere outside Ypres for twenty-four hours while German artillery tried to blow him to pieces. The only thing they actually succeeded in blowing to pieces was his mind. We never grasped such subtleties. To us it was just one of Uncle Harry's turns. And no adult ever spoke about it, much less ever tried to explain it to us. It was as though the poor devil had an unmentionable illness.'

He fell silent, standing motionless beside the dribbling fountain, smoking his cheroot and looking back at the terrace as though watching some significant action in a play.

'And so with my own uncle?' I asked. 'The Vetrano killings?'

'So you *were* alluding to that earlier. I wondered. You know about his involvement.'

'I found out. Lara and I talked about it.'

'Did you?' Arden-Tillyard looked sideways at me. 'But do you know the whole story?'

There was a long and, it seemed, carefully constructed pause. Hewison's voice came across the gardens: 'Leave me be! I'm not a fucking child!' Someone, perhaps Jane, was trying to persuade him to bed.

Finally Arden-Tillyard said: 'Lara's father was killed by the partisans, in reprisal for the Vetrano massacre.'

Again the reflective pull on the cheroot. He examined the thing, decided it was almost finished, and put its glowing tip into the water of the fountain. There was a faint, angry hiss.

'I don't know the details; not sure I want to. But it seems he was some kind of Fascist, on the Grand Council or whatever they called it. At least that is what I gather.'

'From whom?' I felt a confused anger, directed at Lara as much as anyone. I had thought myself party to her confidence and I found disillusion a bitter thing.

'That is what Jane told me.'

'Jane MacAllister of SOE,' I said with deliberate sarcasm.

Arden-Tillyard looked at me. His eyes, I had noticed, were sharp and penetrating, quite at variance with his languid manner. 'You have been quite curious about this, haven't you? What can be your motive, I wonder?'

The question lay between us without any answer being offered. It was he who eventually broke the silence:

'Of course it should all be past by now, but we never seem to let things die, do we? Why does the past seem such a fascinating place? Why is it that we attach importance to what happened to other people thirty years or three thousand years ago? Why do we hunt so enthusiastically the old barbaric works of slaughter?'

He scuffed his foot in the gravel, almost the gesture of a child faced with a question beyond his answering.

'Isn't it to understand?'

'Is that it? Understanding. But do we ever understand, I wonder? However much we pick it over do we ever understand? Look at the great themes: tragedy, fate, all that kind of nonsense. Take the greatest of them all if you like: the Trojan War. What do the archaeologists find? A habitation level – Troy VIIa – which was nothing but an impoverished fortress covering five acres; no evidence that there was such a thing as a war with the Greeks: rather, much evidence that there could not have been, at least not in Homer's terms. No, the drama which you read is Homer's alone, not Agamemnon's or Priam's. Then again, think how magnificent Hitler will appear in a thousand years' time: he will have become a great tragic figure instead of the deranged son of a minor civil servant. The reality, always, is rather mundane; bathos rather than pathos, I'm afraid.'

'And the death of Lara's father at the hands of David's partisans? That?'

'That as well. Squalid rather than tragic, I expect.' Arden-Tillyard paused for a moment. 'I forgot to say something about dotty old Uncle Harry. After they dug him out of his trench at Ypres they awarded him the Victoria Cross. It seems that he had been terrifically brave.'

He looked up with a smile, task complete. 'I think we might return to the company now.'

Taking my arm he began to guide me back towards the lights. We reached the terrace just as the van Dorens got my uncle up the stairs and into the loggia above. He was shouting at Charles. From where we were we could hear Jane's voice, as brisk and efficient as a nurse's, punctuating his shouts.

'I would like a glass of port,' Arden-Tillyard announced. 'And so would Anthony here. Port from Oporto, not that frightful sweet stuff from Lake Bolsena which David goes on about.'

There was uneasy laughter at his lèse-majesté, but he had jolted them into action. Somebody sat Lara down and pushed a drink into her hand. Meredith began to tell a long and involved story about his problems with the Italian language which won more laughter than it deserved. People rallied round, placated each other's fears, closed ranks.

I went over to sit beside Lara.

'Why did you tell him about the wedding?'

She looked pleadingly at me. 'I didn't tell him, Anthony.'

I couldn't see how to believe her. She had only told me a half-truth about the Vetrano killings and now she was compounding that half-truth with a lie. But I felt a shameful sense of triumph: to have caught her out gave me some kind of hold over her, caught her up in a small web of obligation.

'Then who?'

She looked miserable. 'Not me.'

The van Dorens returned from their mission.

'Last drink and then to bed,' Charles announced. 'It will be a long day tomorrow.' It was unclear whether he was speaking for himself or the whole company. It would have been in keeping with his schoolmasterly manner if he had been issuing a general edict.

I waited for Lara to say more, but she had fallen silent, staring at the glass in her hand. 'I don't really want this.'

I took it from her gently. 'We'll talk tomorrow,' I said.

In the morning everyone seemed to have forgotten the tensions of the previous evening. Only Hewison himself had not appeared. At the back of the Villa Meredith was rallying his followers, while Charles directed the loading of the Land Rovers with all the weary sarcasm of a schoolteacher:

'Oh, *do* come on, Hannah. For God's sake, we'll be here all day.'

I found Lara in an empty room, a scullery or something, at the back of the building. She looked tired, as though she had spent the whole night awake.

'I know you won't believe me, but I didn't tell him anything,' she said.

I shrugged. 'It hardly matters. A small thing.'

Outside, the vehicles were starting up; inside, our small conflict had worked a change, tipped us over a borderline. She wanted me to believe her.

'You must, Anthony. I would not have given him that kind of weapon. I know him too well.'

'Then it can only have been Elwyn Davies. He was the only person we ever told as far as I remember, but that was years ago. He would have known all this time.'

She looked relieved. 'He must have. It's not unlike David to use something that someone did or said years ago. He never forgets.'

'And that explains last night's performance?'

'Maybe.' She smiled wearily. 'You've seen how he can be, how things affect him. That grave they discovered . . .' Her voice trailed away. She seemed to be casting around for coherent ideas and finding none to hand. 'He can be a difficult man to live with.'

We might have left it at that, at a neutral remark about a man who was assuredly not neutral, but neither of us made a move to go. We were standing close, close enough for me to sense her warmth and catch her faint scent, close enough to worry that the door might open and someone appear. And there was the insidious intrusion of self.

'Have I outstayed my welcome?'

She looked up quickly. 'Don't leave.' Her tone was too urgent and her words too personal, but it was too late to have it otherwise. 'He won't think about it, you'll see.'

'That's easy for you to say. You belong here. I'm only here on sufferance.'

'Believe me it's true. Please don't go now.' Then she reached out and took my hands.

Was this how she had held on to Uncle David at the end of his visits to Sabazia fifteen years ago when she was only a girl, and her mother was looking on anxiously? And had he felt then a similar confusion of emotions as I now felt, similar conflicts? This was the first time we had been alone together since my previous visit to the Villa, and all that time I had known that this would happen, that I would find myself standing on the borderline which convention had drawn between us and wanting only to step over.

I raised her hands and held them before my face as though to examine the fact of our contact. Her fingers were very slender, the nails almond-shaped; not at all the kind of hands one would expect on someone who helped out with the digging.

'I won't go.'

A car horn sounded outside and a car door slammed.

'Someone's coming.'

We were conspirators, united by a moment's intention to betray. I leant forward to consummate it, to kiss first her fingers and then her mouth.

Jane's voice called from somewhere beyond the door: 'Anthony, where the devil are you?'

I let Lara's hand go. There was something behind her smile, a complex of emotions which I couldn't read.

'Go,' she said. 'Go now before she comes.'

We had connived at secrecy.

That morning I got up the hillside to have a look at the interior of the tomb: a low cave with a thin layer of dust on the floor. The beam from my torch swept around the walls and over the remains. The bones looked more vegetable than animal, like a random scatter of twigs and sticks; but the skulls were unmistakable. They were nightmare things with dislocated jaws and vacant orbits, and crania pierced by ugly holes. After recognizing them it was easier to identify the rest: the ribs like crushed basket-work, the femurs drawn up to the chins, the pelvic girdles like shallow bowls of terracotta. There were even hands and feet visible in the dust, carpals and metacarpals, tarsals and metatarsals lying in exact, articulate juxtaposition.

I looked at them for a long time, and wondered.

Hewison appeared at the excavation after lunch. He was the same as ever: dominant, acerbic, incessantly energetic. He even organized the television camera below the new-found grave so that he could pronounce his opinion:

'This mass burial almost certainly dates to the time of Lucri's confrontation with Rome. Before the Romans came there is little if any sign of violence in Etruria, and to my knowledge no traces of this kind of atrocity have ever been found. Yet here we have a dozen or more people murdered. Cast archaeology aside for a moment and turn to Livy and you will see that such outrages were a feature of the war with Rome. Livy, Book seven, if you want a reference.'

Charles was shaking his head and tutting at such wild speculation. The shadows of the previous evening seemed to have fled and David Hewison was once again the focus of all activity at the dig, the totem figure around which all the others danced. He even came over to me and clapped a hand on my shoulder.

'What do you say to that?'

'You're probably right.'

'Probably, probably. You are as evasive as Charles.'

We walked away from the tomb, back along the now well-beaten path which followed the stream bank. I wondered whether he was attempting to apologize.

'Do you know I saw myself in a historical light when I first came here? During the war, I mean. You know that, that I was here then?' It was the first time that he had ever alluded to it.

'I've heard something, a family story.'

He repeated my words with amusement. 'A family story. I wonder what they made out of it? Anyway, the truth was that I felt that I could break out of the treadmill of the war, be out on my own, use my imagination as well as what little courage I could muster to work according to my own lights. Above all I could cease to be just another pawn in the hands of the bloody generals.'

'And instead?'

He laughed. 'Instead.'

We had reached the point where the stream had to be crossed by stepping stones. He balanced across and, turning, put out a hand to help me. The gesture was almost solicitous. 'We should build some kind of bridge here,' he said, but he had not forgotten my question. As we began to climb through the trees, he returned to the subject.

'Instead I found myself a victim just as much as anyone else, but with no one else to blame. Philosophically the choice is simple. Man is either a victim of circumstance, or a victim of himself. Either way he is a victim.'

A group of volunteers was coming down through the trees from the *tendopoli*, carrying picks and shovels to begin clearing the landslide from below the tomb. Hewison exchanged a few words with them, and I noticed what had struck me before, that people had an air of unease when he spoke with them, that he lacked the common touch; and for the first time I felt sorry for him. Just like his elder brother he was trapped inside a persona of his own making, a man behind a mask.

'In what way were you victim?' I asked.

He frowned and shook his head. 'I'm just saying that none of us can stand aside, none of us can escape. Think about it when you see those skeletons in that tomb.' His half-hooded eyes suddenly opened fully, searching my face for any reaction. 'Think about it when next you visit the mausoleum at Vetrano. Forget all pious intentions: what would you have done *then*, not now? And not you as an over-privileged European liberal of the post-war period, but you as a Roman soldier of the fourth century BC or a German soldier of the twentieth century AD. What would you have done then?'

We had been climbing through the trees and now we reached the edge of the wood, in view of the top of the plateau and the track which led from the excavation to the main road. Lara's red Renault was moving along the track, trailing a plume of dust. She must have caught sight of us on the hillside below because the car came to a halt.

My uncle stopped abruptly. 'I must apologize for last night,' he said. There was an unexpected humility about him, as though he had been working up to this. 'I behaved intolerably I believe, but . . .' If he had been looking for a justification he did not find one. He shook his massive head. There was sweat glistening on his forehead and he raised his hands to wipe it away. 'It is difficult to talk about these things. One forgets . . . You know how it is when you wake from a dream? You know? You don't remember exactly, just impressions and hints, just . . .' He made a vague gesture, looking for under-standing.

I nodded.

'Well, that's it, that is what it's like. Like waking from a dream. A nightmare.'

He turned and went on up the hill, a massive figure labouring over the rough path. Despite the fact that Lara had climbed out of the car and was waiting for him at the top, he seemed very solitary on the hillside.

*

It was difficult to see Lara on her own. The next day I deliberately did not go to the dig, but even then I could only snatch a conversation with her as she worked amongst the fruit trees behind the Villa.

It was a scene like many I remembered from the old days at Poggio Sanssieve: a dozen labourers up amongst the trees, bringing cases of fruit down to the edge of the orchard to be weighed on a massive beam balance. Palmiro stood beside his mother to record everything in a leather-bound register: apricots, peaches, nectarines, the weights against the names of the piece-workers.

'I heard that David apologized to you,' Lara said. 'A rare thing, an apology. A family privilege perhaps.' She was wearing dungarees and a khaki shirt which might have come from an army surplus store. In London she would have been high fashion but for the dark patches of sweat beneath her arms.

'I'd have thought that family would have been the last people to win an apology.'

She smiled vaguely. Her mind was on the harvest. She called instructions to one group of pickers to move to another row, then went over to check Palmiro's register. I sensed her enjoyment of the task.

She glanced up. 'Do you want to help?'

'Do I get piece-rate?'

She laughed. Together we walked up between the trees. They were pruned little bigger than bushes to make picking easier. She pointed out the varieties as we walked, explained the details of the soil and the differences of the slopes. Behind us we could see down onto the roofs of the Villa, a mosaic of abstract colours ranging from palest salmon pink to a dark autumnal red, a composition of slopes and planes like an abstract painting.

We worked together for about half an hour and there was little talk between us and no hint at all of how it had been the previous morning. There was simply the picking. It was hot and tiring, just like Meredith's tavern, just as mind-dulling.

'David hates this kind of thing,' she said at one point. 'Physical labour. There's nothing noble about it, he says. It just stunts the mind.'

'That's just what I enjoy about the digging. It's a blessing not to have to think.'

She looked at me quickly but said nothing. The picking went on. Peach scent hung in the air around us. Our hands were sticky with the juice and our comfort threatened by wasps, but I was happy in her company. It was only when she called a rest that there was an intrusion.

'Why didn't you tell me about your father?' I asked.

Her expression was instantly suspicious. 'Who did?'

'Francis, that evening.'

'What did he say?'

'That your father was killed, in revenge for the massacre.'

She seemed about to speak, then thought better of it. A dark line of anger had appeared down either side of her mouth. Without a word she picked up the case we had been filling and walked away down the hillside. At the balance she weighed the fruit, sliding the brass weights along the beam with a slick efficiency, like a teller counting bank notes.

TEKEL, I thought. Thou art weighed in the balance and found wanting. I went over to her, wishing I had never spoken. She spoke without looking round, spoke in her careful English so that neither Palmiro nor his mother would understand.

'Why are you so curious about the past?'

'I don't want to intrude, but I do want to understand. I want to understand you. And David.'

She turned to look at me. Her expression was unnerving. 'The problem with archaeology, the thing that has always worried me, is that whatever you try to understand you end up by destroying.'

'I don't want to destroy.'

'Neither do the archaeologists.'

She turned to Palmiro's mother. 'I'm coming back.'

I followed her along the edge of the orchard and away from the picking. Once we were out of earshot she lapsed back into Italian.

'So what do you want to know, Anthony? Yes, my father was murdered. He was a Fascist, a *repubblichino* in fact, which is worse because half the country was Fascist during the monarchy whereas only the' – she made a deprecating gesture

146

– 'the idiots and the criminals stood by Mussolini when he set up the Republic of Salò. So he was a *repubblichino*, while my mother helped the partisans, David's little group. You could say that my father remained loyal to his cause even when the whole thing was hopeless, while she turned away. That was what she felt anyhow.'

'She sounds very courageous to me.'

Lara laughed humourlessly. 'I lived with it all my childhood, her sense of betrayal. I don't think she ever forgave herself, which was why she was so hard and unmoving, why she would never accept anything from David, why she died in pain rather than have proper treatment for her illness; and why she would not accept my feelings for him.'

She led me across the stony ground to where a dry-stone wall marked the edge of the orchard, out of sight of the pickers. I felt like an onlooker at an accident, unable to identify the margin between compassion and vulgar curiosity. Through her I could see her mother, previously imagined dying of stomach cancer in a room in the *Castello*, then as a freedom fighter, now as a woman fighting a bitter battle between belief and loyalty, a bitter battle which no longer seems to be part of this century. Who now cares about loyalty or keeps any faith?

'And your father remained a Fascist to the end?'

'I believe so. He never lost his faith.'

'It sounds like blind faith to me.'

'You can call it what you like. He died for it. When the hostages were murdered the partisans grabbed the first revenge they could. My father happened to have come down from the north just at that moment –'

'So he was an innocent victim?'

'Not innocent. No one past the age of reason is innocent. But I suppose his only direct guilt was that of being a fool.' She looked at me with a bitter little smile. 'Although in Italy that can be a capital crime. They kidnapped him and tried him and shot him. And that was that.'

'But your mother was a part of the group –'

'Don't be so naïve. It was civil war, dear Anthony, it wasn't like England's crusade against the Nazis. It was civil war. Things like that happened. A man against his father, a daughter

147

against her mother, isn't that it? If you want to find out don't ask me, ask my brother Gianluca. He was there.' She had sat down on a part of the wall where some of the stones had fallen away. Looking up at me she spoke with a faintly mocking tone which I did not understand at the time. 'I'm sure Gianluca will be able to tell you everything.'

Like all Italians she could smile easily enough. Her smile was lovely: it took in her green eyes, her flushed cheeks, her curved and articulate mouth, her whole personality. There was nothing false about it, but I knew she could turn it off as though with a switch.

'Do you still love David?' I asked.

The smile became a laugh. 'Yes, of course. Do you wish that I didn't?'

'Don't be absurd.'

'I thought that maybe you were jealous.'

'I am.'

She sat on a flat slab amongst the small stone fall with her feet swinging and her heels kicking against the rocks, and her voice quite without emotion.

'When I first saw you, when you first came to the Villa, do you know what I thought? I thought, it's David. It was something about the way you were standing, looking around. Not a facial resemblance at all, more an attitude, a sense of ownership. I sat in the drawing room watching you and thinking, how like David.'

'You seemed so impersonal.'

'I was afraid.'

'Afraid?'

'That we'd end up talking like this.' She pushed herself to her feet. 'And now we have.' She reached up and kissed me very softly on the mouth, and then equally gently she pushed me away. 'After you did that yesterday I made up my mind to ask you to go away. But now I find that I can't.'

Then she turned and set off back to where the picking was underway.

The excavation of the burial chamber was conducted with the patience of a surgical operation. First the position of each and

148

every bone was plotted; then they were labelled and lifted onto beds of tissue paper and carried down to waiting boxes; and finally every milligram of dust in the chamber was sifted. And when the television man asked Jane for an opinion on the pathetic burial she looked knowing, just like a surgeon, and, just like a surgeon, reserved her prognosis.

'We must wait on the tests. And then all the radiometric dating and fluorine analysis in the world will give us only a very rough idea.'

'But why do you think they were killed?' asked the television man.

'Why? Good heavens, I've no idea. How on earth can you find out something like that?'

In the event it was Francis Arden-Tillyard who produced his results before any of the laboratories.

'The chamber was cut at the time of the most recent tombs at Lucri, at the beginning of the fourth century BC,' he declared. 'Which gives us a *terminus post quem* for the burial. An analysis of the chisel-marks of the chamber reveals a strong positive correlation with those of early fourth-century tombs.' To anyone who showed any interest he would display a mass of statistical data. 'It is a most rigorous argument,' he insisted, 'most rigorous. I am talking about ninety-five per cent confidence limits.'

'There are no limits at all to Francis's confidence,' Jane remarked dryly. Among the excavators 'chisel-marks' became a catch-phrase.

# XIV

## *Winter 1943/44*

THE railway lines gleamed like polished pewter in the
moonlight. From the break of the trees where he stood they
curved away and onto the bridge, sliding between the gaunt
framework of girders and converging into the shadows of
the far side. Above the track, above the steel superstructure,
the silhouette of the acropolis – that was how he always
thought of it now – blocked out a large area of the night
sky. Up there amongst the sepulchral mounds of the old city
Orlandi ought to be getting his men into position. They
would be crouching down behind the broken coaming
which had once been an Etruscan wall, with their weapons
nosing down at the narrow valley and the station of
Vetrano.

He turned to his two companions. '*Va bene?*'

Their faces were blackened with camouflage cream but he
could see their teeth gleaming white as they grinned back at
him.

'*Va bene.*'

He had chosen them himself, two of the steadiest of
Orlandi's band, an ex-infantry *sergente* and a man who had
been a pay clerk in the Regia Aeronautica. The *sergente* was a
stern, middle-aged man from Molise who frequently be-
moaned the failure of the monarchy. 'They have betrayed us,'
he would say. 'The House of Savoy is finished. Deserted by
their natural leaders what choice do the people have but to
take power in their own hands?' He did not seem a very
convincing or convinced Communist. The pay clerk on the
other hand merely shrugged and smiled at any talk of politics:

he was a musician, and on the subject of late baroque chamber music he would wax long and lyrical.

Hewison looked towards the acropolis. In the moonlight he could see the jagged rocks which dropped down from the plateau across the path of the railway, but from where he stood the cutting through the rocks was obscured by the bridge itself. He hoped, he prayed, that the curve of the bridge would give him some cover when he went to work out there on the steel plates, and that the rush of the river a hundred feet below the rails would hide any sound he might make; and that he would just be able to plant his charges and get out of the place. To his shame he realized that he didn't really care whether the damn thing would actually work when the next train came along. Survival in the next half-hour was his only concern.

The luminous hands of his watch had reached three o'clock.

'Weapons safe,' he whispered. The Sten gun was notoriously unsafe. In a training session near the Club he had seen an entire magazine sprayed into the air after someone had jumped from a truck with a Sten on 'fire'. It was not an experience he wished to repeat now. He checked the weapons just to make sure.

'*In bocc'al lupo*,' he whispered. 'Let's go.'

His companions slithered down the bank in his wake. Their boots crunched on the gravel chippings of the railway bed.

'Keep to the sleepers. Less noise.'

The three men advanced along the line, tripping from sleeper to sleeper like women wearing hobble skirts. For an awful moment Hewison had to fight down a fit of giggles; then they were walking out onto the bridge with the river gleaming through the gaps in the steel plates beneath their feet and the girders forming a crude trellis-work above their heads, and he couldn't see the joke any more.

Halfway across the bridge he stopped. As his companions moved off the track to take up their positions one of them tripped against the rail. The sound reverberated in the steel framework all around them like an echo in a cathedral.

'Quiet!' he whispered. He crouched down by the rail. Ahead of him the cutting in the rock was clearly visible, but through it there were only dense shadows. Nothing moved. The station building was just out of sight around a slight curve. On a winter's night like this no doubt the guards were inside, huddled round a fire.

With infinite care he unslung his Sten gun and laid it beside him on the steel. Then he opened his kitbag and set to work.

The fixing of the charges took twenty minutes of fumbling in the darkness, working by feel and disjointed memories of the sabotage course at the Club. He had done some practice in a darkened room at the Casolare, but that had been unreal, like reading through a play. This was the first performance, with no dress rehearsal.

First he moulded the plastic explosive beneath the rails in two places, two pounds or so each, the distance apart a few feet more than the wheel base of the engines which used the line. The socialist railway official had provided that information. He gauged the distance by counting sleepers, crouched beside the line and acutely aware of the opening at the far end of the bridge. The river rushed below him, the wind ruffled the trees on the hillside behind, and nothing stirred in the direction of the station.

Once the plastic was in place he began to link the charges up with cordtex fuse. That took time, agonizing time working with cold fingers against the cold steel, struggling with black insulating tape to stick the fuse against the underside of the rails. His companions grunted and shifted like tethered animals in the darkness behind him.

Finally he fitted a pressure detonator in the centre of the rail and joined the cordtex to it. His watch said three-twenty. There was still no movement at the far end of the bridge.

'We've done it,' he whispered. 'Let's get out of it.'

They made their way back along the steel plates, each careful tread a triumph of self-control, the embankment at the end of the bridge like a shoreline. When their feet touched the chippings once again it was like feeling the sea bed rising up under them. They scrambled up off the track and into the trees.

'I need a crap,' the pay clerk whispered.

The enterprise lurched into farce.

'Then have a bloody crap, but for God's sake be quick about it. We don't want to hang around here.'

Exhausted, Hewison and the *sergente* slumped down at the edge of the trees. The other man blundered amongst the bushes further up the hillside. They laughed with the breaking of tension. 'We're okay,' the *sergente* said. 'We've done it. Another five minutes and *il Volpe* will withdraw. Perfect timing.'

Hewison nodded. His head was throbbing but he felt a stir of achievement. Of course a train still had to pass over the pressure detonator and of course the whole thing had to work, but at least he had done it. Even if the charges failed to go off no one could take that away from him.

It was then that the first shot sounded.

'*Porca Madonna*, what's that?'

They scrambled to their feet, grabbing their guns. The pay clerk emerged from behind a bush with his trousers round his ankles.

'Wipe your arse and come over here!'

The man stumbled to join them. Like rats from a hole they peered out from the trees.

For what seemed ages nothing more happened. Then there was a sudden burst of automatic fire; some shouting; more firing. A stream of tracer bullets spangled the night sky above the acropolis like fireworks.

'That's finished it,' the *sergente* muttered. 'We might as well have stayed at home.'

Hewison made his decision then, if decision, with its implications of thought and consideration and judgement, is not too misleading a word. He began scrabbling in his kitbag.

'Give me a light here,' he demanded.

'What are you doing?'

'Just give me a bloody light.'

From a packet he selected a time pencil, colour-coded for two minutes. Had he paused to reflect he would have abandoned the whole idea, not through fear, although any pause would have allowed fear to intrude, but through plain common sense. There was no point in what he was doing.

'You two stay here and cover me. You do not fire unless you see me in danger, and then make sure you fire bloody high! Understand, sergeant?' He hoped that the use of the man's former rank would bring with it memories of military obedience and discipline. 'I'll only take a few minutes.'

He slithered back down the embankment. As his feet hit the chippings there was more firing from the direction of the station. He ignored the sleepers and began to run as fast as he had ever run in his life. His boots pounded on the stones, then rang on the steel plates of the bridge. Silence was of no matter now. At one point he caught his foot on something and sprawled headlong, but immediately he was up again and running. Another spray of tracer bullets erupted into the air above the acropolis. The racket rang around the hills, drowning the sound of the river, drowning the noise of the wind, drowning the pounding of his feet, drowning even his terror.

He skidded to a halt beside the pressure detonator. This time he turned his torch on. By its light it only took seconds to rip the detonator from the cordtex and put the time pencil in its place. 'Never forget to activate it,' he heard the voice of some long-forgotten instructor say. He gave the pencil a sharp twist, then put it gently down beside the track. 'And never run,' the voice said. 'There's always enough time. You don't want to sprain your fucking ankle two yards away from the fucking thing, do you?'

He began to run, the metal ringing under his boots. Behind him there was another burst of fire. He reached the bank, scrambled up to the trees, grabbed his kitbag, and shouted to the other two.

'Let's get out of here!'

They followed him up the hillside. The firing ceased as they struggled through the trees. It seemed an age before they heard the ringing explosion which told them that the line was cut, but it was hardly a victory: it would not take a repair crew more than a couple of hours to repair the damage.

'What the hell happened?' the pay clerk kept asking. 'What the hell happened?'

'We cocked it up,' Hewison answered him. 'And we haven't heard the last of it either.'

154

# XV

On a hillside overlooking Viterbo – Viterbo with the Roman walls, Viterbo of the mediaeval quarter which looks like a stage set for *Romeo and Juliet*, Viterbo where four thirteenth-century popes were elected and Henry of Cornwall was murdered by Simon de Montfort's sons – on a hillside overlooking all this, Gianluca Alessio's house proclaimed the twentieth century as stridently as a neon sign. It was an uneasy blend of concrete bunker and plate-glass aquarium, set amongst sloping lawns and framed by the drapery of weeping willows. There was nothing so vulgar as a flower in sight.

'I look for purity of line,' its owner said, 'the purity of Brancusi or Mondrian. I cannot abide the past, with all its *clutter*.'

He was, of course, the second witness at The Wedding. He had a complexion as perfectly grained as cream laid paper, and clothes as plain as the lines of his house: plain, handmade black shoes, plain grey trousers, plain mauve sweater, plain white silk shirt.

'Everything must be simple,' he insisted, although it was plain, surely, that nothing was.

He stood to receive me with a faint and ironical smile which I recognized well in Lara. He gave the impression that to get this far into the sanctuary, past the anonymous, oracular voice which had spoken from a metal grille beside the main gate, past the exquisite youth who had stood attendance at the front door, through the interior spaces gleaming with pink and grey granite, past gravel beds in which angular members of the cactus family posed like exponents of modern ballet, was all to be accounted a triumph.

'Welcome to the penetralia,' he said. He rested his right

hand on the flank of a piece of abstract bronze, and dismissed my escort with a soft 'Grazie, Claudio' which was at once gracious and imperative. His eyes followed the youth's departing figure for a trifle longer than one might have expected.

'A late Boccioni,' he said. He was not referring to the youth. He gave the bronze a faint slap as though it were a departing buttock. 'A priceless piece. I love that word, don't you Mr . . . Lessing, is it? It is one of those delightful linguistic moments when everything is subtly *right*, because of course there *is* no price that I could attach to it.' His fingers ran across the metal surface, smoothing into a dimple, drifting delicately across a ridge. 'Nothing would induce me to surrender it. It occupies this particular space as though the space itself were created solely for its occupation, don't you agree?'

'It's very fine. And important, I would think.'

'You know Boccioni?'

'I've seen some of his work. My grandfather collected modern Italian art. I think there were some pieces by Boccioni.'

'Of course, you are a relative of David's.'

'His nephew.' I examined the bronze more dutifully than enthusiastically. There was about the piece a suggestion of recumbent torso, a hint of a head, curves and folds that were something like drapery. Like so much Italian art from that period it seemed a sham.

'It was possibly the last major piece he ever created,' Gianluca explained. 'Uncertainly dated to nineteen fourteen. He was, of course, killed when he was only thirty-four.'

'In the war?'

'During the war, but not in action. The advantage of being killed during a war is that people always imagine you died a hero. Didn't Rupert Brooke gain reputation in the same way? There is something implausible about ordinary death in the midst of so much deliberate slaughter, isn't there?'

'What is it called?'

The man looked very tired, tired rather than world-weary, which might so easily have been a pose. This was the person whom Elwyn Davies had described as a most courageous boy.

'It is entitled "Youth",' he replied.

He led me away from the sculpture to a space – rooms did not have any existence in this house – where there were low sofas and lower glass tables and a scattering of expensive art books.

'Now how can I help you? Please sit down and tell me what I can do. On the telephone my dear sister was . . . shall we say, evasive?'

I shrugged awkwardly, not knowing how to answer. 'I'm interested in a piece of history. I think you know something about it.'

Gianluca folded himself into one of the sofas, adjusting his trousers over his knees, settling himself as carefully as someone arranging flowers in a vase.

'History, Mr Lessing? Or may I call you by your first name? My sister told me it was Anthony. So, Anthony, you wish to know about history; but I am afraid I am not a historian. Surely you want one of David's legion of experts for that. I am a simple publisher of not-so-simple books. If you wish to know about Italian poetry of the late twentieth century, then I can help; if you are interested in our list of works of literary and art criticism, then I can help; if you wish to buy some truly exquisite art books,' he waved a hand at the volumes strewn across the tables, 'then I can help. But I know nothing of history.'

He smiled patiently. A cat had come to sit on his lap, a fluffy, indolent beast who settled there as though by right. Gianluca's fingers disappeared amongst its fur.

'Lara didn't explain? I mean recent history. History of which you have personal memory.'

His eyebrows arched upwards. The quizzical expression was, in an incongruous way, almost a caricature of Lara's gentle irony. I was certain that he knew full well why I was there. 'But you can hardly expect me to consider that history.'

I smiled. 'I work in the family business. In commerce anything older than five years becomes history. Until then it is merely out of date.'

The reply was calculated to please him, and it worked. He nodded in satisfaction. 'You do not sound too sympathetic.'

'Sympathy has nothing to do with it. We don't make medicines and all the rest out of a sense of vocation or anything. David's elder brother has it perfectly: "Our business is not to make pharmaceuticals; it is to make a profit."'

'But that is precisely what I admire about commerce, Anthony. It is so beautifully honest. No bogus preoccupation with doing good.' Gianluca smiled, showing cool white teeth against the perfect texture of his skin.

The exquisite Claudio appeared. We waited and watched while he served us coffee with something of the silent ritual of a Japanese tea ceremony. When he had withdrawn Gianluca looked up. His expression was that of a man who faces the doctor and knows already what he is going to be told, a brave smile, but a knowing one; and no optimism.

'Now the history,' he said, 'of which I have personal memory. But remember Anthony, *nessun maggior dolor*, there is no greater pain than to recall one's youth in old age.'

I smiled reassuringly. I was acutely aware of the man's fragility. In some way he seemed to be a counterpoise to my uncle, a man of equal but quite opposite eccentricity, a man whose mind teetered, like David Hewison's, on a hard fulcrum of pain. 'Believe me, I don't want to cause any undue stress.'

'What, Anthony, does "due stress" involve?'

'Well, I would like to know something about the war.'

'Go on.'

'I understand that Lara's father, your father, was killed during the war, somewhere near here. He was, so I believe, a prominent member of the Fascist party –'

Gianluca waved his hand dismissively. 'The history books will tell you that. What you are trying to say is that he was murdered, by partisans.'

'And that you and your mother helped in the partisan movement.'

His look was bleak, the quiet despair of the condemned man. 'Why evade the issue? Say that both I and my mother worked with those very murderers.'

'Please believe that I don't want to upset you or hurt you. I just want to understand.'

Gianluca moved his head slowly. For a moment I thought he was in pain, but then I understood that he was nodding.

'Yes, I can sympathize with that,' he said quietly. 'I too have always wanted to understand, and yet I find that such a desire is never susceptible to logical explanation.' He smiled his thin smile. 'Why do I wish to understand a particular quirk in human behaviour? I have no idea. My understanding will not change it. Why do I wish to understand how a piece of religious doctrine can have risen from the formlessness of man's primitive beliefs, for example? My knowledge will neither change the doctrine, nor help me to believe it. It will change nothing. And yet I wish to understand such things. Illogical, no?

'Perhaps knowledge itself has intrinsic value?' He shook his head sadly in reply to his own question. 'Knowledge is what knowledge does. If it enables you to make a medicine which will cure a disease, well and good. If it enables you to kill people efficiently, well and good. If it enables you to understand something for its own sake . . . boh!' He held out his hands in the familiar, Roman gesture of hopelessness. 'The idea that knowledge has intrinsic worth is a familiar romantic conceit, isn't it? Beauty is truth, truth beauty; rubbish like that. I am afraid it has no currency in the harsh world of the twentieth century.'

He was silent. From another part of the house the clacking of typewriter keys could be heard, perhaps the beautiful Claudio earning his keep. The sound was not intrusive; somehow it served to heighten the silence around Gianluca.

'We are different kinds of man, Anthony,' he said quietly. 'Perhaps you don't understand that a man like me becomes so familiar with pain that he becomes inured to it. I have known such pain since I was a boy. It is always there, but long ago I learned to live with it. So do not worry about my pain.'

He began to stroke the cat gently, rhythmically, as though it were a palliative. 'You talk of my mother and my father. Doubtless you would also like to hear about my brother-in-law? He was involved in the band called "Fabiomassimo".' He looked up. 'I thought so. So there you have the principal actors in the little drama. Naturally we have to add a few small parts – a rough and ready selection of partisans, embryo politicians, the village doctor, the odd *contadino*, even, I suppose, some German soldiers – but none of them will distract attention from the principals.'

He picked the cat up from his lap and placed it on the floor. The animal stood motionless, unable to comprehend this assault on its comfort. Gianluca crossed his legs and settled cushions at his back. 'Yes, David Hewison was part of "Fabiomassimo". One might almost say that he was the founder of the group, although many of the elements were there before his arrival. It was David who was the catalyst.' His expression was one of faint self-mockery. 'He was god-like, you see. Heroic in the classical sense. A Perseus. A man who swept down from the skies at the very moment of our greatest need, when everything around us was chaos and the ordinary decencies of society had been thrown aside, when we had almost descended into anarchy.

'Into the midst of this chaos came David. It was he who gave us hope that honour had not entirely deserted us, that Italians could at least attempt to hold their heads up again. Because, you see, he was Italian. We knew that as soon as he spoke. He was no foreigner condescending to us, but one of us, speaking our language better than most of us, knowing our country as few of us comprehended it. A hero and an Italian! Imagine that against a background of a weak and vacillating king, of irresolute and cowardly generals, of rampaging huns.'

Gianluca chuckled softly. 'Do you know I used to watch him talking with the gods? You see he kept one of his radios in the attic of our family home in Sabazia – has Lara shown it to you? I thought she might have – and I would sit and listen as he communed with the gods of war a thousand miles away in Algiers. And then his prayers would be answered, which almost never seems to happen with gods, and there would follow a magical shower of gifts from the heavens: guns, bullets, explosives, but, even more magical than that, boots and clothing and food. A veritable shower of gold. Can you imagine his effect on us, Anthony, can you imagine?'

Irony was only brushed lightly over the surface of his narrative. It was possible to see the reality beneath.

'My father was away at the time. I don't know what your knowledge of those confused times is, Anthony. Doubtless you have done some reading, and maybe heard something from your Italian relatives. Anyway, after Mussolini was snatched from his captivity in the Abruzzi mountains he was taken to Hitler, and the Nazis later set him up in the north as head of a new Italian Fascist state, the *Repubblica Sociale Italiana*, the Republic of Salò. It was there that my father had gone at the end of September 1943, with words like *virtù* and *onore* on his lips.'

An expression of distaste had passed across Gianluca's face, but whether it was directed towards the Republic of Salò, or his father, or the concepts of virtue and honour, was not certain. 'So my mother – and I – were in a curiously secure position from which to offer help to Allied prisoners of war who were on the run, and later to the partisans. We were the family of a renowned Fascist and therefore free from the attentions of the *squadristi* or even the German SD. And we had special privileges: a telephone which worked, a petrol ration, that kind of thing; and of course certain connections which brought in valuable information.'

'But your father knew nothing of this, of your mother's involvement with the anti-Fascists?'

'Do you mean, was he a secret sympathizer? Oh no.' Gianluca shook his head sadly. 'No, no, no. He was a man who remained deluded until the end, locked up in a kind of fantasy which bore more relation to the *Chanson de Roland* than to any understanding of what Fascism was all about. I suppose such iron-bound delusion made it easier for my mother to deceive him.'

'And what happened in the end to the group?'

He pursed his lips and considered the past. 'Of course "Fabiomassimo" ended with the liberation.' The word was delivered with heavy irony. 'That must have been a few days after the Allied entry into Rome in June 1944. As far as I remember it was the French colonial troops, the Goums, who moved through the area: they were worse than the SS by all accounts. "Fabiomassimo" rose openly to aid them against the retreating Germans. But I only heard about all that second hand, because we had already gone to Rome. Anyway, by that stage my mother was not really in a position to take an active part in any partisan group.'

I must have looked blank.

'She was with child, my dear boy. My sister.' Gianluca smiled humourlessly and patted his stomach.

'Of course. I forgot. One tends to forget that the ordinary things of life go on in war.'

He raised his eyebrows. 'Does one?' He laughed at my discomfiture. 'In fact we had been in the city for some time when the Allies arrived, living in our apartment there. I still own it as a matter of fact.'

'So your sister was born in Rome?'

He inclined his head. 'That autumn. She is *una vera romana.*'

We were silent for a minute, as though we both acknowledged that we had skirted around the central incident, which was not a question of birth but of death. Finally it was I who moved the conversation back in time.

'All this was after the Vetrano massacre, wasn't it?'

Gianluca nodded heavily. 'It was all long after the Vetrano massacre. That came at the beginning of the year after an attack on the railway bridge. Do you know the one, beneath David's acropolis? Of course you do. In the manner of many such things it was horribly bungled – it is only in American war films that episodes like that end up with glory and destruction. All that happened here was the death of two German soldiers and an Italian railway worker.'

'I understand that the Americans finally destroyed the bridge.'

'I expect they did: they destroyed most things. By then the Germans had already taken hostages and the bridge itself had ceased to matter. They took five for each victim of the raid. Do you not find it an exquisite irony that the Italian railway man was ranked as equal to the German soldiers? At least in death.'

'And what about your father?'

'Oh, he was never equal.' He laughed softly at the idea. It was unclear from his tone whether he valued him above or below. 'I suppose in many ways my father was a dangerous innocent. His final act was his undoing, because he arrived from the north at the very moment when the hostages had been taken and the partisans were casting around for something to do. It was the idea of the communist leader Agostino Orlandi, I believe.'

'His family works at the Villa Rasenna.'

Gianluca chuckled. 'Naturally. David always had a soft spot for Agostino and his family. He was not a bad man, a simple, courageous man in fact, but not a man of great intelligence. After the war he became a local politician, an *assessore comunale* of some kind for a while; but he was never a success. Then,' he put his head back reflectively and tapped his lips with a long forefinger, 'then there was another man whom I only saw once or twice, called Tobaldi, Tobardi, something of that kind. He was an outsider, a party man from the north. We always suspected that he had more real power than Orlandi.' He seemed to contemplate these spectral figures from the past with genuine amusement.

'And the Communists carried out the kidnapping of your father?'

'Certainly. They took him just after he reached home.'

'And David played no part in the affair?'

'In the kidnap? No. I believe that he opposed the whole idea, and he was not, is not, a man who would go against his own ideas. As, no doubt, you understand.'

A suspicion was growing in my mind. 'You said your father went north in the previous year, in September. Was this the first time he had come back home?'

Gianluca's expression was alight with amusement now. 'It was indeed. We had expected him at Christmas, but then he was called away to Germany. To judge by a letter we received from him he was very proud of that. So we passed Christmas on our own – with David anyway – and when my father finally came back it was the first time for four months.'

'And the partisans kidnapped him soon after he arrived. How soon? Days? Hours?'

He was watching me carefully, sensing how close I was to the nub of the matter. 'He arrived in the afternoon, a bitterly cold day, I remember. There had been some snow.

Early the same evening they . . . invaded the house and took him.'

'The same evening?'

'The same evening.'

Something sounded in my mind, the faint echo of a thought which I did not dare pursue. 'So they must have been prepared, must have had word that he would be there.'

The man's expression faded slightly, as though something had disappointed him. 'Oh yes,' he said. 'David told them.'

'David?'

The faint, ironical smile, so reminiscent of Lara's. 'Does that seem like betrayal?'

'It seems, at least, compromising.'

The man shook his head in the manner of a tutor correcting a pupil. 'That is a fault which all historians make, to assume an insight into the motives from a knowledge of the bare facts. A man is capable of committing the basest of imaginable acts for the most exalted of reasons. I do not for one moment believe that David Hewison intended harm to my father. Of course he felt guilt. It is in the nature of man to feel guilt about things he cannot help. Isn't that where the Church wins all the time? It was perhaps to expiate that guilt that David himself told me what had happened.'

It was impossible to read any bitterness in his expression. The façade was almost perfect, tempered over the years until it was as hard as steel. 'Naturally I had seen little of my father in those war years. I felt distant from him . . . emotionally as well as physically. I think what damage there was had already been done, during his life rather than at the end of it; but of course I wept when David told me everything.' The bleak smile, the hard shell, shining brightly with use. 'And understood as well. It is only through suffering that you understand, Anthony, because through suffering you lose all defences. Perhaps that means nothing to you? It was through suffering that day that I understood, it was weeping in David's arms that I confronted myself. Then it only remained for me to do the next and necessary thing: endure.'

'And in retrospect no blame attaches to David?'

'To David? How could it?' He spread his hands open. There

was something infinitely tender about the gesture, as though he were displaying his wounds to my gaze. 'You see, he was my first lover.'

The typewriter clacked away in the distance. Now I could hear another sound as well, an exterior sound like a faint wash of rain: the sprays playing over the rich, velvet lawns of Gianluca Alessio's garden. I found these two sounds very easy things to focus my attention on, easier than the figure of the man in elegant grey trousers and pale mauve sweater who sat directly opposite me, easier far than the tortured complexities of a past which was not my own.

'And then there was just the waiting for the inevitable,' Gianluca continued evenly. 'They kept him up in the hills at their hideout – the Casolare. You can find it on any good map – and made demands of the German authorities that everyone knew were impossible. In the event the Germans killed the hostages at Vetrano and moved against the Casolare the next day; but of course they did not really expect to rescue my father. To them he was just one more Italian. Exactly how he was killed we never found out. Even if he knew, David never said. "Executed in the name of the Italian People" was the formula.'

He shook his head at my expression. 'Worse things happened, Anthony, much, much worse. Expressions of sympathy are out of place. Now let me finish the story as we have got this far, and then you may go; and make out of it what you will.'

He breathed in deeply and gazed at a point some way above my head, as though to find images of the past pictured there. If there had been a momentary betrayal of emotion, his face was once more smooth and composed.

'We left Sabazia the day after hearing of my father's murder. It was not David who brought the news this time. I forget who now. We fled to Rome by car and took refuge in our apartment near Piazza Navona, as I have told you. There we existed until the Americans arrived. About "Fabiomassimo" we heard little and none of it first hand. I understand that it was dispersed for a while, but soon enough it reformed and was able to play some part in the war at the very end. I suppose it gave some people back their honour, if honour still meant anything by then. But for us in Rome concerns were more basic: to find enough food. Food was very short in the city in those days and with my mother pregnant a good diet was essential. In retrospect the search for food seems to have occupied my every waking moment.'

'But you did return to Sabazia.'

'Do you find that strange? Of course we went back. It was the house of my mother's family, her home from when she was a girl.'

'Not your father's?'

'No, no. He was from the north, the Veneto. Not from this part of the world at all. Yes, we went back the next spring when my sister was a few months old.' Gianluca's smile was back in place once more, tinged with mockery. 'I see that mention of her interests you. Are you rather fond of her perhaps?'

I shifted slightly under his impassive gaze. 'I can't deny that she is fascinating.'

He nodded, still smiling. 'Fascinating. That is exactly what your uncle found, long ago now. *Incantevole*.'

'When did he come back?'

Gianluca's gaze moved away until he was staring reflectively out of one of the plate-glass windows onto the sweeping lawns. 'When did David come back? Oh, not for some time, not for some time. We had almost forgotten him.' He nodded, as though agreeing with that judgement. 'In nineteen forty-seven, it would have been. At first an occasional visitor, but then gradually more frequent, until finally in those difficult years he became something of a provider for our little family: the sometime god become godfather, if you like; revealed in all his splendour as a man of wealth.' He smiled his thin smile once more. 'Revealed as a man whose will has never been thwarted.'

# XVI

## *Winter 1943/44*

WHEN the group reformed hours later at the Casolare Hewison attempted to discover what had happened. It was difficult to break through the euphoria.

'A victory for the forces of liberation!' Orlandi announced repeatedly.

'A hammer-blow by the proletarian revolution!' countered Tobasi.

It was unclear exactly in what the victory consisted, or where the hammer-blow had fallen: all they could say was that there had been a lot of shooting. Hewison made a vain attempt to count the number of rounds expended – the kind of thing one was meant to do after an action – but it proved an impossible undertaking. The issue of magazines had been haphazard, their use profligate, their return to the 'armoury' random. The men just stood around grinning vaguely and shrugging off his questions. After all, they were veterans now.

What he could establish for certain was that, apart from a couple of splinter wounds, none of the group had been hurt. Crouched down behind the stretch of Etruscan wall and looking down onto the station, they had at least been in a secure position. On the other hand their estimates of enemy casualties varied wildly, the only certain victim being the unfortunate man – German? No one could even be sure about that – who had started the whole skirmish by wandering down the track towards the bridge.

'He had heard you at work,' Orlandi asserted.

'But the shooting started minutes after we had finished. We were back in the woods by then. Gino had even gone for a crap.'

Again the shrug, the ultimate obstruction to any enquiry, the fortress wall against which neither battering-ram nor mining would prevail.

'Boh,' answered Orlandi, expressing the completeness of Roman indifference in that single, impenetrable plosive.

That morning, vague and clumsy from exhaustion, Hewison went down from the hills to Sabazia, to try to obtain some news. He had half-expected to find soldiers there, *squadristi* if not Germans, but the village was as desolate as ever on its pinnacle of rock. As usual he entered the *Castello* through the postern gate. To the unknowing eye it was just a rough cave cut into the rock on which the village was built, the kind which the *contadini* used for storing their tools. There were some ancient farm implements, a few bales of straw, a pile of logs and vine prunings; and no sign of the door at the back which led up through the rock and into the cellars of the house.

He found Doctor Pellegrino in the drawing room with Clara.

'There are Germans in Vetrano. Everywhere.' The man's face was grey with anxiety. 'I barely got through the road blocks. It is all finished.'

Hewison was angry. 'It is not all finished. It has barely begun. What do you expect them to do, call a public *festa*? What can you tell me about their casualties?'

'There are many stories, but the official one is that three were killed. One of them was an Italian, a railway man.'

'They have taken hostages,' said Clara. Her voice was quite calm and flat, as though she was mentioning yet another item of food which could no longer be found in the shops. 'Fifteen of them, at random. Five for each man killed at the station. So you see that at least in death an Italian ranks equal to a German. Apparently they are holding them in the orphanage.'

The doctor added, 'They have been making announcements everywhere in the name of the German military command. They will restore the hostages to their families –'

Hewison finished his sentence, '– in exchange for the murderers.'

Pellegrino nodded miserably. 'They call them terrorists, terrorists and traitors.'

It was not difficult to picture it, possible even to feel some of the impotent terror of the hostages – old men and boys because there were no young men left, all powerless to do anything but cringe. It was all part of the logic of this kind of war, what he had been taught to expect. 'In Greece,' they had told him at the Club, 'the Communist partisans have deliberately incited atrocities against the civilian population, on the grounds that it reinforces the people's hatred and resolve. Of course that is not our style.' Not our style.

'We will just have to sit it out,' he said.

'And the hostages?' The doctor's tone was accusing.

Hewison gave no answer.

The doctor left shortly afterwards. He had a patient to attend to in the village, and then the road blocks to face. He went out like an old man, tired and drawn.

'I hope he doesn't go to pieces.'

'He's a good man,' Clara replied, but that was not really the point at issue.

'There has been no sign of the Germans here?'

'Not yet. Perhaps they won't come. Vetrano is the obvious place and nobody ever bothers with Sabazia. I don't think they are looking for anything so what's the point?' She was beautifully composed, like a ballerina executing some complex and difficult passage. Her hair drawn tightly back from her face emphasized her calm austerity. Her hands lay in her lap, lightly clasped, at peace.

'You won't have heard the other news, I don't suppose. The Allies have landed, south of the city at Nettuno.'

He felt curiously indifferent, as though rather than a mere sixty-five miles away it was on another continent. 'Maybe there's hope then.'

'Maybe.' She did not seem convinced. 'What will you do now?'

'Go back to the Casolare. Wait.'

She nodded, as though that were a wise and clever decision. 'My husband gets here tomorrow, or the day after. One can't be sure these days. He said for a few days only. I don't know whether the landings will make any difference.' She made a small gesture which may have been one of uncertainty, may have been of despair.

Hewison felt anger again. 'He is a fool not to get out. It's crazy now, pointless. Anyone can see that. Even a fool like Mussolini, except that he has no choice.'

She sighed wearily. 'I've told you, David, I've told you. He believes in it all.'

'In what? Taking hostages? Shooting innocent people?'

'Was the railway man guilty?' she asked. Her eyes were hard and dry, as though she had already wept all the tears there were to weep.

'They have taken fifteen hostages against our surrender.'

The news stunned them to a momentary silence. Then some of them, those who came from Vetrano, began to shout: 'Names? Do you know who? Who have they taken?'

But he could tell them nothing more. Anyway they would find out soon enough when somebody came across the hills from the town bringing the full story. Doubtless there would be a poster with a list of names which they could crowd round and discover uncle and great-uncle, nephew and cousin, in one case a son, in another a father. But for the moment there was a blessed anonymity about it all.

'This will reinforce the people's resolve,' Tobasi exclaimed. 'Their revolutionary spirit will be tempered in the furnace of suffering.'

'Why don't you fuck off?' someone suggested. 'You don't have people there.'

The men began to bicker. Orlandi sat in his usual place beside the fire and contemplated the imminent disintegration of his group with a calm expression. When he finally spoke his voice brought the argument stumbling into silence.

'This is precisely what the Germans wish to happen. We meet with the first misfortune, and you are ready to cave in like children.' He added, with an emphasis which did not miss its target, 'It is precisely what the Germans *expect* to happen. They expect the forces of Italian liberation to be no more resolute than the forces of Italian Fascism were. They expect us to collapse as we collapsed after September the eighth, as we collapsed in Greece and Albania and Libya. They despise us. Is that what we want?'

'Well, what the bugger do we do?' someone asked.

It was not Orlandi, but Tobasi who answered. 'We respond in kind,' he said. 'They take hostages; we take hostages.'

'Kesselring perhaps?' a sarcastic voice suggested. Tobasi ignored it.

'Alessio,' he said. 'Vincenzo Alessio.'

For the first time in his life Hewison found himself at a loss. He had been reared in a world of certainties, certainties of opinion and faith, of wealth and education, of both present and future existence. In all matters he had known the right way to behave and the right opinion to express, and unlike the fanatic or the bigot he had been able to support such certainties with eloquent and elegant reasoning. Naturally doubts existed, but they were doubts voiced in a manner whose careful subjunctives somehow converted them into certainties. 'One might suppose that . . .' dominated 'I don't know . . .' His creed was that everything, every mystery, every irrationality, even every religious doubt, will ultimately surrender before the force of pure reason.

The truth was, he had never really been confronted with a moral dilemma.

Now, in the face of Tobasi's proposal he felt nothing but an amorphous mess of conflicting motives, of emotions so mixed that he could barely identify them. In the seething of his mind half a dozen different arguments floated to the surface like scum, but he had lost the knack of expressing them. Anything he said was either ignored, or dismissed by Tobasi with biting, off-hand sarcasm.

'You are suddenly an English gentleman again, are you? But then you don't have relatives in the town either.' And, 'If she's a true anti-Fascist she will accept it.'

'That might well be, but –' But he did not know. He did not know what her feelings were for him, for her husband, for anything; nor his for her. Or even whether feelings even mattered against the bizarre logic of this war. Just once some kind of emotion had taken hold of them, one evening when they had been alone together in the *Castello*. Like children they had fumbled with each other's bodies, and she had lain passively beneath him while he spent himself inside her; but the moment seemed divorced from reality, a curiosity which had nothing to do with their real feelings for each other. 'That was foolish,' she had said afterwards, almost as though it had been an accident. 'We had no right to do it.'

Thus his emotions lacked any sense of logic. In his dilemma he clung to abrogation of all responsibility as though it were a kind of religious faith: this was Tobasi's war, Orlandi's war, their civil war; it was for them to decide. Personal feelings had no part to play. And thus, suppressed by his mind, his inner conflicts manifested themselves in his body: he felt sick. While he was listening to their planning his head was reeling and his stomach churning, but whether from revulsion or excitement he could not say. Nausea is a crude sensation.

'When does he get here?'

'Come on. You are the one who always talks to her. When does he come?'

'I don't know. She said . . . I don't know.'

'This is a popular decision. It might save innocent lives for the price of putting one guilty one at risk, and you say you don't know.'

'Christ alive, I don't know! She doesn't know.'

'But we have moved the radio out, so it must be soon.'

'She said . . .'

'*What* did she say? What?'

'She said tomorrow, or the day after.'

There was an awful hiatus. In that time he went about the ordinary, petty things of his strange life: conducting a weapons check, running weapons classes, even leading an expedition to plant mines on the Vetrano road. He also composed and transmitted a report on the attack on the station, a transmission which lasted longer than the prescribed five minutes. In it he mentioned the hostages and asked whether a leaflet drop could be made over Vetrano to claim responsibility for the attack on behalf of a British commando.

The answer came two days later, by which time it was too late anyway, but no, it was not possible. All aircraft were involved in supporting the bridgehead at Anzio where Kesselring had succeeded in mounting a counter-attack. As he unravelled the cypher groups the word 'sorry' emerged in clear. Davies was sorry. But by that time they had already had Alessio shut away in a back room of the Casolare and the whole thing had gathered a momentum of its own.

# XVII

I FIND it difficult to recall what my feelings were when I returned from seeing Gianluca. I retreated to my room in the Villa. For a time I struggled fruitlessly with thoughts which I could barely comprehend, a dreadful, amorphous mess of emotion in which there were elements of anger and pity and hate and fear, and something which I hesitated to try to put a name to at the time but which was, I suppose, love; but how I might act I had no idea. Moral outrage and self-interest and plain self-righteousness chased each other through my mind, but they left me impotent.

Only after I had been there a long while did I notice the book. It was a plain-bound volume without a dust cover and it was lying on the pillow of my bed. I looked at it dumbly, wondering what its significance could be. The title along the spine – *History as the Story of Liberty* – barely meant anything to me; the author, Benedetto Croce, was little more than a name. But when I reached out for it I found that there was a leather bookmark between its pages, and this sentence underlined in pencil:

'History is its own mystic Dionysos, its own suffering Christ, redeemer of sins.'

I puzzled over it a long while, trying to comprehend it as one might try to understand a newspaper headline in a foreign language. The phrase 'redeemer of sins' sounded loudly in my mind. Did history simply redeem sins by distance, by a kind of moral statute of limitations, or was it that an understanding of the historical context expunges any guilt from an act?

I was hardly in the mood for intellectual games. My state of mind was such that it took me a long time to understand that that was not why the book was there.

Outside, the hard enamel blue of summer had gone. The sky had clouded over and a hot southern wind, a *scirocco*, was gathering amongst the pines and rushing through the oaks and cypresses at the garden's edge. Along the path leading down through the trees the sound of the wind was as loud as a cascade of water.

I reached the clearing expecting to find her there: but there was only the margin of trees, the stream running through the grass, the spout of solidified lava with the cave at its base. Inside the cave the Dionysos still stood in the shadows. Nothing had changed. There was that same organic wholeness of rock and stone, the same hidden knowledge in the smile, the same bizarre wand clutched in his right hand.

I wondered whether I had mistaken her message, until I heard a footfall behind me.

I turned. She stood silhouetted in the brilliant light of the entrance, her face and expression quite invisible.

'I wondered if you would come,' she said. Her tone was faintly amused, as though even now she was preparing for an escape, a recourse to laughter if the circumstances should warrant it.

'You have spoken with Gianluca. How did you find him?'

She walked into the cave and went up to the statue. In one hand she had some ivy leaves threaded into a circlet. As she reached up to place them in position on the statue's head her skirt, pulled tight against her body, drew up to show the pale backs of her thighs. I found the movement painfully tender, with all the ingenuousness of a young girl; but there was nothing ingenuous about the god, now crowned with living ivy, looking ironically back at her.

'He seems a sad man.'

'Does he?' She turned. 'Anyway, was your curiosity satisfied?'

'I'm not sure that satisfied is quite the right word.'

She smiled a bitter little smile. 'No, maybe not.' She looked around the cave, then back at me. 'What about my message?'

'Croce?'

'Yes. What did you make of it?'

I shrugged, impatient with the game. 'Do we still talk about sin these days? Isn't it rather unfashionable?'

'There are many unfashionable things which are none the less true.'

'And how do you feel about David's sins, then? Are they redeemed?'

She walked past me and out into the daylight. I was happy to follow her, to escape the malign influence of the god. She stood looking out over the valley to the hills of the far side where grey *maremmano* cattle grazed amongst the oak scrub. In the distance they looked like lice on the back of a vast, dormant animal.

'So he told you about him and David?'

'That they were lovers? Yes, he told me.'

She turned.

'Is that all?' If she had ever been the young schoolgirl, she wasn't now. Her features looked suddenly old, much older than her years. 'He said nothing about my mother?'

I shook my head. I suppose I had already guessed.

'Well, it was all three of us, Anthony, all three. My mother, Gianluca, and I. She never said anything herself, but one day when I had had a row with her, oh, over the usual kind of thing, David told me: "You ought to know, Lara, that once I had another Toy. Once your mother was my Toy as well."'

I opened my mouth to speak but she put up her hand to stop me. 'Don't say anything, Anthony. Please don't reduce it all to a matter of moral outrage. Morality has nothing to do with it.'

'What does then?'

She shrugged. The gesture was not one of indifference but of pure incomprehension. I went up to her and touched her cheek, and she grasped my hand as a child clutches an adult's, suddenly and desperately.

'Can you understand what possession means, Anthony? Complete possession? Can you see that David possessed us totally, from that moment before my birth when he came to Gianluca and my mother from the sky? Since then I sometimes feel that we have never really existed except as possessions of his, spiritual and physical possessions. Toys. That was why she refused his help when she was ill, but she was deceiving

176

herself if she thought she could escape. The only way she had to escape was to die.'

'And what am I? An escape as well?'

'That's cruel.'

'But is it true?'

'Perhaps. I don't have any clever answers left.'

She seemed suddenly very tired. She moved nearer me and I put my arms round her to give her some kind of comfort. Through her shirt I could feel the flesh of her arms and back, the edges and curves of her bones. My face was buried in the hollow of her neck and I breathed in her scent, a rich amalgam of perfumes that was uniquely hers, that was a statement of her sexual identity which filled my head and drove out any shreds of rational thought which might have remained to me. I whispered something which was, I suppose, a declaration of my love. She made a sound like a small cry of pain and turned her face upwards. We kissed. I had dreamt that something like this would happen but the reality was more potent and somehow less credible than any dream. I could not believe the softness of her mouth or the quickness of her fingers at my clothes or the heaviness of her body as it pressed me down to the ground. I could not believe that she was naked and kneeling astride me, with her breasts swaying as she moved and her thighs clinging to mine. I could not believe the all-consuming vortex which she had become.

In memory it all seems mere seconds, and purely animal. But at the time we lay outside time, and the purely animal thing we did with each other elevated us far above the material into a world of spiritual wholeness where I had never been before. Or perhaps all that is just an illusion, a trick played upon us by our bodies, which are more powerful by far than our minds. I don't know. I don't know whether to elevate the memory or dismiss it as pure sensation, but I do know that when it was over she looked at me with a great sadness; and she must have seen the same look in my face for she put out her finger and touched my lips as though to stop me speaking.

'I know,' she said. 'I know,' as one might talk to a child in pain. And indeed I did feel an acute pain like that of a bereavement, because for precious moments not only had I known her more perfectly than I had ever known anyone else, but I had actually *been* her, a part of her as vital as any organ. Yet now we were lying side by side in the grass amongst the debris of our clothing, and that moment's annihilation of self was nothing more than an uncertain memory.

She smiled sadly. 'We'd better get dressed.'

We got up and began to gather up our clothes. I watched her as she stooped, and loved the sight of her body, the sway of her breasts, the curve of her hips, the dark mass of hair between her thighs. But now I watched her as I had Helen or any other woman; and however much I might wish it otherwise there was suddenly something desperately mundane about us: two adulterers tidying away the evidence.

'What if someone had seen us?'

She shrugged, waiting for me to finish.

'What now?' I asked.

'What do you expect?'

'We must talk.'

'Must we?' She laughed faintly, buttoning up her shirt and tucking it into her skirt. 'What good will that do? Will words explain anything? Will reducing us all to the abstracts of popular psychology make anything better?'

'No, but –'

'But what? Can't we just be happy with what we had here? Isn't that enough?'

'No it's not,' I said.

'Well, it's all we've got. Now come, and don't be foolish.'

Like any suppliant I was powerless. I steadied her as she slipped her shoes on, laughed with her as she over-balanced and stumbled, and then took her hand to go back through the trees, feeling childishly reassured by that contact with her, and correspondingly cast adrift when we came into the shade of the box hedges at the edge of the garden and she let my hand go.

'We can't be seen like this,' she said. She laughed and reached up to kiss me on the cheek. 'We must be aunt and nephew again.'

But although we laughed together her expression had a distant quality to it, as though our intimacy was already stored away in a remote part of her mind where it might be inspected occasionally, fondly but without too great a passion, and where it could do no harm. And I understood that, although I had had possession of her for a moment, she had been David Hewison's since childhood. He had lain with her when her breasts were still budding and her hips were narrow and her body hair was no more than floss. She was not just his possession, she was his creation. I think it was from that moment that I began to hate him.

When I got back to my room a trivial little memory stirred amongst the confusion inside me. I went over to the bookcase and pulled out the copy of *Four Quartets* which I had looked at weeks ago.

'H.D.H. to L.A. You are the music while the music lasts.'

But it was not L.A. It was a simple ambiguity of the handwriting. The first letter was not a sharp acute, not even a right angle. It was a curve like a bent elbow. 'To C .A.' Clara Alessio.

The next days passed in a curious way. Life proceeded as normal – the evenings at the Villa, the sweat-ridden days at the dig – but I felt dissociated from all that was going on around me. In a way it was like suffering from a kind of exhaustion; or being under the influence of a mild drug, a hallucinogen which gave me visions which I knew I had to call reality, whilst denying me something far more real which I knew was only a dream.

Lara was both the reality and the dream. I had a dream image of her naked against me and all-consuming; and a real image of her as once again the mistress of the house, focus of the Villa, hostess to a disparate group of academics, wife of David Hewison; and the two images did not coincide. She smiled at me, but remotely; talked with me, but only in an allusive, ironical manner which did not allow me near the quick of her; and evaded me when I tried to be alone with her. That moment outside the cave might never have occurred, or rather it had occurred and by its disturbing power it had sent us fleeing from its reality. You can always deny responsibility for your dreams: within the gothic architecture of orthodox theology they cannot themselves carry the stigma of sin.

I was almost glad when David suggested a new job for me.

'You are wasted at the moment,' he said one lunchtime. We were talking in a corner of the mess tent, in the nebulous light which came through the canvas. It was hot. Around us was the noise of sixty people eating. 'You tell me that you work for the publicity department or something, so why not employ your talents for us?'

'Tell me how.'

'Deal with that awful man Harris and his damned exhibition, liaise with him on our behalf. Someone will have to or they'll be doing whatever the hell they please.'

Ever since he had made the apology his attitude towards me had changed. It was as though our little conflict and reconciliation had broken through one of those unseen barriers with which my family has so long divided itself up into small parcels of antagonism. I would not describe this new attitude as friendly. Few people had a relationship with him which involved the equality of friendship. It was more as though he had accepted our blood relationship in a formal and rather old-fashioned way: he had become faintly patronizing, avuncular. Ironically it was at the very time when I had learned to hate him that I had become the first member of the family with whom he had had any relationship other than the merely litigious for a decade or more.

'It's about time you did something really useful for the excavation, something more than navvying.'

'I enjoy the navvying.'

He looked at me in surprise. 'What the devil has enjoyment got to do with it?'

'He's offered me a job,' I told Lara, catching her alone for the first time. 'He wants me to work with Harris on the exhibition. He says I'm to keep an eye on the man.'

'You'll become a member of the excavation staff if you're not careful.'

'That's hardly a joke. Charles said the Trust would pay me consultancy fees. Should I accept? It'll mean going to Florence.'

She looked back at me with her impassive expression. 'How do you feel about it?'

Ironically what had been a complete and shameless intimacy between us had now become a kind of obstacle, a nucleus which threw out its own gravitational field and drew towards it every partial intimacy until finally we seemed to be left with nothing, not even an easy familiarity. It had become like talking to a stranger.

'You know how I feel.'

'And you know how I feel, Anthony.'

'Do I? You've given me little indication.'

For the first time I saw her angry. 'How can you be so stupid?'

'I'm not stupid, just frightened to lose you.'

'Then you *are* stupid.'

It was the first time I had seen her angry, and also the first time I had been angry with her. I don't really remember what we said to each other, but I do know that like most rows it did not clear the air.

The next day I told David that I would take the job on, but I also made a condition.

'Harris's plans look as though they come from a British Council training manual. There's no excitement, no focus. The public will just wander round, mouth a few platitudes, and wander out again. We need something they won't forget.'

He looked suspicious. 'What do you suggest?'

'The jewellery and the portrait of Lara. I want to use the two together, a full-length reproduction of the portrait and the jewellery together in the innermost room.' I showed him on the plans. 'Nothing else to clutter the place up. Just the jewellery and the portrait.'

'But the portrait has no validity as a reconstruction. It's pure artistic fancy.'

'That doesn't matter. It will create a sensation.'

'I don't want a sensation. You cannot turn twenty-five years of painstaking work into a sensation.'

'But it *is* a sensation. I've heard you yourself talk about it, not in dry-as-dust terms like the others, but as a drama.'

He grunted, but I could see I had flattered him. Charles was dry-as-dust, Meredith was dry-as-dust, the rest were dry-as-dust, but not he.

'How would you do it then?'

I explained. 'Any information – description, details of provenance, date, all that sort of thing – would be kept outside the room. Inside there'd be just the jewellery laid out on a black ground, and the portrait behind it. Pitch dark except for two spotlights. Yes, of course it would be a bit theatrical, but then the Etruscans themselves were theatrical, weren't they?'

Hewison nodded. 'Histrionic. Did you know it's an Etruscan word? *Ister*, a player. Livy Book eleven, when the Romans imported Etruscan dancers and players to placate the gods during an epidemic. And the acting mask as well, the *persona*. Etruscan *phersu, phersuna*. You are quite right, quite right.'

'So, what do you think?'

He looked at me curiously. 'Would I want Lara's image paraded for the world to gawp at?'

'Surely you have no need to be jealous.'

His look was unnerving, as though he was trying to read my thoughts.

'All right,' he said at last. 'Go ahead and do it.'

When the day came for me to leave for Florence I found Lara in the drawing room. I noticed that she was wearing the same dress as she had worn on my first arrival at the Villa. Perhaps because of that there was a hint of finality about our leave-taking.

'Full circle,' I said.

'Perhaps we have not even left the second.'

The allusion was to Dante. 'Which was that?'

She shook her head. By her feet the chimera snarled at me for my ignorance. 'When will you come back?'

I tried to judge her tone. She had a startling ability to hold herself in check, to shutter her emotions away.

'I don't know. I have to do something about my work soon. If I just remain drifting around Honjohn will be demanding my resignation.'

'Perhaps it would be best to give it to him.'

'That's what Helen always wanted.'

The name brought silence. She looked down at her feet, at the chimera, then up again quickly. 'I expect you will be back soon.' She was smiling, more openly this time, holding out her hands to me in a formal and rather quaint gesture which seemed to have been practised, like a stage direction. I took her hands and as I leant to kiss her she averted her face just a fraction so that even that was equivocal. My lips met the corners of her mouth; not totally impersonal, but no suggestion of what had actually taken place.

Then I remembered. 'It's Francesca da Rimini, isn't it? The second circle.'

It was not exactly fear which I saw in her expression, but the kind of confused pain one sees in an invalid's eyes, the kind of pain I used to see in my mother's. And her smile was an invalid's smile as well, an attempt to laugh it off.

'Yes,' she said. 'Francesca da Rimini.'

The last sight I had of her was as I left the Villa. I looked back and caught sight of her face at one of the windows, staring through the reflection of the sky. She seemed impossibly remote.

# XVIII

## *Winter 1943/44*

ALESSIO was an impressive-looking man. He was tall, taller than anyone of the Partisan group except Hewison, and massive in his dominance of others. When he had first been unhooded in the presence of his captors he had looked at them with an expression of mingled amusement and derision, and Hewison had recognized the look of a man whose creed is more powerful than any temporal adversity.

'You are a prisoner of the *Comitato per Liberazione Nazionale*,' Orlandi had declared grandly. Alessio's eyebrows, arcs of steely grey hair, rose in affected surprise. 'You will be treated well despite your membership of the traitorous Fascist government and, at such a time as the innocent hostages now being held by your German masters in Vetrano are released, you will be released. If the same hostages are murdered, then you will be tried by a revolutionary court. These facts will be conveyed to the German military command forthwith. Do you have anything to say?'

Alessio's eyes held not a trace of hesitation, not a glimmer of fear. He turned his head to survey the circle of partisans as though reviewing a rather slovenly squad of soldiers. His profile was the kind to appeal to the Fascist mind: aquiline and predatory. In his own time he turned back to Orlandi.

'By what legal authority are you constituted?'

'By the Will of the People.'

Alessio smiled. 'The people,' he repeated. His tone hovered between disdain and disbelief. 'Every rogue in history has appealed to the will of the people.'

They led him to his cell. This was a small room at the back

of the Casolare, a bare box of rough-plastered stone walls and cracked cement floor. On one wall there was a scrawled slogan, relic of some long-forgotten assignation: *Evangela ti amo*. With his head almost touching the roof, Alessio stood in his immaculate grey suit at the centre of this cell.

'Take his tie and belt,' Orlandi commanded.

The prisoner gestured his guards away. It was noteworthy that they obeyed him instantly. With his own hands he removed the offending articles and handed them to Orlandi.

'Do not imagine for one moment that I will cheat you of your revenge. I am not a man to commit suicide.' He glanced around his cell. 'May I have a chair, a bed, something?'

'We live simply here. I will see what can be done, but do not expect much.'

Alessio's smile was tauntingly composed, the smile of a man who faces martyrdom for his faith. 'Assuredly I do not expect much.'

It was the first time Hewison had ever seen her angry. Her eyes were hard, her lips were like flint.

'Why should I ever have trusted anyone?' she asked. 'Orlandi, or you, or anyone? Why should I have supposed that my own misery might be left for me to deal with alone?'

She turned away from him and stood looking out of the window onto the moat below and the tops of the lemon trees.

'Why did I ever think that something called decency might still exist? I have been as naïve as Vincenzo himself.'

Her fingers were knotted tight, forced down by her side as though otherwise they might break away from her control. He expected her to weep, but her tears were under as tight control as her fists. When she spoke again it was more quietly, almost reflectively, at the pale reflection of herself in the window pane.

'I suppose that it is as much my fault as anyone else's. Like anyone else in this damned war I put ideas before people. That is what war is all about, isn't it? Ideas before people. Oh, not necessarily grand ideas; mean, squalid little stratagems as often as not, expedients. The idea that I should make love to you for example. An expedient made possible only by the war, a way of quietening our pain for a moment. More than anything else in human affairs war is the practice of expediency, isn't it? Anything is lawful, but not everything is expedient.'

She nodded at her reflection, as though a clear understanding had just dawned. 'Of all the disciples Paul was the one who was fighting a war, wasn't he? The man who reduced love to a weapon.'

She turned towards Hewison. Her finger pointed. 'And you.' Her mind seemed savage and erratic, like a prisoner locked inside the cage of her body. 'And you,' she repeated. 'I had expected you to be above all this, above all our filth. A god descended from the sky.' She laughed bitterly. 'You are just a pathetic victim like any of the others, aren't you? Just another name on another tomb.'

'You really expected any different?'

'I hoped, yes. Without much evidence I had hoped. I thought I saw in you a disinterested quality, a nobility which is rare in this country.'

He was reminded of her husband's *virtù*. Their mediaeval modes of thought bore little relationship to the war which the men up in the Casolare were starting to fight, which the Germans and the Allies were already fighting at Cassino and Anzio.

'Nobility is rather a quaint word,' he said.

'Goodness, then; or does that sound too old-fashioned as well? Certainly it is a rare quality in Italy at the best of times. An Italian is always interested, always adding up his gains and losses. Judgement for an Italian has always been mere calculation. But I had thought you different, capable perhaps of choosing the good and the right, rather than the merely expedient. Now my eyes are opened.'

'This war has disposed of a whole range of illusions, hasn't it? Now it has disposed of your illusions about me.'

'Indeed.' She picked distractedly at the wool of her dress, an old dress now, three or fours years old; a sign of the war. He watched her small, repetitive movement and thought how she had lain quite still beneath him while he had spent himself inside her, but had grabbed him towards her when he had been about to pull away. And now that moment of terrifying intimacy was lost.

'Do you still love him?'

She turned her eyes on him as though they were weapons. 'Love?' she asked. 'Why do you ask about love? What can you know of it? You cannot use just one word for such a complex thing, so better use none. Don't hedge me about with words.'

'We hedge our entire lives with words. What else do we have?'

'That's like explaining to a prisoner that he has always got bars.'

She fell silent. He wondered whether he ought to leave her, but he did not want to. Leaving her now, leaving the *Castello* now would, he felt sure, be leaving it for ever.

He asked, 'Where is Gianluca?'

She waved a hand vaguely. The gesture might have been meant to indicate the warren of rooms and passages beyond the door, but it might also have been a gesture of dismissal.

'How has he taken it?'

'How the hell do you think he has taken it?' she almost shouted. 'He doesn't know whether to love or hate his father. He's nothing but a child, and he is having to deal with emotions which would destroy an adult. How the hell do you think he has taken it?'

She began to weep now, silently, without expression, the tears running over the sharp contours of her face and gathering in the corners of her mouth. Like a paper mask in the rain, her expression seemed on the edge of dissolution.

'I will go and see him,' he said. 'Talk to him. Do what I can.'

'Haven't you already failed to do that?' she asked.

Battalion Kleber of the Fourth Parachute Division of the German army had reached Vetrano in the early morning. After spending the night on the road down from Perugia the men were exhausted and glad of the opportunity to rest. Before leaving their headquarters they had been told they would continue on through Rome immediately in order to plug the defences at the new beachhead around Anzio. The sudden order diverting them to Vetrano had brought an unexpected and welcome respite. The men were all veterans and too familiar with the ways of the war not to know that soon enough they would be in the front line, and too wise not to treasure a delay. Long ago they had learned to live for the moment.

Their commanding officer, a Bavarian who had been a schoolmaster in peace time, found the delay frustrating. No more than his men did he have ideas of death or glory in the face of the Americans in front of Anzio, but he did have clear ideas about how to run an army. One way was not to change orders at the last moment on what he guessed to be little more than a whim.

'There is an intelligence report,' he had informed his company commanders, 'that the present landings at Nettuno and Anzio are no more than diversionary. The main strike will come around Civitavecchia, once our defences have been drawn south. Therefore we have to stand by.'

This kind of frustration was bad enough, but what was even worse, what was the kind of thing that drove an experienced soldier to distraction, and what was so typical of this damned country he had been forced to defend, was that in merely pausing for a while at an insignificant little town he had become embroiled in a local problem. In a haze of tiredness he had spent the morning trying to get through to regional military headquarters at Viterbo, and army headquarters at Soratte, and even his own divisional headquarters in Perugia. But no one wished to know. With tens of thousands of enemy troops streaming ashore within sixty miles of Rome perhaps this was understandable; but it did not help him. He sat behind a desk in the municipal offices of Vetrano and tried to bring his brain to focus on the problem. By his side was the aged Captain who was in command of Vetrano. In front of him was the Fascist mayor. In the orphanage across the road fifteen citizens of Vetrano – a pathetic group, he had to admit – were imprisoned under the guns of his men. In the village church nearby lay the corpses of two German soldiers who were nothing to do with him, and one Italian railway worker who was even less so. And somewhere out in the hills were terrorists of the kind he had heard about in Greece and fought against in Jugoslavia, men who were only too willing to shelter behind the anonymity of civilian clothes when it was convenient and plead combatant status when things went against them. His own men wore uniform all the time. They were proud of it and they never wished to hide it. They were not saints, but they were honourable. And as they had brought the bodies along the track from the railway station they had been angry.

Major Kleber thought of some of his men who had been enticed into a house with offers of sex by two Jugoslav girls, and then had been shot in the back; and he tried not to think of the fifteen civilians he had imprisoned in the orphanage.

'Who is this Vincenzo Alessio?' he asked again of the *sindaco*.

'He is a man of great importance,' the man replied for the dozenth time. 'A friend of Il Duce himself, a member of the Grand Council, a man who has been presented to the Führer and all the other luminaries of the German Reich. And he is also a friend of the common man. And a good Christian,' the *sindaco* added, knowing that Major Kleber had been seen in the church saying a prayer beside the bodies of the dead men.

'So if he is so important why the devil can't I get any sense out of anyone?' the Major asked, more of himself than of the Italian. And he felt tiredness pressing down on him.

Outside it was windy and raining. Eighty miles to the south other battalions of the Fourth Parachute Division were facing the British Brigade of Guards on the Via Anziate, but here in Vetrano he was waiting for a second landing which he knew would never come and worrying about a handful of Italians who he knew did not matter.

'Try again,' he said to his signals sergeant. 'Try to raise Grottaferrata. Try to get General Schlemmer on the line.'

The next day Battalion Kleber was ordered south to the beachhead. The staff officer at army headquarters who gave the order did not express much interest in the Major's local problem.

'It's your affair,' he said. 'I can't bother the Field-Marshal with that kind of thing at a moment like this.'

'But I need advice.'

'Advice? Get rid of them. They deserve anything that comes to them.'

'I'm worried. The Geneva Convention . . .'

'Major, the Geneva Convention says nothing about civilians being given guns and told to shoot uniformed combatants in the back. The Geneva Convention says nothing about the indiscriminate bombing of civilians. The Geneva Convention says nothing about an awful lot that is happening at the moment. Geneva is in Switzerland and Switzerland isn't fighting this bloody war.'

'Would the Field-Marshal authorize me to do it?'

'The Field-Marshal has expressed his loathing of guerrilla warfare. He has said, unofficially, that the male population ought to be made to suffer the consequences.'

'So I shoot them?'

'That, Major, is for you to decide. All I am interested in is that you move down towards the beachhead immediately.'

So the battalion prepared to move, but before it left the town Major Kleber gave orders that the fifteen hostages being held in the orphanage be taken out and executed.

'If they think we are just going to sit by while our men get shot in the back by civilians, then they can think again,' he said to the Captain. He was exhausted and he was angry, as much at the circumstances as at any particular person or persons.

So the fifteen citizens of Vetrano, who until that moment had done nothing to impress themselves on history, were marched out into the fields just to the north of the town while the whole battalion was stood to in the streets. The townspeople were ordered to remain indoors. So no one saw the hostages lined up against a dry-stone wall, nor the two paratroopers cock their sub-machine guns and level them at the victims and fire, nor the commander of the execution squad go forward and check each body for any sign of life and shoot two men in the back of the head when he found that they were still breathing. But they heard the firing plain enough and they knew.

A runner brought news of the killings to the Casolare. Orlandi and Hewison received the news outside the house. It was not unexpected, and Orlandi's nod as he heard the man's breathless report may have been a nod of fatalistic acquiescence.

'So we will have to kill Alessio,' said Tobasi, who had emerged from the building on hearing the messenger outside.

'Try him,' Hewison said. 'We will have to try him, remember? Crimes against the Italian people was the formula, I believe.'

Why clinging to a kind of ersatz legality was so important he was not sure. It was perhaps a kind of sentimental regard for a type of behaviour which had once been considered the norm, pre-war ideas of justice and morality. After all there was nothing particularly just about staging a trial in order to kill a man for a crime he had not committed, indeed a crime which didn't even exist in any civilized legal code. A muddled form of justice was worse, surely, than no justice at all.

'That is nothing more than a formality.'

'Nevertheless.'

Tobasi glared at him. 'It will be a revolutionary trial,' he said enigmatically.

# XIX

THE exhibition was to take place in an echoing, sixteenth-century *palazzo* near Santa Maria Novella. When I got there work was already under way and in the care of the ubiquitous Harris and an energetic girl from the *Ministero per i Beni Culturali* called Anna. There was not a great deal for me to do, beyond act as an ambassador for David.

'What would *Signor* Evison prefer? Would *Signor* Evison like these over here?' they would ask as though I were he. My opinions, delivered for the most part off the cuff, were taken to be the word of the man himself. I was struck by the irony, but happy enough with the role. It was cool beneath the high ceilings of the *palazzo*, cool and somehow soothing. I was quite content to hang around and watch while workmen assembled display cases or manoeuvred information boards into position with Mr Harris worrying at their heels. And I could see from the start that Anna was fully in command.

'That's just what I thought,' she said when I explained how I wanted the jewellery displayed. 'The original plans were about as exciting as a plate of cold *polenta*. And the portrait is a brilliant idea.'

When the portrait arrived two of the workmen brought it up from the street. Like men carrying the image of a saint in a procession they shouldered it and marched up the stairs. We all watched. There was a faint sense of ritual as they eased it through doorways and around the glass cases and into the inner chamber of the exhibition area. Once it was hung they stood back so that the faithful might press forward to see.

The face looked out at us like the face of an Egyptian mummy, a stylized image of the real thing; beautiful but dead.

Anna nodded in satisfaction. One of the workmen pronounced it '*Bellissima*'.

When the others had gone I found an opportunity to go back into the room by myself, to pay homage or last respects I wasn't sure. I felt in a kind of limbo; but limbo is the first circle of Dante's hell and at least with Lara I had qualified for the second. Dante reserved that circle for the *peccator carnali* who 'had allowed appetite to suppress their reason'. The original Italian is perhaps a little obscure, so I offer my own translation. I had found a second-hand copy of *Inferno* on a bookstall in the Piazza Ognissanti and I rediscovered the ugly aptness of the story of Francesca da Rimini. Surprised in adultery by her husband, the deformed Gianciotto Malatesta, Lord of Rimini, she was murdered together with her lover. *Trucidati*, said the notes in my copy. Her lover was Gianciotto's brother, Paolo. Dante blames allegorical Love for the whole affair, leaving the lovers languishing in hell and yet somehow innocent; but whom do you blame in the twentieth century?

I had no answers. In mediaeval times the wicked were always ugly or deformed, and by all accounts Gianciotto Malatesta was both, which must have made it even easier; but nowadays we look more for deformity of the mind and are less certain when we have found it. We have inherited so much that it becomes impossible to judge anything, lest our judgement seem narrow or tendentious or intolerant. But I found it difficult to sit before that painting of Lara and not hate David Hewison for what he had done.

A week later Francis and Goffredo Macchioni arrived with the exhibits. Two large vans blocked the street outside the *palazzo* while workmen humped heavy packing cases up the staircase. There were dispatch notes to check and receipts to sign, artifacts – some no bigger than a farthing – to be locked and sealed in their cases, alarm systems to be activated. From now on there were guards around the place. Mr Harris fussed.

'You've built up quite a little empire here, I see,' Francis said to me. 'Must be a family trait.'

The jewellery came in an armoured van with an armed escort.

'A fantastic sum,' said Harris to anyone who would listen. 'Quite fantastic.'

Unpacking it was like excavating it, peeling away layers of dross until the gold leaf lay exposed in its bed of tissue paper, smiling its secret smile. There was a sharp intake of breath from the people who were watching. In the two thousand years since a goldsmith had beaten it out and encrusted it with intricate spirals and arabesques of gold granulation it had lost none of its potency.

Anna eased the scallop-shaped pectoral up and held it against her chest. She smiled round at us.

'*Come va?*'

'For God's sake be careful,' warned Harris.

Someone else said, '*Benone*,' and Macchioni bowed to her: '*Una regina.*'

'But not as beautiful as the *signora* in the painting,' she added wryly.

No one answered that. Together she and Goffredo laid out the pieces in the inner sanctum beneath the portrait of Lara. Under the spotlights the metal gleamed a thick, butter yellow. An electrician connected up wires to infra-red sensors which clicked and blinked in the shadows whenever anyone passed through their beams. They were like small, malevolent demons guarding the shrine. That afternoon when they were tested they screamed and shrieked throughout the building like banshees.

After that our work seemed done and I went out for a stroll with Francis. The streets had come out in a rash of posters:

*LUCRI. IL TESORO DI UNA CITTÀ ETRUSCA*, they announced in gold letters. The background was matt black. The pectoral and fillet shone out from the darkness.

'*In anteprima*', said a newspaper headline. '*La Ricchezza Etrusca*'.

The city was at its worst, overhot and overcrowded. It is not the city of the Renaissance. That is a fallacy engendered by the architecture and encouraged by the tourist agencies. In reality it is the city of the Grand Duchy, stale and reactionary. Like any old crone it can grab you by the sleeve and talk about the good old days, but it doesn't really remember them any more than you do. I hated the place. Perhaps it was a desire to escape it that made me suggest to Francis that we get out for an afternoon and visit Poggio Sanssieve.

'The family mausoleum? My word, I'd love to.'

So next morning I hired a car and in the dead time after lunch we drove out along the north bank of the Arno to Pontassieve.

EVISON FARMACEUTICI, a sky sign announced to the world.

The road wound through the dispiriting town, then opened out into the Sieve valley. There were people fishing on the weir above the town just where I used to fish with the *fattore* of Poggio Sanssieve. I remember crouching in the curve of a willow trunk to watch the fish rising, learning to identify the flies and select the correct lure. An arcane and useless piece of knowledge which has quite deserted me now. Only one name stays in my memory: *friganea*. But what it refers to and when I might use it I no longer have any idea. The perspectives of time shift so suddenly: fifteen years ago when I had been at university those days seemed recent; now they were as distant as sepia photographs in a book about the last century: the old *fattore* dead, Nonna Angelica dead, my mother dead, Helen gone. But Lara rediscovered, and with her another past.

'My goodness,' said Francis at the very same curve in the road where Helen had exclaimed 'Good God Almighty!' fifteen years earlier. The Villa had come into sight. In English the word 'villa' has been irrevocably compromised. Until that moment Helen had never quite believed my stories of a Renaissance *palazzo*. It was a shock to see the truth, the great, ornate galleon of a place riding high on its terraced hillside above the valley floor.

'The story is that it was designed by Giuliano Sangallo,' I said to Francis. With Helen I had felt a need to apologize: 'But they always say that kind of thing,' and she had retorted, 'Not about semi-detached houses in Purley they don't.'

'It was by way of a dowry for my grandmother. Probably more of a millstone round the neck than a buoyant asset, but my grandfather could afford to keep millstones afloat.'

'Obviously a family weakness,' Francis observed.

It was to this house that my grandmother retreated after my grandfather's death in 1956. She was running from a Britain which she admired but had never come to understand, to an Italy which was changing beyond her comprehension. And it was here that my mother and I travelled almost every summer in order to try and preserve her illusions. For my mother the task was always too great. After a few days she would abandon the place in order to pursue her *dolce vita* in Rome, leaving me to pass lonely weeks in the company of the gardeners or the maids, or acrimonious ones if my cousins were staying. Here I had lost my virginity to the *fattore*'s granddaughter, and my illusions about my family, at almost the same time.

It wasn't until my grandmother died that the inevitable changes came. Thomas had the building restored and converted into a conference centre and company showpiece – 'putting the family assets to work' was how he described it – and so now the lawns at the side were artfully paved with hollow bricks in order to keep the grass while yet allowing rows of executive Alfa Romeos and Lancias to park there. Now the hall had the shadowy quiet of an over-expensive hotel and the rooms were discreetly signed – *Sala di Riunione, Gabinetti, Tavola Calda* – for the groups of grey-suited men and women who conducted earnest conversations at the *Punto di Incontri* or laughed too loudly at the American Bar. Now it all seemed like a meticulously accurate reconstruction by a film company of the Poggio Sanssieve which I had known, which had been identical in geography, almost identical in furnishing and fittings – although then they had been dull and dusty – but peopled instead by ageing retainers and clumsy village girls, and pervaded by Nonna Angelica's presence – a kind of smell, an amalgam of sweet, old-fashioned perfume and damp decay.

'We'll stay for dinner,' I told the man at the desk.

'Very good, sir. Do I bill Head Office?'

'Yes. The public relations account.'

Francis chuckled into his moustache.

'It's good to see you back, sir. I hope you aren't disturbed by the sales conference.'

'I'm sure we won't be.'

I showed Francis the *salone grande*. He looked around with amused delight at the massive baroque furniture, at the painted *cassoni*, at the intricately carved ceiling, at the paintings – 'School of Perugino', 'After Della Francesca', 'Attributed to Martini', Madonnas and Saints all of them, all except for the two portraits on either side of the fireplace which were by Orpen, and showed Sir Gordon Hewison, Bart. and Lady Hewison, both staring back at you as though you had committed a grave solecism.

'My grandparents,' I said. 'He's the one who went gaga. I expect David has mentioned him during one of his diatribes.'

'So that must be Nonna Angelica, of whom one hears far more. And the gentleman in the hall?'

'David's brother, Thomas. Sir Thomas, second Bart. Doubtless Honjohn will appear soon enough.'

'Honjohn?'

'My cousin. A company joke. Not the kind you repeat to his face.'

He examined the painting of my grandfather for a while. 'One sees a likeness, between him and David, I mean. The eyes. And that way of holding his head. No wonder David calls it the family mausoleum.'

'There's more.'

We went through the glass doors and onto the back terrace. The parterre gardens had never, never been so splendid in the past; nor so dead. To one side, behind a screen of cypresses, was the chapel – *Capella di Santa Rosa,* a discreet sign indicated – where I and my cousins had stuttered out confessions under Nonna Angelica's stern eye, where doubtless Thomas and David and my mother had received similar training in their day, and where finally, and with a faint feeling of getting our own back, we had buried her alongside the founder of the feast.

But it was here also, a mere three months ago, that I had watched my mother's coffin being interred at the culmination of a journey in which nightmare had alternated with pure farce. While battling with forms of the most exalted ghoulishness and officials of infinite obfuscation, I had wondered whether that final clause in my mother's will – 'That my body be laid to rest beside my parents at Poggio Sanssieve' – had been by way of a practical joke. After all, sentimentality about the family had never been part of her make-up and she had always professed a loathing for the place.

Anyway, there she was beneath a slab of marble as white as snow:

FELICITY PERPETUA.
BELOVED DAUGHTER AND DEVOTED MOTHER.
'FOR SHE LOVED MUCH'

The epitaph was my choice, my last joke.

'So this is what David has spent all his life escaping,' murmured Francis. 'It is seductive, isn't it?'

I agreed. Seductive was exactly the word. But the trouble with seduction is that you never know the cost when you are being shown the goods. Prostitution is more honest.

We ate dinner on the terrace surrounded by the noise of the sales conference delegates.

'We ought to drink a toast,' Francis announced, raising his glass. 'To the Hewison fortune, perhaps, the fount of all our present riches.'

We drank.

'A dull enough toast really,' he added thoughtfully. 'Mercenary. Better drink to a beautiful woman.' He eyed me over the top of his glass. 'Perhaps Lara.'

'Perhaps.'

'You seem much taken with her.'

'She is a striking woman.' I replaced my glass carefully. 'A shade tragic. Fey.'

'You think so?' Francis stroked his moustache. 'Perhaps you are right. But very lovely. You seem quite fond.'

Had he guessed something? His eyes looked brightly out of that languid, slightly effeminate face.

'I am.' I stood on the edge of confession, wanting to talk about her to someone, not certain of his own loyalties.

'And David? How do you find your uncle?'

I hesitated. 'He disturbs me. Maybe frightens is the right word.'

'Oh yes, exactly. Frightens. There is something profoundly frightening about a man who combines intellectual strength with physical strength, and binds it all together with a touch of . . . shall I be kind and say, aggression? It is almost a blessing to find a weakness; but in a way David's weakness is almost more frightening than his strengths: a sense of guilt is a terrifying thing, don't you think?'

He sipped from his glass with great concentration. 'And the man is a Papist. I wouldn't wish to offend you, but I have always associated Protestants with guilt and Papists with cheerful iniquity. The Arden-Tillyards are Church of England of course, which is neither. Or both, depending on your point of view.'

There was a pause while a waiter appeared with the roast quail we had ordered.

'Maybe David has lapsed too far,' he continued when the man had gone. 'Too far for a good purging at the confessional.' He chuckled in that peculiar manner of his, as though at a private joke. 'I like that word, purging. It has wonderful echoes of mediaeval medicine about it: laxative, cathartic and drastic. Maybe confession is merely cathartic and what poor David needs is a good dose of drastic.'

'Would that have done Uncle Harry any good?'

He looked up from his food. 'That's the problem with those mediaeval prescriptions: kill or cure. I'm certain that it would have done for Uncle Harry far quicker than his heart ever did. But has modern medicine given anything in its place? Does it have any cures for the spirit or the soul, or whatever? Does Hewison Pharmaceuticals produce a cure for *angst*?'

'It has tried,' I answered gloomily. 'It's trying still. Pills to pick you up, pills to ease you down, pills to knock you sideways. My mother knew all about them. Blessed are the pill-makers, Helen used to say, for they shall inherit the earth; blessed are the pill-takers, for they shall see God. She wasn't being funny.'

'Helen?'

'My wife. Was my wife, is my wife, I'm not really sure what now.'

Francis pondered. 'And now what will you do, Anthony, once the exhibition is set up?' He dissected a quail with immense care. 'Is your own *angst* cured? Do you return to the manufacture of pills?'

I laughed. 'That's the question I've been trying to answer. Do you realize that I am completely free? I'm in a condition which most people would envy, and I find the prospect appalling.' I itemized my freedoms: from wife and family, from geographical ties, from financial constraints, from ambition. 'But you see, with no constraints . . . adrift!' I made a waving gesture with my hand. It might have signified a drunk wandering down a street or a sail flapping in the wind: as indeterminate as my mood.

'And you came to Lucri looking for constraints?'

'Something. A vague idea. Memories. I don't really know. I sound inarticulate.'

'Most people do when they try to explain themselves.'

We ate in silence for a while. The noise from the conference delegates around us increased. Having all the usual constraints waiting for them at home they found their present freedoms merely titillating. One thing to be cast adrift within sight of land, quite another to be far, far out in the middle of the ocean.

'And Lara. Is she a constraint?'

He went on blithely picking over the little corpse of his third quail.

'What do you mean?'

'Oh come, come, Anthony. In a small community like ours one notices things: a look, a gesture. Don't they have a term for it nowadays? Body language.'

'And how has this language been interpreted?' I felt angry, conscious of talk that had been going on behind my back.

'Imprecisely, I suppose. As a budding intimacy perhaps? Maybe innocent enough at the moment, but dangerous, very dangerous. I think you have done the best thing by leaving.'

'I'm not sure that I have left.'

'Haven't you?' He looked up with a quick smile. 'Then I would make up my mind if I were you. And, if I may be so bold as to proffer advice, don't run away with the idea that in these enlightened or degenerate days sexual jealousy has somehow been emasculated. Appropriate word. Perhaps it can no longer start a Trojan war; but a mere Agamemnon . . . with ease.'

I asked, 'What the hell do you know, Francis?' and he looked at me with a shake of his head.

'Know, Anthony? I know nothing; except that Lucri is a very important piece of work and David is a very remarkable man. But, as you know, there is a weakness in him, a flaw. I don't pretend to be either psychologist or priest . . . but I would not wish to see him destroyed.'

'Hasn't he done his share of destroying?'

'You are not implying revenge, are you?'

'Don't be ridiculous.'

'Because I can sympathize with you. I can see how conversation with Gianluca – yes, I know you have seen him – coupled with a love for Lara and maybe a fear of David, all these might add up to the irrational: a crusade, or worse, something absurd and quixotic like the rescue of fair lady. But really all you could achieve is a great deal of damage, a great deal of misery.'

'You are talking as though I were a child.'

He denied it gently. 'Not you in particular, Anthony. I always think that the biggest mistake most people make is to suppose there is something called "growing up".'

'But you have grown up, of course.'

He ignored my anger. 'Maybe I have, but really it is something negative, a deficiency, like being crippled. I can stand aside and watch the other take part. I can try to imagine what it is like, but I can never experience it for myself.' He shook his head. 'No depths, but no heights either.'

'So how can you judge?'

'Judge, Anthony? For heaven's sake don't deny me that. It's the only thing I *can* do.' He pushed his plate aside. 'Would you mind if I smoke? I need the comfort of a teat.'

I watched his hands. They were long and delicate, almost like the skeletal things I had seen in the mass grave. Blood did not seem to flow beneath their skin. They shook slightly as he manipulated a cheroot and struck a match. The match flared.

He inhaled, then blew a stream of smoke out into the darkness away from our table.

'What is it about this country?' he asked softly, expecting no answer, watching the dissolution of the smoke. 'It seems a place where anything can happen – the very worst and the very best, too often at the same time. It throws a kind of magnetic field around it, doesn't it? A magnetic field with innocence at one pole and corruption at the other, and the wretched people strung out in between like little vibrating compass needles. Corrupt innocence, innocent corruption. From Dante to D'Annunzio; from the Emperor Hadrian to the Emperor Mussolini; from Saint Augustine to Saint Savonarola. And right at the opposite poles those rare creatures who become myths: Saint Francis, Saint Clare and a few others on one side; the Emperor Nero, the Borgia pope, a few others on the other.'

He laughed quietly into the night. 'The only ones who can stand aside are those who were born under Saturn, like me. Lead. Non-magnetic. Most of the Anglo–Saxon world. They are the grown-ups.'

'And where does Lara come?'

'Oh, she is in the magnetic field all right, towards the pole of innocence I suppose you'd say, but with that seed of corruption within her. David on the other hand . . .' He shook his head sorrowfully, like a physician who holds out no hope.

From one of the tables behind us there came a shriek of laughter – male, female, it was impossible to tell. Francis looked at me and raised his eyebrows as though to say 'there you are'; and I thought of Helen and how she had betrayed me, and wondered if Francis were not right. For Helen it had not mattered. It was neither good nor bad; merely convenient. It wasn't an act which had existed on a scale of moral values at all.

'You know I'm sleeping with Pat, don't you, Anthony?' was what she had said, as she might have remarked, 'I went to the library today.'

'Surely you can say the same about any country, any people.'

'Not the Anglo–Saxon world for certain. Our existence is very different: we exist on a ladder of status, the status of rank in Britain, of money in the States. It doesn't really matter how you achieve the status. Certainly morality has little to do with it.'

The game amused him. 'How easy it is to invent little systems to explain mankind. How plausible. Can't you see Harris on my ladder of status? All the rungs are greased. He scrabbles and scrabbles and as soon as he rises up he slithers back down again, sometimes back to below the point from where he has just come. They'll probably post him back to England and put him in charge of a book store or something.' He blew smoke, as though at the wretched Harris struggling up his ladder.

'And where do you come, Francis?'

'Me?' He considered a moment. 'Let's see: middle academic, in a rather esoteric field. That's quite high. You see, the British idea of rank still has remarkably little to do with money. I might only earn the salary of a . . . oh, detective-inspector, car salesman, I don't know, but in terms of status' – he looked over his shoulder down onto the ground as though looking down from a great height – 'I can just about see the tops of their heads, way, way below. And there's Harris, incidentally.'

He threw back his head and laughed, and the sound brought a hush to the other tables.

# XX

# *Winter 1943/44*

THE revolutionary trial was a grim affair. The rough deal table which had previously graced the main room of the Casolare and imbued it with a certain peasant honesty was now draped with a red cloth. A line of chairs had been placed behind it for the 'Representatives of the People', and a single chair had been placed in front of it for the defendant. And two men were stationed against the side walls at forty-five degrees to Alessio to cover him with their Sten guns.

It was, of course, a sham; but at the time, and indeed later, Hewison could not really imagine an alternative which would not have been even more hypocritical. Paradoxically there was something almost honest about the whole thing, beginning at the beginning with the President's opening remarks: 'Vincenzo Alessio, representative of the puppet government of the Fascist criminal Mussolini, you are here to be tried and condemned to death in the name of the Italian people . . .' etcetera, etcetera. At least he was not mincing his words.

And neither was Alessio himself, who merely retorted that the presently constituted court had no authority under any code of justice and was therefore not worthy of his recognition. 'And furthermore could you ask your men to put their guns down?' He added with heavy irony: 'I know that I am going to die anyway, but I would like to be prepared for the event. At the moment I feel it may well be sudden and unannounced.'

The request was granted.

The trial had no particular form to it, but it was cloaked in a kind of instinctive ritual, as though there is ingrained in each human a natural sense of the solemnity which is proper to such things as funerals and marriages and judicial murder. The proceedings were conducted under the aegis of Orlandi as President of the Court, and the prosecution was in the care of the ideologue, Tobasi. Somehow this man contrived to rise above the absurd platitudes of his previous utterances: his accusations against Alessio took on a mystic, almost hieratic quality, like the chantings of a priest. They became, by their pure intangibility, rather magnificent. Of course it was a prosecution case that did not require an answer, any more than the Canon of the Mass requires an answer, but nevertheless Hewison felt constrained to do something. So it was he who broke up the flow of Tobasi's eloquence to ask questions and make objections, it was he who found himself suggesting an appeal to higher authority, it was he, in all, who became *de facto* if not *de jure* the man's defence counsel. By so doing it was clear to him that he was gaining little. Alessio viewed him with complete indifference, while the partisans muttered amongst themselves that Egisto seemed to be little more than a Fascist sympathizer and Tobasi openly despised him for his role. Nevertheless, with the desperation of a temperance preacher outside a public house, he persisted. Eventually he was even able to persuade the court that he should be allowed some time alone with the defendant so that together they might discuss matters.

Even this was futile. Alessio merely sat on the wooden box which had been provided as a seat in his little cell, and stared straight ahead at '*Evangela ti amo*' and paid no heed to Hewison's pleas. It was only when he had given up all his efforts that Alessio looked directly at him for the first time.

'Are you the one who has been at my house?'

He smiled at Hewison's consternation. 'Don't worry, she did not betray you. Someone in the village. Anyway I can see it is you. I was told someone *alto, bello*, which will serve as a description, I suppose.' He watched Hewison carefully, their roles suddenly, incongruously reversed. Outside the cell was Orlandi's revolutionary court waiting to condemn him to death, yet here he was examining Hewison with all the minuteness of a judge examining a witness.

'Are you her lover?'

'What on earth do you mean?'

Alessio laughed softly. 'I imagine you know very well what I mean. Look, I will not survive this, we both know that. Believe it or not, there are things that matter more to me than my own life: Clara for one, whatever you may think; my son for another. When one is in this kind of situation,' he gestured eloquently around the cell, 'you grab whatever opportunity arises. I know well enough that what I am saying guarantees, should I ever need such a guarantee, that I will be killed, but that hardly matters. So tell me, are you her lover?'

Hewison stumbled with embarrassment, thinking of that one time. 'I suppose so. We once . . .'

'Just once?' Alessio laughed without humour. 'Yes, it would not be the kind of thing she would take easily to.' He nodded thoughtfully. 'Betrayal is not the kind of thing she would enjoy, so perhaps just once is best. It has the air of a momentary failing about it, doesn't it? You can excuse just once. Go to confession and be done with it. But more than once begins to look like deliberation, plotting, calculation even. For more than once you need to sow the little networks of lies to justify yourselves to each other and to the world. Perhaps it is those lies which weigh on the conscience more than the act which engenders them.'

He paused, regarding Hewison bleakly, as a man might assess the strength of the last straw which he has to clutch at. 'If I were not in this absurd situation I would say to you – as man to man, I mean, not as jealous husband – stay with just once. You have the moment, for what it is worth – it's a frightening moment in many ways, isn't it, that total, shameless abandonment inside another? – and what you don't have is the disillusion. That comes later when you come to understand that actually you have abandoned nothing. I sound cynical. My whole life has been a battle against cynicism, you know; yet here I am at the very end of it being as cynical as anyone. Does one account that a failure?'

He saw that Hewison was about to speak and held up his hand. 'No, wait. Hear me out. I know that you will say that there was a huge measure of cynicism in Fascism, and I won't

206

deny it: the animals like Ciano. But now all that is purged. The Duce is never cynical. Neither was Giovanni Gentile. The true believers. I am one such. Should I say, was? There was no cynicism in my politics, and yet now I surprise myself sounding cynical in my private life.'

He shook his head despairingly. 'I sound hysterical, don't I? I sound like a man whose mind is going, but I'm not. That is why I'm saying these things, to show you that there is nothing but purity in my mind, no attempt at deceit. I say this: take her. She will be vulnerable if the Communists win, and I can see that you are not one of them. So do not be happy with just once. Look after her for me. And Gianluca. A young boy, so directionless at the moment. A difficult age, I suppose, and perhaps I am mostly to blame. He needs a father's presence, don't you think?'

He looked up from where he sat. 'Could you do that? You are on the other side of adolescence, so he will look up to you, I am sure. And you are not a Communist, that is important. I fear desperately that Gianluca may be seduced by Communism, you know? The influence of a man who has more sense than that . . . and then not to be on his own with his mother. Not natural, that. It can make a boy . . . you understand what I mean.'

He watched Hewison move to the door. His expression was close to panic. 'Or are you one of those modern liberals which are the curse of your nation?'

Hewison paused. 'My nation?'

'England. I can see that plainly enough now. England is the only country in which people go to war for nothing more convincing than pure expedience. The advantage of that is that you can always walk away from the consequences when it suits you. Are you like that? A man who, like his country, has no standards that are not dictated by pure pragmatism? A country which professes Christianity while embracing Stalin's Russia, a man who visits the church in Sabazia to make his confession, yet fights with Communists. Are you one of those, Egisto or whatever you are called, a modern liberal with your heart as empty as a tomb? Good God, you make me sick.'

Hewison watched him from the door, a figure in a battered grey suit hunched forward on his wooden box with his face in

his hands. Something about the way he held himself reminded
him of Gianluca. He went out into the cold sunlight, shutting
the door behind him.

'Let's get on with it,' he said to Tobasi.

# XXI

I HAD a picture of Lara in my mind; not the portrait in the exhibition, but my last sight of her as I left the Villa Rasenna, her face seen milkily through an upper window looking out. It was to that image I spoke on the telephone two days before the exhibition opened. Her voice was remote, blurred by reflections of other voices on the line, dulled by her own sense of finality.

'Will David be at the opening? Goffredo says not, but people suggested I ring.'

'I don't think he will. It's not the kind of thing that he likes.'

'And you?'

There was a pause. The hateful telephone in which you receive only the single dimension of sound, and that reduced by electronics to a mere semblance of the real thing. What was her expression? The pause seemed hostile, a faint hissing in the earpiece which must have been electrical interference but sounded like an angry exhalation of breath. Somewhere in the far electronic distance a voice twittered unintelligibly.

'I don't think so, Anthony. It would be difficult.'

For an instant I was angry: 'For God's sake, Lara –' and then the anger evaporated. You can't, I reflected, blame a prisoner for not leaving her cell. 'You'd enjoy it.'

'I'm sure I would.'

Pause.

'Look, I've decided' – I hadn't, but important decisions are usually made on the spur of the moment – 'I'm going back to London. To try and sort things out. Back to defending the empire of pills against the forces of darkness.'

'Oh.'

Even that told me nothing.

'So, I'll be in touch.'

'Yes.'

'Give my regards ... oh, you know the kind of thing. Thanks.'

'Of course.'

'Pity you can't come. Goodbye.'

'Goodbye.'

There; the final tenuous thread snapped. It had taken little effort.

'He'll not come,' I told Francis.

'Never thought he would.'

'What a pity, what a great pity,' Harris complained. 'Such a great man. So important in our links: a perfect blending of cultures.'

'Nor Lara.'

Francis smiled encouragingly, actually put out a hand and patted my shoulder. 'Better that way.'

The last things were being put in order, the labels checked for accuracy – 'Seventh century!' Goffredo kept protesting about something. 'It cannot be sixth. Seventh! I have to check everything, everything' – while I wandered around the rooms, peering at the glass cubes in which Lucri's treasures waited for the public: the migraine patterns of the early pottery, the sinuous elegance of the black-figure ware, the iron-grey of the *bucchero*, delicate little bronze figurines, a group of exquisitely chased bronze mirrors, a scattering of fibulae, brooches, rings. They were all very lovely but, out of context, somehow sterile.

The Etruscan Pantheon was peopled by gods who can be related to Latin deities – Menvra: Minerva; Uni: Juno; Turan: Venus – together with a host of nameless demons. Examples of these adorned the pediment and formed the Antifixes of Lucri's principal temple.

Beside this notice stood a leering terracotta face, eyes popping, tongue protruding, teeth as sharp and predatory as a tiger's. Was this the image of Etruscan nightmares?

In another glass cube I found: Bronze Chimera. circa 500 BC.

Its lion head snarled as violently as ever, in protest, I

presumed, at the nameless forces which had condemned it to this hybrid existence; but I noticed now that the goat head had a dull resignation about it. It had surrendered.

'Like Battersea Dogs' Home,' said Francis at my side. 'Who would ever take him home to the children?'

The next room had plaster models of the excavation zones, a reconstruction of a trench to show the stratigraphy of the site, all the details which the public would glance over but never read; the room beyond housed a reconstructed tomb, with the grave goods lying around the sarcophagus as though in the dust of centuries. Then there was the man in blue uniform with a pistol on his hip and past him, through a dark doorway, the gleam of gold.

From where I stood I could see Lara's face hanging in the shadows just beyond the guard's shoulder.

The official opening was in the cool of the evening. It was a tedious event in which local dignitaries made interminable speeches and nobody looked at any of the exhibits except the famous gold-work. People jostled around the display cases like guests at a cocktail party. Flashlights exploded. The guards looked nervous, as though the last people they trusted were the *sindaco* or the superintendent of archaeology or the gentlemen of the press. Anna, wearing a new pair of jeans and a gold tee shirt, was interviewed by a women's magazine.

'Would you love to own jewellery like the Lucri treasure?' they asked her.

'No,' she replied.

Afterwards we went for a meal at the restaurant where we had lunched during the weeks of preparation. Goffredo got slightly drunk and made a proposal to Anna which she deflected more delicately than she had the enquiries of the female journalist. Francis became even more languid and rambling than usual until by the end of the evening it was almost impossible to get him to finish a sentence.

'Hewison Pharmaceuticals will pay!' I announced as the bill came. We cheered. There was an end-of-term feeling to the whole evening. Even Harris was casting discretion to the winds.

Later we all went back to Anna's flat, a two-bedroomed place which she shared with another girl. There was a terrace which looked across the roofs: Brunelleschi's dome and Giotto's *campanile*, the tower of the Palazzo Vecchio beyond.

'The most famous skyline in the world,' said Harris.

'What about New York?' Francis retorted.

'The Valley of the Kings.'

'Doesn't count. Not a city.'

'Venice then.'

Goffredo was fiddling incompetently with a record player and suddenly the room filled with the noise of Greek folk music.

'Athens!' he said triumphantly. 'The Acropolis!'

Anna and I left them to their meandering argument and went into her bedroom. She was quiet and methodical, to my relief neither talking nor pretending.

'There,' she said when we had finished. It was like making love to Helen.

I had booked a ticket on the afternoon train to Milan. In the morning I went round to the exhibition to see how things were going.

Goffredo looked half asleep. 'Where did you get to last night?' he asked. Had he been too drunk even to notice?

'I've come to say goodbye.'

A good crowd was milling through the rooms, Germans and Americans prominent among the foreigners.

'Would that look good back home,' said one blue rinse, peering at the chimera. 'Honey, would that look good as a door stop.'

At the door to the inner room the guards were marshalling a queue to see the gold. They were allowing them in four at a time. Minnesota complained to Düsseldorf: 'Why don't they have a bigger gallery?'

I turned away. It all seemed very remote now, nothing to do with Lara or the Villa Rasenna or anything. Things that become public property seem to lose any personal association they may once have had. Like Poggio Sanssieve.

By the ticket desk there was Harris with some guests whom he had been showing around. There were introductions.

'I'm going,' I said to him. 'Back to England.'

'This is *Signor* Tobasi.'

I nodded at the man. 'I'm saying goodbye, I'm afraid.'

'I am an old friend of Mr Hewison's,' the man said. 'This is a very fine display of his life's work.'

'It's just scraping the surface really. If you haven't already you should visit Lucri itself.'

The man smiled smugly. 'Perhaps.' He was small and squat, with a clipped beard and a panama hat now hiding his bald scalp in preparation for the sun outside. There was something almost Slavic about his appearance. I watched him go carefully down the stairs, testing each step with his toe before committing his weight to it.

Tobasi. The name seemed familiar.

'Well, goodbye, Harris.'

I didn't even know Harris's Christian name. He was the kind of man who went through life being addressed by surname alone; the kind of man who never seems to know anyone well enough to be on first name terms. I imagined that even his wife would long ago – as soon as the children came – have abandoned Alexander or whatever in favour of 'Father'. We shook hands with some affection, fellow workers, fellow victims of David Hewison's wrath, since the previous evening fellow carousers.

He glanced at his watch. 'Don't be late.'

'The train doesn't leave until after lunch.'

'Still.'

I turned and went down the stairs. And then I remembered. I took the stairs two, three at a time, dashed out onto the pavement. The sun was blinding. Cars were jammed into the street outside. There was hooting. Pedestrians threaded their way through like people in a maze.

Up towards Santa Maria Novella, nothing. Towards Piazza Goldoni a distant panama hat just disappearing. I ran. I thought I had lost him in the chaos of the square, but the hat was there again, turning onto the Lungarno. I caught up with him by the bridge.

'*Signor* Tobasi!'
'*Signor* Tobasi!'

He stopped and turned. I was running with sweat. His expression, curious and amused, made me feel foolish. Was I in pursuit of a phantom, here in the summer heat of Florence with the traffic grinding past on the Lungarno?

'Tobardi, Tobaldi, something of the kind,' Gianluca's voice whispered.

'David Hewison. I wanted to ask you something about him.'

'Please.' He inclined his head. He seemed a figure at odds with his surroundings, his shabby linen suit, his goatee beard and narrow, nervous eyes not Italian at all. I suddenly understood that what I had thought of as middle European was actually Jewish.

'If you are going my way?' He doffed his hat and indicated the bridge. 'There is a little place where I take my lunch.'

'Did you know Hewison during the war?' I asked as we walked. 'Were you one of the partisans?'

He raised his eyebrows and made a curious snuffling noise which might have been laughter, but he didn't answer. On the far side of the bridge he led the way to a drab little bar where they greeted him as '*professore*'.

'I like it because it is so bad,' he explained with another little snuffle. 'All the Florentine elegance nauseates me.'

His English was heavily accented and spoken with all the care of someone who has learned the language from books. Throughout our conversation he insisted on speaking the language in preference to Italian. He was of that particular cast of personality which thrives on the awkward and the dissenting: a doctrinaire Marxist in the west, he would be a liberal democrat in Russia; a Jew in the street, he would be a gentile in the synagogue. One had to disagree with him to get him to agree, and show no interest in order to awaken his.

'I am a philosopher,' he declared in the tone of one who expects a denial.

'Were you also one of Hewison's partisans?' I asked.

He sipped at a glass of white wine. The barman had come round to our table with a plate of bread rolls. Tobasi levered one open with his thumb to examine the contents. They seemed to meet with his approval.

'I would describe him as one of *my* partisans,' he said through a mouthful. He peered down and picked crumbs from his beard.

'But you fought with him?'

'By mere coincidence. What is the English saying? Necessity makes strange bedfellows?'

'I think it is misery.'

'Better. *Miseria* will do much better.' He took another mouthful. 'Do you know Italy well, Mr . . . ?'

'Lessing. Anthony Lessing. Well enough. My grandmother was Italian.'

'And what is your interest in this?'

'I am David Hewison's nephew.'

'Ah. I thought I detected the odour of journalism. But instead it is,' he made a disparaging face, 'a family interest. Well then, perhaps you will understand a little when I use the word *miseria*. It is the principal feature in the history of the Italian peoples, Mr Lessing. And when a people faces misery that is when it confronts it's destiny. Every such time this has happened in Italy the people have been *ingannata*.' He glared at me, not finding the English word.

'Betrayed.'

'Betrayed!' he repeated loudly. Bits of bread roll flecked the table in front of him. 'Italy is crushed by her burden of unfulfilled history, Mr Lessing. You should know. We even have a name for the phenomenon: *qualunquismo*. The Anglo-Saxons make a virtue of it and call it "business as usual", but *noi altri* cannot make a virtue of popular sentiment. Business as usual becomes for us "the usual reactionary ideas imposed in the usual reactionary way".'

'Are you a Communist?'

Tobasi chuckled. 'What does that mean, eh? *Anzi*, what do you mean by it?'

He hardly waited for an answer. 'In the days when I knew your uncle I could have answered yes to many more versions of that question than I can now. But since Togliatti's betrayal of the Italian proletariat . . .' He snorted indignantly. 'However it is of those times that you ask, times when I truly believed that we had it in our power to fulfil Italy's destiny, so you make take the answer as yes.'

'And did you fight in the partisan group called "Fabiomassimo"?'

The man's mouth turned down. 'That name. Yes, I was with them. I was sent down from the north, from Milano to help organize the south, the *gruppi di azione patriottica*. You must understand we were the only political party with any real organization at that time: we were the standard-bearers of anti-Fascism. We could bring the northern factories out on strike. We could organize absenteeism, sabotage. We had cells all over the north and therefore we could move around with relative safety. Twenty years under Fascism had taught us valuable lessons in the art of survival, so when the resistance groups started the only effective ones were those of the Party.'

I had the clear impression that all this had seethed in his mind for years, that for decades since the war it had bubbled up again, died away again, over and over like a natural ferment, doubtless being subtly transformed in the process.

'And what did I find on this mission to the south? I found a rabble of so-called Communists led by a man called Orlandi, a group of ineffectual liberals, a woman who was the wife of a *repubblichino*, and the Englishman. It was the Englishman who ruled, I saw that straight away. He had power over them, the usual capitalistic power of money of course, because he came with the support of the American war machine; but, more than that, he had the power of personality, a sort of inner conviction which they all bowed to.'

Tobasi stroked his beard lovingly. His eyes were bright with triumph. 'It was only I who saw that the conviction was founded on nothing.'

He paused, as though to let that insight impress itself on me.

'It is a northern disease, Mr Lessing. Maybe you can understand, maybe not. In the south it is impossible to be motivated by no philosophy whatever. That is why, despite all the corruption, we are still basically a religious people whether we call our religion Christianity or Communism. Between the Communist Party and the Christian Democrat

Party you have some seventy per cent of the popular vote, and both are confessional parties. But what declaration of faith do your political parties in England demand, eh? A belief in decency and fair play.' He laughed.

'You were talking about Hewison.'

Tobasi nodded. 'Exactly. Hewison had no faith at all; maybe a burnt-out Catholicism, but no real faith. A dead ember. And yet he ran "Fabiomassimo" with all the energy of a missionary, as though he believed in what he was doing. But for me it was quite different. I had a faith, and you must remember that at the time we also had the example of Marshal Tito to inspire us. We saw ourselves at the door of the great Italian revolution in which the old liberals who had betrayed Italy in the past would be cast aside onto the ruins of Fascism. We believed that we were fulfilling our history, Mr Lessing.'

Tobasi waved his bread roll at me. He seemed a faintly ridiculous figure delivering a street corner oration across a café table, but perhaps all the other audience had fled. He bit into his roll again. 'And there was the reactionary Hewison in charge. I saw my task as taking control from him.'

It was not difficult to imagine a power struggle between the two men, the Jewish activist from the north whose mind was steeped in the arcane lore of international Communism, and the English officer whose motives were as obscure as those of the rest of his race.

'And you succeeded?'

A wordless shrug. He chewed and drank, and pushed the remaining roll towards me.

'What defence does such a man possess when faced with conviction?' he asked. 'Hewison was still obsessed with the problems of personal morality although he had lost any basis for it. The classic dilemma of modern western man, don't you agree? Whereas I was, shall we say, inspired by history? For me all morality, every human relationship, was tested against that simple standard: would it move us one millimetre nearer the historical revolution? How do you think a man like Hewison could survive in the face of that?'

I had no doubt. I watched him curiously, this artifact from Hewison's past which chance had thrown up in front of me like a potsherd thrown up by a plough. Behind his ridiculous exterior there was something hard and cold about him, something quite ruthless.

'What can you tell me about Alessio?' I asked abruptly.

The man paused, with glass raised and lips open. Then slowly, watching me all the time, he drank.

'You have the manner of a lawyer, Mr Lessing.'

'I'm not one.'

'But what is your interest, I wonder? Just devotion to your relative? Or something else?'

'I know his son, Alessio's son.'

He nodded thoughtfully. 'And what have you learned from him?'

'That his father was a Fascist. That the partisans took him hostage.'

'You know why?'

'In reprisal for the hostages of Vetrano.'

'Possibly.' Tobasi drained his glass. 'Partly,' he corrected.

'There was another reason?'

'Motives in war are never very simple. There may have been a dozen other reasons.'

'Is it any different in peace time?'

'Probably not. But the revolutionary situation makes things more acute. For example,' he waved his hand. 'For example, Hewison's commitment to our cause was of great concern then. It was a matter of the utmost significance, a matter of life and death.'

'Was it ever in doubt?'

Tobasi sniffed. 'Perhaps you do not know he was the lover of your friend's mother.'

He looked for a reaction but I denied him the satisfaction.

'Does that have anything to do with it? I understand she was not in sympathy with her husband's cause. She was a dedicated partisan.'

'Possibly,' repeated Tobasi.

'Did you have any evidence to the contrary?'

'She was a liberal. That is always evidence to the contrary.'

'So the kidnapping of her husband was partly to test Clara Alessio?'

218

'Another reason, if you like.'

'In fact Alessio's kidnap was as much to test people as to free the hostages of Vetrano?'

'Oh, certainly. Surely you do not imagine that we were so naïve as to think that the Germans would worry about Alessio? No, no. The kidnap was really to temper the steel, to harden the committed and to expose the waverers.'

'And did it work?'

Tobasi seemed to savour the question. 'I would say, excellently. The Alessio woman, your friend's mother, was exposed as a weak link. She broke.' He gestured vaguely. 'She ran away to hide in Rome or something. And Hewison proved himself.'

'How?'

Tobasi's lips widened to display a sandwich filling of yellow teeth. His eyes swam with tears of amusement. 'We put Alessio before a revolutionary court. We tried him as a traitor to the Italian people. And naturally it was Hewison who defended him: the Englishman seeing that fair play was done right up to the end.'

'But he failed?'

'Failed?'

'In his defence of the man.'

'Failed?' Tobasi repeated. He had picked up a toothpick. Now, with great care, he began to probe his teeth. 'No, I wouldn't say he failed at all,' he said. 'I'd say he succeeded admirably. You see, it was Hewison who carried out the execution. Hewison shot Alessio.'

# XXII

# *Winter 1943/44*

THE People's Court never reconvened. In the sky above the wooded hills, well below the cloud base, there was an aircraft flying. It buzzed and whirred like an ill-designed toy. Its undercarriage hung below its fuselage like the legs of some monstrous crane fly. Its cockpit – plain enough through binoculars – looked as though it had been designed by a firm of glasshouse suppliers rather than aeronautical engineers. It was hardly to be accounted a warplane, yet somehow its very innocence, its clumsiness, its absurdity all gave it a sinister cast. Its very lack of threat threatened.

'A *deus ex machina*,' murmured Hewison, handing the binoculars back to Orlandi.

'A what?'

'A Fieseler Storch. I think perhaps we had better move from here.'

'Move?'

'It's looking for us.'

'How do you know that?'

'Well, they are hardly looking for General Alexander. Anyway we can't take any risks.'

There was some protest but he insisted. 'Our only strength is our weakness,' he said, knowing that paradox would appeal. 'A willow bends in the wind but always survives. It is the oak which the storm destroys.'

Rhetoric like that swayed Orlandi. It was a curious trait of the Italian character which Hewison had long ago understood: presented with a reasoned argument the instinct was to marshal a counter-argument; presented with a piece of imagery, however feeble, the average man would agree.

'But first we must execute the Fascist,' protested Tobasi.

'There is no time to finish the trial. If we move we move at once. If they know we are here . . .' He let his words trail away meaningfully.

Orlandi said, 'I know where we can go. They'll never find him.'

'We should kill him now. What the hell does the trial matter?'

'But you agreed to the trial.'

'A willow bends with the wind,' Tobasi retorted. 'Why should you stand by the man in this way?'

Why indeed? 'Because we are fighting for decent values, not for the values of arbitrary arrest and arbitrary killing.' He could hear Clara answering that one.

'I know where we can take him,' insisted Orlandi. 'Not too far away from here. Caves.'

They heard the sound of the other aircraft even as they made their way through the woods. It was a much louder sound than the Storch's, much more the heavy roar of a warplane.

'A bomber,' suggested Tobasi, but no bombs fell. Standing amongst the bare trees with a thin drizzle coming down through the branches and riming their clothes like a heavy dew they listened anxiously; but no explosions came.

'What then?'

Someone, a surly youth nicknamed Berlicche, said the dread word 'Paratroopers'.

Hewison shrugged. 'Maybe it's just a coincidence.' The aircraft had made its pass. The noise of its engines was fading towards the south. 'Let's get a move on.'

So they went on. The march was slow and tedious, made slower and more tedious by the reappearance of the Fieseler Storch circling over the bare winter woods, now coming low to examine a hut which might house fugitive partisans, now circling away over a hill where movement – a fox? a boar? – had been spotted amongst the undergrowth, but always in the vicinity, searching. There was an oppressive quality about the presence of that aircraft, a teutonic determination which reminded Hewison of a fox hunt he had once witnessed in Tuscany as a child: men in heavy coats and wide-brimmed hats standing at the entrance to an earth waiting for the terriers to do their work; men digging laboriously when the dogs could do no more; spades rising and falling over a bloodied corpse. He felt the same sense of inevitability now.

'Paratroopers,' Berlicche had said, and somehow he sensed them behind them in the woods, remorseless as a nightmare, grim men in grey with a job to do.

The march went on. Orlandi took the lead with his men, then Alessio stumbling along between two guards, then Hewison, then Tobasi at the back. The party ploughed through deep leaf mould, battled through trackless brambles and scrub, slogged up hills whose summits were tree-clad and featureless, pushed down into valleys which seemed not to have been visited by man for centuries. They heard nothing behind them, but the word 'paratroopers', once uttered and never repeated, drove them on.

Alessio began to tire. At one point he had to stop in order to be sick. His cheeks were grey and a thin foam of spittle had gathered at the corners of his mouth. His breathing came short and harsh as he crouched over his vomit.

'He needs a rest.'

'There's no time to rest. It's not far now.'

The roles had been neatly reversed. Orlandi was now the advocate of flight, Hewison the champion of waiting. From behind Tobasi said, 'If he's a problem we can always leave him.' He did not mean alive.

Hewison took Alessio by the elbow to help him up. The man wiped specks of vomit from his chin and regarded Hewison with irony.

'I was right about you, wasn't I? You are different. You stand aside from all this.' He made a gesture which implied more than the woodland and the band of dirty partisans who stood around him in a circle. He meant the war, Italy's own civil war. 'You *are* English.'

Hewison pushed at the man. '*Andiamo. Forza.*'

The partisans were watching the two men with curiosity. Orlandi urged them on.

Alessio nodded at his own judgement. 'I might have guessed American, but you have a European subtlety which the transatlantics lack. It can only be English.'

'I'm Italian.'

'Oh partly, I'm sure.' Alessio stumbled forward in the wake of the partisans. He managed a glance over his shoulder. 'You couldn't speak the language as you do without being part Italian. Brought up here, I suppose. But not wholly Italian. There's no involvement, no passion in you. You're a hybrid.'

'Shut up!' Tobasi shouted.

'A hybrid Italian,' Alessio went on. 'A chimera.'

'Shut up, you bastard!' Tobasi pushed forward past Hewison and swung his Sten gun into Alessio's back. The man grunted in pain and fell forward onto his knees. Hewison put out a hand to stop another blow.

'Leave him. That's what he wants.'

'It's what he'll get.' Tobasi's eyes were bright with hate, his mouth compressed.

'Leave him.' Hewison took the prisoner's elbow and helped him up again. Alessio smiled through his pain as though he had won a victory. He walked on in silence.

Later they halted beside a stream where years ago nameless people had constructed a boulder dam. It was a fine piece of work which must once have held back a head of water for a mill race. Amongst the bushes was the ruin of a building. Large grey millstones lay half-buried in the grass.

'*La mola*,' announced Orlandi.

There was a cascade of water through a breach in the dam. The roar of the falling water was loud enough to force him to shout. 'We go on up the stream.'

A circuitous path led up from the ruin. Hewison stood for a moment where he could get a view back some of the way they had come, at a country once settled and fertile, once a nucleus of civilization in the barbarian peninsula, now haunted by its past only because modern man had given it no present; at least nothing beyond their own savage little war.

Tobasi was waiting impatiently for him to move.

Up above the dam the river had cut a deep gorge. It was tree-filled and loud with the sound of water. The sense of architectural eternity about the place lived in a strange harmony with its air of decay: the cliffs of brown tuff at once impervious to change and as transient as dust; the river which slid between them both feeble and a vehicle of destruction.

'The caves are further up,' Orlandi called.

Of course they were not natural caves. Like the eyes and mouths of carnival masks they stared vacantly out of the blank rock walls, partly obscured by the vegetation which clung to the rock and approachable only over a pile of mossy boulders. Of course they were Etruscan tombs.

'They are perfectly dry,' Orlandi shouted. 'And unless you know they are here . . .'

He led the way up over the boulders, followed by his band of partisans humping their meagre equipment. It was difficult getting Alessio to follow. The rocks were slippery and he was only wearing town shoes. Hanging onto Hewison's arm he slithered and struggled, and when they finally got him up and onto the ledge he was pale and winded, barely able to stand.

While Hewison watched over the prisoner the rest of the group held a hurried meeting. Hewison felt that he had finally lost hold over them, that his power had been drained away from him by his defence of Alessio and by the subtle machinations of Tobasi. And he felt tired, physically tired of struggling through this damned wilderness, but also tired of Alessio's voice, tired of his taunts and his ironies, tired of having to be understanding towards a man whom he had disliked ever since Clara had first spoken of him; tired too of having to admit to himself that Alessio was not the insensitive fool that he had always imagined.

There was, he knew, an easy way out. When Orlandi and Tobasi came from the meeting he offered no protest.

'Take him then,' he said turning away towards the mouth of the cave. 'Take him and do what you like.'

But Tobasi grabbed his sleeve. He was smiling, shaking his head.

'I'm sorry, I'm not too familiar with the gospels. How does it go? "I am innocent of this Man's blood: you see to it." Is that correct? He was right, you know? What he said about

224

you. You aren't an Italian, you are a hybrid. You are neither for us nor against us: you are just playing this for games.'

With an air of finality he pushed Hewison back towards the prisoner. 'Well now the games are finished, *signor ibrido*. Now you can kill him.'

Then he left Hewison and the prisoner alone on the ledge and went into the cave where the others were waiting.

Alessio looked up at Hewison. Even at a moment like this he contrived an ironical smile. 'Is this what you expected, Englishman?' he asked. 'Is this what you expected when you set out to war?'

'Shut up.'

'Is it what Clara expected when she set out to betray me?'

'She didn't set out to betray you. There was nothing you can blame her for.'

'Oh, but I don't blame her. I sympathize. The flesh is always weak, isn't it? But what you are about to do cannot be passed off as a momentary weakness of the flesh. Now you are going to damn your soul.'

There was a silence. A cold wind was buffeting the ledge and Hewison shivered. He tried to gather his thoughts into some kind of order, but for once he failed. His circumstances were far beyond appeals to reason. He had stepped into a world of pure chaos.

'Let's get on with it,' he said, as though he was referring to something distasteful but quite ordinary. He pulled Alessio to his feet.

A path of sorts led diagonally upwards through the trees from where they stood, presumably the traces of a way which had once given access to the tombs from the higher ground. Hewison urged Alessio towards it. He had a vague sense that death, like birth and love, was something that demanded privacy.

As they went Tobasi called from the cave, 'I'll give you five minutes.'

The two men stumbled and slithered in the leaf mould, pulling themselves up on branches and roots, clambering over more boulders. After a while there was a small clearing guarded by an outcrop of rock. The rock was split at its base by a narrow cave from which a small spring issued. Alessio stumbled into the space and sat down on a boulder beside the stream.

'So,' he said. He sat with his back towards Hewison, staring across the gorge to the far side. His grey hair was plastered against his scalp. His suit was muddied, torn at one elbow and sodden up to the knees. He was shivering slightly, from fear or cold or an amalgam of both Hewison could not say. Hewison rather thought not fear; it was he who was shivering from fear. He wondered how much time had already passed and he glanced at his watch before realizing that he had not looked at it at the beginning and that what it said meant nothing. Did time pass quickly or slowly in circumstances such as these? He had no means of knowing. Nothing they had taught him at the Club said anything about this.

Unexpectedly Alessio looked round at him.

'Give me a few moments, if you please. In the absence of a priest . . .' He attempted a smile. His face was grey, slick with sweat, but paradoxically he seemed far more composed than Hewison felt.

'Of course.'

'Ever a gentleman, *la mia chimera*.' When he had used the word before it had sounded abusive, but this time the possessive pronoun gave it an oddly affectionate sound, like a father talking to a son. He turned back towards the view across the valley and sat still for some time, his elbows on his knees, his hands clasped beneath his chin. And while Alessio sat and prayed, or whatever it was he was doing, Hewison thought of Clara and Gianluca: Clara pale and naked, splayed open before him; Gianluca on his knees in front of him, begging.

After a while, still without taking his eyes from the view before him, Alessio said, 'Thank you.'

Hewison fumbled with the flap of his webbing holster. He drew his automatic pistol and slid the action back to cock it. With one hand he pulled his scarf from his neck and wrapped it clumsily around the weapon to deaden the sound. Then, holding the gun with both hands as he had been taught, he took two steps nearer the prisoner. Alessio must have heard all this, but he made no move. His very immobility was a kind of reproach.

With the muzzle of his pistol one foot from the back of Alessio's head and Clara's image still in his mind, Hewison fired.

The shot, barely muffled by the scarf, rang around the valley. Long after the whole thing was over, to Hewison's mind the sound still seemed to be there, detached from its origins, ringing around the landscape. The impact knocked Alessio from his seat and flung him forward and down the slope. He came to a stop with his limbs folded under him and his head resting against a stone, his face half turned sideways. Hewison ran down to him. His features were crumpled into the grass, but a single eye looked out at what remained of his world.

Before anything could happen, before that single, accusing eye could blink or the crumpled mouth move, Hewison placed the muzzle of his pistol against Alessio's temple and fired again.

# XXIII

'HEWISON shot Alessio.'

The train wound its way up to the Fréjus tunnel, rocking from side to side on the curves, while Tobasi's face smiled at me out of the darkness of my sleeping compartment.

'Hewison shot Alessio.'

I dozed fitfully, waking into a half-consciousness that seemed full of fear, falling back into a sleep that was nightmare: the shabby bar, the shabby little man disposing of dog-eared bread rolls and moral dilemmas with equanimity. The simple standard.

But nothing was simple.

'Hewison shot Alessio.'

I felt like a voyeur, like someone who has discovered a peep-hole through into the next room and stays there for days with his eye glued to it, watching. Where did that metaphor come from? For a while in my insomnia I pursued that irrelevance before turning back to the central fact: there was the peep-hole; and beyond it not the next room with whatever mundane little dramas went on there, but the past. Hewison's past. I was a voyeur of that past, with my eye pressed to the hole and my breath coming short and sharp and desperately suppressed lest the protagonists should hear and make my single hungry eye part of their existence.

The sensation both thrilled and shamed me. I peered through the hole and watched David Hewison take possession of a family, an entire family: their bodies, their souls, and finally, for that is total possession, their deaths. The present survivors were doomed as surely as the past victims. Lara's face bled tears at me and said, 'The only way she had to fight against it was to die,' but that did not make her any less a

228

victim. Knowing that you have a disease is no cure; it may be that it is the principal symptom.

Disease was the right metaphor: possession from within, the inexorable metastasis of a cancer, drawing corruption from healthy tissue and laying the body waste exactly as it had laid waste Lara's mother, or my mother. Lara's face bled tears at me, but her face lay beyond the milky white reflection of the window pane like a face seen through the pale stuff of a shroud.

I wondered whether I might not be the physician with the cure to hand – or the exorcist.

'*Exorciso te, immundissime spiritus, in nomine Domini nostri Jesu Christi.*'

My emotions were drawn in primary colours and bold shapes: hate for David Hewison, love for Lara, pity for Gianluca; no compromises.

'Can you understand what possession means?'

I felt I could.

CHAMBÉRY, said the name board outside my window. The air was cold. I watched a solitary railway worker clump along the platform dragging a water hose behind him. He fixed it beneath the carriage with a sullen efficiency, banging at the fitting. Knock! Knock! Faith here's an equivocator . . .

I fell asleep as the train began to move once more, and through my sleep David Hewison floated down beneath a white moon to take possession while I invaded his room at Poggio Sanssieve once again, going through the clothes in his wardrobe, going through the cupboards, going through the drawers, finding once again the revolver. I raised it and cocked it once more, but this time I pointed it at a man called Alessio and blew his brains out.

Dawn was the low hills of Burgundy and my reflection floating in the glass, and a headache. There is nothing more mundane than morning on a train. The sleeping car attendant brought fresh orange juice and aspirin. He looked sympathetic. The more you tip me the more sympathetic I'll be.

The train shuddered over the points and rattled through the purlieus of Dijon, and the distance behind was a palpable thing, a ribbon of railway line telescoping out, shifting the

229

Villa Rasenna further and further back in perspective, diminishing it with each mile covered. A train journey is itself an experience. It drums itself into the mind with its complex syncopation, its shifting and swaying, its litany of passing names, its changing cast of characters. By the time the train was sliding along under a leaden sky and the names glimpsed through the windows were Etaples, Abbeville, Boulogne-sur-Mer, Lucri seemed impossibly remote.

EVITEZ L'ODEUR AVEC EVIT-O. LABORATOIRES HEWISON. REIMS.

The cry of gulls and the taste of salt. England was that smear of shadow on a grey horizon; Italy did not exist.

It was this sense of remoteness which allowed me the pretence of reconstructing some kind of life in London. I looked up old friends, visited old haunts, made one or two new acquaintances; but I never really believed in my efforts. For days on end, aside from my work, I saw no one. In a more acute way than ever before I felt a sensation of being cast adrift, and what seemed like order and method in my life was actually, if I examined it carefully, pure chaos: like crystals dissolving in water or smoke spreading through a room. My course through the chaos was a random one to which I could give a spurious sense of purpose only in retrospect. I felt all the time that I was waiting for something to happen.

I wrote a brief letter to Anna and to my surprise received a reply, a post-card of the Florence skyline, almost the view from her flat. The message was bright and friendly:

'Ciao. *La mostra va benissimo. Ora è deciso che si inizierà a Roma il 24 gennaio. Ci vediamo? Anna.*'

The exhibition was going well and would be opening in Rome on 24 January. Would she see me there?

My letter to David and Lara vanished without trace, like a stone dropped into a deep well.

'I feel that I must make a positive effort to start again,' I had written, 'but I will always owe both of you, and Lucri, an enormous debt because you gave me something new to work for just when I needed it. I think of the Villa Rasenna and everyone there with great affection.'

Nothing I wrote was exactly untrue; but nothing came near the real truth.

The apotheosis of David Hewison took place just when the autumn was crumbling into an early winter. I suppose it was exactly the moment for something exotic, something a bit magical, something from a warm, southern climate to capture the public imagination. The prosaically-titled television documentary 'Lucri: an Etruscan Town Revealed' seemed to provide the very thing.

The whole affair acquired a momentum of its own. Local librarians found themselves pestered for books on the Etruscans. The Etruscan rooms at the British Museum became a significant centre of attraction, drawing crowds of children away from the mummies and the Rosetta stone and Lord Elgin's plunder. Those few people who had had the good fortune to have visited the painted tombs at Tarquinia or the necropolis of Cerveteri found themselves called on to air their scant knowledge at parties and in the pub. A travel firm included amongst its offerings for next summer 'An Etruscan Adventure'. A major fashion designer announced that he was into the Etruscan look. I viewed the whole thing with a mixture of amusement and disquiet.

When I opened a newspaper one Sunday morning and found David Hewison staring out at me from the cover of the colour supplement it was like taking the lid off a coffin.

DAVID HEWISON: A SECOND ARTHUR EVANS? the title asked from a piece of dead space beside the man's right knee. The picture itself was not a thing to be passed over lightly: his gaunt frame was exaggerated by a wide-angled lens, his face stared out at the reader with the over-stated proportions of an Aztec mask. In his hands was a muddied bronze figurine which he cradled gently, like a baby just rescued from an earthquaked house. The background was the stones and trenches of the excavation and, beyond, the holm oaks and cliffs of the necropolis.

Quite deliberately I avoided seeing the television film when it was broadcast, but on a visit to Guerdon House we all found ourselves watching a televised talk in which Francis Arden-

Tillyard appeared with the Italian Cultural Attaché and the Keeper of Etruscan Antiquities at the British Museum, discussing the importance of the Anglo-Italian archaeologist David Hewison and the possibility of bringing the Lucri exhibition to London.

'After all,' said the presenter, 'such treasures belong to the world, don't they?'

The British Museum man, thinking of the Elgin Marbles, nodded emphatically.

'Not when we've poured so much money into finding them,' muttered Honjohn.

At his wife's insistence I had already given a carefully edited account of my experiences at Lucri, the kind of thing Harris would have liked: 'an excavation of world importance.'

'Sounds wild fun,' Rosamund declared. 'And what about the love child?'

'What on earth do you mean?'

'The wife. Isn't she a delicious little peasant girl?'

'Rosamund,' I had answered her, 'we are none of us boys and girls any longer. She's no more a girl than you are, and less of a peasant.'

'Anthony!'

'Well, it was a stupid thing to say.'

Cordiality balanced on a razor's edge and Honjohn was constrained to take me aside, muttering about the shock of my mother's death and the great unity of the family. Rosamund retired in dudgeon.

'How are your affairs, old chap?' Honjohn enquired nervously. I laughed, but he didn't see the joke. 'We are all awfully sorry about your marriage, old fellow. My father is particularly sympathetic. But let's be honest, we never did think her as exactly – how shall I put it? Suitable.'

'I'm sure you didn't. But I was in love with her.'

He pondered this for a moment. 'Thing is, Anthony, just between you and me of course, I don't really think that's the point. I can't really say that I have ever been in love with Rosamund, not *in love* as you might say. I look upon marriage more as a kind of contract which parties negotiate in full awareness of the implications, and so does she. Now I think that this is only being realistic. Of course there's nothing to stop love being a clause in the contract, nothing at all. But I don't think you want to make it the *only* clause, if you see what I mean. Then if the . . .' His voice died away. A dreadful thought had occurred to him. 'I say, there's not going to be a divorce, is there?'

'Divorce? Does it matter, John? We weren't married in church so I don't see that a divorce should offend the family sensibilities.'

I could see him struggling with the theological implications. 'No, I suppose not. It was different with Aunt Felicity, but then you could say that in her case the contract was flawed from the beginning.'

'What do you mean by that?'

'Well, he was a Protestant, wasn't he, your father?'

I laughed at his absurdity. 'I don't think it was any contract that was flawed. I think it was my mother herself.'

Even against his sentimental regard for the dead he had to admit the truth in that. He sighed deeply and shook his head. 'First your mother, now you. I wonder if it runs in the family.'

During Prime Minister's question time two days later a Liberal member of Parliament put down a question asking whether, in view of the sad neglect of one of Britain's greatest academic luminaries and mindful of his most gallant war record as well as his selfless dedication of a personal fortune to the furthering of human knowledge, it was not high time that H.D.Hewison be given some official recognition by her Majesty's government. The Prime Minister replied in anodyne terms. At the same time *The Times* ran a leading article on British archaeology since the war, while the *Times* Diary revealed that Hugh David Hewison had once served as an officer of the Special Operations Executive, and observed that a combination of scholarship and irregular warfare was a not uncommon feature of British History. To a list which included Sir Richard Burton, T.E. Lawrence and W.F. Deakin, asserted the diarist, the name of H.D. Hewison could be added.

My disquiet turned to foreboding as my office began to receive enquiries from the Press. I knew the signs well enough. Like dogs around a buried corpse the Press scratched and nosed, sensing that there was something there beyond the elegant musings of the *Times* diarist and the imprecations of Liberal members of Parliament.

WAR HERO ARCHAEOLOGIST ESTRANGED FROM PILL FAMILY, a tabloid newspaper shouted from its middle pages.

> The heir to one of Britain's largest fortunes denies that there is any bad blood between ex-secret agent Hugh Hewison and the famous family which funds his life's work. But reliable sources admit that the world important excavation which the prodigal son has been undertaking for the last two decades is proving a serious drain on the . . .

And so on. Ironically it appeared beside a Ban-O advertisement, but this time Ban-O could not work its magic and cover the stench. Hewison Pharmaceuticals Ordinary Shares dropped a dozen points on the stock market and Honjohn summoned me to his office.

'Was it you?'

'Don't be absurd, John.'

'My father is furious.'

'I'm sure he is.'

'Family loyalty and all that.'

'I said it wasn't me.'

He eyed me as though I were an unreliable cow, likely to give him a kick in the groin just as he was emphasizing some attractive feature to a dealer.

'Then I have to believe you.' For Honjohn the simple fact was that I had been to the Villa Rasenna and in some alchemic way my unnatural presence there must have stirred the whole thing up.

'There were television people all over the place when I was there,' I protested. 'Press, cameras, the lot. He's been discovered, that's all. These things happen. And the tabloids have to have a bit more.'

'But why now? Why now after twenty years? I haven't told my father but I happen to know that you have been acting as public relations officer to Uncle David.' His voice had grown shrill and his farmer's face had acquired a healthy flush. 'It is a gross disloyalty, even a breach of contract.'

'How the devil do you know about it? Anyway it was perfectly innocent, nothing more than helping him out with this exhibition in Florence, along with the British Council. Good God, John, you're becoming paranoid.'

He stiffened. 'I'm not.'

A portrait of Sir Gordon stared down at him and reminded him of insanity. He walked away to stare out of the window and worry about his mental health.

'Then for God's sake stop worrying about plots and believe the truth. All that has happened is that the Press has scratched around a bit and come up with a hand.'

He turned. 'What is that supposed to mean?'

I was feeling angry and confused. 'I mean that if we're unlucky they might dig up the whole corpse.'

He didn't answer. I wonder if he had any idea what I meant.

It was winter. The weather was wet and sour. In the parks the trees lost their leaves and almost simultaneously the shops put on their seasonal tawdry of tinsel, cottonwool and neon. The interest of the popular Press in David Hewison died away as I had supposed it would, but he was not altogether forgotten in other ways. A feature in a magazine entitled 'The Hundred Men and Women of the Year' had David Hewison's face peering out uneasily between an American physicist who had discovered yet another fundamental particle and a French anthropologist who had pushed man's origins yet another million years back into the Pleistocene. The potted biography beneath the picture gave a bare outline of his work and dubbed him 'the most significant figure in archaeology since Sir Leonard Woolley'.

Rosamund rang to invite me for 'family Christmas at Guerdon. You'll come? Super.' So I suppose that I had been forgiven and the family still considered me worth saving.

The same day a letter arrived at the office bearing a Vatican City stamp and postmark.

'Greetings from the pope?' asked one of the secretaries.

The handwriting – that convoluted script which is typically Italian – was not familiar. My Christian name was misspelt. I remember sitting and staring at the address and wondering whether this was what I had been waiting for, even wondering whether I should open it. My hands shook as I did.

Inside there was a card showing Fra Angelico's Annunciation. On the back was scrawled, 'Caro Antony' and a conventional greeting – 'Felice Natale e Buon Anno' or something which I barely read – 'con affetto, Lara.'

But underneath she had added:

'Nessun maggior dolore
Che ricordarsi del tempo felice
Nella miseria.'

Francesca da Rimini's poignant words from the second circle of hell:

'There is no greater sorrow
Than to remember happy times
In misery.'

The poignancy of innocence, the sweetness of corruption. I thought of Francis leaning back in his chair and staring out into the darkness of the gardens at Poggio Sanssieve.

'Innocence at one pole and corruption at the other, and the wretched people strung out between . . .'

I read the words over, absorbing the shape of her handwriting more than anything, making its unfamiliar curves and flourishes a part of my experience of her just as I had the curves and hollows of her body, because the words themselves I knew well enough, knew them as a cry from the second circle of hell, but as a cry without a shadow of repentance.

Christmas was an uneasy few days dominated by the presence of David's brother Thomas, a man whose power had always been wielded through the mechanisms of finance and management rather than by force of personality, a grey eminence with no one to stand behind but himself. There was no mention of my aberration, my visit to David, but the fact of it seemed to hang over the festivities as a threat.

One evening, finding himself alone with me, Thomas took it upon himself to talk as father to son – 'for surely I am as near as anything a father to you.'

'I feel for you, my boy,' he said. 'I feel for you in the loss of your wife as well as the loss of your mother. These things happen, oh indeed, these things happen, and it is up to us to face them like . . .' here he paused, not quite knowing what like. 'Crusaders,' he decided at last. 'Crusaders, obeying orders and staying firm in the Faith. As your mother did, sticking at it to the end.'

And I saw my mother, a Belsen figure with scrubbed scalp and wasted limbs, shuffling down the corridor of the hospice and clutching her midriff to herself as though clutching a great treasure. But actually she was clutching her liver, the organ which finally betrayed her.

'Loyalty is what matters,' asserted my uncle. 'Loyalty to our Faith and to our family, whatever might have happened in the past. Loyalty.'

And indeed he was right. Loyalty is the great watchword. It ought to be displayed in mighty letters in every factory of Hewison Pharmaceuticals, above the ranks of women popping blister packs of 'female endocrine regulant' pills into boxes labelled 'Gynotrol':

Loyalty and Hard Work.

Motivated by this loyalty on Christmas Eve we went as a family to midnight Mass at Welwyn Garden City, to the church which Sir Gordon Hewison had had constructed out of red brick and loyalty to Rome near the Hewison Laboratories. There is a Hewison chapel in the church, a kind of twentieth-century chantry where masses are said for his soul and Nonna Angelica's. Above the altar is a stained glass window showing a plague-ridden Saint Roch with his dog, along with the exhortation to be 'loyal unto God'. Saint Roch is showing the plague spot on his knee. The piece of bread in the dog's mouth looks suspiciously like a box of pills.

It was during that service, kneeling down like some caricature of a crusader knight, that I made up my mind where my own loyalties lay.

# XXIV

As soon as I arrived in Rome I found the number of the British Council and telephoned Harris.

His tone was an uneasy blend of surprise and suspicion. 'Where are you?'

'Here in Rome. I thought I'd get to the opening of the exhibition.'

'Yes, of course.' There was a pause which I didn't bother to fill. 'Actually we've got a do at the Council the evening before. Actually we're showing that television documentary they were making in the summer, remember? Perhaps you saw it in England.'

'I managed to miss it.'

'Oh.'

'But I'd like to see it now.'

'Yes. There's a bit of a reception afterwards, you know the kind of thing. H.E. will be there, and the Minister.'

'Church or State?'

'What?'

'It doesn't matter. Will Hewison come?'

'He's been invited.'

'With Lara?'

'Lara?'

'His wife.'

'Of course. How silly. Yes, naturally. They're both on the list, but I haven't heard anything.'

'And I'm invited?'

'I suppose so. I can add your name to the list if you want. Yes, that'd be a good idea.' He sounded relieved, as though that had got him out of any further obligations. Perhaps memories of the last evening in Florence were an embarrassment. 'Well, I won't keep you,' he said, as though it was he who had telephoned. 'See you then.'

Then I dialled the number of the Villa Rasenna. The phone rang for a long time before anyone answered and then it was only Rosa. Lara was at the dig and was not expected until the evening.

'Is she well?' I asked stupidly. I could sense puzzlement in Rosa's reply. Certainly she was well.

I felt an absurd resentment that her life might be continuing as normal without my being there to witness it, almost as though I had imagined her in some kind of limbo all this time, still staring out of the upper window after me.

'Good,' I said. 'I'll ring back later then. Tell her I rang.'

I left the hotel and went for an aimless walk around the streets, ending up, like so many tourists, in Piazza Venezia. Beneath the balcony from which Mussolini had harangued the crowds I watched the traffic swirl past and up towards the marble confection of the Victor Emmanuel monument. There were military buses parked there and soldiers forming up on the steps for some kind of ceremony.

'Anzio,' said a *carabiniere* at the police barriers when I asked. 'The anniversary of the landings.'

The twenty-second of January.

An NCO was trying to get soldiers into some kind of order. They were national servicemen and not very adept. Behind and above them was the tomb of the unknown soldier, its perpetual flame flickering faintly in the milky sunlight. Over everything rose the great cliff of the monument itself, *L'Altare della Patria*, white and glittering and hollow inside, like meringue. Hidden behind it, with an irony which struck me even as a child, stands the Aracoeli, the Altar of Heaven, and below that the beautiful *piazza* from where the Emperor Marcus Aurelius, the most perfect pagan, addresses the world from horseback.

Rome is a preposterous city, a colossal fluke, a scrap heap of every past and every idea which Europe has ever suffered. Here you can have anything you please, any epoch, any philosophy, any political system. Any illusion too. Somewhere amongst my papers is a photograph which has always

followed me around, which for a long time was the picture I
kept pinned on the inside of my locker door at school, a
photograph of my mother and me posing beneath the Marcus
Aurelius statue. The colours are fading now, but not the
memory. It was, I suppose, the only summer when she did not
leave me at Poggio Sanssieve.

'You should come and join us, Jack,' she had said.

Jack, behind the camera, had only laughed. 'Not yet.'

'How would you like Jack to join us?' she asked me. 'Not
just now, but forever? How would you like Jack as a new
father?'

I knew what they did. At the hotel her room was next to
mine. The walls were thin and I could hear them plainly
enough every night. It was as though he was attacking her,
kicking her onto the bed, pummelling her and driving cries
from her with every blow; but I knew it was not that. I knew
what it was.

'Not at all,' I answered.

Jack had laughed awkwardly and pressed the shutter
release, thus preserving for posterity my wooden certainty and
my mother's nervous smile. In my schoolboy slang a 'jack' was
an erection. I did not see him again after that particular
holiday and when she next came to visit me at school she was
accompanied by a younger man, altogether more beautiful
than Jack, altogether less interested in her young son.

Was I, just as my mother had been, in pursuit of an illusion
here?

On my return to the hotel I rang the Villa again and this time
it was Lara who answered.

'*Pronto?*' I could recognize her voice in just that one word.

'It's Anthony.'

'Rosa said you had rung.' Her voice was as toneless as if she
were dealing with a wrong number.

'I'm in Rome. I wondered whether you received the invitation from the British Council.'

'Yes we did. Some time ago.'

I swallowed the thing in my throat. 'Will you be coming?'

'Some people will be. Jane and Charles and others.'

'But will you?'

'What?'

We spoke over each other, the inevitable confusion of the machine.

'Sorry, what did you say, Lara? I didn't catch it.'

'David says he can't be bothered with all this nonsense.'

'But you, will you be there? I want to see you.'

'Maybe, Anthony.'

'Please.'

'I'll try. Anyway the others will be there, but I'll try.'

'I'm not interested in the others.'

Then she laughed. 'I'll try.'

'Do. *Ciao*.'

'Goodbye, Anthony.'

'*Ciao*.' Which comes from Venetian dialect and means *schiavo*, slave. Your slave.

The lecture room at the British Council was almost full. There were a few Italians, many people from the English expatriate community, some African students, a leavening of clerical grey. The nuns looked like schoolmistresses of the nineteen-fifties, with only discreet crucifixes pinned to their jackets to proclaim their vocations. The priests were loud and jovial and hoped that people would find them rather liberal. I pushed through the crowd looking for Lara, but although it was a quarter of an hour after the scheduled start there was no sign of her. I noticed Jane in one corner talking patiently to two ancient ladies, and Charles pontificating to someone I recognized from the television crew. But there was no Lara.

Harris emerged from amongst the press. He had the distracted air of a weak swimmer just out of his depth. As he caught my eye he nodded a greeting, but he was struggling after a more important catch. Goffredo Macchioni was more welcoming, clasping both my hands in his and claiming me for a *un vecchio amico*.

'I am most sorry that *Signor* 'Ewison is not here,' he complained. 'He is too modest about his achievements, too modest. A great man.'

I thought of what I knew. The knowledge ticked away in my mind like a bomb. 'And Lara?'

'*Come?*'

But Harris was swimming back towards us with a big fish in tow.

'His Excellency, *Signor* Macchioni. His Excellency.'

Like many a British Ambassador this one lent a faintly colonial air to the proceedings. His words seemed to come from a prepared speech, the kind of thing one says to the natives. One sensed the ghost of the punkah wallah haunting him.

'Excellent demonstration of the cultural and commercial ties between our nations. I gather that Italian television is interested in it. I'm sure the whole thing will go swimmingly.'

And then Macchioni had been edged away from me to take his seat up at the front, and there was nothing to do but find myself a place and scan the audience for the last time, hopelessly. I felt faintly sick. I thought of what I knew, of what her face had been like looking out through the window at my departure, of her Christmas card which might have meant nothing, of her awful wooden voice on the telephone. I was, I suppose, clutching at straws. By now I had a handful of them, all knotted together and twisted into a corn doll whose shape was a grotesque caricature of Lara. But behind that the figure of David Hewison loomed vast and all-consuming, reducing me to the dimension of a child playing about his feet. As the audience's mutterings died away and the house lights dimmed I resigned myself to the fact that she was not coming, and the anger I felt was a petulant, child's anger directed at him.

The screen at the far end of the room lit up. It showed a track of bleak, scrub-covered hills. The camera began a slow pan leftwards while an asthmatic flute began to play a meandering tune.

'This,' said a voice in the darkness, 'is Tuscia. It is an Italy which few Italians know and the foreign visitor rarely sees, an Italy which lies a bare forty miles from the centre of Rome and nowadays is almost devoid of settlement. Yet here, two thousand five hundred years ago, lay the heartland of a great and beautiful civilization which taught the infant Rome all that she knew of religion and art and governance, and which was in turn destroyed by her pupil. Rome turned to Greece and aped her beauty. Etruria she desolated.'

The view shifted across hills and woods and valleys which I recognized almost with pain, until in the foreground there was a network of stones and the temple of Turan. The picture lunged forward. Full face, a terracotta demon leered out of the screen at us.

A thrill ran through the audience, and the voice of David Hewison sounded through the room saying, 'It is not a dead past, it is more a living thing, a resurrection.'

There was the figure of Charles pointing out the structure of the excavation in the manner of an army officer indicating battle lines, there was Meredith muttering over a fragmented pot, there was Goffredo taking the audience for a walk through the *tendopoli*, talking about the way the small army of volunteers had laboured over Lucri for so many summers. I even caught a glimpse of myself, sun-scorched and ragged amongst the ruins. The audience in the lecture room was silent. It was the animated conversation of the Villa Rasenna which flooded the darkened room, that arcane talk which the microphones had eavesdropped with such care one evening: Francis demolishing the reputation of some unfortunate archaeologist who, thanks to careful editing, would remain forever anonymous, Meredith telling an elaborate and faintly indecent joke about votive objects, Jane arguing a point about dating, Lara drifting into the picture with a word in Italian to her husband. The camera hung on Lara for a moment, and in my own mind the image remained long after the picture had changed.

But the image which stayed with me was a composite, made up of the spectrum of her moods and manners, concocted from my varied perceptions of her, her smell and taste, the smooth fabric of her skin, the structure of her limbs and body, the range of her expressions and the whole span of her thoughts. While the film ran on I saw only Lara, until once again she occupied the screen, but now in the form of the portrait, standing in hieratic robes with the Lucri jewellery gleaming against her skin and the voice of the commentator asking, 'Was this the treasure of an Etruscan priestess?'

The house lights came up with the applause. Some enthusiasts cried, 'Bravo!' The television director stood to acknowledge the clapping. Mr Harris was smiling in triumph.

Out of some instinct I half-rose in my seat and looked round at the blinking faces and the beating hands, and there she was, at the back of the room near the door, watching.

The audience was beginning to break up. Someone caught my elbow and said, 'Anthony, I didn't expect to see you here,' and I smiled hastily at a half-familiar face. Harris was edging his way down the aisle with the British Ambassador and the Minister. Precedence and politeness were battling for supremacy. They kept getting jammed between the two banks of chairs.

'There's Anthony Lessing,' said Charles's voice from somewhere behind me. I ignored him and pushed through the rows of people to Lara's side. She smiled a neutral, distant smile as I reached forward to kiss her.

'There's some kind of reception now, I think', I said. 'Are you staying?'

'I don't know. I . . .'

'I must talk with you alone somewhere.'

People seemed to be staring at us. The place suddenly seemed an awful crush of milling bodies, a trap. An anxious Mr Harris hove in sight with his two guests.

'Mr Lessing –' His expression was that of an irate governess about to say, 'Where are your manners?' In my determination to get to Lara's side I must have committed some awful solecism, but I was beyond caring.

'Can we get away from here?' I asked her.

Then Harris saw who it was. The effect was dramatic. He folded. Someone had tugged the stopper out of his belly and all the air rushed out in an explosive 'Oh!' Bereft of all support his arms tucked in towards his midriff. His neck folded so that his head started to settle sideways on his shoulders and for a delightful moment it seemed that he must entirely deflate there and then in the midst of his kingdom, to become a crumpled rubber heap on the floor over which the British Ambassador would step with diplomatic aplomb, hand held out towards Lara.

Regrettably some reservoir of British Council hot air was magically tapped. At the last possible moment Mr Harris reflated with an 'honoured guest' on his lips and an indulgent smile on his face:

'Ambassador, may I present . . .'

I suppose Harris's intervention had saved me from disaster. Like an anarchist who has planted a bomb which has failed to detonate I could walk quietly away and the thing might never have been.

'Didn't expect to see you here, Anthony,' Charles was saying in an indignant tone, as though he had been excluded from a secret. 'Quite a surprise, I must say.'

'It was quite a surprise to me really. Spur of the moment.'

'What spurred you, I wonder?'

I smiled at him. He could think what he liked. In Charles's hands the truth would be mauled beyond all recognition. 'I got fed up with the English weather.'

'Huh. I'm going back to it tomorrow. Something at Cambridge; what they call, with awe-inspiring accuracy, a symposium. All wine and waffle I always say.'

People edged around tables of tired-looking canapés and juggled with glasses of wine. Jane regarded me with a far more perceptive eye than did Charles.

'So the nephew returns,' she said. 'I had been wondering when,' and I had the feeling that with her no secrets existed, that she saw through every subterfuge. 'Francis says you did a wonderful job in Florence.'

What else had he said, I wondered? How much of our talk that evening at Poggio Sanssieve had found its origin in Jane's careful manipulations? I dismissed my efforts as of no account, which was true enough, and my flight back to England as motivated by a desire to 'sort things out'.

'Incidentally, I met a man in Florence who knew David during the war. Tobasi. Does the name mean anything to you?'

She was, I suppose, trained to it; or maybe it was only ever the ones like her whom Elwyn Davies and his kind recruited. There was nothing in her expression, no hint of recognition.

'David knows people all over the place.'

I nodded. Someone interrupted us and I took the opportunity to slip away. Jane watched me as I went but she was well trapped and couldn't follow. With little ceremony I extricated Lara from the grasp of some of the British Embassy staff.

'You were rude to them,' she said as I led her from the room, but I didn't really care. The door to the Council library was open. Inside there was the dusty smell of books and an atmosphere of impoverished learning. A notice forbade readers either to fall asleep or to remove their shoes.

'You were rude to Mr Harris as well.'

'I expect he will be in here soon with an eviction order.'

She smiled. All my intentions in distant England had come to this moment, with Lara watching me with that ironical smile and my knowledge pulsing inside my head like a migraine.

'Why didn't you come back from Florence?' she asked.

'Did you expect me to? I told you on the 'phone.'

She shrugged. 'I didn't know what to expect.'

She wandered away from me along a row of books. They all seemed to be either dark brown or dark blue, the common denominators of the book-binding trade. Her fingers must have drifted over a few million words before she pulled one volume out and flicked distractedly through it.

'When I was a child,' she said, 'I used to open the Bible like this when I wanted an answer to my problems. Just where it came open. You could always find the answer you were looking for if you were prepared to cheat a bit.'

'What answer are you looking for now?'

Her face puckered slightly, an expression which reminded me of that photograph of her as a girl. 'That's when the system lets you down, when you don't know the answer already.'

Then she read from the book she had taken: 'Those who have loved exceedingly can hate as much as they have loved.'

'That doesn't sound like the Bible.'

She glanced at the spine. 'It's not, so it doesn't count. *The Politics of Aristotle*.' She returned the book to its shelf and spoke while still facing away from me.

'When Francis came back from Florence he said that you had had a love affair there.'

'Francis is a poisonous bastard.'

'But is it true?' She looked round at me. There was no accusation, just that expression of faint irony, infinitely more disturbing than anger or jealousy.

'It was you,' I replied. 'Every minute of it was you, not her.'

'That's not very kind to her.'

'Who said anyone was being kind?'

We watched each other, words apart. The library door opened, allowing in a burst of sound from the reception like the outside world intruding upon a tomb. Someone looked in, said, 'I'm sorry,' and retreated.

'So tell me why you have come back now,' Lara asked, and I didn't know how to reply. Declarations of love are outmoded nowadays, as dead as museum exhibits, substituted by brightly-packaged declarations of lust. Love, with all its implications of faith and eternity and progeny, has become an embarrassment.

'What you wrote on your Christmas card.'

'*Il tempo felice*?'

I nodded.

'But at least Francesca could claim that she had never loved her husband. Her betrayal was a betrayal of a code . . .'

'And vows.'

'Yes, vows. Very mediaeval. Whereas –'

'You love David.'

'Yes, I love David.' She was smiling, not her childlike smile. No innocence there now. 'And you.'

The atmosphere in the library was suffocating. I felt like an asthmatic struggling to draw air against a constriction in my chest, suffocated by the name of David Hewison just as Lara was, fighting against it as she wasn't.

'I met a man called Tobasi in Florence,' I said deliberately. 'He knew David during the war.'

At that moment the door opened again and there, like a *deus ex machina*, was Harris: Harris indignant, Harris suspicious, Harris puzzled by a mood he sensed but did not understand. Harris with the Minister for Culture at his shoulder.

'The Minister is about to depart.'

We came out into the hallway like guilty children. The

247

Minister was effusive. He had decided that a stilted blend of English and Italian fitted the occasion and he drove this language mercilessly through every obstacle. Our discomfiture was no hindrance.

'*Un opera d'arte, una* creation,' he exclaimed. '*Signor* Evison is a man of *grandezza*, a great Italian, *un grand' inglese. Come siamo* fortunate to know him.'

'How kind,' replied Lara.

The Minister raised her hand and brought his mouth to within an inch of her smooth knuckles. I watched in fascination, remembering her hands and what they had done with me.

'*Enchanté,*' the man said, as though to demonstrate trilingualism. Then he swept out of the building with minions scurrying in his wake like minnows following a large carp.

'David loathes him,' Lara remarked, but Harris knew better.

'Very significant. Within the coalition, if you take my meaning. And now, if you will excuse me, I must return . . .'

Muttering threats against librarians who leave doors unlocked he left us on our own in the hall. It was an absurdly baroque place. Above our heads allegorical figures, doubtless with names like Faith and Piety and Hope, cavorted across a domed ceiling. On the walls were mirrors framed with gilt wreaths and supported by gilt *putti*. I could see our figures reflected in the glass as though I was looking at them through a window: a rather pale man whose drawn face suggested that he was recovering from an illness, and a dark-haired woman whose solemn expression might have been interpreted as concern for the man's health. But mirrors only give an illusion of depth. Looking straight at her I knew that what looked like concern was only confusion.

'What were you saying?' she asked.

'It doesn't matter. Nothing important.'

A man from the *Soprintendenza Archeologica* approached us. '*La Signora* 'Ewison? We met once at the Villa Rasenna.'

I watched her construct a smile. 'Of course. It was the season before last, wasn't it? When the Minister visited.'

The man was flattered by being remembered. His English had deserted him and he slipped into Italian, talking animatedly about Lucri and David Hewison, drawing Lara away.

Through the door into the reception I could see Jane watching us and I wondered whether she had sent him. I was becoming paranoid. I touched Lara's arm.

'Can I come and see you?'

She looked round. Her expression was difficult to read, just a surface thing like the reflections in the mirror. For a moment I feared she would refuse.

'Yes, of course.'

'*Una casa bellissima*,' the man said, as though he too were fishing for an invitation. '*Bellissima*.'

'Telephone me,' she said. 'Telephone me tomorrow.'

Then she was gone, through the door into the reception, drawn by the man who was saying, 'I must introduce you to my wife.'

# XXV

## *Spring 1945*

ONE morning a large Humber edged its way into the main *piazza* of the village of Sabazia. It was painted olive drab and it bore a sign saying, 'Allied Control Commission' on its front bumper. At the wheel was a young woman driver wearing the khaki uniform of the First Aid Nursing Yeomanry. Her only passenger was a Major of the Royal Army Service Corps.

A few villagers stood at the edge of the square and watched in silence as the car parked in front of the church. The occupants climbed out. Italians have a natural sensitivity to oddities. There was, the onlookers felt, something odd about the couple from the car, the small, dark Major who might almost have been Neopolitan and the tall woman whose mass of sandy-coloured hair was only approximately pinned up into her cap and whose pale skin was dusted with that mark of the far north of Europe, freckles. Odder still than their appearance was the fact that the man emerged from the car first and held open the door for his driver.

The strangers looked around curiously, then advanced on the little bar.

'Can you tell me where the *Castello* is? The home of *Signora* Alessio,' the Major asked one of the customers. His Italian was perfectly accurate but marred by a heavy foreign accent. That was excuse enough for the customer to shrug ignorance in that unfathomable manner which is peculiar to the Mediterranean peasant.

'Bloody fool,' said the Major, in English, with a smile.

As he looked at his companion with an expression of

resignation two little boys ran up to him with the universal cry of greeting for Allied soldiers: 'Candy?'

The Major looked helpless. The *signora* of the bar emerged to order the two children away, but the Major's driver stopped them.

'Look what I've got,' she said. From the depths of the canvas bag which she carried over her shoulder she produced a tin of evaporated milk. 'Are you brothers?' Her accent was less marked than the Major's, her manner with the children somehow sisterly rather than motherly.

'Cousins.'

'Then there are two.' As though by magic another tin appeared. 'But you must take them to your mothers.'

The boys hesitated, looking dubiously at the tins and trying to decide how they ranked on a scale which included chewing gum and candy.

'Better than sweets,' the woman assured them.

She watched them run away across the *piazza*, then turned to the *signora* of the bar. '*Il Castello?*'

The *signora* gave instructions. All eyes followed the two strangers as they walked away down Via Vittorio Veneto to the *piazzetta* where the single holm oak grew.

'Quite a fortress,' the Major observed, looking up at the impressive façade. The curious accent he had when speaking Italian revealed itself as Welsh when he was speaking English. 'Ghibelline crenellations – unusual for this part of the world, one would think. Quite a hideout David found.'

The two visitors crossed the bridge to the main door. The Major tugged at the bell pull and after a minute a young maid answered. She looked wide-eyed at the uniformed figures.

'Is *Signora* Alessio at home? We are officers of the British Army. We would like to speak with her.' The Major smiled what he hoped was a reassuring smile. The maid looked dumbly back at him.

'There's nothing to worry about,' said the Major's companion. 'We are friends.'

'A moment.'

Gently but firmly the door was shut in their faces.

'As bad as trying to get into Baker Street,' said the Major with a wry smile.

A few minutes later the maid returned and ushered them into the gloomy hallway. They followed her upstairs and along a corridor to a bare reception room where, her son by her side and her baby daughter in her arms, Clara Alessio stood to meet them. A poignant little group.

'My name is Griffiths,' said the Major. 'This is Janet MacAlpine. We are colleagues of the man you knew as Egisto Pascucci; close colleagues.'

The woman looked back at her two visitors without expression. She had a closed, rather narrow face, a face which was not lacking in beauty but which was drawn tight as though against a hostile world.

'You had better sit down,' she said.

After a dozen visits of this kind her behaviour was familiar enough to the Major. People whose lives had depended on secrecy in the last few years had found that habit hard to break. A brutal natural selection had eliminated the garrulous ones.

'We have come,' he shrugged at the anticipated inadequacy of his words, 'to thank you for your work and to see if there is anything we can do to help you at the moment. Unofficially, of course. We are not,' he smiled encouragingly, 'very official people.'

The boy was about seventeen, Griffiths guessed. A fine-looking boy with his mother's elegant bone structure. The baby, even now grabbing with tiny fist at its mother's neck, seemed less than a year old; but he was not adept at estimating such things.

'What a lovely baby,' said Janet. 'A little boy?'

'A girl.'

'How many months?' She went over and gurgled at it. The baby looked back with blank incomprehension.

'Six.'

'What is she called?'

'Lara.' The woman watched as Janet tried to evoke a smile from the baby. 'How do I know you are who you say you are?' she asked.

'You have a telephone. If you call the Allied Control Commission in Rome and ask to be put through to the Inter-Services Research Bureau they will vouch for us.'

Clara did not bother. Instead she pulled a chair out from the table behind her and sat down.

'May I?' Janet held out her hands.

Clara surrendered her daughter. Something about Janet, maybe her cap, maybe her uniform, upset the baby. It began to cry, a small, thin protest like the mewing of a cat.

'There, there,' Janet said in English. 'There, there.' But the baby did not stop crying until it had been restored to its mother.

'Is he still alive?' Clara asked.

'Egisto? Yes he is.'

Did a small hint of relief come into her expression? Impossible to be sure.

'At the moment he is in England. I expect he will be going back to civilian life. I expect we all will soon enough.'

'What is his real name?'

'Ah.' Common enough. Griffiths wondered what lay behind her toneless questions. 'I'm afraid we are not author-ized to release such information. I know that sounds dread-fully bureaucratic, but I suspect it is the only way. You may imagine . . .' His voice trailed away. He looked at the baby, then at Janet.

Janet smiled confidently. 'Of course he will be perfectly free to contact you once he has been demobilized.'

'Of course. Do I have a similar freedom of choice?'

'Ah. We could, if you wish it, convey a message . . .'

For the first time she smiled, but a thin, humourless smile. 'I didn't mean that.'

'Of course not.' Griffiths looked relieved. 'Ah, I understand that your husband is dead, *signora*.'

'He was murdered, Mr Griffiths or whatever your name is. He was murdered by the partisans with whom I worked.'

'So I believe, so I believe. You can imagine how sorry I am. Not the kind of thing we encouraged but . . .' He spread his hands helplessly. 'The war.'

'Yes.'

'However, to think of the present. It must be difficult for you on your own. To make ends . . .' Too late did he realize that he had embarked on the literal translation of a colloquialism which did not go into Italian. He recovered hastily. 'To cover your costs. Food, clothing. We would not want a comrade-in-arms to be in difficulty. We have some funds –'

Clara shook her head. 'I am no different from the other people in the village, Mr Griffiths, better off than most. I would not wish for any special treatment.'

'Quite so. Quite so. If there is anything that you can think of . . .'

'Nothing that would not apply to every village in Italy, I imagine.'

'Of course.' He reached into the top pocket of his battle-dress and pulled out a card. 'If you should need any help do not hesitate to get in touch. Just ask for me by name at this number.'

She took the card. 'It says Captain,' she stumbled over the pronunciation, 'Upritchard here.'

'Ah.' Griffiths laughed awkwardly. 'Yes, well that's me. Or rather it isn't me either. We all of us have so many different identities that it's difficult to get it right. Either name will do. Whatever you do, though, don't use my real name: they won't recognize it.'

Finally he had got her to unbend. She smiled properly now, in genuine amusement, and her face was momentarily beautiful. 'I don't know your real name, Mr Griffiths, so how could I?'

'How absurd! Of course not. Major,' he corrected, 'not Mister. Major Davies, that's the real one. I always reckon it's anonymous enough as it is. Like being called Rossi. Who needs cover names?'

'Major Davies.' She nodded thoughtfully, then turned to the woman. 'And you. I suppose you are not Janet, either. Are you perhaps Jane?'

Davies' companion looked nonplussed.

'There is just one other thing,' Davies said quickly. 'When everything finally gets sorted out I imagine there will be some kind of official thanks: a letter, possibly even a decoration . . . these things aren't up to us.'

'Not a medal, Mr Davies. I don't really think I would want anything like that.'

He shook his head. 'Probably not,' he said. Then he stood up. 'Well, if there's nothing more we'd better be going. We have a number of people to see. A Doctor Pellegrino for one. A *Signor* Orlandi. Others.'

'I'm sure.'

The two visitors shook hands formally with both Clara and Gianluca.

'You never know, we might well meet again,' Davies said. 'I'm not a soldier really, you see. I'm a classical archaeologist in real life. If you can call that real. I've done quite a bit of work in Rome. I might well be back, who knows?'

She smiled at him, a reflective smile which he could not quite fathom out.

'Who knows?' she repeated.

# XXVI

I DROVE north from Rome. The weather had deteriorated from the false spring of the last few days. Now it was as uncertain as my feelings, veering between light and dark, between banks of cloud sliding in from the Tyrrhenian Sea trailing skirts of rain, and skies of that luminous silver blue which is so different from the hard blue of the summer that it might be another element altogether.

I followed the Via Cassia as it rose up over the high ground of the Campagna. All the modern building was clustered along the roadside: beyond it the land was almost unaffected by development. Even here, so close to the city, the twentieth century has not really permeated the landscape. It is a thin overpainting inexpertly and patchily applied, a modern imposition just as the two-thousand-year-old road is an ancient imposition. As I drove I could imagine David Hewison's insistent voice, the rounded vowels, the forcibly articulated consonants, delivering judgements like blows with a cudgel:

'Conquest, my dear fellow, pure colonial conquest. The white Americans did it with the railways, the Romans did it with their roads; just as the present Italian governments are conquering the South with the *autostrada*.'

The irony is that even now, two thousand years after its victory has been won, for those with a grain of sensitivity towards the past the road is still as plain a mark of subjugation as a scar across a slave's back.

I stopped for coffee at a shabby bar which proclaimed itself of the 'Quarto Secolo', a claim which was plainly idiotic, but probably true. Inside, a group of roadworkers were drinking a mid-morning coffee and *grappa* and arguing about the coming weekend's football. Their voices rose and fell in the swaggering tones and truncated inflexions of the Roman dialect, a city dialect which has spread out into the Campagna, spread and spread until now it laps halfway into Etruria itself.

Outside, the sky had darkened and rain had begun to fall. I felt the weight of the past pressing down on me – the greater past of which the roadworkers were an almost emblematic fragment, and my own fragile little past which was now mingled with David Hewison's and Lara's. I wondered whether I should drink my coffee, go back to the car I had hired and return to the city.

The roadworkers' argument grumbled on. They were the descendants of those men who had first laid the road across the desolated fields of Etruria, ignoring the valleys where the old ways had run and by-passing with a sullen, conqueror's deliberation the great city of Veii which had ruled here. Their ancestors had dug the ditches and pounded the gravel and settled the massive basalt slabs into place, and thus destroyed a people more surely than any army.

One of them was voicing hesitant support for the Lazio football team.

'*Che cazzo!*' his mate shouted. '*È più forte la Roma!*'

I smiled. That was it, wasn't it? As the echoes of that past tragedy grew fainter they are heard only as the notes of vulgar comedy, the rivalry of football teams. That was Croce's redeemer of sins. *È più forte la Roma.* Now we can wring our hands over violence in the football stadium and forget about the two-thousand-year dead, the destruction of a culture.

I paid for my coffee and went out into the rain, thinking of Lara and Hewison, and Gianluca and Clara, and wondering when their small tragedy would ever metamorphose into comedy. The process was surely quicker for lesser things. Adolescent pains become the jokes of middle age. Just as now I could smile wryly at the thought of Helen when once I had wept, so one day soon I would laugh. It would be the same for Lara.

I got back into the car and pulled out into the traffic. I almost turned back towards the city.

*

At the top of the avenue the Villa Rasenna stood behind its screen of umbrella pines in marvellous counterpoise to my own disquiet. It calmed me. The house seemed unmoving and unmoved. It had the quiet sensation of the centuries about it, a sense of agelessness acquired through age, a rocklike passivity which had given it resilience against every human current flowing past. It was an observer, not a protagonist. I recalled clearly the curiosity with which I had first viewed the place almost a year earlier, stumping up the avenue with a suitcase in my hand while wondering vaguely about a lost relative and his relationship with my mother. Then I had seen the house as a kind of metaphor, a contrast to Poggio Sanssieve. But now I saw it almost as a deity, a cult object standing above the tide of human affairs and looking down on me as though at a piece of flotsam swirling around its base.

Lara met me in the entrance, coming down the stairs as soon as I pushed open the door. We kissed softly, like one-time lovers remembering in that gentle gesture a small moment of carnal violence.

'I thought you wouldn't come.'

I was surprised at the warmth of her greeting. I felt things welling up and bursting inside my chest.

'Is there anyone here?' I asked.

'No one.'

I grabbed her wrist and pulled her towards me. I wanted her there and then, while the relief at my arrival still showed in her eyes.

She turned her head away from me. 'Don't be stupid, Anthony.'

'Where is David?'

'At the dig. With all this rain there is lots of work to be done, reinforcing trenches, that kind of thing. Jane is there too, and one or two others. Meredith.'

'Do they know I will be here?'

'I mentioned it. Jane said . . .'

'What did Jane say?'

'She said you were dangerous.'

'What the hell did she mean by that?'

'I don't know.' She pulled free of my grasp and went up the stairs. 'I don't know, Anthony. I don't know anything.' I followed her into the drawing room. A log fire was burning in the grate. She went and poked at it aimlessly.

'You're trying to ignore the truth,' I told her.

'Isn't that the recipe for happiness?' she replied without conviction. 'Did I tell you he received a letter from the British Ambassador? Apparently the Prime Minister's office wished to know whether he would accept a . . .' she waved a hand vaguely, 'CD, CB something. An award.'

'CBE, I expect. You are trying to change the subject.'

'Yes. He tore the letter up.' She looked down at her hands as though expecting to find the pieces there. 'He hates what has happened. He hates the intrusion, people asking him questions, taking photographs.'

'Perhaps he is frightened of what they might ask.'

'What do you mean?'

'Nothing in particular. You know what the Press is like.'

'Not really. How have things been with you? Have you seen your wife?'

It was like talking to a stranger. 'Just once, to discuss division of the spoils.'

'Spoils? That sounds bitter.'

'Not really, just tired.'

'Of what?'

'The whole rigmarole, the memories. It hasn't yet become a joke.'

'Do such things?'

'They do in time, don't they?'

'But you loved her?'

'Not in the way I love you.'

I saw her flinch, but whether at my words or at the sound of a car outside I could not be sure. We stood silently while feet pounded up the stairs towards us and the door was flung open. David Hewison stood in the entrance in muddy boots and dripping anorak.

'What? Are you here?' He advanced on us massively, hand outstretched. 'Is it good to see you? I don't know. Better than a whole lot of gossip columnists anyway. Jane says you are in love with my wife, but I don't see why that should put me off, do you? We have tastes in common.'

He turned to kiss Lara, calling her 'Toy' and patting her cheek. 'Bloody weather. I left them all blundering about in the mud like Filippo Argenti. I didn't want to leave him alone with you for too long.' His laughter was to show that it didn't mean anything. Nothing was difficult for him, nothing was not a mere game. 'So tell me why you have abandoned the world of pills and placebos once again.'

'I thought I'd see the exhibition. Spur of the moment.'

'The exhibition's not here.'

'That's not very kind, David,' Lara said. 'Anthony's always welcome here.'

He smiled at me. 'My wife welcomes you. Your feelings are reciprocated, you see? When you left she never stopped talking about you, did you, Toy?'

She coloured slightly. For a moment it seemed that the whole conversation was going to blow up into a squalid marital dispute. His mood was more erratic than I had ever seen, the undercurrents of bitterness closer to the surface than ever before. I wondered whether he was quite sane.

'Anthony is the only member of your family I have ever known,' Lara said quietly. 'Is it wrong that I should be fond of him?'

'I consider it wrong to be fond of any of them,' he replied. His expression insisted that it was all a joke. 'So tell me, nephew, how has the family reacted to my new-won fame?'

And I found myself trying to placate him, slanting the story so that it would appeal most:

'They seem appalled for the most part. I spent Christmas at Guerdon House so I saw it all: little huddled conferences to discuss what to do, occasional careful interrogations of me as the only first-hand witness, attempts to keep it all from Uncle Thomas. It's as though you've contracted some unspeakable disease.'

I mentioned the newspaper story which had affected Hewison shares, and Honjohn's accusations of disloyalty. It all seemed to please him as I knew it would.

'So there's something to be said for popular fame after all.

260

One can put up with 'phone calls from journalists craving audience or letters from Prime Ministers offering gew-gaws, even bloody travel agents if it all makes the family shudder. And what about my senile brother?'

'He never mentions you. It's as though you didn't exist.'

He nodded thoughtfully, rocking slightly on the balls of his feet, contemplating the next move in a war of attrition whose motives seemed so confused as to be incomprehensible, so distant as to be irrelevant. And I hated him for the casualty which his war had caused: Lara sitting in the chair beside him with her face like an invalid's.

'Of course I threw their bloody CBE back at them,' he announced suddenly. 'But what if they had offered a knighthood, eh? What then?' He laughed again, but there was something splintered about his laughter, about his whole mood, like an old wooden beam under great strain. 'Now that would have made Sir Thomas's eyes water, wouldn't it?'

In the fire there was a massive glowing log lying across the andirons, flaking white squames of ash as though sloughing off a skin. Lara watched it patiently. The line down the margin of her cheek from the wing of her nose to the corner of her mouth, usually no more than a faint shadow, was now deeply drawn. She looked older than her years, old and defeated.

'I saw Francis a month ago,' I remarked.

She looked up for a moment.

'That damned aesthete?' Hewison asked. 'Did you?'

'On television.'

'Television.' Repeated thus in Hewison's tones the word took on an almost symbolic meaning, as though emblematic of the world which existed outside the confines of the Villa Rasenna and the Lucri excavation, a world from which he was entirely exiled but which had now come searching for him. 'On television,' he repeated, as though talking of marvels. 'And was he talking about me?'

'About Lucri and the Etruscans, and you of course.'

'The second Arthur Evans.'

'You read that, did you?'

'I heard about it. It seems absurd. They want to take it from me, you see, all that I have created here. The family want it, the academics want it, the journalists want it, everyone. They want to create things according to their own prejudices. Arthur Evans, T.E. Lawrence, whatever is to hand. They want to consume the person and spit out a kind of parody, so that what remains is theirs. Possession is ten tenths of their law, dear nephew. And yours.' He turned to look directly at me. 'Only you don't want my fame.'

Lara stood up. 'I think I ought to show Anthony to his room now, David. And you ought to go and change out of those wet clothes otherwise you'll catch cold.'

He hesitated. I saw his eyes moving from his wife to me and back again, like a bear watching two dogs moving around him just out of reach. His mood seemed balanced on a razor's edge.

'Why don't you have a hot bath?' she asked.

He nodded at me. 'There. She is like a mother to me.'

I had my old room. Its features – the bedside lamp with its wicker shade, the Piranesi engravings on the wall, the bookshelf with its small collection of guest-room books – had lost their impersonality and somehow become more familiar to me than my bedroom in my own house; especially now with Lara standing looking out of the window, waiting for me to speak.

I humped my suitcase onto the bed.

'He knows,' I said.

She made a slight movement of her shoulders, but said nothing. I could see the milky reflection of her face in the glass, through it the dark green of the cypress trees at the border of the garden swaying in the wind. The window pane was running with rain and the water distorted the view, blurred it and ran it like watercolour so that only her reflection was constant.

'You shouldn't have come.'

'I think I should.'

I remembered the photograph in Hewison's study, the fifteen-year-old girl with her face alight with joy and her mind suffused with the glow of what had just taken place in a pink-walled room – empty now, the wallpaper peeling in great

262

swathes, the dust lying thick on the floor – in the *Castello*, an initiation into a mystic world conducted by the man who stood with a camera to preserve the flower of her new innocence for as long as silver lasts on paper, which is not very long when measured against time at Lucri.

'There is no future for you here. It is finished.'

She laughed. 'I think when I first saw you I knew that finally you would do that.'

'Do what?'

'Try to offer me a future.'

She turned and looked at me. A furrow of concentration was drawn down between her dark eyebrows. 'But you're too late. By my whole life too late.'

I felt an impotent anger. I knew I was strong. My knowledge made me strong, but only in the way that the brutal are strong. I had weapons, potent weapons, but with weapons you can only threaten or destroy, nothing else. Powers of persuasion I did not possess.

'You cannot detach me from my past.'

I felt suffocated by repetition. 'You only have to try.'

'I tried, Anthony.' She shut her eyes for a moment. 'I tried on that afternoon, and all I succeeded in doing was trapping you as well.'

'Then let's both get out of the trap.'

She shook her head. 'Do you know what date it is tomorrow?'

It took a moment to bring my mind into focus. 'Date? What are you talking about?' But it was as I uttered the last word that I understood.

'The twenty-sixth,' she said. 'The twenty-sixth of January.'

'Tomorrow,' Hewison announced loudly, 'is the day of the Fifteen Martyrs of Vetrano. Does that not have a marvellous and mediaeval ring to it? The Martyrs of Vetrano.' He relished the phrase. Around the table anxious faces watched him: Jane, Lara, Meredith, Hannah, three others whom I only half-remembered from the summer. Lara's lips moved faintly, as though in prayer.

'It brings to mind images of virginal maidens with their eyes turned up to heaven and their ears hardened by Faith against the oaths and blasphemies of the rabble, doesn't it? Of course that impression is quite wrong. No martyrs here, not "martyr" with its origins in *martys*, witness. Our fifteen weren't bearing witness to any faith, beyond the dull faith of peasant obedience. Obedient unto death, with no options, my dears. None whatever.'

'Why the hell don't they leave it alone?' said Hannah unexpectedly. 'What good does it do now after all these years? I think –'

Hewison's expression barely flickered. 'You don't think, my dear, except to get your chronologies muddled.'

The girl winced as he swept her intervention aside.

'Sheep, not martyrs. The Fifteen Sheep of Vetrano. Now it sounds more like a nursery rhyme. Perhaps one day that is what it will become, a nursery rhyme.' He began to recite, half-singing, waving a hand in time with the words:

> 'Little Bo-Peep lost fifteen sheep,
> And didn't know where to find them,
> Have a look round,
> They're stuck in the ground,
> Where nobody needs to mind them.

'How's that?' He laughed humourlessly. 'Pretty tasteless, I'd say, but then so are bands and wreath-laying and all that. Which is what they all do.' He directed his stare at me. 'Do you want to see? It would appeal to a publicity man. Doubtless you will be able to descry some cheapjack moral in the thing. Shall we go tomorrow and pay homage to the fifteen sheep?'

'David!' Lara protested.

'No! You shall not have your way! It will be a treat for my nephew, to see us scratching at our sores. We will go.'

'I'm not sure I –'

'Of course you want to go. It fascinates you, my dear fellow, fascinates you. I know it. Let us go then, you and I, and see how the bands parp and the little children clap and the big children shed a tear or two. Lovely stuff. Nothing, absolutely nothing, like a good weep for making you think you have a profound mind.'

Jane's voice cut through his words. 'David, don't be so damned puerile! And you,' she turned on me, 'why the hell don't you show some tact and go back to England? Leave us alone.'

'Leave us alone?' My uncle laughed. 'But how can he leave us alone now? He is part of us, whether we like it or not. Part of us. Isn't that right, Lara? Cleaved unto us body and soul.'

We went to Vetrano the next morning, just the three of us jostling together on the front seat of one of the Land Rovers. Jane had gone off to the dig after declaring the whole idea childish. Her departure seemed to amuse Hewison. He had the ponderous gaiety of an invalid out on a jaunt and away from his nurse for the first time in months.

'I will drive,' he insisted when it seemed that Lara wanted to. 'I will scatter my enemies before me.'

Sitting at the steering wheel he fumbled with the ignition key, stabbing it randomly at the lock until it went home and cursing it all the time for conspiring against him. There was that erratic quality about his mood, something fragmented about the way he spoke and his manner as though somewhere deep inside him something had broken.

Lara climbed in beside him. 'Do you really want to go, David? Wouldn't you be happier if we stayed and did some work at the dig?'

The engine started. He pumped the accelerator. The engine note rose and fell. 'What is it about women,' he asked me over the noise. 'What is it that aggravates so? Is it their eternal concern for others, their loathsome sympathy, their armfuls of compassion? You ought to know.'

'They have more charity than us.'

'Ha! Charity. But look what they have done to it: degraded it from a kind of love to an odious condescension which they wield like a weapon.'

He swung the Land Rover down the avenue towards the road. 'No, not a weapon. A net, a web. They snare you in it.'

The vehicle lurched onto the road. 'I have spent my life in

women's snares, you know. My mother, your grandmother, was an Italian mother *per eccellènza*, the kind of woman who, under the guise of worship, rules you.'

We had heard it all before but that didn't deter him. The vehicle swung around the curves of the road, whilst he recited his litany. 'And then the war,' he said, 'and other women to ensnare me.'

I saw Lara bite her lip. The Land Rover bumped across the ruts where the tarmac lay over the old railway lines and there had once been a level crossing. The tracks ran through brambles to our left, towards the valley of the Carema and the railway station and the girder bridge.

'The first time I ever passed along here was in the back of old Doctor Pellegrino's car,' he said unexpectedly. 'He was taking me to meet your mother.'

Lara said quickly, 'Pellegrino was a dear old man, the old-fashioned kind of doctor who knew more about people than about medicine. Who is to say they are not the best?' But David's mind had already jumped to another subject.

'This was the way the legions came, you know. Tramp, tramp, tramp. Drums beating and cymbals crashing and standards waving in the air. A grim lot, with the smell of plunder in their nostrils and a fat city just ahead of them. I wonder how many of Lucri's people died? A few hundred? A thousand? Few enough by modern standards, no doubt. No doubt the modern historians would reduce it all to size like they do with everything else. Homer's Troy was only a fortress with a few hundred people, Marathon was a skirmish on the far borders of the Persian Empire which Darius would have barely noticed, that kind of thing. It's the modern fashion to measure tragedy numerically, you see. That's what democracy means. By those standards we are of no significance here, against Treblinka or Auschwitz for example. Here we only managed fifteen.'

'David.' Lara's tone was weary.

'There. I've offended modern sensibilities by talking the truth. But I'll not shut up. I'll make it clearer: we live in what you might call the Statistical Age, in which people only count numbers. It is only now, now that we can destroy millions at a stroke, that it has been decided that war is not such a fine thing after all. Because of the numbers likely to get killed. That is the sum total of our morality.'

The Land Rover began to slow as the road climbed towards the ugly modern buildings on the edge of the town. There was the sign in four languages saying Welcome to Vetrano, and beyond it a poster evoking the powers of Evit-O in solving all your social problems.

'But it doesn't really matter how you die,' he said. 'Tomorrow in a nuclear flash, today of cancer, two thousand years ago by a sword, or thirty years ago by a bullet. For the victim it is still the end of the world.'

We drove into the *piazza*. There was a crowd over by the war memorial. To one side stood a wooden rostrum decked out with red white and green bunting, flanked by a squad of soldiers and a *Carabiniere* band. The crowd was milling about irresolutely, as though nobody expected much to happen but no one wanted to leave in case it did. A flatulent sound came across the open space as the bandsmen began to tune their instruments.

'Do you really want to see this, David?' Lara asked.

'Your guest, my dear, your guest.'

'He wouldn't mind.'

'We must do our duty as hosts.' He had adopted the patient manner of an adult talking to a child. 'This is a bit of local colour, a fragment of local history. We will watch the ceremony.'

He parked the vehicle and climbed out, slamming the door behind him.

From the entrance to a nearby butcher's shop an old woman watched us. She turned to call into the interior and another, younger woman pushed aside the plastic fly-curtain to join her. She was wiping her hands massively on a bloody rag. Hewison turned towards them and made a little bow. The younger woman nodded in return, but the older one just looked back at him impassively, like someone who has not understood.

'What do they think of me, do you suppose?' Hewison asked. 'What dark thoughts stir in the depths of their cyclopean minds?' He gave a jaunty little wave and turned away, and I heard him murmur, 'I will devour you last of all. That shall be my gift.'

We crossed the *piazza*. On the war memorial Italy, in classical draperies, bowed her bland head over the engraved names of the '*Gloriosi Caduti*'. There were two lists of names, one conspicuously an addendum to the other, as though the commemorators of the first conflict had genuinely believed it to be the war to end all wars and had therefore failed to make provision for the next. The names, hedged around with stone cannon, furled pennants, crossed rifles and swords, all the paraphernalia of monumental warfare, brought the words memorial and marmoreal together in a tasteless sculptural pun. It would do in Italian as well, I thought: *marmoreo and memoria*.

More people joined the crowd behind, jostling me against Lara. She smiled over her shoulder, as though the contact was reassuring.

'*Signora Lara*,' said someone behind her. '*Come sta? È tanto che non la vediamo.*'

There was an ambivalent mixture of church and state about the gathering, with a surpliced priest and a flock of acolytes forming up beside the soldiers. The mood was part ritual, part *festa*, wholly equivocal towards the little tragedy which it was recording.

'A far cry from Remembrance Day in Britain,' I whispered to Lara.

There was a sudden stir of directed interest amongst the crowd as a portly man, gift-wrapped in *tricolore* ribbon, climbed onto the rostrum.

'*Il sindaco*,' Lara said.

The mayor turned to face his constituents. The bandmaster raised his baton and the band – a toyshop confection of black, silver and red – struck up the jaunty tune which betrayed itself as the national anthem by bringing the soldiers to the present and a doughty group of civilians formed up beside the priest to the salute.

'Veterans of the Resistance,' Lara explained.

The mayor laid his hand on his heart. Someone in the crowd said, 'He's checking his wallet.'

There was laughter, quickly hushed to silence. Lara giggled. For a moment she had forgotten the brooding presence of her husband, forgotten the tensions which permeated the man like static electricity and flowed over into her own life to charge it too with the awful energies of fear and guilt. For a moment she was just a young woman standing against me in the crowd.

I looked round, but the people massing at my back were all strangers. David Hewison was no longer in sight.

From the rostrum the mayor began to make a speech. No one in the crowd listened to him with particular attention, yet no one actually ignored him. Occasionally, when he uttered a word like *libertà* or *democrazia* or *sacrificio*, there was a murmur of something like approval from the audience, as though those words at least meant something to them; or maybe, like people listening to an old story, they were merely reacting to familiarity. When finally he finished he received a perfunctory round of applause which suggested that he had somehow got things more or less right. He nodded in agreement at the faces below him, then struggled down from his perch.

There followed a brief pause while things were sorted out, and then the ruling triumvirate of *sindaco*, parish priest and *maresciallo* of *Carabinieri* set off at the head of the procession. They crossed the *piazza* and headed for the orphanage. The acolytes came after, then the band, then the squad of awkward soldiery, then the veterans of the Resistance, and behind them all the townspeople pushing and shoving across the open space like sheep.

As the procession converged into the Via dei Quindici Martiri the numbers seemed suddenly to multiply. A mass of humanity jostled between the houses. Someone began to shout directions like a steward in a football crowd. People waved and pointed from the windows up above.

I noticed an antithesis of the ages: the children were laughing, but the old people wiped their eyes, remembering perhaps a smaller procession marching along the same road when it was called Via Giuseppe Verdi or some such, and simply led out of the town to the fields and the *macchia-*

covered hills. But then, of course, the children would have wept as well.

'Where's David?' Lara asked. She was turning round to try and spot him above the heads.

'I can't see him.'

Her expression said, 'I knew this would happen.'

'Should I go and look for him?'

Wearily she shook her head. 'Leave him. He'll go for a walk or something, and meet us back at the Land Rover.'

'What does he feel?'

She blinked and moved her head sideways, as though evading a blow. 'What does he feel?' she repeated, as though mere repetition of the question might bring an answer to light.

The procession had reached the mausoleum. It broke up and shuffled into the little garden, the bandsmen wielding their instruments over their heads like pieces of awkward plumbing. A young priest was marshalling his catechumens into some kind of order beside the soldiers.

'He just hates all this.' She gestured at the milling crowd.

'But these are the people who remember.' I had noticed a group clustering behind the parish priest and the mayor, women hunched beneath black shawls, men with black armbands: the relatives. 'What could be more appropriate?'

'But he would like to forget. Of course he can't, and the idea that he wants to fills him with guilt but . . . if he only could, if he only could.'

She clenched her fist and raised it to her mouth, biting the knuckles so that her teeth made small, curved depressions in the skin. I reached up and took hold of the knotted fist, brought it down to my side and held it tightly against me. I could feel the dampness of her saliva on my fingers.

At that moment the band broke into a brassy rendering of the Jews' Chorus from *Nabucco*, the crowd broke into applause, and the parish priest and the mayor, church and state, stepped forward to lead the mourners into the darkness of the mausoleum.

Lara looked round with a tight smile. I had taken her hand in cold deliberation to try and make her understand my presence beside her, but I also knew in that moment when she looked at me while some of the crowd were singing along with the band – for the chorus from *Nabucco* is better loved than any national anthem – that the possession of which she had spoken was complete. Lying with me that once, when she had given everything that she owned in body, had not broken the possession so why should holding her hand like this, secretly in the crowd as the singing of '*Va' pensier*' came to an end and, bathetically, the catechumens broke into a shrill hymn about *Gesù Divino*, why should this? Why should anything? Why should I be able to strip away the overburden of a past which had pressed down on her mind so long that the two things, the past and the small mineral gleam of her own identity, had become one thing, as indissoluble as the frozen lava which lay beneath the arx of Lucri.

'*Non ci sta il Signor Davide?*' asked a face in the crowd.

She clung to my hand, clung to it like a child. '*Ci stava, pero se n'è andato . . .*'

'*Peccato.*' The face glanced at me, nodded, turned back.

'Let's go,' Lara said quietly, letting slip my hand.

We walked away down the Via Dei Quindici Martiri towards the centre of the town, with the discordant piping of the children's choir following us:

'*Resta con noi,*
*Non ci lasciar,*
*E la notte non più scenderà.*'

Hewison was not at the Land Rover. The *piazza* was almost deserted, the war memorial at the back abandoned to its own remote irrelevance. Even the butcher's shop beside the vehicle was closed.

'The whole town seems to have gone.'

'Of course.'

We waited around uncertainly, not saying much. There were two coaches by the municipal building, one painted military khaki, the other dark blue with the word *Carabinieri* down the side in white. The two drivers smoked and talked, waiting for the reappearance of the soldiers and the band. They were outsiders with no interest in this trivial little ceremony. The empty *piazza* with the two uninterested coach drivers and the shuttered shops seemed sadder by far than the gathering at the mausoleum; as though the modern town might be there at the memorial, but the ghosts of the fifteen martyrs still hung around the square as doubtless they had done in their lives, sitting at the plain tables outside the bars, drinking cloudy wine and arguing about things they never really understood; least of all the reason for their dying.

'What do they think of him?' I asked at one point but received little more than a shrug in reply.

'How does it matter what they think? Most of them don't understand and anyway Italians are very adept at shrugging off the past.' She looked round the square helplessly. 'But where is he?'

'Shall we drive around and see if we can find him?'

She shook her head.

From behind the orphanage came the sound of a solitary trumpet playing a maudlin piece which I recognized because it had once been a popular success: *Il Silenzio*.

'They have finished.'

Hewison appeared last of all, after the soldiers and the band had debouched from between the crowded buildings and gone over to the coaches, after the priest and acolytes had crossed the *piazza* to the church, and the mayor to the *Municipio*, after the people had diffused out from around the mausoleum to repopulate the town and return it to its present. He came from the street beside the butcher's shop, from quite a different direction from everyone else, and he gave us a humourless little wave as he approached.

'Where have you been, David?' She reached up and kissed him. It was the first time I had ever seen her make any spontaneous display of affection towards him. He smiled and patted her cheek, but gave no reply.

'The duty to the guest is done, his morbid curiosity is satisfied and we can lock away our guilt for another year.' He climbed into the Land Rover. 'Will no man say Amen?'

# XXVII

THE Villa seemed a great echoing museum which for once not even Hewison was capable of filling. He took himself off somewhere 'to do some work. You can have her to yourself', and so I found myself alone with Lara. He knew about us and he didn't care. Against that indifference I was powerless, powerless to take her from him, powerless to stir him even to jealousy.

I watched her sitting at a desk in the drawing room, writing some letters. She was quite oblivious to my eyes on her and to the faint ticking of the bomb which lay in my mind. I watched her writing, watched the faint straining forward of that body whose heaviness I had once borne for what I could now no longer recall as anything more than a single evanescent minute. True love, I had always been taught by people who never seemed to practise it, is entirely selfless. I knew that I should leave her now and drive the two hours back to Rome, consigning her memory to that part of the mind which deals with nostalgia, only occasionally taking it out to mull over it with the obsessive minuteness of an archaeologist handling some treasured artifact, trying to read a significance into it, trying to see a pattern.

I wondered what the pattern was. Was Tobasi part of it? Was Elwyn Davies, chuckling over his memories? Was the now long-dead hostage called Alessio, whose Christian name I did not even know? Was a woman called Clara, dying in an agony of cancer? Was my mother? Or the fifteen corpses of Vetrano?

But the pattern was none of these people, either alive or dead, but just a collection of memories in various minds, like a scattering of autumnal leaves which describe no pattern

273

whatever except a random one, but upon which a human being can impose a pattern which is nothing more than the pattern of his own mind. And I knew I could be part of this non-existent pattern, this pattern-to-be which I might make. Mere memory would be no use. It would be something like a piece of buried metal, that oxidizes away bit by bit until it is no longer recognizable. That is why you can bear tragedy, because you are left with only the rusted memory, not the original polished reality with its bright cutting edge. I did not want that.

Hewison drank too much at dinner that evening. There was Lara's expression of concern, the others' dull expressions of embarrassment, Jane's attempts to stop him; and the splintered words from the man's own mouth sweeping like shrapnel across the table. Meredith and his helpers left the table at the earliest opportunity. Outside it was raining heavily. They excused themselves by referring to the rain and talking about an early rise tomorrow, lots of work to do if the weather goes on like this.

'It rained four point three centimetres in twenty-four hours last Thursday,' Meredith observed, escaping with relief. 'Imagine.'

So the four of us were left around the table, to imagine four point three centimetres or not, as we wished.

'I presume you are leaving tomorrow,' Jane said to me. 'Can you take some mail to post in England?'

Hewison laughed. 'Him leaving? Is he? Do you think he has sucked us dry yet?' His laugh was a knowing one, as though he had discovered a secret. 'I know how his mind works, my dear Jane. Do you know the plant broomrape? That is what he reminds me of. Broomrape. It has rather splendid flowers, almost orchid-like, I suppose, but if you examine it carefully you notice something wrong with the plant: it has no leaves, no leaves at all. Parasitic, you see, uses its roots to penetrate other, perfectly normal plants and draw the juices out of them. Entirely parasitic.'

'David, you are being offensive.' Lara was angry, her lips white and compressed.

274

He spoke pointedly to Jane. 'She leaps to his defence. I suppose she enjoys his attentions. But she is wrong to suppose that he is offended. You are not, are you?'

I shrugged. 'Not particularly. I just think you are being unfair, that's all.'

'I think not. But perhaps you see it from a different point of view. You tell me what you want from us then.'

'I think it is time we all went to bed,' Jane said in her finest schoolmistress voice. 'A long day tomorrow.'

'But Anthony and I have only just begun, isn't that right, nephew? And we are certainly not going to break off because of the exhortations of my warder. Now tell me, Anthony, what is it that you want? My wife? Or is it less straightforward than that, less simple than pure libido?'

I said nothing. I sat and watched the man at the head of the table — we were sitting asymmetrically at one end of a table which only a few months before had seated sixteen — and reflected that in some ways he was like one of those old and ruined animals you see in the zoo, an old lion perhaps, with teeth worn and broken and coat shabby and any instinct for survival which there may once have been long ago exhausted. But of course, unlike the lion, Hewison's bars — there all around him plain enough to see — were self-created. Then I thought, maybe they are surrounding me as well.

'I don't know what I want,' I answered eventually, and brought a derisive laugh from my uncle.

He pushed himself away from the table, like a judge rising and with his ponderous movement raising the whole court. 'A spoilt brat, who's had too much already.'

I followed him out of the dining room. Lara hesitated, watching the two of us anxiously.

Jane asked, 'Are you all right?' and the question was curiously indeterminate, directed neither at one nor the other, nor specific in what respect we might or might not be all right. I think she sensed that for the moment her control over Hewison had gone.

'Of course I'm all right,' he answered roughly. As though to demonstrate that this was so he even paused and waited for me to join him, and put a hand on my shoulder. 'Do you think

I might devour him alive, my beloved nephew? All I wish to do is breathe fire over him.' And he laughed as he led me across the *loggia* and into the drawing room.

An evening of strong contrasts: the storm outside, the shabby stillness within; Hewison loud and voluble, demolishing Charles for his pusillanimity, Elwyn for his dry-as-a-stick celibacy, Jane for her meddling; or soft and thoughtful, almost maudlin when he spoke of Clara or Lara. And contrasts between the sudden flashes of understanding which came to me but gave no more of a view than the flashes of lightning which lit up the world outside, and the darkness through which I stumbled most of the time trying to follow him.

'. . . it started at Djemila, I suppose. It was Djemila, wasn't it? One of those North African sites anyway . . . with Jane. There was a French Army unit nearby where we stayed the night. They were a relief once you got them off politics, Darlan, De Gaulle, Laval, that kind of thing. Knew how to talk about something other than sex and horses which is all the British ever seemed to think about. Better educational system, you see . . . more encouragement to think for yourself. And naturally Jane was *simpatica*, spoke, speaks I presume but I haven't heard it in years, spoke it like a native. The language. What about you?'

'When was this?'

'When?' He laughed. 'Pleistocene period. Aeons ago.'

'The war?'

'The war.' He thought a moment. 'We've shrunk from the war, haven't we? It's all history now, we say, and hope that that will lay it to rest. Let's worry about the future. But you see,' he sat forward eagerly, suddenly almost sober, 'we have confused two things: the war as history, and the war as myth. The war as history is something we can safely leave to the historians, let them maul it about like dogs with a bone; but the war as myth will stay with us for ever, even if we think we forget it. You understand what I mean by myth? These days one wonders. Even Charles will say, "that's a myth", when what he means is "a lie".

'Look at the Trojan cycle, the eternal war in the back-ground, its origins lost to memory, its end somewhere in the future, its significance only in its eternity.' His hand waved back and forth across the centuries, across the millennia. 'How will the men of the future, if men of the future there be, view our century of war, do you think? Will they even be able to distinguish two separate events, or will it just be seen as an endless conflict, an eternity of conflict with the German tribes? How often the diets of Poland have been polluted with blood and the more numerous compelled to yield to the more violent! How often Hector's body has been dragged through the dust and Odysseus set to wander the world! And you ask, was it the war?'

He chuckled over his image of his century, and his place in it. I tried to pull him back from his ramblings. 'What started there, at Djemila?'

'What indeed? She asked me to marry her, you know? Which was strictly against the bloody rules. Damn the bloody rules, Elwyn's bloody rules. I told him later, told him she pulled her knickers down in my room in that Free French mess. Some surprise that, black lace knickers under a khaki skirt. Not what you'd expect to find. Do you know what he said?'

He looked at me as though for an answer. I shook my head.

'Against the rules, that's what he said. Against the rules. That was in Bari. Against the rules. They had rules about where you could take your knickers down and in front of whom. Imagine. Nobody below field rank, I presume. Must have been written by Elwyn himself, only an old queer could do such a thing.'

'Elwyn?'

'Didn't you know? Oh yes, Elwyn. For entirely classical reasons, I imagine.' He spluttered with laughter. 'I didn't miss her, you know? That's what made me realize. Didn't miss her at all.'

'Miss her?'

'Jane. Because of Clara.'

'Tell me about Clara.'

He looked suddenly suspicious. 'Why should I confess to you? But who knows? Maybe I will. It's a Catholic failing isn't it, an ingrained habit you never lose even when all the other stuff – mass, communion, prayer – even when all that has gone?'

But no confession came.

'Clara,' I prompted him. He repeated the name as though it was a surprise.

'Clara. I spent two months in and out of her house, you know? Two months seeing her almost every day and trying to pretend that she was a mother figure to me, twenty years older, another man's wife, *divieto di accesso*.' He laughed. 'But in the end it was she who said, "Come and show me what you did with Jane."'

We sat silently for a while with that confession between us.

'And her husband?'

'Oh, him. He was away, away in the north with the government. One of Mussolini's cronies. She was on her own.'

I laughed. 'You had her to yourself?'

His eyes snapped into focus. 'She wasn't a tart. Not like your mother. It tortured her, the idea that she had betrayed her husband. She wanted to do it, and she did it, and she hated herself for it.'

'So what happened?'

'She went. Went to Rome. Left me alone.'

The little manipulations of arithmetic worked through my mind, the months slipping one after the other like abacus beads, backwards and forwards, backwards and forwards, until, through a blur of drink, I saw in startling clarity what I suppose I had always dimly understood and never wished to face, ever since talking with Gianluca all those months ago. The beads clicked backwards and forwards through my still reluctant mind while Hewison's voice rambled on. And always they gave the same answer.

'Where did you go this morning when we waited for you?' I asked.

'Go?' He seemed puzzled. 'Go? Why, nowhere. I just wandered around,' a vague wave of his hand in a vague circle, 'by the back streets until I came to the mausoleum. A

278

gruesome name if there ever was. Good King Mausolus. And watched men saluting and trumpets parping. And when they had finished and all gone away I went in and tried to say a prayer. Shouting in the dark to keep my courage up, maybe.'

'I saw your signature in the book. Last year's, I mean.'

'Did you now? It is rather like putting your name to a manifesto, knowing, or at least hoping that no one will read it.'

'Why should you hope that?'

'Because one does not like to advertise one's own inadequacy.'

I watched his slumped figure with something close to sympathy. Once I thought I hated the man. Now the realization had come to me that far from hating him, far from envying him his possession of Lara, far from anything like that, I almost loved him; rather as a son, I supposed – without much conviction because without any experience – might love a father. I didn't want to destroy him. I wanted to succeed him, and to love him despite my succession, to revere him and honour him in my victory, to worship the vanquished. It would be a conquest akin to that of love where the triumph is at once a victory and a surrender, where the victim is the victor and the conqueror is conquered. Perhaps somehow I could explain my feelings to him. Perhaps these awful moments of intimacy could be transformed into something close to courtship. Perhaps my words would do justice to the exquisite pain my new understanding brought me.

'Do you realize what this place has come to mean to me?' I asked. 'Do you realize how fond I am of you?'

He looked up quickly, his eyes disturbingly clear.

'Me? Do you mean me, or do you mean Lara?'

'You. Plural. Lara and you, and the Villa. You know what I mean.'

'No.' The eyes were quite unhooded now, stripped of their heavy layer of intoxication, as bright and penetrating as when he was at his work. And his face seemed to have grown huge, as huge as a statue's head, as vast and numinous as a totem.

'Are you and Lara lovers?' he asked.

'No.'

279

Ponderously the head nodded, as though there were a ghost in the machine. He smiled. 'So you have been.' It was not a question. It relieved me of the need to confess. 'I can tell by your tone, you see: a denial with no surprise, no indignation behind it; confident in its superficial truth, but not confident enough to be outraged. Perhaps I should have been a lawyer, a barrister-at-law exposing the little evasions which are never exactly lies. Instead I'm a bloody archaeologist. It must have been last summer, but not for long. How often? Christ alive, I sound like a confessor now. How often, eh? Just once?'

'Just once.'

And he began to laugh, his great racking laugh, a consumptive's laugh. Tears slopped from his eyes down his cheeks and when finally he brought himself under control he was pale and shaking, like someone who has just suffered a fit.

'I'm sorry. You mustn't think I am laughing at you, either of you. You can be assured of that. I was laughing at the past. I think perhaps that one has the right to laugh at one's faith occasionally. Jews always tell the best Jewish jokes, so they say. You must allow me to laugh at the past.'

We sat silently for a while, with Hewison mulling over the amusing past. Every so often a small bubble of laughter escaped from him like steam escaping from a safety valve. He would give a little snort and his whole frame would shake. I had the vague idea that I should try to get him away from his drink and to bed, but instead I said, without any particular preparation:

'There's something I wanted to ask you about the past, your past.'

'Go ahead.'

I put my glass down. I had drunk too much. There was a throbbing in my head, the beat of a pulse ticking in my ears so loudly that it almost drowned the sound of my own words.

'Those people whose deaths were commemorated today . . .'

'*I quindici martiri.*'

'Exactly. There was another one, wasn't there? Another death I mean.'

He laughed. 'Another death? Dear God, Anthony, don't be so naïve. There were millions of deaths, millions of them.'

'I mean another particular one, one we did not commemorate today. I'm talking about Lara's father. Where is the memorial to his death?'

I had forgotten the bomb, but as Hewison pushed himself forward in his chair I found the thing in my grasp. I watched him carefully, saw his tongue run across his lips, saw the movement of his throat as he swallowed, and the cast in his eyes which might have been hate, and I felt the weight of the bomb. A bomb, I knew, was a weapon which cannot be directed, which destroys at random.

'What do you mean?' he asked, looming towards me dangerously.

I felt fear, but fear for my uncle as much as fear for myself. And I understood – vaguely because my mind was deafened by the ticking of the bomb – that he too was afraid.

'When I was in Florence,' I said, 'I met a man called Tobasi. He told me about Alessio's death. You killed him. First you had his wife, and then you killed him.'

The bomb exploded: a white flash, a waft of heat, a shock blast, then the smashing of glass and the tearing of woodwork and the crash of falling masonry. From somewhere beyond the dust and the smoke the figure of David Hewison peered down at me.

'Where is the memorial to his death?' I repeated.

There was silence as the dust settled. Somewhere out of sight water flowed from a broken pipe. Hewison was on his feet swaying slightly amongst the debris, but otherwise apparently unhurt. He spoke in a voice which was steady and unslurred.

'I commemorate his death. Not just one day a year but every day of my life.' He was still holding his glass. Cautiously he placed it on the table. 'Merely by being alive I commemorate his death. Merely by being alive.'

He stepped carefully over the wreckage and headed for the door. At one point he stumbled, as though he had suffered an injury after all. Or maybe he had just tripped. At the door he paused beside the portrait of Lara and looked at me. The great mask of his face was drawn in harsh tones of white and black and red, carnival or funeral.

'I wonder, Anthony, whether in your smug little life you have ever felt anything at all. I wonder whether you even felt anything when you fucked my wife.'

I closed my eyes. Now the fear was gone and I felt only pity.

'Your wife, David?' I asked him quietly. 'Your wife? But she's not your wife, is she? She's your daughter. Your bloody daughter.'

Long after his departure I sat motionless in my chair. I was wondering what I had said and, conscious that it amounted to some kind of disaster, why I had said it. That was difficult. Motives for a crime are one thing, but motives for ordinary, squalid domestic behaviour are quite another. And then, are motives causes? An intriguing problem, that. The words reverberated in my head like an examination question: motive is both efficient and final cause; discuss. Had I spoken like that to David just because I was drunk, or was I drunk because I had known that I would speak like that? Motive is both efficient and final curse. If you can predict the future then it has already become the past.

I felt on the edge of some kind of crisis. I was not yet hearing voices, but I had begun listening for them: Elwyn's offering nothing but taunting irony, Gianluca's offering despair as a form of consolation, Lara's offering obsession as a comfort. And David's? Now I could see that the chimera beside his armchair was moving. Its lean ribcage was gently expanding and contracting, its muzzle quivering with awareness. They were the subtle movements of a sleeping cat or a baby in a cot, movements which are sensed as much as seen. If I sat still any longer it would step towards me.

I pushed myself up out of my chair and went over to touch the cool bronze, just to make sure. Once I had sorted out the intricacies of balance the movement did me good, quietened the voices. I patted the inert bronze head affectionately. My head was clearer now. Those gleaming canines would never pierce my flesh.

For a moment I looked at the portrait of Lara, waiting for it to say something. Then I went out.

The *loggia* was shadowed grey and black, as damp as a well. The rain had stopped. I stood by the balustrade and looked down into the empty axis of the house. In the darkness the fountain sounded much louder than during the daytime. Was that the running water I had heard, the broken pipe? I smiled. The bomb. How could I ever take stock of the damage? Carefully I stumbled to my bedroom.

# XXVIII

SOMETHING disturbed me the next morning before I had fully woken up. Perhaps it was just the sounds within the Villa. So much was it a place of rhythm and habit that anything out of the ordinary struck one immediately. I lay in bed and listened to a complex of sound which was subtly different, like a minute change in a familiar music score. There was a buzz of hurried conversation somewhere outside my room, a sudden flurry of footsteps. At the back of the Villa someone called loudly, then a car door slammed and an engine roared into life.

I turned over and scrabbled for my watch, knowing from the darkness of the window that it would say something like six o'clock, and that that would do nothing to still the faint unease which fluttered in my gut. My head was throbbing. Just as I swung my legs onto the floor someone knocked at the door. I pulled the sheet across my lap.

'Come in.'

It was Lara. Her face was drawn, the face which had looked at the ceremony at Vetrano yesterday, the same face which had looked down at me from the portrait in the drawing room last night.

'David has gone,' she said.

'Gone?' For an absurd moment I thought she meant dead.

'Disappeared. His bed was not slept in . . . one of the Land Rovers is missing.' She made a helpless gesture, as though scattering something in front of her. 'Did anything happen last night, before you went to bed. What did he do?'

I shrugged. 'I thought he had gone to bed. We'd both drunk a bit, talked about things, personal things, you know. It was mostly he who did the talking.'

284

She nodded. We could hear a car driving round to the front of the house. 'Palmiro. I've told him to go to Sabazia. Jane has already gone to Vetrano.'

'Has he ever done this kind of thing before? Disappeared, I mean. Pushed off somewhere.'

She didn't answer me. 'You'd better put some clothes on,' she said. 'We're going to Lucri.'

It had started to rain again. The *tendopoli* had the mournful look of an abandoned army camp, the troops gone, the war moved on somewhere else. Only the watchman was there, picking his way through the puddles to check the huts in the thin dawn light. Most of the tents had been taken down: rectangular patches of almost bare earth showed where they had been. Parked beside the watchman's Fiat was the missing Land Rover.

'Have you seen *Signor* 'Ewison?' Lara asked.

The man pointed down the Decumanus Maximus. 'Earlier this morning,' he said. 'I was woken by the lights.'

Lara set off down the path. I hurried to catch her up. 'Should we go after him like this?' I asked, taking her by the arm. 'Aren't we treating him like a child?'

She looked at me without breaking her stride. 'A child.'

The excavation was desolate. It lay under the thin drizzle like a set for a film about the First World War, a maze of trenches amongst the mud, the puddles the colour and texture of milky tea. Above the trees the gaunt walls of the necropolis threw her voice back unanswered.

'David!'

'David!'

I followed her along the duckboards towards the arx. We clambered up through the trees. Up on the summit plateau the rain teemed down, threshing at the grass, spouting from the eaves of TEMPIO IIA, TEMPIO PUTATIVO DI TURAN (AFRODITE), 6° SECOLO AC., spewing from the lips of the gargoyles like vomit. The massive block of the Tolfa Hills was a vague, two-dimensional shape through the wall of falling water. No one moved on the plateau. No one answered her shouts.

'David!'
'David!'
We sheltered for a while in the pronaos of the temple. It was like standing in a bus shelter in some depressing, half-built, half-demolished suburb. Nothing moved across the desolation of foundation stones and streets. As the rain eased we left our refuge and picked our way back down through the entrance pylon.

'Where is he?' she wondered aloud, standing where three ways diverged: rightwards back to the main excavation, straight on up to the necropolis summit, leftwards down towards the abandoned railway line. 'Where is he?'

Without answering her own question or waiting for an answer she turned left and went down through the trees, trudging in the deep oak leaf mould. From the midst of a thicket a cow watched us with that strange impassivity which has so often been interpreted as wisdom, but which would nowadays be dismissed, paradoxically, as stupidity. Her great Minoan head turned to see the two humans pass by.

'Why on earth should he be down here?' I called. I was following in her wake, stumbling in the wet and cursing the fact that I had not bothered to find some rubber boots.

'Why,' she repeated.

The stream was fuller than I had seen it before. Lara splashed across, then waited while I jumped inexpertly from boulder to boulder, slithered and plunged one leg knee-deep into the water.

'Hurry up.'

'This is idiotic,' I shouted.

'Yes.' But she was already scrambling up the mud of the far slope and onto the railway embankment. I hurried after her. Up on the line she was walking between the rails, stepping rapidly from sleeper to sleeper, occasionally slipping and stumbling down onto the grey chippings. I followed with difficulty, the banal problem of how to walk along a railway line building up in my mind to the proportions of an obsession: when I attempted a natural stride I was forced to alternate between sleeper and chippings and every few steps one foot landed exactly on the edge of a sleeper; when I shortened my stride to walk on the sleepers alone, as Lara was, I felt that I was hobbled like a horse. I stumbled and swore and changed step and slithered behind her, and tried to ignore the ghosts around me.

The platforms and the abandoned railway station loomed ahead of us through the rain.

VETRANO, announced the yellow tiles across the front of the building. Ceramics never lose their gay insouciance. They gave a cheerful, irrepressible display of optimism to the scene, as though perhaps a bell would ring to signal the arrival of a train, and passengers would shuffle forward to the platform edge in anticipation. But of course optimism was misplaced. Like the arx looming over it from the left, this narrow world between cliff and lava slope was peopled only by the insubstantial impressions which the inhabitants of the past make upon the present. No ticket collector now, no porter, no station-master; no German soldiers either, stamping up and down in the cold and the monotony of guard duty and dully unaware of the men watching them from amongst the trees at the top of the cliff. None of these things – instead a mute cow peered out from the *Sala Attesa* – but perhaps their imprints, faint and elusive in the damp air, like the imprint of an ancient body in the earth of a burial pit.

A second cow shouldered her way off the tracks ahead of Lara – two tracks between the platforms here, so that an up train might pass a down train – and loped with surprising grace up onto the main platform, then away behind the building and down the rough path which led through a desolate valley and up over desolate hills for six kilometres before reaching Vetrano where there was a *Palazzo Municipale*, an *Orfanotrofio*, and *Ufficio Pro Loco*, half a dozen shops, two butchers, a pharmacy, three bars, and a Via dei Quindici Martiri with a small chapel and fifteen names.

'Why here?' I asked again, pointlessly, to Lara's back.

At the far end of the platform was an old cast-iron water pump. She stopped beside this, one hand raised to touch the rusted column, her manner not one of indecision but more of preparation. The gaunt structure hung over her like a sculpture of a giant bird.

I came up to her and touched her shoulder. 'Lara, let's go back. This is stupid.'

She looked ahead down the converging lines. A hundred yards further on the rocks of the arx crowded from the left directly across the path of the railway, bare and jagged like the vertebral column of a vast, dormant archosaur. The stream curved away from them, running under the line to make a wider detour around the outcrop, but the present century is impatient of natural obstacles: the railway cut straight through the rock barrier. It was towards this deep notch that Lara was staring, towards the space which its vertical sides framed, towards the intricate girder-work of the bridge which part lay within this frame.

Her face was wet with rain. A strand of damp hair was plastered across her forehead and down one cheek like a scar.

'I heard a story once,' she said. 'Was it a film, perhaps? I don't know. About a man who had lost his memory. The police arrested him and he found himself charged with a murder he could not remember. He was tried, convicted, and finally executed for this murder, but all the time he had no memory of it at all, no memory of anything. Was he guilty? That was the point of the story. Was he guilty? If you forget aren't you, automatically, forgiven? Isn't that drinking from Lethe?'

Her face had been in profile, but now she turned towards me with the smile which reminded me of her brother, the irony, the faint mockery. 'Of course the corollary of that idea is obvious: if you do remember then you are automatically guilty.'

I said, stupidly, 'It's more than thirty years ago now,' and she laughed.

'An age.' Then she took her hand from the iron column of the water pump. 'Come on.'

Her manner was matter of fact, as though she was now resolved. She led the way along the platform and down onto the stone chippings again. The cutting through the rock opened for us like jaws. We passed through from the narrow valley into the great open spaces of the bridge.

A wind dashed drizzle against our faces. We reached the girders, stood suspended between the stone prow of the arx behind us and the wooded hills of the far side of the valley, between the grey snake of the river below the rails and the milk-white shroud of the sky above the roof of girders. The bridge swirled vertiginously, caught between the contrary motions of river and cloud, like a piece of flotsam in a whirlpool. Soughing through the girders the wind snatched at Lara's mouth so that the words 'David! David!' repeated over and over seemed like small rags of smoke blowing away down wind, each one replaced by another, the supply apparently inexhaustible, the meaning uncomprehended even by the thing for which they were intended, a grey-brown hunch of clothes and limbs on the bank far below, the colour exactly of the mud and vegetation on which it lay, and the water which surged past it as though trying to pluck it away.

# XXIX

'DAVID?' Orlandi roared with laughter. 'For me it'll always be Egisto. And what's the other name?'

'Hewison.'

'What kind of name is that?' He tried to get his mouth round the sound, failing as Italians always did with the aspirate and the semivowel. But he was not a stupid man. 'I've heard it before somewhere.'

'Evison.'

'Medicines. Soap.'

'Exactly.'

'Your family?'

'My family.'

'You're a bloody capitalist!' He roared with laughter again, and this time drew his mother into the joke. She looked round from the stove where a vast pan of *fettucini* was on the boil.

'There's another capitalist who's helped us,' she observed. 'What do your Russians do?'

'Inspire us, *mamma*, inspire us.'

'They don't inspire me.'

The *pasta* came. The two men sat opposite each other and began to eat, glancing up every now and again as though to convince themselves that it was all true. From time to time Orlandi shook his head as though in disbelief.

'We thought we'd never see you again. Back to your own, we thought, back to England where everyone is rich.'

'My own are here,' Hewison replied; which was taken to be a complimentary pleasantry but won favour for all that.

'And have you seen anyone else?'

'No one.'

'You've not been to Sabazia?' Orlandi's expression was of

studied innocence, but both knew what was meant.

'Not yet. I have written.'

'She replied?'

'Yes.'

There was a significant pause. His mother served their food and for a while they ate in silence. But when she left the room on some errand Orlandi took a drink of wine and deliberately wiped his mouth on a napkin. 'How does she feel about . . . ?'

'Things like that are difficult to read in letters.'

Orlandi shook his head. 'It should never have happened, never have happened.'

'But it did.'

'That fool Tobasi.'

The name brought a silence. On the table between them was a photograph of a group of men in battledress jackets and black berets standing in front of the Victor Emmanuel monument. They had their arms around each other's shoulders. One or two raised victory signs. 'You should have been there,' Orlandi had said when showing it. 'It was your victory just as much as ours.' He was the one in the middle, the one with the scarf around his neck.

'Do you know she had another child?' Orlandi asked, not wanting to pursue the question of Tobasi any further. 'A little girl.'

'So I believe.'

'Did she tell you?'

The two men's eyes met across the table. 'She told me,' Hewison said. 'She said she is called Lara. It sounds like an Etruscan name. That's what she wrote.'

Orlandi nodded as though a great political truth had just been uttered.

'Etruscan. And we killed her father.'

'I,' Hewison corrected him. 'I killed her father.'

'We all did. You were the one who wanted a fair trial, but we all killed him. Or better,' he added, a good idea occurring to him, 'better say the war killed him. How can you apportion blame during a war, eh?'

'That's easy,' Hewison replied. 'The difficulty is bearing the guilt.'

The mother came back then and the conversation changed tack into pure reminiscence, a satisfying blend of memory and wishful thinking and pure fancy which turns agony, which cannot be borne for long, into the exquisite but quite innocuous pain of nostalgia.

'Do you remember old Pellegrino? Carrying explosive around in his medical bag? He still works here, you know. You ought to go and see him.'

'I expect I will.'

'And Gino –'

'The musician –'

'Trying to play the concertina –'

'But he wasn't as good as that illiterate old shepherd. Gino was the one who came with me on the bridge raid, remember? He was having a crap when the shooting started.'

'A crap!'

'Came out of the trees with his trousers round his ankles.' Hewison pushed his legs out, ankles together, and pointed. 'Round his ankles.'

Orlandi spluttered with laughter. 'Trying to fight a war with his trousers round his ankles.'

'Might as well have crapped on the Germans.'

And they both began laughing. They laughed and laughed until the tears came and their ribs hurt, laughed and laughed while the mother looked on with her mouth compressed into an expression of 'there they go, making fools of themselves', laughed and laughed until Orlandi said:

'They were times, eh? Times to remember.'

And Hewison found himself agreeing. But his own memory was not selective like other people's memories seemed to be. He could not remember Gino without the bridge, the bridge without the shooting, the shooting without the murder of the hostages, the hostages without Alessio's crumpled face amongst the wet grass with its eye looking out on the world, waiting. He could not remember Jane without Clara, Clara without Gianluca. He could not divide his memory into small compartments because his memory was not the contents but the recalling, and in this it was merciless. It was like a living organism growing out through all his experiences, feeding on them but never consuming them, growing from one to the other, but never able to diminish any of them.

'Times to remember,' he agreed. But that was because he had no choice.

Rounding the curve of the hill he came into sight of the house. They had never used it during the war because it had been too close to the road and too conspicuous, but he remembered it well. And now . . . he stopped the car and looked up at the building almost with a sense of ownership, with a faint smile of pride; and then a moment's anxiety.

He climbed out of the car and opened the gate, then got back in and drove up the rough drive. A glance from this distance told him straight away that his fears were groundless. Nothing had happened to the place in the last three years, nothing except three more years of decay. He looked up at dusty, broken windows, at pointing which was badly in need of repair, at roof tiles which had slid off in some recent storm and exposed wood beneath.

The main door was closed by nothing more than a twist of stout wire. He opened it and stepped through into the entrance. There was the smell of farmyard about the place, the smell of straw and manure. Stacked against one wall were some rakes and something that looked remarkably like a winnowing-fan. In the courtyard beyond there was an ancient harrow and a broken, rusty tractor, the kind with metal wheels which look like mediaeval torture instruments. Along one side bales of hay were piled under the arches. It was much as he remembered.

Satisfied now, he went back outside and followed the side of the house round to where ruined hedges guarded the mournful relics of the gardens. Traces of a geometry of paths and a pattern of beds remained. At the centre was an old stone fountain with a group of dolphins sporting around the bowl. It was broken and parched. There was no means of telling when it had last worked. He walked past the fountain towards the far border of the garden breathing in the dark smell of leaf mould which hung about the place, and that scent which he recognized from Poggio Sanssieve, the scent of box. For a long time he stood at the break in the hedges and looked along the path slanting down through the trees. He knew where it went, knew what was there, as both part of the hillside and part of his own memory.

Afterwards he drove to the village. Nothing had changed here either. At the foot of the ramp he pulled onto the verge to let a horse and cart come down. He wondered whether the driver would be anyone he remembered but, except for those like Orlandi whom he had known well, three years were enough to merge all individual faces into one general face in his memory, like time smoothing out the features of a sculpture until it no longer has any particular identity, but gets reduced to Portrait of an Unknown Man. The cart driver presented just such a general peasant face to the world, staring back at him with curiosity because he was a stranger and seated in a car rather than because he was recognized.

Within the village walls was the mediaeval greyness and the sensation of suffocation which he remembered so vividly. From the top of the church steps he regarded the place with a kind of controlled horror, wondering whether he should continue or whether the sensible thing to do would be to turn round there and then and go back the way he had come.

It was the face which moved him on. Disembodied by shadows it stared out of the door of the shop. It watched him. It was neither male nor female, neither particularly young nor particularly old, neither hostile nor friendly; but it seemed to know. Its passivity, the movement of its tongue and the slow settling of its lips, the faint opening of its nostrils as it breathed in, the blink of its eyes all seemed to challenge him to act.

He turned away and set off down Via Vittorio Veneto towards the *Castello*.

The maid who answered the door had been a runner for Orlandi's group. Then she had been a chit of a thirteen-year-old who would dart through the woods like a squirrel with messages for the partisans, or sidle her way through a Fascist road block like a thief, carrying plastic explosive in her bag. Now she was almost adult, and pretty in her budding maturity. She stood at the door with a broom in her hand and her mouth open in astonishment.

'I want to see *Signora* Clara. Is she in?'

'Yes, *signore*.'

'Can I come in?'

'Of course, *signore*.'

The maid stood aside.

'You had better go and tell her I am here, that I would like to see her.'

'Of course, *signore*.'

He waited in the hallway. It was a full five minutes before Clara appeared and when she came she seemed older than he remembered, thinner and sallower of complexion; with her hair pulled back into a single plait she had something of the look of a schoolmistress about her.

'So here you are,' she said. 'Why did you take so long?'

Her tone of voice was flat and dull, as though all the waiting had exhausted her. As so often before he felt totally inadequate in her presence, a boy faced with a woman, a boy who had yet lain with her and given her that animal satisfaction which she had cried out for and which, surely, boys cannot give.

'Why so long?' she repeated.

'I explained, didn't I? In my letters.'

'You never really explained anything. You just made statements.'

'I wanted you to have time. And me.'

'What has time got to do with it?' She turned away from him and went over to the window from where she could look down into the moat, where the lemon trees grew. 'What has time got to do with it?' she repeated.

'Your daughter –'

'Lara.'

'Where is she?'

'She goes to the nuns in Vetrano twice a week. It's good for her to be with children of her own age a bit.'

'How is she?'

'Beautiful, much more beautiful than her mother.' Still she stared out of the window. 'She's yours, you know.'

'I had guessed. I want to –'

295

'Don't make offers. They wouldn't be accepted.'

'Why not?'

She turned, laughing humourlessly. 'What are you? Twenty-eight? I'm old enough to be your mother. It would look absurd. And then . . .'

'What?'

She stood looking at him for a long while without speaking. He could see the conflict in her face, the battle between what they had once known and what had come later, and suddenly he understood the significance of her pause. She could shrug her shoulders at his question and dismiss it all as of no matter, claim that time had passed and things had a different perspective now; and then they could chat together in a neutral way, and he could promise more of the assistance which she had already turned down in her letters; and when a decent interval had passed he could rise and make his apologies – 'quite a drive back to the city . . . lights not too good on this old wreck I've bought' – and that would be that. Or . . .

'Why didn't you stop them?'

'I tried. Or at least I tried to offer him some defence. But you know how things were. It's easy to put it all into order after the event, but the reality was never like that, was it?'

'What was the reality?' Her mouth was clenched tight and her face had taken on that ugly cast which had frightened him when he had first seen it. 'What was the reality, Egisto, or David, or whatever it is I should call you now?'

'The reality is that I killed him.'

Her expression did not waver.

'I killed him.'

She shook her head. 'You can't say that. We killed him, you and I and circumstance. We killed him.'

'I killed him.'

Did she understand the meaning of the words? She took a step towards me and I could see she was weeping now, the tears running down her cheeks, her eyes raw, the whole mask about to dissolve. She grabbed at my arms, not in a gesture of either anger or affection but more in the way that someone drowning would grab at a support. 'We killed him,' she said.

'We killed him.' And she began to shake me as though I were an insolent child who would not listen to what she had said:

'We killed him, both of us. Like Jane said.'

'How can you apportion blame like that?' I asked her gently.

Outside it was already dark. We were alone for the first time since the morning, shut away in the once-anonymous guest room which had become my own over the last months, battened against the world. That morning we had struggled through the rain and mud to help bring his body up from the banks of the river to the ruins of the *tendopoli* where it could be loaded into one of the Land Rovers. In death his massive form had taken on a perversity all of its own. It slithered out of our grasp, pulling us this way and that as though it still possessed a kind of life, a final determination to play us as puppets. No one spoke a word on the journey back from the site. At the Villa Rosa and her mother were weeping hysterically.

Then had come the intrusion of strangers, the officials, the journalists asking the same questions over and over again, first at the hospital, later at the *Carabinieri* station where a *maresciallo* took down our statements in laborious longhand, later still back at the Villa when a senior officer appeared from the Headquarters in Viterbo. The telephone never ceased ringing. It became an incongruous background note to the whole day, a silly, insistent trill which only came to an end when someone thought to leave it off the hook.

'You drove him to it,' Jane shouted at me. 'It's all your fault, you selfish bastard! You as good as murdered him. You killed him, both of you!'

The *carabiniere* officer looked embarrassed. 'It must have been a terrible accident.' He slapped his leather gloves against the side of one immaculate, red-striped trouser leg. 'It must have been an accident. Wet rails, mud on his shoes: it's obvious. Such a great man.'

From beside the fire the chimera had snarled at him, as doubtless it was snarling now in the darkness of the drawing room.

'You cannot blame yourself,' I told Lara. 'Whatever Jane says.'

She had become quiet. She had wept all the tears she had to weep and her face had taken on a parched and withered look. We examined each other wearily, as survivors from a disaster.

'What's the point?' she asked.

It was then that she came to me, gently and passively, not with love but rather as though she was fulfilling part of a ritual. Seeds sown long ago germinate and blossom and die, but they have made other seeds whose time will come sooner or later; and so it goes on. Full circle.